The PANGAEA SOLUTION

Solve the Equation...

Save the World

CHARLES JACOBS

Published 2020

Printed in the United States of America
Print ISBN: 978-1-951490-28-7
Ebook ISBN: 978-1-951490-29-4

Publisher Information:
DartFrog Books
4697 Main Street
Manchester Center, VT 05255

www.DartFrogBooks.com

THANK YOU...

I 'd like to thank the following people for their help over the years with this book.

Foremost, I'd like to thank my wife, Kim, for agreeing to let me leave my corporate job and venture out as an independent consultant in order to free up time and give me the flexibility to pursue my writing. I'd also like to thank Sandra Gunselman, a PhD geneticist who reviewed the book from a technical standpoint, correcting technical points, and, most significantly, suggesting a better mutation than the one I'd come up with And, finally, I want to thank Whitney Davis (of Whitney Davis Literary), for a level of enthusiasm and commitment that went well beyond what I expected from a paid editor.

I also want to acknowledge everyone else who volunteered to read the book at various stages of completion and offer thoughts and edits: (in rough chronological order) Amber Thacker, Marc Reid, Lisa McKenzie (author of the blog, *mslabrat.com*), Tracee de Hahn (author of *Swiss Vendetta*, and *A Well-Timed Murder*), Kim van Alkemade (author of *Orphan Eight*, and *Bachelor Girl*), Nicole Murphy, O.M. Faure (author of *The Beautiful Ones* trilogy and *The Cassandra Programme* Series), and Liz Kelley.

In the countryside, the night has a heartbeat;
Its pulse, a symphony of tones and overtones, rhythmic and melodic;
Its performers, a universe of throbbing insects, hot with passion
and calling through the darkness;
And in the stillness, against the barren silence, its din becomes a
roar, all-encompassing, deafening;
Until, broken by a single whisper, it fades into nothing.

0. ONE SOUND IN THE NIGHT

S till wearing her blood-streaked prom dress, Kay Westfield sat on the porch swing of the sagging farmhouse where she lived and waited for the police to arrive. She heard a footstep at the screen door to her right, and she knew her father must be standing there, judging her, but she was too angry even to look at him.

Not only had he refused to believe her, he'd actually laughed in her face. She knew it would be different, though, when the police arrived. They saw bizarre things all the time. Any minute now, two or three squad cars would come driving up with their lights flashing and their sirens blaring, and she'd tell them the whole story. And when her father saw how seriously they took her, he'd realize he'd been wrong, and he'd have to admit she was no longer the little girl he thought she was.

Kay pulled her long legs up on the swing and hugged her knees to her chest. Behind her, the full moon glowed on the western horizon, and, to the east where she stared, the black basalt of the night sky was beginning to fade into indigo. For just a moment she let her mind drift, losing herself in the rising and falling of the crickets' song.

The sky was growing perceptibly lighter, and Kay could just make out the silhouette of trees in the Andersens' farm in the distance. Mrs. Andersen would be waking up about now and making coffee for Mr. Andersen. Betty Andersen would be getting home from the prom soon too, if she hadn't already. What would Betty think when she heard about this? Somewhere behind the barn, a horse snorted and stamped its feet. *It must be wonderful to have a mother*, she thought.

Senior prom was supposed to be special and sweet. "A Night to Remember." That's what the prom committee had named it. What a joke! After a year of being cattle-herded from class to class with no social events other than sports games and boring, uncomfortable *dates*, prom was the big chance to be an adult. Ever since spring, it was all that anyone in the senior class talked about. Who are you going to prom with? What are you going to wear? Where are you going to dinner? It was probably the same all over the country, she thought, only worse in a little farm town like Ivesdale, Illinois.

Kay thought about how she had spent all afternoon getting ready. Her best friend, Susan, had let her use some of her perfume–real perfume from France–and had even given her a pair of red lace panties that she'd bought for her in one of *those* stores at a mall in Champaign, the county seat fifteen miles to the northeast. But John, her date, hadn't even waited until the dance had begun before he'd started drinking. By the time the band quit, he'd downed almost half a bottle of Jack Daniels, and, twenty minutes later, he'd puked all over his rented tuxedo and passed out on the grass. After that, she had been on her own. So much for a night of romance.

Just then, Kay saw the twin cones of a car's headlights cross the rise by the Andersens' farm and dip down on the dirt road that led to her house. Why only one car? And why didn't it have its lights and sirens on?

Kay heard her father step outside, letting the screen door snap closed behind him with a whip-like crack. He trod past her down the creaking stairs, tucking his dirty shirt into the waistband of his gray-green trousers. He spat on the ground. Lifting his gaze to the approaching headlights, he turned his cap around so the visor pointed forward.

A minute later, a big, dark blue sedan pulled into the pool of light from the porch lamp and eased to a stop in front of the house, the tires scrunching loudly on the loose gravel. The car door squeaked opened, and a middle-aged man in a suit climbed out. Not bothering to switch off the engine, he swung the door shut and walked slowly toward Mr. Westfield. With his necktie and polished shoes, and his longish blond hair fluttering in the breeze, he looked rather dashing for a policeman. Kay suddenly noticed the smell of manure blowing in from the cattle barn and cringed.

Mr. Westfield extended his hand. "Chip Westfield. Sorry to drag you out here at this hour."

"Deputy Kresge," Kay heard the policeman introduce himself. The two men walked back to the house.

"This is my daughter, Kay," Mr. Westfield said. "She's the one who called."

"Let's go inside and sit down," the deputy suggested. "And then let's see if we can sort this out."

"Git inside," Mr. Westfield ordered Kay as he opened the screen door. She stood up, smoothed down the front of her stained gown and pushed her way past him. It was hot inside, and the house smelled like damp newspapers. Mr. Westfield held the door for the policeman, who nodded his thanks.

Kay looked around the drab room and wondered what sort of

impression it made. He must think we're slobs, she thought. She sat in the chair near the door so the deputy would have to face toward the window and away from the piles of junk in the back hallway. Mr. Westfield stood by the hall entrance and looked down at his daughter.

"Tell him what happened. Tell him the truth this time."

Kay glared at her father; then she turned to the deputy and took a deep breath. "Well, you see—" she began, staring into a pair of cobalt eyes.

"Sorry to interrupt," the officer cut in, smiling apologetically. "First off, can I get your full name?"

"Katherine Elizabeth Westfield," she told him. "People call me Kay."

"And how old are you, Kay?"

"I'm eighteen. Well, almost eighteen."

"Are you a student at the high school?"

"Yes, that's right. I graduate next week."

"Good," he said. "Now tell me what this trouble was."

"Okay," she began. "Let me tell you what happened. I went to the prom tonight–last night–with a guy named John. John Dorringer. Soon after the dance, he got . . . tired . . . and went home early. I spent the rest of the evening at some of the post-parties they have. You know, at people's houses. About four o'clock, I was getting tired too, so I decided to drive home—"

"In *his* truck!" her father interjected.

"He was too tired to drive, so I had to drive him home!" she snapped.

Mr. Westfield let out a disgusted hiss and stared at the ceiling, barely containing his frustration. The policeman frowned slightly then looked up at Mr. Westfield. "You know what I'd just love right now?" the deputy said. "A big cup of coffee. Do you have any?"

"I could make some," Mr. Westfield offered before he realized he would have to leave the room to do so. He hesitated for a second, then, reconsidering, hurried down to the kitchen in back.

No longer suffering under her father's glare, Kay continued quickly. "On my way back home, a deer ran in front of me. I swerved so I wouldn't hit it. The truck sort of . . . skidded——you know, like it's going to spin around. So I turned the steering wheel back the other way, only I guess I turned too hard, and the truck went off the side of the road and hit a chain-link fence. When I got out and looked at the fence, I realized I'd busted a hole through it."

"So you were alone at this point?" The policeman was scribbling notes on a small pad.

"Yes," she told him, wishing her father had been this interested.

"Then what did you do?" He asked, looking up, his intense eyes staring through hers.

"Well, I didn't just want to leave it. I mean, there was a hole in the fence, and I didn't want whatever was inside to get out. Especially from *that* farm."

"What farm is that?"

"Mr. Feldmann's farm. He's some crazy professor at the University in Champaign. He does strange research on plants and animals. I've heard stories about him before. Everyone has. But I never believed them till tonight." She noticed he'd quit writing in his notebook.

"What exactly did you see?"

"Well, I could see the farmhouse in the distance, so I decided to crawl through the hole in the fence and go tell Mr. Feldmann what had happened. I must have cut myself," she said, lifting her dress up to her knee and showing him the gash on her calf. "I hoped he wouldn't be too mad. When I got to the house, I heard people out back, so I walked around to where they were. And that's when I saw what was going on. It was really freaky. Like, there was an airplane there, a small one, but it didn't have any wings. I mean, they'd been removed."

"Are you sure it was a plane? Could it have been something else?"

"No. I'm sure it was a plane. Besides, that wasn't the only thing that was strange. There was a long row of cages with animals in them, too—a whole row of them down this sort of road on the farm." She saw the detective set his notebook in his lap.

For a moment, the whole scene played out again in her mind—the muffled thud, followed by the brilliant flash of the explosion and the shock wave that had knocked her backward to the ground.

"And then the plane blew up." She paused for effect, but the sheriff just sat quietly listening. "And these guys were standing around with weird masks on—like gas masks—only bigger. And then the animals started dying, and the men were just taking notes. About the animals, I think."

"They didn't notice you standing there?"

"No. I was in the shadows."

"And you were definitely alone?" Something in his voice had changed.

"Yes. I told you that. My date went home early because he felt sick."

"Sick? I thought you said he got tired."

"Tired because he was sick," she blurted out, realizing how lame that sounded. "After that, I got scared and ran back to the truck. Then I drove home and called you."

"How much did you have to drink tonight?"

"Nothing."

"Nothing at all?" he asked incredulously. "I can test you right here."

She glanced down the hall to make sure her father wasn't

coming, then she said softly, "Well, maybe just a little." (The cop picked up his notebook and wrote *that* down.) "But that was before midnight. And that has nothing to do with—"

Just then, Mr. Westfield came back to the room with two cups of coffee. He set one on the table next to the officer, then walked over to the couch and sat down. "She tell you what happened?"

The deputy nodded and closed his notebook. He took a sip of coffee and told Mr. Westfield it tasted great. Then he looked at Kay for a second before returning his attention to Mr. Westfield. "Let me tell you what I think happened tonight. Your daughter and her date did what all kids do at the prom. They dance. They go for a drive afterward. Then they park in the country and have a little beer. Then it's time to leave, only her date's had a bit much to drink, so Kay decides she's going to drive. But she's unfamiliar with the truck, and maybe she's had a bit too much beer too, and she runs into the fence. The kids can't tell anyone what really happened, so Kay drives her date home, then waits till she's sobered up and comes home herself."

Kay's mouth dropped open in disbelief. "*That's* not what happened! If you go there right now I'm sure you can still find the plane."

The deputy gave Kay a patronizing smile and turned to her father. "We got a report this evening that a propane tank exploded at Dr. Feldmann's farm. I'm sure that's what she saw."

"It was not! I *know* what a plane looks like. I've taken flight lessons. I'm going to be a pilot someday, you know."

The policeman smiled as if to say, "Of course you are." Mr. Westfield nodded knowingly to the deputy.

"I did just about the same thing when I was in high school," the officer said. "Only I didn't say anything about exploding airplanes and dead animals."

"But it *did* happen! Someone has to do something about him! He's crazy. You need to go there right now!" She tried not to cry, but the tears rolled down her cheeks anyway, and that made her feel all the more ashamed and embarrassed.

"Look," the deputy said, sounding very fatherly himself. "I can talk to Dr. Feldmann. He's a reasonable guy. If I explain how sorry the kids are and tell him they promise to stay away from the farm, I think he just might not make you pay to fix the fence."

Mr. Westfield's lips peeled back into a smile that crinkled his steady, gray eyes, obviously pleased to hear that.

Mr. Westfield thanked the deputy and showed him to the door. "Sorry to drag you out here so early," he apologized.

"Quite alright," the deputy responded. "It just wouldn't be good to go and make a lot of trouble over this. Dr. Feldmann is a very important man. No one got hurt much. Best to just forget it. Kids do the craziest things."

Mr. Westfield stood and watched through the screen as the police car drove away. When the car dipped over the shallow hill and disappeared into the reddening horizon, he turned to Kay. "Don't *ever* embarrass me like that again! Now go to bed, young lady. I'll deal with you when you get up."

"Embarrass *you*? I can't believe you let him do that to *me*! I'm not making this up!"

"Go to bed! I said I'll deal with you later."

With a "harrumph" of disgust, Kay hiked up the stairs to her bedroom and slammed the door. Pulling down the flowered shades on the windows, she stripped down to her bra and underwear—throwing the blood-stained dress in a heap on the hardwood floor—and climbed under the covers.

Well she *was* going to make a fuss about it, she decided. Somehow she'd show her father that she was right.

As drowsiness poured over her in lolling waves, she considered various alternatives, but they all just seemed to end in even more embarrassment. She finally drifted off into a restless sleep as the morning sun rose over the waking prairie.

1. BANKER'S HOURS

David Blum, dressed in a navy blue suit, white shirt, and red Hermes tie, stood in the library-like main room of Chadwick & Sons, Dealer in Rare Coins and Medals, and stared out through the barred windows at Victoria Embankment and the River Thames beyond. John Chadwick, the fourth generation in the business, had gone to the basement safe to retrieve a collection of Tokugawa-era Japanese *obans*—hand-rolled gold coins the size of small pancakes. The set had hammered for 2.6 million dollars to a floor-bidder in a recent auction, but the winner had failed to make payment, and now Chadwick, presumably the under-bidder, was offering them to Blum in a private sale for 2.5 million dollars.

After a short while, John, a spindly man with thinning gray hair and oversized black-framed glasses, returned carrying a red lacquered wooden box the size of a lunch pail. He set it down in the pool of sunlight on the table and lifted the lid. The light struck the surface of the first oval coin and glared back into David's eyes. Sliding his six-foot frame into the cane chair in front of him and careful to handle the coins only by their edges, Blum separated the rest from their jute tissue paper wrappers and laid them out across the leather-topped table.

The *obans*, spread in front of him like golden serving dishes, were some of the most beautiful coins he had ever seen, and it intrigued him to think that one of these very pieces might have once paid the dowry on a shogun's daughter or been used to buy the services of a samurai army.

At moments like this, Blum couldn't help but marvel at the life he'd created for himself. With his recent promotion to senior advisor in Regency Bank's Chicago office (at the unprecedented age of just thirty-eight), he now managed almost two billion dollars for some of the world's most wealthy (and secretive) individuals. In addition to paying a handsome salary, the job sent him traveling the globe, visiting art galleries, vintage car auctions, and coin dealers like Chadwick.

Not that any of that was enough to impress his father.

"I can see that you're satisfied with their condition," John stated flatly. "I *have* come across individual coins in higher grades, but never together in a set like this. I dare say this may be the last complete collection you or I ever see outside of a museum. Quite a find really. Shame about the chap at the auction. Seems he got a bit carried away. When it came time to make payment, he was, shall we say, pecuniarily embarrassed."

Blum sat back in his chair and swept away an errant lock of black hair that had fallen over his right eye. "A phenomenal set," he said. He nodded to himself. "I'm sure my client will be pleased." He glanced at his gold Daytona chronograph and added six hours. "I can have the funds wired to you within the hour, and I'll arrange for a bonded courier to retrieve the coins this afternoon. It will help if you can have the VAT forms ready when he arrives."

"Splendid," John replied.

The two spent a few minutes catching up on what would appear at Chadwick's next auction. When they were finished, Blum hailed a cab to Regency's headquarters in the West End, where he arranged for payment and retrieval of the coins. Then, his work completed, he spent the rest of the afternoon browsing through antiquarian bookstores in Cecil Court.

Blum treated himself to an early dinner of duck a l'orange and a celebratory bottle of 2005 Armand Rousseau Chambertin. (*Wait until accounts payable saw that on his expense report!*) Then, feeling rather content, he returned to the Cadogan Hotel and pushed his way through the heavy, wood-framed revolving door. He smiled at the heavyset young man behind the main counter.

The receptionist smiled back. "Good evening, Mr. Blum."

At the mention of the name, the concierge standing at the end of the counter looked up. "Pardon me. Mr. Blum, is it?"

David nodded. "Yes?"

"I have a message for you, sir. I was just going to take it up to your room." The older, gray-haired man, dressed in a dark, teal-blue uniform, turned a small piece of paper around in his hand and screwed up his eyes. "You're to call your Aunt Shelly. She left a number."

He had his aunt's number in his cell phone, but he took the note anyway and thanked the man.

The phone at the desk rang. The concierge answered it and signaled to Blum as he nodded several times. Holding his hand over the receiver, the concierge whispered, "It's your aunt again, Mr. Blum. Would you like to take the call here?"

Blum frowned. He couldn't remember the last time she had

called him, let alone twice in one evening. It sounded serious. "No. I'll take it in my room. Can you transfer it there?"

"Certainly, sir. I'll connect it straight away."

Blum skipped the cage-like elevator and jogged up the stairs to his room on the second floor. On the way down the carpeted hallway, he absently glanced at the slip of paper. The number was wrong. Not even the right area code. Then it hit him. It was his father's phone number.

What was Shelly doing in Champaign? His father hadn't mentioned she was coming to visit. Was that why he'd called the other night?

Blum shut the door to his room and answered the already ringing phone. He heard a scratchy voice say, "David?"

"Aunt Shelly?"

"Oh Davie," she sobbed. "I...I..."

"What is it? What's wrong?"

"It's your father."

Blum's body tensed. "Dad? What about him?" He'd seemed fine when Blum had talked to him a week earlier. "Is he okay?" His heart pounded.

"He's dead, Davie," Shelly said, through her sobs.

Blum's knees went weak, and he sank to the floor. Trying not to let his voice crack, he asked, "How did it happen?"

"It was his heart. He had a heart attack. The sheriff found him in his car by the side of the road. He must've known something was wrong and pulled over."

"In his car? But he doesn't have a license anymore. He hasn't driven in almost five years." A sudden flash of optimism embraced him. "Are you sure it was him? He lets people borrow his car sometimes. Maybe it was somebody else." That had to be it. It was all a big mistake. His aunt must have overreacted.

"I had to identify the body, Davie. It was definitely Solomon." He heard her voice tremble. "It was horrible. I tried to reach you over the weekend, but I must have had an old number. I called your office first thing this morning, and they said you were out of the country. I didn't know what to do, so I flew up here to Champaign. I finally got the number for your hotel from your assistant."

Blum sank back on the carpeted floor and rested his elbows on his knees. "What can I do?" he asked with resignation.

"Nothing right now. I think we can have the funeral on Wednesday, if you can make it."

"Of course. I can fly back to Chicago tomorrow morning. I'll need to stop by my apartment, but I can drive down and be in Champaign tomorrow night."

Having talked about it, Shelly sounded stronger. "I'm very sorry, Davie."

"Me too," he said. "Thank you for taking care of things. I'll see you tomorrow night."

He heard the call disconnect but didn't put the phone down. Instead, he tried to lose himself in the dull buzz of the dial tone—crawl inside the dark, electronic world on the other side and slip down the smooth, spiral slide into a deep sleep. It wasn't until the line went completely dead that he returned the handset to the cradle, and then, for the first time since adolescence, David Blum began to cry.

2. SUCH A SHAME

After a somber graveside service, David and his aunt, both sweating in unseasonably hot black and gray, walked between the two rows of mourners who offered their condolences in hushed tones. Blum recognized some of his father's colleagues from the university, as well as a few neighbors and friends.

As the crowd broke up and people headed to their cars, Blum wandered back through the cemetery to his father's grave. He pulled a folding chair up to the edge and sat down. For the next hour he remained there, bathed in the speckled late-afternoon sun that filtered through the full trees overhead. Consumed by his incredible loss, he reached up and grasped his shirt pocket. Pulling softly at first, then harder, he tore it back and let the flap hang loose.

Blum's mind drifted to his mother's death, and he recalled the same stabbing emptiness he'd felt then. Only six at the time, he'd found her unconscious on the kitchen floor when he'd come in from playing outside on a fall afternoon. He remembered how quiet the house seemed. Frightened, but not knowing what to do, he simply cradled her head and stroked her hair for more than an hour until his dad came home. She died on the way to the hospital.

Later, he overheard the doctor tell his father that she might have lived had if she'd made it to the emergency room sooner. Convinced it was his fault, nothing his dad said could console him. Looking back, he realized those were probably the last tender moments he'd had with his father. Shortly after that, a wall seemed to go up between them, and David had always wondered if his father had blamed him for his mother's death after all. Nothing else seemed to explain the man's transformation.

When at last a funeral-worker came to complete the burial, David stood up and walked to the parking lot without looking back. In no particular hurry to leave, he unsnapped the tonneau cover on his black AC Cobra and stowed it in the trunk before climbing in and firing up the engine. With the rumbling V8 barely idling, he rolled down the gravel driveway and turned south toward town.

As he cruised along, he was surprised to see how much the area had grown since he'd moved away. What had been just another one of the mile-spaced county roads that cut the countryside into a checkerboard of soybean and corn fields now teemed with gas stations, motels, and strip malls. The "twin cities" of Champaign and Urbana—literally across the street from each other—were no longer the sleepy college community he remembered.

Twenty minutes later, after making his way through the familiar streets of western Champaign, he arrived at his childhood home and parked in the driveway. As he entered the kitchen through the side entrance, the familiarity of everything inside—the butcher-block table, the faint smell of cedar, the feeling of the linoleum tile under his feet—reminded him of his childhood and embraced him with a soothing nostalgia tinged with melancholy.

Making his way to the front hall, he greeted a few of the guests who had stopped by for a small reception. Barely into the introductions, he heard the gong of the doorbell. When he opened the heavy front door, he faced a young man—no more than twenty-five—dressed in tattered jeans and a T-shirt.

The fellow combed back a curly mop of straw-colored hair with his fingers. "Is David Blum here?" he asked, stealing a nervous glance past Blum at the guests in the entry hall.

"I'm David."

The guy looked relieved. "Here," he said, handing Blum a sealed red envelope. "This is from a friend of mine. He said it's very important that you get it."

"That was thoughtful. Would you like to come in? We've got food and drinks."

"No thanks. I have to get going."

"Well, thanks for the card," Blum called to the fellow, who was already mounting a bicycle at the end of the walkway. The young man nodded and pedaled off, almost side-swiping a silver sedan that was cruising past.

Blum wondered why the guy was so uncomfortable dropping off a condolence card. Some people were just funny about funerals, he supposed. He tossed the envelope onto the stack that had collected on a table in the hallway, squared the untidy pile, and then stepped into the brightly lit room to greet the other visitors.

An hour later, after taking time to chat with each of the guests, Blum began to feel drained and went to the kitchen to grab a beer. When he walked into the room, he was surprised to find an older, silver-haired gentleman, dressed in black trousers, a gray jacket, and a wrinkled white shirt, helping himself to a glass of milk from the refrigerator.

"Excuse me," Blum said. "Can I help you with something?"

The fellow turned. His clear, gray eyes stared up into Blum's through thick wire-frame glasses. "Ah. You are David, no? Perhaps you recall meeting me? Otto Feldmann." He stuck out his wrinkled, muscular hand, and Blum gave it a few firm pumps. "We had dinner together, you, me, and your father. But that was, what, twenty years ago, no?"

Of course, Blum remembered. Back when he was in college, his father had invited the professor to their house for dinner. He couldn't recall how the two had met; his father had been in political science, but Feldmann was in genetics or something. All three of them had gotten somewhat tipsy on cheap wine and stayed up late discussing how to solve the world's problems. Blum remembered saying some outrageous things, which, to his disappointment, had failed to get a rise out of his stoic father.

"You know, your father spoke of you all the time," Feldmann told him.

"Is that so?" Blum said. Then, to be polite, he added, "My dad talked about you as well."

Feldmann's smile narrowed. "Oh, really? When?"

"Now and then," Blum said, waving his hands to convey vagueness.

"His death must be quite a shock. When did you last speak to your father?"

"A week ago, I guess," Blum replied, puzzled at the question.

Feldmann gulped down the last of the milk from his glass. Some of the liquid clung to his upper lip, giving him a false smile behind which he looked rather cold. "Of course, I'm very sorry about it all," he said. "It's such a shame."

3. A FACE IN THE SHADOWS

After his Aunt Shelly left for the airport the next day, Blum called his office and talked to his admin. Not wanting to burden clients with his personal affairs, he asked her to tell anyone who called that he would still be in London for the next few weeks. Then, powering up his laptop, he spent an hour going through his work and personal emails.

Nothing looked important, save one item from the Champaign County Sheriff's Office. Attached to a short cover message he found a scanned copy of his father's accident report. Blum brought up the document, but it didn't say much. The sheriff had found Solomon Blum in his car at 12:05 a.m. on County Road 500E between 800N and 900N. The location—outside of town—surprised Blum. When his aunt had said, "by the side of the road," he'd pictured a city street. So what the hell *had* made his dad head out into the countryside last Friday night? And in a car he hadn't driven in years? It didn't make sense.

The coroner had estimated the time of death as 9:00 p.m. Cause of death showed "Natural Causes—heart attack." The report ended with, of all things, "License expired. No citation issued."

*

That evening, Blum sat in the living room and began the solemn task of going through the condolence cards. Most people had simply signed their names below pre-printed messages, but a few had taken the time to write rather touching personal thoughts, and more than once he had to stop and take a deep breath before reading on. As he neared the bottom of the stack, he picked up the red envelope delivered by the nervous young man on the bike. He tore open the flap and pulled out a handwritten message.

> Mr. Blum,
> I need to talk to you about what really happened to your father. I was a student of his, and he told me you used to work for the FBI. I know you've since left, but I'm hoping you can still help me. I don't know where else to turn. Please meet me Thursday night at Fortunato's Bar at 9:00 on the third level. You don't know me, but I will recognize you.
> Till tomorrow,
> Hans Meier

Blum sank back in the couch and combed his fingers through his hair. What did the guy mean, "*really* happened to your father?" And what did he think Blum could do about it?

Or was this some sort of sick joke? Blum had never heard his father mention anyone named Hans Meier.

Curious if the guy even existed, he pulled out his phone and brought up a directory. A single listing for "Hans Peter Meier" popped up. Was that the guy? Blum hit "call." The line connected and rang, but no one answered. Deciding it must be an old listing, he hung up.

He read through the note again to make sure he hadn't missed anything. Then it suddenly occurred to him—the note was delivered yesterday. *Today* was Thursday. He checked his watch. 8:40. The aftereffects of jet lag and the funeral had left him completely drained, but he was intrigued to find out what Meier wanted to tell him. He pushed himself out of the couch, grabbed his jacket and keys, and headed for the door.

Blum remembered the route to Fortunato's—a favorite hangout for him back in college—but traffic backed up as he approached campus, and it was a quarter past nine when he finally climbed the carpeted stairs to the cozy third level. Looking around, he could see that little had changed over the years. Secluded booths still lined the walls, and the gas fireplace in the center of the room lent a familiar flickering glow to the tables that surrounded it.

Having no idea what Meier looked like, Blum knew he would have to count on being recognized. He ordered a Beck's at the bar and sat at a well-lit table near the fireplace. As he waited, nursing his beer, he scanned the room, looking for a flash of recognition on anyone's face, but no one paid any attention to him.

Ten minutes later, a man jogged up the stairs and paused on the top step, looking right at him. Blum started to lift his hand to flag the guy's attention, but then, from somewhere behind him, a voice called, "Yo, Kyle! Over here," and the man headed to a table in the back.

Blum scanned the room again, but everyone seemed to be busy chatting in pairs or small groups. He checked his watch. 9:45.

Where the hell was Meier?

Blum walked to the bar and ordered another beer. While he waited for it to arrive, he tried calling Meier again, but this time he got a recording telling him the line was out of order. He paid for his beer and downed a slug. As he turned back around, he spotted a man with black hair sitting in one of the chairs at the table where he'd been sitting.

Finally, Blum thought. *Thank heavens.*

"Hans Meier?" He asked as he approached the man.

The guy turned and scowled. "Who?"

"Hans Meier?"

The guy shook his head. "Nope. Sorry."

With no more empty tables available, Blum returned to the bar and sat on a stool with his back to the counter. He scanned the crowd again, but no one caught his eye.

The clock on the wall told him it was 10:00. Deciding an hour was long enough to wait, he reached for his beer to take a final sip, but then something caught his eye. In the deep shadow of a tall divider on the far side of the room, he noticed the silhouette of a man sitting there—a big guy with a large head and heavy features. As Blum squinted into the dark booth to try to get a look at the man's face, the guy turned slowly toward him. For an instant, the stranger's eyes caught the light from the fireplace and seemed to glow briefly, as if they too were burning. A second later, a waitress approached the booth and set down a fresh beer. As the man in the shadow bent forward to pick up the glass, his face showed briefly in the glow from the fire. Then the waitress stepped to the side and blocked Blum's view. By the time she turned away, the man had withdrawn back into the shadow.

It had been an odd-looking face, Blum thought. A face too large for its body, with thick, scowling lips. Had he been there the whole time? Was *that* Meier? If so, why not come over?

From his limited experience with surveillance, Blum knew how difficult it could be to identify someone from only a photograph. It was possible Meier didn't recognize him after all. On the other hand, it struck him that the man wasn't behaving like someone who was waiting for a first-time meeting—no querying glances or shrugs of dismissal. And why was he hiding in the dark?

Something felt off though about the whole situation. If this was nothing more than an old friend of his father's wanting to talk, why send a note instead of calling? And even if Meier didn't know Blum's number, why the complication of a meeting instead of simply asking Blum to call *him*?

Could it be a set up, he wondered? But for what? And why have him meet in a crowded bar instead of a deserted parking lot? These people are friendly, he told himself. To hell with the guy in the back booth. Probably just looks angry because he frightens women away. Poor bastard.

Even so, Blum began to feel vulnerable sitting there on display, and he realized he was hunching his shoulders—subconsciously protecting his neck. His beer suddenly tasted bitter, and he set it down. He checked his watch. It was almost ten-thirty. Meier wasn't going to show. Time to go.

Blum slid off the bar stool and stood up. As he did, he noticed the man in the shadows start to pivot out of his booth as well. The coincidence of the timing struck a nerve. Crossing the room, he resisted the urge to look back over his shoulder as he started down to the second level. When he turned to descend the next flight, he glanced up and was shocked to see the giant man heading down toward him, jaw clenched and eyes glaring.

Weak from exhaustion, and realizing he was totally unprepared for a confrontation, Blum dashed down the carpeted steps to the ground level. Something told him not to use the front door. Instead, he shoved his way through the crowds of students to the rear emergency exit. Stealing a look back, he spotted his pursuer standing at the bottom of the stairs scanning the room.

Blum hit the release bar on the door and ducked out into the dark alley behind the building. As the alarm blared, he noticed an aproned busboy next to him emptying the trash.

"Hey!" the kid yelled. "What the hell are you doing?"

Blum pushed past the startled figure and jogged down the alley to the lit street beyond.

4. ALL ROADS

The next morning, Blum sat on the back patio, sipping his second cup of coffee. The late-morning sun glared down from a cloudless sky, lighting a bed of lilies at the edge of the sandstone pavers. In the brilliant daylight, his moment of panic the night before seemed like something of an overreaction. The whole encounter could have been just an odd coincidence or a strange misunderstanding. Regardless, Meier had reached out to tell him something important, and David knew he owed it to his father to try to contact Meier in return.

Blum pulled out his phone and tried calling Meier one last time, but the line was still out of order. He brought up the listing for "Hans Peter Meier" again and saw it provided an address—1003 West Nealy, Apartment 14. Of course, Meier could have moved since the entry was last updated, but it was all Blum had to go on.

Blum found Meier's apartment building—a bland cinderblock two-story—on a quiet residential street in central Champaign. Parking his car around the corner, he crossed the gravel lot and entered through a glass door into a lobby that smelled of mildewed carpet and fried food. To his right, a bank of steel mailboxes lined the entire wall. He found number fourteen and was glad to see "Hans Meier" scribbled on a piece of white tape next to it. Seeing number ten at the top of a short flight of stairs to his right, he headed up.

About halfway to the end of the narrow hallway, he spied an open door with 14 on it. He stopped short, though, when he noticed the deadbolt extended and the wood splintered around the knob and jam.

Leaning closer, he heard footsteps inside the apartment crunching on broken glass. The footsteps stopped, and a moment later a male voice muttered, "Jesus Christ. Look at this shit."

Deciding the voice sounded more exasperated than threatening, Blum stepped forward and peered inside. What he saw sent a chill down his spine. The place was completely trashed. Furniture lay overturned and slashed, books and clothes littered the carpet, and light switches and outlets hung from their openings. Blum also spotted a landline phone smashed into four or five pieces.

Out of service was an understatement.

A workman stepped into view. He wore jeans and leather boots, and a tool belt hung around a hairy belly, which spilled out below a tight yellow T-shirt. The guy stopped and picked at his teeth with his thumbnail.

"Jesus H. Christ," the worker muttered again. As the guy turned, he noticed Blum staring. "Hey. You know anything about this?"

Blum shook his head. "What the hell happened?"

"I dunno. Christ. Probably some wild drug party. Fuckin' kids."

"The guy who lives here," Blum said. "You know where he is?"

"No idea."

"So you don't know if he's okay?"

The handyman frowned and approached Blum. "Funny. Cops asked me the same thing."

"Cops?"

"Yeah. Manager called 'em. They just left a minute ago."

"What did *they* do when they saw this?"

"Jack shit, if you ask me. Lazy fuckers looked around. Told me it's not a police matter if someone wants to trash their own crap. 'Malicious mischief,' they called it. Told me to call 'em if the little bastard won't pay for the damage to the walls."

"Huh," Blum said, studying the scene. The slashed couch and torn chairs were old and worn, and the collapsed bookshelves had been cobbled together from cinder blocks and boards. Amidst the low-buck debris, one thing stood out. At the far end of the living room, a high-end audio system stood untouched.

The handyman apparently noticed Blum's interest. "What are *you* looking for?"

"The guy borrowed some books from me," Blum said, thinking quickly. "Never returned them. I really need them back. They're kind of important."

"What about those?" the man said, pointing at a mess of books and papers that littered the floor to the right of the doorway.

Blum perused the titles, which included *Principles of Corn Hybridization* and *Synthesis of Fertilizers from Biological Sources*. Scattered among them he also spotted notebooks labeled with letters and numbers indicating graduate-level courses.

Blum shook his head. "No. These were leather bound." Picking a subject far from anything Meier was likely to have, he added, "And they're about medieval English history. If you find them, I'd appreciate if you'd give me a call."

Blum reached down and pulled a page with writing on it from one of the notebooks on the floor. He wrote a name and number at the bottom and tore it off from the rest of the page. As he handed the slip of paper to the handyman, he crumpled up the remaining portion and casually stuffed the wad into his back pocket.

The handyman studied the paper. "Jack Watson, huh? My name's Jack too."

"Small world," Blum said. "Um, hey . . . mind if I use the bathroom? I gotta take a leak, and I've got a bit of drive ahead of me."

"Okay, I guess. Just make it quick. Manager'll chew my ass if he finds you here."

"Only be a second," Blum said, heading past the filthy kitchen into a short back hallway. As he turned toward the bathroom, he scanned the bedroom and saw more of the same low-budget ilk—battered furniture and simple posters taped to the walls. However, in stark contrast to the living room, nothing there looked disturbed.

A digital clock on a plastic milk crate right inside the bedroom door did catch his eye. The alarm light was on, indicating it was set to go off. Blum glanced over his shoulder. Jack was busy with a tape measure. Blum reached down and pressed the alarm button. 8:00 p.m. showed on the screen. Someone, perhaps the workman, had to have hit the reset button since eight the previous evening or else the clock would still be beeping.

Blum stepped into the cramped bathroom, shut the door and scanned the tiny space. Soap, a comb with blond hairs, and a contact lens case littered the edge of the sink. On a shelf above it, a small tube of mustache wax sat leaking yellow goo. He popped the lids on the contact case and found a pair of pale-blue lenses soaking. Turning, he noticed the tub looked dry, but a washcloth wadded up in the corner still felt wet inside. Blum flushed the toilet to confirm his ruse and opened the door.

As he returned to the hall, he saw a small pad of paper on a table just outside the door. The exposed sheet was blank but appeared to have some writing pressed into it. Intrigued, Blum tore off the top sheet and stuffed it in his pocket; then he returned to the living room where the workman stood measuring part of the wall.

"Have you been in back yet?" Blum asked, pointing over his shoulder to the bedroom.

"Nope. Not yet. Why? Pretty bad?"

"Actually, no."

The handyman snorted. "Well, thank God for small fuckin' favors."

"If you find those books, please call me," Blum said. "I'm up shit creek if I don't get them back."

"You got it," the handyman replied.

Blum nodded and left the apartment. As he made his way across the parking lot, he noticed a blue pickup with "Jack's Handy Work" stenciled on the side, and he chuckled when he noticed the slogan below that. "Always professional. Always cheerful."

Blum strolled up the block to his car and climbed in, all the while trying to piece together the details of what he'd just seen. He guessed that Meier, a graduate student in biology or agriculture, was blond, had a mustache, and most likely was wearing his glasses. Blum also had an idea of what might have happened the night before. As he saw it, Meier, deciding to take a late-day nap, had removed his contacts and set the alarm for eight p.m. to ensure he would make it to Fortunato's by nine. The wet washcloth would have dried after a full day, so, at eight, he must have gotten up and showered. Then, not bothering with his contacts, he'd left for the bar.

Sometime thereafter, someone had jimmied the door and trashed the place. Despite what the police had said, this had not been "malicious mischief." Based on the specific damage he'd seen, it was clear to Blum the apartment had been professionally searched. Moreover, someone bent on destroying the place would have trashed the stereo along with everything else, and a thief would have taken it. Blum guessed that whoever had broken in had left it intact and blasted loud music to drown out the noise while tossing the place. The perpetrator (or perpetrators) must have found something significant in the front room, though, or else the rest of place would have been torn up as well. A police detective wouldn't have missed those clues, but a couple of beat cops apparently had.

Blum pulled out the crumpled page he'd torn from Meier's notebook and compared it to the note the nervous visitor had delivered. He was no handwriting expert, but it appeared to be identical. Which meant Meier *had* written the note.

So why not show up for the meeting?

Blum removed the note pad sheet from his pocket. Tilting it in the harsh sunlight, he caught the relief of writing pressed into it. He couldn't read all of it, but it began with something that could have been "Fortunato's," and seemed to end with "9:00." It could have been Meier who had taken the top sheet—to remind himself of the time—but more likely it had been one of the intruders, aborting the search once he learned about Meier's imminent meeting. And that meant the man he'd spotted in the back booth at Fortunato's must have either been waiting for Meier to arrive or to see who showed up to meet Meier. Neither one bode well for Meier. And it also meant Blum would have to be on his guard, now that he'd been tied to Meier.

So what was the connection between his father, a professor of political science, and Meier, the ag major? His father always seemed to be fighting one lost cause or another. Perhaps the two of them were mixed up in one of those. Only this time maybe the cause had fought back. Blum put both scraps of paper back in his pocket.

What had he learned so far? Something had happened to his father. His father knew Meier. Meier wanted to tell him what happened to his father. Meier had his apartment trashed, probably about the time he was supposed to meet Blum but didn't show. And Meier wanted Blum's help because he used to work for the FBI. So why hadn't Meier gone straight to the FBI? Did Meier think they wouldn't take him seriously? Or, maybe he had, and they hadn't done anything.

Not feeling terribly hungry but realizing he'd skipped breakfast, he drove around until he found a diner. As he waited for his order, it occurred to him that Meier, a struggling grad student, might be receiving some sort of academic assistance, either as a researcher or an instructor. Perhaps someone he worked with knew where he was. Blum dialed university information. The woman who answered gave him the number for the Nealy Street apartment.

"Any chance he has a campus phone number as well?"

"Wait a minute. Yes, he does. There's an office address, too," she added. "Nine two eight Cotespath Hall."

"Cotespath Hall?"

"The Cotespath Hall of Experimental Biology. It's pretty new, I think. A block or two south of the library, right by the old greenhouses on Goodwin."

Blum thanked the woman and hung up just as his food arrived. Relieved to have a lead, and eager to talk to anyone who knew Meier, he wolfed down his sandwich and drove to campus. Finding a garage near the university greenhouses, he wound his way up to the fourth level and parked. When he stepped outside, he spotted a gleaming, ten-story structure across an open quadrangle. Young trees surrounded the building, and a large fountain with "COTESPATH" in brass letters provided a focal point for the circular drive in front. With its black framing and smoked glass, it looked more like an office building than a biology research center.

Blum entered the building into a narrow atrium and rode an elevator to the ninth floor, where it opened onto a well-lit lobby. To the left stood a solid wooden door with a plaque that read, SUITE 900: CENTER FOR SCIENTIFIC RESEARCH—GENETICS.

Opening the door, he found himself in a small, carpeted reception area. At a desk in front of a large window, he spotted a dark-haired woman in a white blouse sitting with her back to him, engrossed in solving a Rubik's cube. Blum glanced at the name plaque. Black letters on a gold background read, "Tina Santini, Administrative Assistant."

The door shut behind him with a loud thud, and, as the lady turned, Blum found himself staring at one of the most striking women he had ever seen. She was in her mid-twenties and had straight black hair that hung down to her shoulders, framing a soft, lean face with intelligent, chocolate-brown eyes. Before Blum could say anything, her desk phone rang. As she turned to answer it, her loose-fitting blouse billowed out just far enough to show off the pleasant effects of a push-up bra.

Spotting a rack of mailboxes on the wall next to him, he scanned the names and found the slot for "H. Meier," right between "V. Lawson" and "S. Muldoon." Meier's appeared to be one of the few empty ones. On inspection, most of the mailboxes had the same memo on top. He stole another glance at the admin and, seeing that she was still on the phone, grabbed one of the sheets. It covered payment policies for the research assistants and was dated August 13, meaning someone had removed Meier's mail earlier that morning.

"Hey, can I help you?" the admin called.

"Yes," Blum said, dropping the memo back into the slot. "I'm looking for Hans Meier."

The mention of Meier's name seemed to surprise her. She put her hand over the mouthpiece of the phone. "Meier? He's not around."

"Do you expect him in today?"

She shrugged. "He didn't show for a meeting this morning. I don't know where he is."

Blum wondered who had taken Meier's mail. "Perhaps he'll be in later?"

"Perhaps," she said. "I'm afraid I didn't catch your name."

Blum decided to tell her the name he'd given the handyman. "My name is—"

"David Blum!" a hearty voice called from behind him. "What brings you here?"

Blum spun around to see Otto Feldmann standing where the hallway met the lobby, his head cocked sideways like a watchful guard dog.

Blum's throat tightened. He coughed to hide his shock. "Professor Feldmann. What a surprise."

The professor strode toward Blum, his white lab coat flapping behind him like the wake of a speedboat.

"He's looking for Meier," the woman said, hanging up the phone.

"Is that right, Tina?" Feldmann turned to Blum. "Why Meier?" Feldmann asked, staring at Blum and waiting for a reply. Tina also seemed to be waiting for his answer.

Blum hesitated. "My father had some of his books, and I wanted to return them. I had no idea he was in your department."

"Really? He borrowed books from Solomon? Where are they?" Feldmann asked. "I can give them to him when he returns."

"Oh . . . at home," Blum said, stumbling for an excuse. "I wasn't sure when I'd find him here, and I didn't want them bouncing around in the trunk."

The phone buzzed, and Tina pushed a button on the console.

"Otto, it's the NIH again."

Feldmann looked annoyed. He thought for a second. Then he turned and put his hand on Blum's shoulder. "Wait here," he said. "I'll only be a minute." To his admin, he added, "I'll take the call in my office." He dashed down the hall and disappeared inside a doorway.

"So your father knew Otto," Tina said. "Were they close?"

"Not particularly. My father was a professor, too. They met years ago."

"Oh," she said. Her cell phone pinged. When she turned to answer it, Blum used the opportunity to back off and collect his thoughts.

God. Talk about lucky. Another second and he would have told her his name was Jack Watson, and Feldmann would have overheard. He'd have had a hell of a time explaining that. Blum sank into a chair and waited for the professor to finish his call. When Feldmann returned, he was shaking his head with frustration.

"I apologize, but the NIH is very concerned, and I must deal with them now. God in heaven, they're all a bunch of nervous old ladies!" He chuckled. "But I'd very much like to catch up with you. How about dinner this weekend?" He pulled a cell phone from his lab coat and checked his calendar. "Sunday? Will you still be in town? I hope you don't have plans."

"That sounds great," Blum said. "Do you have a place in mind? I'm afraid I don't know the restaurants in town anymore."

"Oh, no. I mean a real meal. Come to my house—to my farm. It's only a few miles from town. You have a car, no?" Blum nodded. "Good. Good." Feldmann turned to Tina and stirred the air with his hand. She handed him a Post-It pad and pen, and he wrote down an address. "Here," he said as he tore the top page off. "Google it for directions, but you can't miss it. It has a big fence all the way around—to keep out the squirrels." He laughed. "Say seven o'clock? That should give the chef time to prepare."

"Seven's fine," Blum replied, wondering how a professor could afford his own chef. It could have been a joke about his wife, but Feldmann didn't have a ring on his finger.

Without saying good-bye, Feldmann marched back down the hall to his office.

Blum turned to Tina. "Chef?"

"You're very lucky," she replied. "Not many people get invited to the farm for dinner."

"In that case I'll consider myself special," he said, then, gazing one last time into her dark brown eyes, he smiled and headed for the elevators.

5. FINAL CONTACT

Leaving Cotespath Hall, Blum slipped on a pair of sunglasses and headed back toward his car. It would have been interesting to poke around in Meier's office, but he couldn't think of any easy way to do that. Perhaps an Internet search would provide something instead.

Realizing that the university library was only a few blocks away, and preferring a full-sized screen to the browser on his phone, Blum passed the parking garage and headed north. A few minutes later, he descended the steps to the subterranean library entrance, pushed through the turnstile, and wandered to the back where he found a bank of public computers.

Entering "Hans Meier University of Illinois" into the search line, a list of links popped up immediately. The first entry pointed to a research paper on virus propagation in tomato plants by "Hans Meier and Peter Creighton, University of Illinois, Department of Experimental Biology." The technical jargon in the abstract escaped Blum, but he didn't care. He fished a scrap of paper out of a nearby trash can and scribbled Creighton's name on it. Returning to the search page, he scanned the other entries. Most linked to the same paper, but one item referenced a bridge tournament the prior year where, according to the article, Hans Meier had partnered with someone named Beau Delaney.

Bringing up a fresh search page, Blum entered "Peter Creighton," and, scrolling past entries related to the tomato research paper, he spotted a link to the university phone directory. There he found Creighton's address and phone number, as well as those for Delaney. He copied them down, then made his way up the stairs to the ground-level entryway.

After a short drive a couple of blocks north of campus, Blum turned onto a brick street in a decaying residential area, where towering sycamores covered the roadway in a tunnel-like canopy of crumpled green leaves. Halfway down the block, he located Creighton's apartment, a sandstone cube with grime-covered windows. Parking at the curb, he climbed the cracked concrete steps that led to a glass entry door and tried the knob, but it wouldn't budge. He scanned the corroded aluminum call panel to his left and pressed the button for "P. Creighton."

A second later, a metallic voice rattled, "Yeah? Who is it?"

Blum hesitated. Despite what had just happened in Feldmann's office, he decided not to reveal his real name.

"Jack Warner. I'm a friend of Hans Meier."

Long pause. "So?"

Blum didn't want to have a conversation over the intercom, but asking to be let in would be suspicious. Instead, he held the slip of paper with Creighton's address on it over the microphone and spoke through clenched teeth, hoping his words would sound like gibberish from electrical interference. "I'm trying to get a hold of him . . ." He released the talk button as if the line had disconnected.

"What?" Creighton sounded annoyed.

"Booksh," Blum slurred.

"Hold on a second." The speaker went dead. A moment later a skinny, dark-haired man in blue running shorts, an orange "Go Illini" T-shirt, and bare feet trotted into view. He opened the door but made no attempt to let Blum inside. "*What* were you saying?" He looked about the right age to be a graduate student.

"Sorry to bother you. I have some books to return to Hans Meier. I haven't been able to reach him for a week or so. He told me you two worked on some sort of research together. I was hoping maybe you'd know where he is."

"Like I'd give a rat's ass."

"Excuse me?"

"Look, that research paper was *my* idea. I arranged the funding *and* designed the experiment. We wrote the paper together, and then that bastard goes and submits it with *himself* as first author when department protocol says we list our names alphabetically. So, he's not exactly my best bud anymore. Now . . . If you don't mind . . ."

"Okay. Sorry to bother you," Blum said. Creighton simply grunted and slammed the door.

*

Beau Delaney lived farther from campus in an old, two-story house tucked between well-tended homes, where flower boxes hung below shuttered windows and kids played in trimmed front yards. Blum rang the doorbell and waited.

Moments later, a sandy-haired man in his twenties came to the door. Hairy legs protruded from khaki shorts, and a loose cotton shirt lay unbuttoned halfway down an equally hirsute chest. He flashed a pained smile at Blum and opened the door. They both froze as recognition swept over them.

Beau Delaney was the nervous bicycle-rider who had delivered Meier's note.

Delaney snapped his fingers, apparently trying to remember the name. Blum jumped in. "David Blum. You delivered an envelope to me last Sunday."

Delaney looked around. "Of course. Come on inside." He held the door open.

Blum stepped into a dark foyer that smelled of clean laundry as Delaney turned and climbed an old wooden stairway. Blum followed him to the second-floor landing and into one of the two apartments there. He found himself in a brightly lit living room with an open kitchen at the far end. There was no air conditioning, but a strong breeze blew through the room that ran the full depth of the apartment. Pasta boiled on the stove, and the sweet aroma of marinara filled the air.

Delaney ran to the kitchen and turned down the burners. He stirred the pasta while a Siamese cat eyed him from the low, sage-colored couch. The cat turned its gaze to Blum, twisting its head slightly, and then flew out of the open doorway and down the stairs.

"Um . . ." Blum started to say.

"Don't worry about Misty. She won't get far." Delaney wiped his hands a bit longer than necessary on a towel and came back into the living room. He sighed and pointed to a chair. "Have a seat."

Blum sank into a leather La-Z-Boy. "I need to talk to you about Hans."

Delaney's eyes locked on Blum. "Why? What happened to him?"

"I don't know that anything has, but why do you ask?"

Delaney sighed and shook his head. "Because something's going on, and I have no idea what it is." He took a deep breath and fell into the couch across from Blum. He grabbed a throw cushion and clutched it to his chest. "It's all so strange. Two weeks ago, every-thing was perfectly normal. Then, one night, he came over after working late, and he's tense and detached. The more I pushed him to tell me what's bothering him, the more irritated he got. I finally just dropped it. Then, last Friday, he came over—"

"Friday?" The night Blum's father had died.

"Yeah. Around eight. He seemed less agitated, but still not really relaxed. More like hopeful. We sat around and watched TV till he fell asleep around midnight."

Blum noticed a framed photograph next to his chair of Delaney and a slight guy with blond hair and glasses. He pointed to it. "You two?"

"Yeah. We used to be quite a number, you know." Delaney smiled to himself. "But then he got lost in his research, and our little ro-mance ended about a year ago. We've stayed good friends, though. Anyway, this past Monday—no, Tuesday, he showed up here look-ing scared. He still wouldn't tell me anything, other than some-thing horrible was going to happen. He begged me to let him stay here. Said he was afraid to go back to his apartment. I told him to go to the police if it was that bad, but he refused. Told me the cops are involved somehow in all this."

"The police?"

"Yeah. He made me swear not to call them."

"And you have no idea what 'all this' is?"

"Not a clue." Delaney stood up and started pacing. "Then, on Wednesday afternoon, he was still here, reading the paper, and all of a sudden he asked me what time it was."

Delaney glanced over at the food on the stove. He walked be-hind the counter and stirred the contents of the pots again. Blum followed him and sat on a barstool. "Then what?"

"I told him it was four-thirty, and he looked really disappointed.

He wrote a note, put it in an envelope, and asked me to get it to you at your father's house."

"How did he know my father?"

"He'd been a student in one of your dad's classes back when he was an undergrad. Said he knew you used to work for the FBI and might be able to help him. If I hadn't known how scared he was, I would have told him to deliver it himself. But, at that point, he was pretty much afraid to even go near the front window, so I agreed, and that's how I ended up at your house." He paused briefly. "So, what *did* the note say?"

"It said he wanted to talk to me about my father, and he suggested meeting, but then he didn't show up."

"Have you tried his apartment?"

"He wasn't there," Blum said, not wanting to alarm Delaney any further. "When he gave you the note . . . was that the last time you saw him?"

"No. He spent Wednesday night here too, but I don't think he slept at all. He looked horrible. Said he'd probably come back later, but I haven't seen him since. I tried his number. Recording said it was out of order. Probably forgot to pay his bill again. He's not very good about that." Delaney's voice choked. "When you rang the bell just now, I was praying it was him. I was cooking dinner in case he showed up."

"Anybody else who might be able to help me? I ran into Professor Feldmann, but he didn't seem to know anything."

Delaney rolled his eyes. "I'm not surprised. Hans thinks Feldmann is a god. He lives and dies for the guy's approval, but truth be told, I'd bet Feldmann barely knows who he is."

"What about Peter Creighton."

"Creighton? The guy Hans wrote a paper for?"

"Wrote it *for* him?"

"Yeah. The guy's kind of a doofus. He had a good idea but couldn't follow through on the research, and he can't write a coherent sentence to save his life. Hans gave him joint authorship anyway. It was a gift, but Creighton still felt like Hans dicked him when he didn't give him first author. That was a while ago, though. I doubt the two talk to each other anymore." Delaney fished a teaspoon from a drawer and dipped it in the sauce. He smacked his lips a few times as he tasted it, turned off the burner, and tossed the spoon in the sink.

"Anyone else? Other RAs?"

"There was one guy that Hans mentioned sometimes. Victor something. A post-doc working with Feldmann. They're pretty tight, but I've never met him. He's the one who helped get Hans the position in Feldmann's department."

Delaney turned off the burner for the pasta. He lifted the pot to the sink with an oven mitt and poured the contents into a waiting colander. The stainless-steel sink buckled noisily at the onslaught of steaming water. When he flipped the colander back into the pot, some of the spaghetti spilled onto the floor. "Oh shit," he said absently as he bent down and picked up the errant strands. When Delaney stood up, he had tears in his eyes.

"Poor Hans. I really hope he's okay. I feel like calling the police, but I don't want to break my promise to him. Or make things worse. Besides, I don't even know what I could tell them. I know you're not in the FBI anymore, but do you think you might be able to get any help from them?"

"I was in the financial crimes unit—years ago. Besides, like you . . . what could I really tell them?"

Delaney poured the sauce over the spaghetti and tossed it together. "I don't suppose *you'd* want to stay for dinner? It's only jarred sauce, but . . ."

Blum knew Beau could use some company, but the guilt he felt for not telling him everything he knew was already overwhelming his resolve, and getting the guy more upset wouldn't help anything.

"I have plans," Blum said, "but thanks for the offer. I'll call you when I know something." He scribbled his cell number on the back of one of his business cards and handed it to Delaney. "Give me a call if you hear anything."

Delaney led Blum to the door. "Please let me know if there's something I can do. I really mean that."

"I will. Thanks for talking to me. I'm sure Hans will show up soon."

As Blum walked down the steep stairway, Misty bolted back up and dashed between his legs, almost tripping him headfirst onto the ground-floor landing.

"Oh, there you are," he heard Beau exclaim as the front door closed behind him.

On the way back to his car, Blum recalled that his father had left him a message Saturday at around three a.m. London time saying he needed to talk. Blum had called a few times over the weekend but had only gotten voicemail. Three a.m. in London would have been nine p.m. in Champaign. Had Meier spoken to his dad on Friday, triggering that call? Delaney had also said Meier seemed to feel better that evening, but Tuesday, he'd had a total reversal. What could have happened Tuesday to trigger that?

Then Blum remembered; Tuesday was the day his father's obituary had appeared. Had Meier simply been upset because his chance to reach David had gone away? Or, had he suspected something nefarious had happened?

Blum decided to reach out to his father's doctor, an old family friend, to see if she might have any relevant insights. He left a message with her receptionist and was surprised to get a call back almost immediately. After the doctor conveyed how sad she was about Solomon's passing, Blum asked her what she knew about his father's death. She told him that she hadn't bothered to ask for the death certificate because the cause of death had been deemed natural causes, but she had found heart attack something of shock given his recent physical exam and EKG. Blum thanked her and hung up, wondering more and more if his father really had died of heart failure. Could that be what Meier had meant by *happened to your father?*

*

After dinner, Blum returned to his father's house. By then, the sunlight had completely faded, and the house had grown dark and somber. Blum switched on a few lights around the first floor to lift his spirits.

Knowing his father's idea of wine had been a gallon bottle of "hearty burgundy" that would sit in the kitchen cabinet for months, partly drunk, he headed instead to the liquor cabinet in the corner of the dining room. At least his father had developed a passion for single malts. Blum found a nearly full bottle of Bowmore 18 and poured himself a glass. He took a sip and let the smooth, peaty liquid warm its way down his throat.

Spotting a humidor nestled in the back corner of the cabinet, he lifted the burl-wood lid and selected a cigar at random. "Oliva V," the label read. He gave it a sniff and savored the rich aroma, then he clipped the end and picked up the gold lighter he'd given his father as a retirement gift. He thought about smoking the cigar in the living room—who would care? But, out of respect for the house, he stepped onto the back patio instead.

Sitting in a metal rocker, he lit the cigar and took a sip of the whisky, contemplating how many nights his father had sat in that very spot doing the same thing. As a boy, David would watch him from the window in his bedroom and wonder what his father could possibly think about sitting alone for all those hours.

Before he knew it, his glass was empty, and the cigar was all but a glowing nub. With a chuckle of amusement as he realized he'd just spent the past hour doing exactly what his father had done so many times, he tossed the cigar into the ashtray and headed to bed.

6. AN AMUSING STORY

Blum poured himself a mug of coffee and carried it out to the back patio. As he sipped the coffee, he thought about the relationship between his father and Feldmann. On reflection, his dad hadn't seemed particularly fond of the guy. In fact, other than that one dinner at his dad's house, he couldn't remember the two ever getting together socially. Which made it odd that Feldmann had bothered to come to the funeral. And why would Feldmann invite him to his house for dinner? Even his admin had commented that "Hardly anyone gets invited to the farm."

But Blum couldn't imagine Feldmann was up to anything illegal. The guy seemed perfectly harmless—a doddering old scientist with a demeanor more like a friendly dentist than a criminal. Regardless, Blum decided to poke around online to see if anything interesting surfaced.

Unlike Meier, Feldmann was clearly a celebrity, with thousands of references. Most were for articles from technical journals, but there were a number from popular magazines and newspapers as well. Blum glanced through a few, and they all told a similar story about a poor child from Hungary who'd escaped across the border to Austria during the 1956 uprising. After that, Feldmann had been taken under the wing of a wealthy Jewish family in Cleveland. He had studied at Indiana University where he'd received both his bachelor's and master's degrees in agriculture. From there, he'd studied genetics at Columbia and earned his PhD in 1979. He had joined the faculty at the University of Illinois the next year as an assistant professor. By 1986, he'd been promoted to full professor for his pioneering work in gene splicing. Some of the articles embellished the story more than others, but they all repeated similar facts, as though fed from the same press releases.

Blum scanned a few of the technical articles, but they far exceeded his level of understanding. Finally, on the sixth page of search results, he stumbled across one amusing story from 1999—a slightly snarky article in the *Ivesdale Reporter*, the local paper from a small farm town outside of Champaign. Entitled, "Teenaged Girl Mistakes Burning Propane Tank for Exploding Airplane." The story detailed how a high-school girl had claimed to witness a bizarre explosion at Professor Feldmann's farm. According to the article, she had wandered onto the property after wrecking a pickup truck through his fence in the wee hours of the morning. She stated that she had seen a small plane, curiously devoid of wings, explode while men with gas masks stood around and watched. The resulting smoke had killed a number of animals.

But the sheriff had dismissed her story, commenting that a propane tank had exploded on the professor's farm that night, and that the girl's vision of oddly dressed men was nothing more than the emergency workers trying to extinguish the fire. He implied that the teenager's more sinister interpretation was fueled by alcohol intoxication, considering she had admitted to drinking an unknown amount earlier that night at her prom. The reporter had concluded that "We're all still safe from things that go boom in the night, but perhaps not from hysterical high school girls."

The article included a picture of an overly made-up blonde trying to look years older than she was. She reminded Blum of the sort of girls who'd ignored him in high school. Suddenly, the whole horror of teenage romance came back to him, and he felt a twinge of selfish satisfaction that she'd no doubt been humiliated by the article. Being famous, he decided, must attract a lot of crazy accusations from publicity seekers.

*

Blum spent the afternoon with his father's lawyer, going over the will and signing countless documents to transfer ownership of accounts, or to acknowledge this or that. Still in a daze, he scribbled his name on whatever form the dour man put in front of him. Given what he'd experienced the day before, he half expected the meeting to end with the lawyer handing him a sealed envelope marked, "To be given to my son in the event of my untimely death," that would explain everything, but no such letter materialized.

*

That evening, after a simple dinner at home, Blum grabbed an Oliva and the gold lighter, poured a tall glass of Bowmore, and stepped onto the patio. For almost an hour, he sat there, backlit by the chandelier in the dining room, lost in his thoughts. Was Meier dead or alive? How was Meier's disappearance linked to his father?

Had his father really died of a heart attack? Could you really fake something like that? And what might he be able to learn when he had dinner with Feldmann the next day?

Eventually, the cigar burned down, the scotch glass sat empty, and Blum, deciding he rather liked his father's nightly routine, knew it was time to go to bed.

As he climbed the stairs to the second floor, he heard a car engine start right outside the front of the house. Given the late hour, it struck him as out of place. He jogged to the top of the stairs and rushed to the front bedroom window to get a look at who was out there. However, by the time he pulled back the drape, he only managed to catch a glimpse of the tail end of a silver sedan rounding the corner and speeding away.

7. INFECTION OF SALVATION

D avid Blum hunched over the dining room table, catching up with the endless stream of work emails that poured in daily. His admin had done a great job deflecting most of them, but there were a number he had to handle. It was difficult for him, though. He tried to concentrate, but he found his mind drifting from dividend yields and bond spreads back to the whereabouts of Hans Meier.

He minimized his email and brought up a new browser. Finding the home page for the *News Gazette*, he searched for any article from the past two weeks that mentioned "Hans Meier." NO MATCHES. He tried "dead body" instead. That yielded one story from a week earlier about the dead body of a cat that had clogged a sewer drain, flooding an intersection, but nothing about a human corpse. Entering only "body" brought up entries for auto body repair, and hair conditioner that provided "extra body," but no dead college students.

Resurrecting a practice from his FBI days, Blum grabbed his fountain pen and a blank sheet of paper and began scribbling down the names of everyone that seemed to be involved—Meier, Creighton, Feldmann, Tina Santini, the mysterious man at Fortunato's, Solomon, and even himself. Then he started drawing lines to represent connections between people. (Back in the Bureau he would have done this with photographs and strips of yarn.) Meier knew Blum's father, so he drew a line between their names. Meier had contacted him with the letter, so he drew a line from his name to Meier's. Meier worked in Feldmann's lab. Line. Santini was Feldmann's secretary. Another line.

When he finished, Blum had a mess of names and lines. After studying the human circuit-diagram for a bit, he took a fresh sheet of paper and rearranged the people such that only a few lines crossed each other. What he ended up with looked like a wagon wheel. Lines connected himself, his father, Feldmann, Creighton, and the mystery man into a rough circle. In the center sat Meier's name with spokes radiating outward to everyone else. There were a few gaps, but the message was clear: Meier was the key.

Blum closed his eyes. He pictured Meier leaving his apartment and walking to Fortunato's. After that, he imagined someone breaking into Meier's apartment and tearing apart the living room, dining area, and kitchen. Finally, he pictured the intruder finding the scribbled note, then running to catch Meier before he made it to the bar, leaving the rest of the apartment untouched.

Untouched! What if there was something significant in the bedroom where neither the intruder nor the police had searched? Maybe he could somehow convince the handyman to let him poke around in the bedroom for his supposed books.

Excited at the prospect, Blum drove back to Nealy Street and parked up the block from Meier's apartment. As he approached the parking lot, though, he was disappointed not to see Jack's blue pickup anywhere. Then he remembered. It was Sunday. Jack wouldn't be there. Oh well, he thought, there was always a chance the guy had been sloppy and left the door unlocked.

Blum pulled open the glass door and stepped into the foyer. A few garbled voices filtered out of an apartment downstairs. He climbed the half-flight of stairs and glanced down the hall. No open doors. He crept to Meier's apartment. Hearing no sound from inside, he reached for the knob to see if it was unlocked.

Just as his fingers touched the brass handle, he heard keys clattering on the other side of the flimsy door.

Not Jack. Which meant it could be anyone—even the guy who had trashed the place, and possibly accosted Meier. The knob started to turn. No time to reach the exit. Blum spotted a dark alcove further down the hall and dove into it. The space was barely chest deep. He pressed his sweaty back against a cold steel door and listened. A moment later, the hallway flooded with light as Meier's door opened.

Then Jack's familiar voice rang out. "Yeah. Yeah. I told you I would. Jesus." Blum listened to keys rattling as he tried to think of how he could have missed Jack's truck. "Yup, I finished the skim coat like I said." The rattling stopped. "Not till two?"

He could hear Jack breathing heavily, and he cursed himself for panicking instead of simply knocking on the door, but he knew there was no way he could step out of the shadows now and pretend he hadn't been hiding.

"No, I won't still be here." Pause. "Why? 'Cuz the skim's gotta dry before I can prime it. That's at least four hours." Another pause. "I don't want to wait here for an hour. It's Sunday, and I got other shit to do. If I have to come back, I might as well just stay here. Fuck!" Another beat passed. "Look," Jack said. "You're going to be back here tomorrow morning, right?" A pause. "I'll go over all that with you then." Jack's phone beeped off. "Asshole."

The keys jangled some more, and Blum heard a soft *clink*, followed by footsteps receding down the hall. When he finally heard the main door shut, he stole a glance from his hiding place. The hall was once again deserted.

Returning to the doorway, Blum turned the knob and pulled, but the door wouldn't budge. A quick examination revealed a new deadbolt had been installed and was extended. The hinges looked rather flimsy though, and the pin in the middle one was missing. Blum tried unsuccessfully to remove the top pin with his fingers, but when he pulled at the bottom one, it slid out easily.

Glancing around to make sure he was still alone, he grabbed the knob and gave it another tug. The bottom of the door swung out slightly and then snapped back. He pulled harder. The latch still held, but this time something fell past him to the ground. Blum looked down and spotted a key that Jack must have stashed on top of the doorframe.

Replacing the lower hinge pin, Blum snatched the key off the ground and slipped it into the lock. He retracted the deadbolt and reached for the doorknob, but then he paused. What had seemed like a good idea a moment ago now felt a bit crazy. If he got caught inside, he could be arrested for breaking and entering. And that would get him fired—perhaps even land him in jail. Worse, if Meier turned up dead, the authorities might decide he was somehow involved with *that*.

Blum took a deep breath. No choice, he told himself. He had to do it. Besides, this was Meier's apartment, and, to a large degree, he was doing this for him, too. His mind made up, Blum turned the knob, stepped into the apartment, and quickly locked the door behind him.

The furniture remnants that had been scattered around the room before were now stacked neatly in the center, leaving a three-foot walkway along the walls. Despite the open windows, the room smelled of plaster and paint mixed with the cheesy odor of dirty laundry.

Skipping the outer room, Blum headed straight to the bedroom. With only one small window shut tight, it smelled even mustier than the living room. He checked his watch. Five minutes past one. The caller, whoever it had been, would be there within the hour.

Blum started at the far corner of the room with a dresser and worked his way methodically back toward the entryway, but everywhere he looked, he found only the normal detritus of student living. The dresser held basic clothing, much of it worn, stained, or torn, along with receipts from grocery stores and the campus bookstore. On a small bookcase, he poked through old pens in a dusty coffee cup set between empty beer cans, chip wrappers, and crumpled napkins.

Frustrated, Blum lifted and shook the crumpled bed linens. Something rattled. Yanking back the matted, fleece bedspread, he discovered a pair of keys and a blank, gray plastic card held together by a rubber band. On one of the keys, he saw what seemed to be code numbers engraved on the brass below the U of I logo. Hoping that one of the keys might open Meier's office, he pocketed the set.

His bladder was twinging, but he tried to ignore it.

Eliminating the obvious places, Blum carefully slid out each dresser drawer and searched behind them, but all he discovered was a plastic bag of marijuana. Disappointed, he wrenched the dresser away from the wall and looked underneath. Seeing only an old comb and a D-cell battery, he dragged the dresser back in place, making sure it returned to the same carpet indentation from which it had come. The handyman wasn't going to dust for prints, but he might notice if the furniture had been moved.

Blum checked his watch again. One forty. He was running out

of time, and his bladder was now screaming. Afraid he might do something careless if distracted, he went to use the bathroom. While he stood there, his eyes scanned the room for hiding places. The only potential location seemed to be the medicine cabinet, but a search, including the inside of every pill bottle, yielded nothing.

One forty-five. His shirt clung to his sweat-soaked skin. The man on the phone would be there any minute. He might even be early. Where else to look? He felt around the back edge of the bathroom mirror, but it was clean.

Turning to leave the narrow space, Blum bumped into the towel bar. The thick brass rod attached to the wall between two sconces hit his hip, and he heard plaster crunch. As he recoiled from the sound, the rod fell to the tiled floor with a shattering clang. Nerves buzzing, he quickly snatched it up and tried to reset it, but when he let go, the tube started to fall again.

Maneuvering the rod back for another try, he spied a piece of pastel blue paper protruding from one end. He tugged at it, and a rolled sheet of lined notebook paper, no longer constrained by the tube, unfurled in his hand. Despite the messy lettering, Blum was fairly certain the list of words and phrases was Meier's handwriting.

He looked at his watch. Five till two.

Stuffing the paper into his pocket, he set the towel bar on the floor and headed to the main door. He listened intently for any sounds from the hallway. Hearing none, he inched the door open, stepped through, and quickly shut the door behind him.

When he glanced through the glass wall of the lobby, he saw a man coming up the front walk. Blum locked the deadbolt, slapped the key back on top of the doorjamb, and turned to face the apartment across the hall right as the man reached the entryway.

The lobby door swung open, and a thuggish looking redhead in his late thirties, dressed in tight jeans and a cheap mauve sport coat, bounded up the stairs. Spotting Blum, the man's eyes narrowed.

Without thinking about what might happen next, Blum knocked on the door opposite Meier's. He pretended to ignore what was going on behind him, but sweat was running down his neck and chest, and he hoped the guy wouldn't notice how flushed he was. After a moment of tense silence, he was relieved to hear a key in the lock behind him and the door opening. A second later, as the door slammed shut, Blum let out a heavy sigh.

But then the door in front of him opened, and a bored voice moaned, "What?"

Blum faced an unshaven guy, dressed in white boxers and a yellow T-shirt with Greek letters. The young man looked puzzled and a bit irritated.

. Blum simply shook his head. "Sorry. Wrong address."

The fellow stared at him. "What the fuck, man? I was sleeping."

"Sorry." Blum turned and ambled out of the building to his car.

Ten minutes later, he was sitting in a back booth of a coffee shop on the south end of campus, nursing a large Americano. Ignoring the clatter and hissing of the serving area, he unfolded the sheet of paper he had found in Meier's bathroom and smoothed it out against the varnished wooden tabletop. The writing was sloppy, as though it had been hurriedly penned, and, despite the lined paper, the lettering tilted at odd angles, almost as if the notes had been scribbled in the dark.

Individually, the words seemed to have meaning, but read together, they produced nothing but gibberish:

Pangaea
Six million chosen
Everyone dies
People bury their own

Infection of salvation
Millennium can begin
?Ruhola?

Blum had heard of the first word. Something scientific, he thought, but it could have also been the name of a rock band or a movie, for that matter. The last entry didn't mean anything at all to him, and the question marks seemed to indicate Meier hadn't known what it meant either.

Using the browser on his phone, Blum searched for *Pangaea*. It *was* a scientific term—the name of the original landmass that had split into pieces and drifted around the globe, ultimately forming the present-day continents. So what? And what did the other notations mean?

Six million chosen. Did that somehow refer to the Holocaust? Six million Jews had died. What in the world did that have to do with Pangaea?

Everyone dies. The Holocaust again? If that were the case, why *dies* and not *died*? Blum studied the letters carefully to see if he'd misread it. No. It definitely said "dies." Holocaust II? Six million more Jews? He had no clue.

People bury their own. That sounded bad as well. It might be a reference to some type of mass disposal, but burying six million bodies defied comprehension. Where could anyone do that and get away with it? And how would someone go about killing six million people in a way that left enough of "their own" to dispose of the bodies?

Blum took a deep breath and looked around the room. Here he was dissecting a possible mass murder, surrounded by kids in baggy shorts and T-shirts chattering on about upcoming class schedules and parties. He shook his head in disbelief as he moved on to the next phrase.

Infection of salvation. Salvation meant saving. Some kind of inoculation?

Millennium can begin. Which millennium? The calendar had turned over years ago. And why "*can* begin," instead of "*did* begin" or "*will* begin"? Time marches forward. It doesn't need permission. Again, images of the Holocaust came to Blum. Hitler had planned for his *Tausendjähriges Reich*—a thousand-year kingdom. Was that what it referred to?

And then the last term, "Ruhola." He looked it up on his phone. Links appeared to various Facebook pages, but nothing struck him as an obvious connection. Perhaps one of these people was involved? The search engine also suggested searching on "Ruhollah," which Blum did. That led to articles about Ayatollah Ruhollah Khomeini—the spiritual leader of the 1979 Iranian revolution. Bizarre. He checked his watch. Nearly four-thirty. He needed to get home to shower for his dinner with Feldmann. He folded up the list and tucked it in his pocket.

As he drove west from campus, he wondered why Meier had hidden the list. To protect it? If so, from whom? Or maybe he was concerned about being caught with it? Whatever had worried him, he certainly had gone to great lengths to keep it from being found. Perhaps Blum's trip to Feldmann's farm for dinner would shed some light on why.

8. FOOD TO FEED THE WORLD

A t six o'clock, David Blum stepped out of the shower and dressed in a pair of cream cotton slacks, a pink Oxford shirt, and a pair of loafers. He raided his father's closet for a navy blazer and headed for the garage.

Settling into his roadster's deeply bolstered driver's seat, he pumped the gas pedal a few times to prime the four Weber carburetors, and then, with a twist of the key, the engine practically exploded to life. Amidst the caterwauling of the V8 smashing around the confines of the garage, Blum strapped himself into the four-point harness and eased the cue-ball shift knob forward. As he let out the heavy clutch pedal, the tires chirped briefly as the car bounded out of the garage.

Blum made his way to Springfield Avenue and cruised westward through town, bathed in the music of the finely tuned motor. Once outside the city limits, he pushed the car hard, marveling at the engine's power. The small roadster was a rather crude throwback to the sixties—a brutish engine, two seats, four tires, and a steering wheel—but it drove like a flat-out race car. It felt good to be out in the open, too. There was a freedom in the countryside that he missed in Chicago. Out here, he could see for miles in every direction and know he was absolutely alone. It was a different kind of privacy that people raised in large cities never seemed to understand.

Halfway to Feldmann's farm, Blum zipped past a sign for County Road 500E. The number rang a bell. Pulling onto the gravel shoulder, he used his phone and retrieved the email with the police report he'd received the other day. Exactly as he remembered, the sheriff had found his dad on 500E, between 800N and 900N—only a few miles south of where he sat parked. Blum made a U-turn and headed south on 500E. After passing 900N, he slowed to a crawl. Not sure what exactly he was looking for, he scanned both sides of the road, but nothing stood out. No skid marks. No tire tracks on the shoulder. No damaged foliage. In fact, the mile of gravel-strewn asphalt, flanked by grass and weeds, seemed completely undisturbed.

It looked like any other stretch of road, as far as he could tell. It did strike him as being a particularly isolated spot, though. Late at night, you could probably shoot someone along there, he guessed, and no one would even hear it. Even if they did, the sound would be barely more than a cough by the time it reached the nearest farmhouse. And, besides, no one ever does anything about *one* sound in the night.

So what *had* brought his dad to that spot—voluntarily or otherwise? It *was* approximately halfway between his father's house and Feldmann's farm. Or was that just a coincidence? Anything in Champaign County southwest of town was roughly on the way to the farm. He turned right on 800N and headed off into the glare of the setting sun, as puzzled as when he'd arrived.

A bit later, he arrived at a stop sign where two county roads met. Across the intersection on the right, he spotted a field surrounded by an eight-foot chain-link fence. A spiral tunnel of barbed wire snaked its way along the top of the prison-like barrier that extended out to the west and north as far as he could see. According to the directions, that was Feldmann's farm.

As the significance of such an ominous barrier sank in, Blum's mouth turned down in a wry smile. Must be some mighty big squirrels the professor needed to keep out, he mused.

From the aerial view on his GPS, Blum could see that the main gate lay half a mile straight ahead, but, with a few minutes to spare before seven, he decided to drive the long way around to get a good look at the entire property.

Turning right, he drove north, along the east fence. Despite being the height of the growing season, the fields to his left lay fallow. Only weeds covered the broken soil except where clumps of bramble and bushes had grown. Across the barren terrain, roughly a half mile in, he spotted some buildings, but the sun's glare obscured their details.

At the next intersection a mile ahead, he turned left. Along the initial section of the north perimeter, lush orchards produced what looked like apples by shape, but which were deep purple in color and almost the size of small melons. The weight of the strange orbs bent the branches like willow boughs. Further along, he passed a hundred-foot gap in the grove where an asphalt roadway began fifty yards from the fence. From there, it disappeared into the heat waves rising off the blacktop in the distance, perhaps leading all the way south to the buildings he'd seen before.

As he approached the western side of the north face, the orchard ended, replaced by tall, bushy vines, partly hidden under canopies of mosquito netting. The fabric crawled with inch-long insects, and great clouds of the black bugs flew around the exterior—in some places so thick they completely obscured the netting.

Suddenly, the insects parted, forming a wide funnel that splayed upward as well. Through the center of the gap, a white four-prop drone emerged. It paused briefly, then spun slowly, drifting closer to the fence. After a brief pause, it veered upward to the left and drifted back over the netted forest of vines and disappeared.

At the next intersection Blum slowed and turned south. For another quarter mile, he followed the unbroken fence, passing more of the vines covered with the same insect-swarmed netting, and he wondered what strange attraction the plants held for the bugs. Past the vines, he crossed a small bridge over a narrow creek that ran from the neighboring farm, and a little further, he came upon fat, treelike corn stalks that towered more than four feet over those on the other side of the road. Blum shook his head at the bizarre collection of flora.

His tour completed, he turned and drove on to the entranceway, idling up to the portcullis-like main gates. As he looked around, he noticed two metal posts on either side of him with closed-circuit cameras staring out behind smoked Plexiglas domes. The retina-like lenses pivoted back and forth rhythmically. When the left one scanned past Blum's car, it stopped and backed up. The huge, cycloptic eye seemed to bore into him as it twisted and focused. A moment later, he heard a low, mechanical whine, and the doors pivoted inward on shiny, stainless steel hinges. Blum motored through, and as the gates swung briskly shut behind him, he wondered briefly if Feldmann used them to keep things out, or to keep things in. A quarter mile up the hedge-lined drive, he parked on a circular gravel area behind a black AMG Mercedes sedan whose license plate read "AGRI 1."

Feldmann's house, a typical Midwestern four-square of dark red brick with a black asphalt tile roof and a large porch that extended across the front, appeared to be about a century old. Behind the house, slightly to the left and another hundred yards in, sat an immense, windowless, tan-brick structure the size of a gymnasium. The low sun glinted off a glass and metal greenhouse on its roof.

Halfway to the building, a paved road headed north. On the right side of the asphalt lane stood a wooden barn, and to its left, a long, log-shaped building of corrugated steel, topped by a bright-orange windsock. Blum guessed that the drive served as a runway, and that the steel building was a hangar for a plane—or two, given how large the structure was.

Just as Blum stepped out of his car, the front door of the house swung open, and out strode Feldmann, dressed in khakis and a white shirt with a blue ascot.

"Welcome. Welcome," he said. He walked up to Blum and shook his hand. "I apologize again for not being able to talk with you the other day, but you know how it is. I can't bite the hand that feeds me, and, as you can see," he gestured to all that was around him, "it feeds me very well."

"Of course," Blum said.

Feldmann ran his hand over the aluminum fender of Blum's car. "My goodness. When you said you had a car, you weren't kidding. Is this an original Shelby Cobra?"

"Not quite. Real ones are going for seven figures these days. This is an AC Mark IV. It was a continuation of the Cobra built by Autokraft back in the eighties and sold through Ford dealers."

"How fast will it go?"

"Well, in addition to beefing up the suspension, I had the stock engine heavily modified," Blum said. "I've never topped her out, but I would guess around one-sixty or one-seventy. Fast enough to get me into a lot of trouble. Of course, your car's no slouch, either."

Feldmann nodded at the returned compliment. "If you'd like, we can take a quick tour of some of my experiments. After that, we'll sit for dinner."

"Great," Blum said, remembering Feldmann's "chef" and wondering if the NIH paid for that, too.

Blum let Feldmann lead him around the back of the house. Feldmann, the grand tour guide, described everything with expansive gestures. He told Blum about his research on gene splicing that could, among other things, grow larger strains of crops and livestock on less food. He also described his work on breeding plants that were attractive yet deadly to certain insects in order to act as "death traps" for crop pests. Blum guessed the vines he had seen under the white netting were examples of this. In addition, Feldmann described his work on cross-breeding favorable traits from different plants using gene splicing to avoid cross-species infertility, all of which he dismissed as fairly pedestrian stuff. Blum had trouble keeping up with Feldmann, both in terms of the content of his exposition and the pace with which the professor marched across his property.

"And over here," Feldmann gestured, "is my hangar where I keep my two planes."

"Two planes, huh? What kinds?"

"Well," he said, obviously proud of his toys. "I have a Stearman that's been converted for crop dusting, but of course it's fully capable of aerobatics and can be loads of fun to fly. Only you have to make sure the flow valve is turned off or you'll get a face full of pesticide. Here, let me show it to you,"

Feldmann led Blum into the hangar through a narrow aluminum door near the back corner of the domed building. A jaundicing orange glow of sodium-vapor lights along the ceiling illuminated the interior, and the stale air smelled of motor oil, fertilizer, and gasoline. Inside, two planes stood in view. The closer one was the bi-winged Stearman. On the floor, beneath the plane's front end, sat a tray of cat litter to catch the inevitable drip of oil from the radial engine.

"Have you ever been up in one of these?" Feldmann asked him.

"Only once," Blum replied. "Back in college, a friend of mine took me up. Showed me the whole lot—rolls, loops, even a hammerhead. Breathtaking."

Feldmann looked disappointed that he had missed the opportunity to impress David. "Yes," he said. "It's fun."

"What's that behind it?" Blum asked, pointing to the twin-engine turboprop on the other side of the hangar.

"My basic transportation," Feldmann said. "A Beechcraft King Air C90. I use it to get to conferences and such. Most of the places I go are rural, which makes commercial flying impractical. This plane really does the trick. Would you like to see the inside?"

"Sure," Blum said, trying to sound enthusiastic. He didn't bother to mention that the prior winter a client of his had flown him to Aspen in his King Air for a ski weekend.

The hatch to the plane yawned open, forming a short ladder. Blum climbed up first and stepped into the aircraft. Typically, such a plane would seat six people in relative comfort, but relatively comfortable clearly wasn't good enough for the professor. His cabin had been reconfigured with only three seats—leather easy chairs, really—two facing a low table covered in walnut burl with leather padding around the edges. A deep claret carpet covered the floor, and more walnut burl lined the cabin walls up to the beltline. All told, it was twice as nice as the one in which Blum had flown, and he expressed his admiration to Feldmann, who, still standing at the top of the entry ladder, beamed with pride.

As Blum stepped out of the hatch and descended the aluminum stairs, he heard a man's voice call from behind the Stearman.

"Otto? Are you there?"

"Yes," Feldmann yelled. "What is it?"

"A little problem," the voice said. "I need to talk to you."

Feldmann looked as though he was trying to think of an excuse to dismiss the caller. "Is it important? I'm with our visitor."

"It will just take a few minutes."

Feldmann weighed unknown points and then told Blum to wait—he'd be right back.

With that, Feldmann ambled off around the biplane toward the exit, and Blum heard the hangar door bang shut. Only the sixty-hertz hum of the overhead lights remained.

Blum strolled past the King Air, admiring its lines. When he tired of that, he wandered around the hangar, stopping at a workbench in the back. He studied the various tools, all as clean as surgical instruments and carefully arranged in order by size.

Next to the tool bench he noticed a door, and, on reflection, it occurred to him that the room he was in was actually quite a bit smaller than the building had looked from the outside. Suspecting the door might lead to another room, not just a closet, he tried the knob, but found it locked. He looked at the handset and smiled when he realized how easy it would be to slip the latch.

With no sign of Feldmann, and wondering why an inside door would be kept locked, he plucked a small, slotted screwdriver from the tool rack.

A second later, he felt the latch give way. Nudging open the solid aluminum door, he stepped part way into the dark cavern on the other side. The shaft of light from the doorway illuminated a shiny metal vessel resting on some sort of wheeled frame. At first Blum thought it might be a tanker truck to fuel the planes, but then he noticed small, round windows down the side, making it look like some sort of submarine.

Running his hand along the inside wall, he found a switch and flicked it up. Overhead floodlights flashed on, revealing the fuselage of a business jet chained to a long trailer. The wings had been removed, presumably to fit it in the small space. As he scanned the aluminum body, he spotted a gaping hole through the cargo hatch located right below the tail section. The metal around the fissure bent sharply outward. His scalp began to tingle. Only an explosion could do something like that.

Looking closer, Blum could see that the steel parts around the opening had rusted, and a thick layer of dust had collected on the body. He also noticed dense cobwebs draping the wheels of the trailer.

So, at least that part of the girl's story in the *Ivesdale Reporter* seemed to be true.

Blum heard footsteps.

He flicked off the light and shut the door. Out of the corner of his vision he caught sight of Feldmann stepping around the tail of the Stearman. With no time to return the screwdriver to the tool rack, he tossed it on the workbench and jumped back.

"Sorry to have left you like that," Feldmann apologized. "I hope you weren't bored."

"Oh, no," Blum replied. "I love looking at planes. All kinds."

"Good. Good." Feldmann seemed oblivious to Blum's trespass. He led Blum back out into the orange dusk to tour some of his crops. "These here," he explained, "are experimental corn. Not only do the plants grow faster than normal strains—fast enough to plant twice in one season not too far south of here—they also yield thirty-seven percent more bushels per acre. You'll see how good they taste, too. We're having some for dinner."

"I'm looking forward to it," Blum said, his mind racing with the implications of what he'd seen. What else had the girl in the article claimed? Something about guys in space suits. And a cloud of smoke that killed some animals. What the hell could that have been about?

Having missed what Feldmann had just said, Blum changed the subject. "What's in that big building over there—the one with the glass panels on the roof?"

"Oh, that," Feldmann answered flatly. "It's for some experiments that have to be more carefully controlled. Pretty boring stuff, really." Feldmann turned toward the farmhouse. "That's about it for the walking tour. The rest would require a Jeep. I have some other crops growing around, but most of them are leftovers from old research. You might have seen some as you drove up. Depending on what route you took."

Was that a veiled accusation? Perhaps the drone he'd seen had spotted him, and the caller in the hangar had been reporting Blum's reconnaissance.

Feldmann let it go and instead launched into a short history of the farm.

"I bought this place over thirty years ago to conduct experiments. It's exactly one square mile—six hundred forty acres. At first, I was simply experimenting with hybrid plants—the old-fashioned way, with pollen and seeds and all that. Sort of like trying to find the third root of a six-digit number with paper and pencil nowadays. Then I got involved in genetic manipulation, and my research really got going. Now I'm funded by grants from all over— Department of Agriculture, FDA, NIH, CDC and such."

"What about private companies?"

"Not as much. Those folks want to keep their discoveries to themselves, and I want to publish."

The sun had settled quite low, and the two men walked in the shadow of the barn.

"How did you first meet my father?" Blum asked.

"He never told you? We escaped Hungary together in 1956."

"Really?"

"Yes," Feldmann said. "We met late one night on a rotting pier along the Lafnitz Fluss, a river that runs between Hungary and Austria. I was a little boy. Only six. I think your father was twelve. Both families had made arrangements with an old man who had a boat to get us across the river to escape the Soviets. Solomon had been separated from his father, and he stood there on the dock and refused to leave without him. At first, the boat pilot insisted we all wait. I don't think it was compassion, though. The greedy bastard only wanted to get his money. Finally, when we heard shooting just up the street, we knew the Russians were close, and he insisted we leave. Poor Solomon almost jumped out of the boat to stay behind, but we convinced him that his father would join him on the other side when he could get out of Hungary, too."

"But he didn't," Blum commented.

"No. He didn't. We heard later from another group of refugees that the Soviets had caught up to him. If Solomon hadn't come with us, he no doubt would have been killed too." Feldmann looked away for a second, apparently reliving the experience. "And then . . . let me see . . . I didn't see your father again until 1979, during the Iranian Revolution."

"What?" Blum's brow furrowed. Could that explain *Ruhollah*?

"Your father wrote an opinion piece that got published in *The Atlantic*. The name was familiar. When I took a careful look at the picture of him included with the article, I was sure it was the boy on the boat that I remembered. Illinois was one of a number of schools trying to recruit me, and I tracked down Solomon when I got here."

"And he got you a position here?"

"Well, no. He didn't *get* me a position. But he talked to me about the school and put in a good word for me with the Dean of the College of Sciences. In the end, they made me a great offer."

The pole light by the barn snapped on, bathing the weed-strewn gravel below in a blue-white pool of luminescence. Within seconds, a cloud of moths and small flying beetles collected around the mercury-vapor lamp.

Feldmann gestured toward the small porch at the back of the house. "Please."

As Blum climbed the two concrete steps that led up to the landing, the door opened. An aproned man in his late fifties with close-cropped silver hair stuck his hand out in greeting, his eyes crinkling as he smiled.

"Otto, please introduce me to your guest. I've quite a feast prepared."

"David, this is Jerry, my housekeeper and chef. Jerry, this is David Blum. His father was a friend of mine. He's the one who died recently. I told you about him."

"Yes," Jerry said. "I remember." He turned to Blum. "So sorry."

Blum nodded appreciatively, feeling a wave of sadness. He sniffed back a tear.

"Come inside," Jerry invited.

"Thank you," Blum said, stepping into the kitchen. Savory scents from pots on the stove and the platters set out on the wide soapstone counters mingled, creating an enticing aroma.

"Perhaps you'd like to wash up before dinner," Feldmann offered. "There's a small lavatory through that door across the hall."

Blum stepped into the bathroom and shut the door. As he washed his hands, he stared at his reflection in the mirror and thought again about the plane he'd just seen. Had the explosion been planned, or an accident? Either way, why not have the plane repaired instead of hiding it away all these years? A jet like that, even damaged, had to be worth a million dollars or more.

Perplexed, Blum dried his hands and returned to his hosts.

Jerry joined them for a wonderful dinner of roast venison with porcini mushroom sauce and giant butter-slathered ears of corn. As they dug in, Blum probed further on Feldmann's research.

"The last time we had dinner together, you talked about how you were trying to produce more food. Is that still the goal?"

"Good memory," Feldmann replied. "Yes. Food to feed the world."

"Do you really think that we'll ever be able to feed everyone?"

"Sure. We can do it right now."

"Then why don't we? Money?"

"No. Politics, mostly. Of course there are things like national boundaries and wars that impede things, but in a lot of the so-called developing world, leaders use food as a way to retain power—to reward their friends and punish their enemies—even if it means starving off entire portions of their citizens. In the developed world, it's more a case of stupid, irrational fear of things like bioengineered crops. The same flat-earth science-deniers who think vaccines cause autism worry that genetically modified corn is going to turn us all into mutants. And then they get dim-witted politicians to agree with them."

"You said, 'mostly politics.' What else?"

"Well . . . let me put it this way—how many times a day do you want to eat pond algae and insect larvae?"

"So what is the answer?"

"Well, there's no one answer, and there are other constraints that the world needs to solve as well, like pollution, fresh water, and disease. But the university administration is going to force me to retire next year regardless, so to try to keep them happy till then, I just focus on food."

"Back when I went to school here, the only thing I remember that kept the administration happy was a winning football team," Blum added cynically.

Feldmann's eyes glared. "Exactly!" he said, making menacing stabbing motions at Blum with his knife. "I couldn't agree more. Football is practically a religion around here. You know, sometimes I actually think the university would be happier if I focused my research on breeding larger football players for them instead of feeding starving people."

"Could you actually do that? Engineer larger people?"

"Sure. You simply rewrite the program."

"Program?"

"The genetic program. DNA."

"Just like that?"

"Well, no, of course not *just like that*. It's very . . . delicate. A lot can go wrong, and we're only now figuring out what all of the code does."

"But you're saying you could design a person from scratch?"

"Theoretically. But not practically." Feldmann held up his fork with a piece of meat on it. "That would be like trying to create a new recipe by specifying it at the molecular level. Every single atom—how much and where. Pretty much impossible, no? So what do you do instead? You create a new dish by combining 'ingredients'—venison, mushrooms, maybe some cream—in a new way. In principle, geneticists do something similar. We take strands of DNA that do things we understand and want, then we modify the parts we want to change. In the end, we create a new genome that accomplishes our goal."

"And how do you actually do that?"

Feldmann immediately launched into a short lecture filled with words like "ligand" and "nucleotide" that lost Blum almost as quickly as it started. "And if you want to learn more," he said, in conclusion, "sign up for one of my courses."

"Maybe I will," Blum said. He looked at his watch. Nearly ten, and still no mention of Meier. He wiped the corner of his mouth with his napkin. "Well, that was an excellent dinner. My compliments to the chef." He smiled at Jerry, who beamed back. "And I certainly want to thank you for inviting me, especially on such short notice."

"You're welcome," Feldmann said. "Usually my only dinner companions are Jerry here and the occasional visiting professor."

"And, of course, Lawson," Jerry said.

"Yes," Feldmann grunted, looking intently at Jerry.

"Sometimes," Jerry added, sheepishly.

"Lawson?" Blum asked. He recognized the name from the mailbox next to Meier's at Cotespath Hall.

Feldmann looked as though he needed to explain. "A senior researcher. He's been over to dinner a few times. He has special dietary requirements, so Jerry remembers when he comes."

Blum glanced at Jerry to see his reaction, but the chef simply stared down at his plate.

"So you can see, you're a very welcome guest." Feldmann wiped his mouth and threw his napkin on his plate. "David, I understand you left the FBI. What do you do now?"

"I work for an investment advisor. I help rich people with their money."

"That's quite a change."

"Not really. I was mostly investigating financial crimes at the Bureau."

"And now you're helping people commit them. Hah! Seriously, though, I guess you're taking some time off from work?"

"I'm taking a short leave. Just trying to clear up some things of my father's."

"You must have a bit of time on your hands," Feldmann said. "Tracking dear Meier all over town to return some books—books you didn't even bring with you."

All over town? Did Feldmann know that he'd been to Meier's apartment?

"Your father taught political science," Feldmann stated. "Is that what the books are about?"

"Yes."

"I wonder why Meier would want books like that."

"I don't know," Blum said, feeling the conversation had become something of an interrogation. "Why don't you ask him?"

Feldmann seemed to ponder that. "Perhaps I will," he said. "But now it's getting late, and you have a bit of a drive home. Me, I must get my sleep. I have a lot to do tomorrow. And so I really must wish you a good night and send you on your way."

Blum acted cheery, despite his concern. "Thanks again for dinner."

"The gates will open for you when you approach them," Feldmann explained, as he walked Blum to the door. "But, remember, they open in. Give yourself some room. If you have any trouble with the sensor, press the black button on the post."

"Good night," Blum called, walking to his car and starting the engine. He flicked on the headlights and pulled around to the long drive.

As he headed for the front gate, he got the distinct feeling he was being watched, but he refused to turn around. At the main road, he waited impatiently for the gates to part, but they didn't. A creepy, uneasy feeling came over him, and he hesitated before getting out of the car to press the button on the post. Finally, feeling a little stupid for sitting so long, he shoved open the door and stepped out.

His shoes made a loud scrunch in the gravel. As he walked toward the thin, metal pole with the little box and black button, his gaze was drawn down to the dirt by a clump of heavy bushes. Next to the underbrush, he noticed a strange object that looked like some sort of brown bean pod but as large as a man's shoe. It was hard to make out the details in the dim light, but part of it seemed to be moving. As Blum stepped closer to investigate, the object suddenly rose up on spindly, crab-like legs and scampered into the bushes, antennae waving from side to side.

Blum jumped back, heart pounding.

Lit up in the blinding halo of his headlights and unable to see what other bizarre creatures might be waiting for him in the shadows,

Blum felt naked and vulnerable. He hit the black button and dashed back to his car. As the gates uttered a low whining sound, Blum accelerated quickly, kicking up a spray of gravel and plunging the car through the parting barricades as soon as they spread wide enough to pass. He spun a fast left onto the tar-covered road, floored the accelerator, and didn't lift his right foot until he saw the steely skeleton of the fence disappear in his rear-view mirror.

9. SHADOWS ON THE WALL

B lum sped from Feldmann's farm back to Champaign and didn't slow down until he reached the edge of town. As he neared his father's street, he signaled a left to change lanes, but a red Camaro blocked his path, and he missed the turn. Forced to drive to the next intersection and take a circuitous return route, he ended up approaching the house on a side road. As he passed the garage, he spotted a silver Infiniti sedan parked on the main street off to the right.

Could it be the same car he'd seen driving away the other night?

Suddenly, the image of Delaney swerving on his bike as he left the funeral reception came to mind. Hadn't that been an Infiniti as well? The most likely explanation was that the car belonged to someone in the neighborhood, but given all he'd been through, Blum didn't want to take any chances. He shut off his headlights and let the car coast to a stop. Then he let the car roll back down the slight hill of the street until he was out of sight of the sedan. When he was sure he was blocked from view, he turned the car around and drove to the opposite side of the block.

He parked at the curb in front of a house whose yard he knew backed up to his father's. Then, confirming no one was around, he crossed the sidewalk and followed a flagstone path that led behind the neighbor's garage. Creeping across the rear lawn to the bushes at the far end, he found a gap and crawled through. For a few minutes, he sat there on his haunches and listened. Hearing nothing but crickets, he proceeded across the grass to the rear patio and the French doors that led into the dining room.

He dug into his pocket for the key and inserted it into the lock. But just as he started to turn it, a shadow seemed to flash across the wall in the hallway beyond the dining room.

Blum froze. Had he really just seen that?

Then the shadow bounced by again in the opposite direction.

Someone *was* in the house!

Blum stepped back from the door. His first instinct was to call the police. He grabbed his phone, but before he switched it on, he thought about what Delaney had told him. What if the *wrong* police showed up? Would they come after him too?

But that was stupid, he told himself. There was nothing about this situation to connect him to Meier. This was about someone in *his* house. He ducked around the corner to hide the light from his screen and made the call.

"911. What's your emergency?"

"Someone's broken into my house."

"Are you in danger?"

"No. I'm outside."

"You're not in the house? Is your alarm going off?"

Blum stumbled. "No. I saw a shadow."

"A *shadow*? Did you see an actual intruder?"

"No."

"Is anyone at risk in the house?"

Blum cringed. "No."

"Sir. I've got four lines on hold. I need to hang up now."

"But—"

The line went dead. *Shit*, he cursed silently, knowing he should have waited until he actually saw a person. Or would that be too late? The intruder could be running out the door at that point. And that meant he needed get a look at who was inside first. Taking a deep breath, he crept back to the door and crouched down.

He spent a few minutes staring through the dining room into the front hall to see if the intruder would reveal himself—either crossing the dining room entrance or, better still, actually walking into the room. But nothing happened.

Afraid the intruder may not venture to the back rooms, Blum decided to risk moving to the living room window on the side of the house. From there, he'd be able to see into the front rooms, including the stairs to the second floor. It was risky, though. Despite being out of sight from the Infiniti parked down the block, he'd be completely exposed to anyone approaching from the other direction.

He wiped the sweat from his hands, walked across the patio, and ducked around the corner of the house. From there, he crawled on his hands and knees through the waist-high bushes along the brick façade until he reached the arched window near the front corner. Confirming that the street was deserted, he slowly stood up, careful not to cast a shadow into the interior.

The next few minutes felt like hours as he stared through the window, past the partially drawn drapes, into the dark living room and the lit hallway beyond, waiting for any signs of activity. But nothing moved.

Then, just as he was beginning to suspect the intruder might have gone upstairs, two things happened almost simultaneously. First, a brown-haired man of about thirty walked into the hall from the stairway. Then a second man, taller, with graying hair, stepped into view only a few feet inside the window where Blum stood.

Blum couldn't see the second man's full face—only his profile, backlit from the arched doorway of the living room. Blum watched as the two men conversed. He could only hear a couple of muffled words, but he was pretty sure he heard Feldmann's name.

The man in the hallway walked toward the front door as the man by the window crossed the living room and stepped into the lighted entry. He glanced to the right, and Blum saw his face. Neither man was the one he'd seen in Fortunato's.

Intent on watching the intruders, Blum almost missed a reflection in the window of headlights approaching him from behind. He ducked and let the car pass, but when he looked back inside, both men were gone from view. Then, from around the corner of the house, he heard the front door open and the two men talking to each other, seemingly unconcerned about being noticed. He heard the latch engage and the door lock, and a chill ran down his spine as he realized the men must have gotten a key somehow.

Blum burrowed down as low as he could behind the taller grass at the edge of the lawn and listened intently, trying to discern which direction their footsteps would take them—past the corner of the house where he was, or down the block to the Infiniti. Barely able to breath, he waited. When he was finally convinced their footsteps were fading, he peeked over the dew-speckled grass. No one in sight. Crawling forward, he stole a look around the front corner of the house and saw the two men walking toward the Infiniti. Before they reached the car, the curbside door opened. So, the Infiniti *was* theirs, and someone had been in the car waiting for them.

The younger man climbed into the back seat behind the driver, and the other man sat in the front passenger seat, slamming the door behind him. Blum contemplated rushing out to get a look at the car's plate number but decided it would be too risky. They knew where to find him, and he knew nothing about them.

The Infiniti pulled away from the curb and squealed around the corner onto the side street, its exhaust note rapidly fading away.

Should he call 911 again? After all, he'd just witnessed a crime in progress. But the intruders had left empty-handed as far as he could tell, so what would the police do? No damage done. Nothing stolen. "We've got your statement, Mr. Blum. Keep your eyes open and let us know if they come back." And that would be it.

It unnerved Blum how relaxed the two men had appeared as they strolled back to their car. What *had* they been searching for? Those stupid books he had invented that Feldmann seemed so interested in? Then again, what if they had actually been there to *leave* something? A bug? Surveillance cameras? If their goal had been to harm him, they'd probably still be inside, waiting. Regardless, it was too risky to stay there. He needed to collect his things and find a hotel.

After waiting a while to make sure the Infiniti didn't return, he unlocked the patio door and stepped into the dining room. Wasting no time, he packed up his laptop and charger. Then he ran upstairs, hefted his suit bag on the bed and packed it with the clothing and toiletries he needed. Returning to the dining room, he tossed the leather bag by the computer.

There was one more thing he needed.

When he'd left the FBI, David had given his personal-carry pistol to his dad for safekeeping. Dashing through the kitchen and down the basement stairs to the furnace room, he tugged off a heavy quilt that covered a battered, steel safe. Kneeling down, he spent a minute trying to recall the combination. Then he remembered— his parents' anniversary. He spun through the digits and swung open the heavy door.

Digging around, he found the small, leather bag that held his Kahr MK9. He unzipped the flap and extracted the gun, still nestled in its Lou Alessi shoulder holster. The magazine was empty, but there were two boxes of 9mm hollow-point ammunition in the bag. After filling the magazine with shells, he reinserted it in the pistol. Then, sliding into the leather straps of the holster, he shrugged his shoulders, settling the harness into place. He relocked the safe door, put on his jacket, and jogged upstairs.

Feeling somewhat safer now, he gathered his suit bag and computer case. On a whim, he grabbed the half-full bottle of scotch, a few cigars, and the gold lighter, stashing everything in the suit bag.

Afraid of being seen leaving by the front door but knowing he couldn't drag his luggage back through the bushes, he carried the bags into the hall, through the kitchen and out the side door, heading off around the block to his car.

Blum resisted the urge to simply hop in and drive away. Feeling a little foolish, but knowing he could regret not doing so, he set his luggage on the grass next to the Cobra and began a very thorough search of the car—all around the outside, then, with a small penlight, inside the cabin and under the hood. Not quite satisfied, he removed his jacket and shoulder holster and, lying on his back, slid under the vehicle, checking for anything suspicious there. Finding nothing, he patted himself off and stowed the luggage in the trunk. Finally, holding his breath, he sat down and turned the ignition switch. The engine rumbled to life, and he let out a sigh of relief.

Ten minutes later, he stood in the wood-paneled lobby of the Tudor-styled Greystone Hotel arranging a room from the clearly bored and somewhat indifferent young woman behind the desk. The short sleeves of her light-blue uniform shirt exposed a multi-colored tattoo of a griffin that ran up her left forearm. It seemed to go with her fuchsia-dyed hair and the six studs that pierced each ear.

Blum had cleaned up as best he could, and he'd buttoned his

blazer to try to cover as much of his dirty shirt as possible, but grime from the underside of the Cobra still adorned his collar and shirt cuffs, and, from the way the receptionist kept staring, probably his face as well.

"Car trouble," Blum explained, without being asked.

"Of course," she said. "But I'm afraid I don't have any rooms available. Big out-of-town wedding. The only empty rooms aren't made up, and housekeeping's gone for the night."

"Look," Blum said. "I don't care if the room isn't fixed up. I'll sleep on a bare mattress. I'm dead tired."

"Well," she said, clicking away on her terminal. "Looks like we do have *one* room available. The Baron's Suite. Four hundred a night, though."

"I'll take it. Thank you." Blum set his credit card on the counter.

The receptionist examined the card. "Welcome to the Greystone. I need to see your driver's license. How many nights?"

"At least three or four. I'm not sure. Put me down for five to be safe."

The receptionist began typing again on her terminal.

"Hey," Blum said. "I need to ask you a favor. You see, my girlfriend and I had sort of a fight."

"Fight?"

"Argument. I guess I've been kind of a jerk recently, and she called me out on it." He tried to seem contrite. "I just need a few days to myself to think. She knows I like this hotel, so she'll probably call here, and I don't want to talk to her right now. If we get into it right now, it's only going to be a rehash of the same old stuff. I'm sure you must know how that can be."

The girl's nose wrinkled, and the corner of her lip lifted in a look of disgusted disinterest. "And you're telling me this because . . ."

"Because I would really rather not register under my own name.

You've got my license and credit card. You know who I am. I simply don't want to be bothered. Could you possibly help me out?"

"Sure," she said, still looking bored. "Do it all the time. Only usually there's a hooker standing there, too."

"Don't worry. No hookers. I promise."

She flashed the first hint of a smile. "In your case it might help," she mumbled. "So, what name is it going to be?"

"Uh . . . Jack Wentworth."

Her fingers clacked away at the keyboard. "And how many keys?"

"Just one."

She passed the credit-card sized plastic slab through a coding machine and slipped it into a cardboard holder. "WIFI code is on the inside. Enjoy your stay, Mr., um, Wentworth." She handed him the key folder along with his credit card and license.

"Thank you. I really appreciate all this."

She shrugged. "Whatever."

Blum walked to the elevator and quickly made his way to the overpriced suite. He locked the door and slid a chair under the knob as extra security. Not yet satisfied with the barrier, he put a rolled towel along the crack under the door and then shoved a wad of tissue into the peephole to keep anyone from seeing inside. Probably overreacting, he thought, but it made him feel better.

Only then did he shower, slip on a robe, and pour himself a glass of scotch. It was late, and he'd been through a lot that day, but even after a hot shower and a nightcap, relaxation eluded him. He told himself he was safe in the hotel room, registered under an alias, with his car discretely parked out of view in the underground parking garage. Still, he found himself pacing the room.

He knew he should reach out to the authorities, but he had almost nothing concrete to share with them, other than the break-in. Everything else was simply an odd pile of suspicions. He also had to consider Meier's fear of the police. What if Meier's concerns were founded and he reached out to the wrong policeman? He had to tread carefully.

Crawling into bed, he felt under the pillow to confirm his gun was within reach before turning out the light. One thing was clear— Feldmann was in this up to his eyeballs. Not only was he hiding the plane on his property, but he was also the only one who could have known Blum would be away from his father's house that evening. Blum's hurried drive home must have been faster than Feldmann had anticipated. They probably got the call to take off after Blum had already arrived.

Tomorrow he needed to try to track down that girl—the one who had seen the plane explode—and find out what she knew.

Assuming they hadn't gotten to her first.

10. A GIFT OF DARKNESS

H ans Meier *was* still alive—his frail body huddled in complete darkness, soaking in a puddle of his own blood and urine, desperate for food and water, but somehow still alive. For almost a day now, he had remained like that, dangling from a water pipe with his elbows and ankles bound behind him, half kneeling and half sitting. Powerless to relieve the tension in his bindings, it had been at least twelve hours since he had been able to move his fingers or feel anything at all in his hands and feet.

Even so, despite his desperate state, the darkness of the musty room comforted him; it surrounded and warmed him. Light was what he feared the most. When the lights came on, *they* came. And then they would beat him, and for a long time afterward he would see lights that weren't there—lights like dancing fireflies, spinning in front of his eyes. If it stayed dark long enough, he told himself, he might be able to think; to understand.

From the floor above him, Meier again heard the rumbling foot-steps and strange moans. Some sort of livestock, he'd decided. But then the animals uttered sounds he'd never heard before—certain-ly not on the farm outside Vienna where he'd grown up, or at the zoo where, as a young boy, his mother had taken him on Sundays. He thought about his sweet mother and began to cry.

Suddenly the lights snapped on, and against the lights danced the shadows—big bulbous, bobbing shadows carrying clubs, which to Meier's dulled vision appeared as long, obscene extensions of their arms. And then the beating started again, and Meier screamed—screamed at the pain, screamed to feel better, screamed for his mother.

Now the shadows yelled back at him, too. Demanded answers. Something about books. Did he have any books? Borrowed books. It didn't make any sense. All this agony because of books.

Meier lifted his head in disbelief, and through the cloud of pain he recognized one of the shadows. A friend. Why does he want to hurt me now? Why doesn't he save me?

And then the shadow swung his club at Meier's face and gave him the gift he wanted most of all. Darkness.

11. KYC

A sharp knock on the door startled Blum awake. He bolted upright and reached for his gun. The unfamiliar bed linens, wallpaper, and furniture created a moment of panic until he remembered checking into the hotel. Still a little groggy, he swung out of bed and wrapped himself in the courtesy bathrobe. He pulled the plug from the peephole and peeked out. A white-uniformed man stood by a small cart also draped in white. The lens distorted the fellow's face and made him appear rather comical. Only then did Blum remember the room service order for breakfast he had placed on the doorknob the previous night.

He kicked the towel away from the sill and, stashing the pistol in the robe pocket, he opened the door. "Good morning."

"Good morning, sir." The young man wheeled the cart into the room and lifted the linen cover from the steaming dishes.

Blum yanked a five from his wallet and handed it to the man. Then, after locking the deadbolt, he dove into his food. When he was finished, he pushed the cart back out into the hall.

Despite his mental exhaustion and the realization he too could be in danger, to his surprise he actually felt somewhat excited; not only had the discovery of Feldmann's plane confirmed some of the details from the news article he had found, it gave him the first real lead in his search thus far. He wondered what the high school student had actually witnessed some fifteen years ago. Blum had seen the damaged plane, so he knew that at least that part was true. Had the deputy even investigated? Or had he only called Feldmann and asked what had happened? Perhaps Feldmann had ignited his own propane tank in order to provide a cover story.

Curious what might have happened to the girl, Blum tracked down the article he'd found the day before and got the girl's name—Kay Westfield. Then he tried an Internet search on "Kay Westfield" and "Ivesdale," but only a few references appeared, all dating back a decade or more. One of the links led to a site that included a phone number. Blum called it, but the line was out of service.

Replacing "Ivesdale" with "Champaign Urbana," a number of links appeared, including a listing from a couple of years ago on the First Urbana Bancshares website announcing that Kay Westfield had been appointed Chief Compliance Officer. The picture accompanying the text showed a more mature version of the high school girl he had seen before. Gone were the home perm and insipid grin, replaced by neatly trimmed bangs, a tailored blouse adorned with a pearl necklace, and a professional, "How may I help you?" expression.

Blum clicked on the "About Us" link and scanned down past numerous branch locations before spotting "Urbana Main Office."

He dialed the number, and a pleasant male voice answered, "First Urbana. First in Service. How may I help you today?"

"I'm trying to reach Kay Westfield."

"Just a moment. Please hold."

The line went dead for a few minutes. Then a female voice came on. "Ms. Westfield's office."

"Is Kay Westfield there?" Blum asked.

"Yes, she is in her office, but it looks like she's with someone. May I send you to her voicemail?"

Blum hesitated. "No. I only need to drop something off for her."

"Would you like me to tell her to expect you?"

"That's okay," Blum said. "I'll just stop by."

"Certainly, sir. And all of us at First Urbana hope you have a nice day."

Blum hung up, excited with his good luck. Checking the address for the bank and realizing it was just around the corner from his hotel, he grabbed his jacket and phone. He was nervous about leaving the gun behind, but he couldn't take it into a bank. Glancing around the room for hiding places, he settled on hanging the shoulder holster behind the curtains, where only a determined search would find it.

After a short walk, he pushed through the main entrance to the marble-tiled interior and inquired about Kay Westfield. The smiley receptionist escorted him past the tellers to a hallway that fronted glassed-in rooms. At the end of the corridor, the man stopped at a large, corner office and gestured toward the door. Through the glass wall, Blum spied a thirty-something woman in a black jacket and white blouse, her blond hair falling around her black-framed glasses as she leaned forward, reading something.

"This is Ms. Westfield," the man said, and it struck Blum that Kay Westfield still used her maiden name.

Blum thanked the man and knocked on the door. The woman looked up and waved him in. She had a tall face, with a longish, straight nose and full lips. Her hair, now parted left of center, hung down to her shoulders in a loose, slightly unkempt, waterfall of dirty blond.

"Yes?" she prompted, somewhat distracted. She removed her reading glasses. "What can I do for you? Mister . . ."

He stared into a pair of sapphire-blue eyes. "Blum. David Blum." This was clearly the same woman he'd seen in the photographs—the impish teen in the newspaper and the collected female executive on her company website—but neither image had captured the animated intelligence in her gaze, and he found her much more attractive than he had expected.

She leaned forward slightly. "Yes?"

"I need to talk to you about something that happened a while ago. Back in 1999." He paused to judge her reaction, as he took a seat across from her desk.

She squinted. "1999. I was in *high school.*" She shook her head in disbelief. "I don't understand."

Blum wasn't sure she'd believe the whole truth. "I'm working on an investigation that involves Professor Otto Feldmann. I understand you witnessed an incident on his property back in 1999."

Her eyes narrowed. "Are you a policeman?"

"No."

"Private investigator?"

Blum nodded. "I'm trying to find a missing person. Someone connected to Feldmann. I came across the article about what happened and what you saw, but I need some more details."

"Why is this suddenly relevant now?" The phone rang, but she ignored it.

"Because," Blum continued, "from what I read, the reporter didn't seem to believe you. I'm sure he left out things you told him. And I simply want to get those details. They might be helpful."

"Why would *you* believe me?"

The phone rang again. Kay stared at the console as it lit up, presumably to see who was calling, but once again she made no effort to answer it.

"Because I was at Feldmann's farm, and I saw some strange things."

Her eyes widened, and her expression softened. She started to speak, but then stopped. "Look. I'm rather busy . . ."

"You could be very helpful," Blum said, looking for a hint of assent.

"Well," she said, letting out a slow sigh. "I've got some time at noon. That's only about an hour from now. Can we meet for coffee then?"

"Sure," Blum said. "Where?"

"Bean There. It's a coffee shop a few blocks west of here on Main Street."

"It's called *what?*"

"Bean There." She laughed. "Stupid name. Good coffee. I'll tell you what I can, but it *was* a long time ago."

"Anything would be appreciated." Blum stood up. "See you in about an hour then. Thank you."

She started to stand, but her phone rang again. She picked up the receiver and settled back into her chair. Smiling politely, she waved good-bye as Blum nodded and left.

Wandering along Main Street, he passed a hodge-podge of old and new storefronts until he spotted the coffee shop's green awning that hung over a scattering of black, wrought iron bistro tables. He pushed through the glass door into the white-tiled interior, past rows of more bistro tables to a counter at the rear of the shop. Over a cacophony of chatter, hissing espresso machines, and clinking coffee cups, he ordered a large Americano and carried the tall ceramic mug back outside, parking himself in the shade of the awning. Sipping his coffee and staring absently at the passing cars, he contemplated how much to tell Kay. Better to tread carefully so he didn't scare her off, he decided.

With some time to kill, decided to take another look at Meier's list of cryptic terms.

Pangaea
Six million chosen
Everyone dies
People bury their own
Infection of salvation
Millennium can begin
?Ruhola?

What could they possible mean all together? In Pangaea, six million chosen people would die by an infection of salvation and be buried by their own, so the millennium could begin. And what the hell did *Ruhola* mean?

Next, he tried stringing together the first letters. PSEPIMR. Rearranging the letters gave him PREPISM, MISPREP, PRESPIM, and other meaningless combinations.

He realized he didn't even know how old the note was. It could have been written years ago, stuffed into the towel bar before Meier even moved in. But, no—the handwriting was clearly the same as in Meier's note. Of course, the note might have nothing to do with Feldmann, his father's death, or Meier's disappearance.

Having finished his coffee, Blum put the note away and stepped inside to set the empty mug in a bus bin. As he turned back to the main entrance, he saw Kay standing inside the front door, purse in hand, scanning the room. Their eyes met, and she lifted her hand in acknowledgement and walked towards him.

"I'm early," she said. "And hungrier than I thought I would be. Why don't we grab some lunch?"

"How about the Courier Café, if it's still around. I used to like to go there when I was here in college."

"Yeah, it's still here," she said, smiling warmly, leading him out the front door. "So where do you live now?"

"Chicago, but my work has me traveling a lot."

"As a detective?"

"For now," he said, realizing he hadn't thought out what all he was going to tell her. He hated to lie. "How long have you worked at the bank?"

"I guess thirteen years now." She turned the corner, and Blum followed her up the street.

"Where were you before that?"

"College," she replied. "SIU. How about you?"

"U of I. I did a stint with the FBI, and then I got a job in investments." Blum swallowed. "Now I'm doing some investigative work." At least that wasn't a total lie.

"And you're investigating Otto Feldmann?"

"In part. I'm trying to locate someone who is connected to Feldmann. I came across the article in the *Ivesdale Reporter*, but I wanted to get the details from you directly."

"Here we are," she announced, pointing to the corner door of the converted brownstone that had once housed the offices of the now-defunct *Courier* newspaper.

Blum followed her up the sandstone blocks, admiring how the soft folds of her floral skirt swayed with the motion of her hips and brushed against her legs. They sat in a polished-wood booth by a large window. A waiter descended on them almost immediately, handing out two menus and filling their empty glasses with ice water.

"Can I get you something to drink?"

Blum looked at Kay.

"Sparkling water with lime," she replied.

"Ginger ale for me," Blum said.

After the waiter wandered off, the look of professional inquiry returned to Kay's face. "So what exactly do you want to know?"

"I'm trying to locate a guy named Hans Meier. Ever heard of him?"

"No."

"In tracking him down, I've crossed paths with Professor Feldmann. While I don't have anything to directly tie him to Meier's disappearance, I've discovered some things about Feldmann that concern me, and I want to learn more. So, if you don't mind, why don't you tell me what really happened that night when you were on his farm."

She scrunched up her sharp nose and absently brushed her hair behind her left ear as she collected her thoughts.

"Like I told the reporter, it was after my senior prom—"

"Your date was with you when this happened?"

"No. He got drunk before the band even started. Later, he threw up all over himself and passed out in the grass outside the gym, so I had to drive him home in his pickup." She paused for a second, and then shook her head, laughing. "What a turd! I thought he was going to be my knight in shining armor, and instead I have to save his sorry ass. You know, it's amazing how much irresponsibility can seem like maturity when you're only eighteen. Anyway, I sort of dumped him by his front door and headed home."

"What time was that?"

"About four in the morning. As I was passing Mr. Feldmann's farm, I saw two yellow dots in the road. It took me a second to realize they were deer eyes. I swerved, but the deer turned the same direction, so I yanked the wheel the other way." Kay was gesturing as if holding a steering wheel. "That made the back end of the truck sort of go sideways, and I ran off the road and smashed into the fence. I banged up my face and arms, and I was bleeding, but—it's funny—mostly I was just scared of getting in trouble."

"Then what did you do?"

"Well, I should've gone home, but for some stupid reason I decided I needed to tell Feldmann what I'd done. I remember being worried I'd let his livestock out. I could see lights on in the farmhouse, but the main entrance was almost a mile away by road, so I decided to crawl through the hole I'd made and walk there across the field."

"So, were there any animals?"

"No. Not that I saw. Other than the ones in the cages. I'd heard talk about him raising weird animals, but I'd always assumed those stories were just kids trying to scare each other. Even so, I kept my eyes open."

"I'm confused . . . why didn't you just drive to the front?"

"Engine wouldn't start. Must've only been flooded because it worked later. Anyway, as I approached the house, I could hear people talking, so I walked around back. It took me a minute to realize what I was looking at. At first, I even wondered if they were filming a movie or something; it was so unreal."

"Like what exactly?"

"Well, there were these two guys wearing protective gear—white, plasticky jumpsuits with hoods. And they had gas masks on. They were standing in the light by the barn looking down a paved road. And spaced along the road were these crates with some kind of animals in them that looked like giant rats."

"Spaced? You mean they were set in specific places?"

"Yeah. That's what it looked like anyway. All lined up, about fifty feet apart. A dozen or more from what I could see. And they were numbered, starting with one on the closest cage and counting up from there."

"Did the guys see you?"

"No. They were staring away from me. Plus I was standing in a shadow."

"What happened then?"

"Well, I knew I'd made a mistake by going there. I should have left right away, but I just stood there, frozen. Then I heard a muffled bang off to my right." She took a sip from her drink. "And I looked over, and that's when I noticed the plane."

"Do you remember what kind of plane?"

"A tiny jet. Maybe a Cessna Citation, if you know what that is. It was chained down to some sort of trailer, and the wings were missing." Blum felt goose bumps on his arms. "I couldn't figure out what the noise had been, but I was sure it must've come from the plane."

"Did the guys in the white suits do anything about the noise?"

"I'm sure they must have heard it, but I wasn't looking at them at that point, and before I could look back, the plane kind of exploded." Kay glanced around, as if concerned someone could hear her. "I saw a huge flash. And then, half a second later, a big boom—you know, like at the fireworks, where you see the flash before you hear the bang, and then it hits you in the stomach. Only this one was *really* loud, and the shock knocked me over backward."

"Were you hurt?"

"I got scratched up a bit, and I had the wind knocked out of me. I've never been so scared. I was sure they'd seen me, but as my vision cleared, I could see they weren't even looking at me—or the plane. They were just staring down the roadway and watching this trail of smoke drift toward the cages. Right after that, the animals started dying."

"Wow. What did the guys do then?"

"They just stood there! And one of them was taking notes on a clipboard. They must have known exactly what was going to happen. I can still remember the sound of the first animal screeching and banging around in the cage. It was actually a relief when I saw it die."

"So, none of the smoke reached you? You weren't affected?"

"No. The wind was blowing it away from me, thank God."

"Could you hear anything the men were saying?"

"No. They were too far away, and my ears were still ringing. Besides, at that point I just turned and ran back to the truck as best I could with heels on. Then I got the hell out of there."

"No one followed you?"

"Like I said, I don't think they ever knew I was there."

"The hole from the explosion—where was it on the plane?"

"At the back," she said. "Right below the horizontal stabilizer. I'm guessing that's where the cargo hold was. Why?"

Blum was surprised to hear her say horizontal stabilizer instead of just tail.

"Because I saw a plane in Feldmann's hangar—a small business jet with a hole right below the, uh, horizontal stabilizer. Clearly caused by some sort of explosion."

"He *showed* that to you?"

"No. But he left me alone for a while in his hangar, and I poked around. I discovered a back room with the plane in it. I'm sure it's the one you saw." He took a drink. "And what happened after that? You drove home?"

"Yeah. The truck was banged up, but it started fine. My dad was waiting up for me, and I told him what'd happened." She snorted. "He must have thought I was high or something. I mean, I don't know what I was expecting him to do—hug me, call the police, drive back to Feldmann's farm and confront him—but he just laughed at me and told me I had a ridiculous imagination."

The waiter returned with their food, and Kay sat quiet until he left.

"I was so pissed I practically spat on him," she admitted, taking a bite of her salad. "I was still scared that the poison might reach the next farm, so I called the police. I was sure they would take me seriously, but the deputy who showed up just listened to me and then told my dad he thought I'd made up the whole thing. He said a propane tank had exploded on Feldmann's farm, and that must've been what I saw."

"And your mother? What did she think?"

Kay looked down. "My mother died when I was eleven."

Blum paused, trying to think of something to say. "I'm sorry. My mother died when I was six." They both sat awkwardly still until Blum broke the silence. "So, um, how did the newspaper get the story?"

"From me," she said sheepishly. "I wasn't going to give up, so I called the paper. I was hoping maybe if they reported what had happened, the cops would finally have to do something."

"And instead, the reporter made fun of you, huh?"

"Yeah. It was really embarrassing."

"Did you see a propane tank anywhere?"

"No. It could have been somewhere else, but it's certainly not what I saw."

"You think maybe the cop was lying?"

"I doubt he ever went to the farm. Probably just believed what Feldmann told him on the phone. I don't know."

"And the poison? No issue of anyone downwind being affected?"

"Not that I ever heard about."

For a few minutes, they ate in silence.

"You mentioned rumors about strange animals," Blum said, after a while. "Anything in particular?"

"Oh, there was some story about a pig with a human head. You know, the kind of crap kids say to freak each other out."

"Anything about large insects?"

"No, why?"

Blum shrugged. "Just wondering. Have you ever come across Feldmann since then?"

"Not in person," she said. "For years I tried to forget about him and that farm. But about seven or eight years ago, when I first became a compliance officer, I was doing a KYC review—that means Know Your Customer—on a non-profit, and it turned out that the outfit was funding Feldmann's research."

Blum knew all about KYC reviews—the regulatory requirement

for banks to verify who their customers were, and, more impor-
tantly, where they got their money. "Would that have been CSR?
The Center for Scientific Research?"

She squinted. "That sounds about right."

"Did you find anything interesting in the review?"

"No. It all checked out. I'm really not even supposed to be talking
to you about this." She looked away and stared out the window.

He decided to try a different angle. "By any chance, does the
word Pangaea mean anything to you?" Blum studied her face but
saw no reaction.

"No. What's that?" she asked, returning her gaze to him.

"I'm not sure. What about Ruhola?"

"What?"

"Ruhola. I may not be pronouncing it right."

"Why are you asking me this?"

"I came across a note that had some words on it, including those
two."

"What else did it say?"

"Just more gibberish." He picked up the last bit of quiche on his
fork. "Out of curiosity, how did you end up in banking?"

"The bank was recruiting on campus, so I interviewed and got
an offer. At the time, I think I accepted simply to piss off my dad.
He *hates* bankers. Some bullshit about Jews controlling the financial world. I don't know. I quit talking to him years ago. But then I
found I was pretty good at credit and finance, and I was certainly
better with people than I thought I would be."

When the waiter returned with their check Blum tore a scrap
from the bottom and wrote out his phone number. "Here," he said,
handing it to Kay. "If you think of anything else that could be helpful, please give me a call. I'm running out of leads."

She studied the number before opening her purse and placing

it inside. Digging further into the purse, she extracted a business card and handed it to Blum.

"In case *you* have any more questions. My cell number is at the bottom." Her offer seemed genuine. "Not that I know much that's useful."

They shook hands in front of the restaurant and parted. As Blum headed to his hotel, he mentally replayed the conversation they'd had. Her description of the explosion certainly seemed to match what he'd seen in Feldmann's hangar. After listening to her story, it all pointed to some sort of test as to whether a poison could be distributed from a plane, and that was certainly something serious enough to get someone killed. So why was Kay Westfield still alive, given what she had apparently witnessed, yet his father, who probably hadn't seen Feldmann in years, had possibly been murdered? Not to mention the fact that Meier had gone missing. Perhaps Kay had been that *one* sound in the night—the one no one does anything about. Meier and his father had been sounds two and three, and they weren't being ignored.

Blum returned to his room. He briefly considered going for a swim to try to unwind, but the lingering effects of the past few days were taking their toll. Instead, he lay down on the couch and closed his eyes. As he dozed off, he tried to make sense of exploding planes, poison gasses, *Pangaea*, *Ruhola*, and burglars in his father's house. But mostly he thought about the very charming Kay Westfield.

12. A FAMILIAR NAME

Blum stared at his reflection in the glass entry door to Cotespath Hall, pretending to peer into the interior. Standing close enough that no one could see what he was doing, he reached into his pocket and extracted the keys he'd taken from Meier's apartment. He tried the first one. It slid easily into the lock and turned smoothly, releasing the latch. He smiled to himself, but his momentary celebration ended when he spotted a security camera mounted above the lobby elevators, pointing directly at him.

Shit. How could he have missed that before? Even if the second key opened Meier's office, it didn't matter if he couldn't find a way past the security cameras. Better to come back later to scout for another way in, though; if he was being watched, it wouldn't look good to be seen going from door to door.

Blum left and drove to a Greek diner. Right as he took his first bite of gyros, his phone rang.

"Hello?"

"Hey. It's Kay Westfield. Am I interrupting?"

He set down his sandwich and wiped his mouth. "Not at all. What's up?"

"Well . . . I just wanted to tell you that our talk yesterday got me thinking, and, well, I remembered a couple of things. Not sure if they'll be useful or not. Perhaps we could, um, get together, and I can tell you . . ."

Blum smiled. "That would be great. Do you want to meet at the Bean There?"

"No. I'm sick of that place. Besides, I'm going to be busy with my church group this afternoon, so I've got to work through lunch. Could we maybe do dinner?"

"That'd be fine," he said, trying to sound blasé.

"Good. Why don't you pick me up? Is that alright?"

"Of course. Where?"

"Sunny Ridge Village. It's a condo development on Springfield, just west of Mattis. Unit 8C."

"Would six work?"

"Hmm. Better make it seven. I'll see you then. Bye." She hung up before he could say another word.

More information? Or was she asking him out? He smiled to himself. Either way, he'd get to have dinner with her.

Blum spent the afternoon trading emails, washing clothes in the hotel laundry room, and paying bills. He also checked his work emails, including one from his boss asking him when he was coming back to work.

Blum stumbled over his answer, agonizing over whether to just call the authorities and tell them what he suspected. But which authorities? Meier had told Delaney that he was worried about the police. Perhaps the FBI was a safer bet. Unfortunately, Blum couldn't think of anyone there he could completely trust. When he'd left, Petersen, his boss, had so tarnished his reputation that

Blum had even wondered if they would poison his background check for the job at Regency. And, besides, the strongest evidence he had that anything serious was going on was the list he'd stolen from Meier's apartment. To share that, he'd have to concede his own crimes. He could claim he found it in his father's house, but that might make his dad out to be one of the criminals. No, he concluded; he could only go to the FBI with a complete case—one that didn't rely on his testimony as an admitted burglar.

Blum replied to his supervisor's email with a vague reference to wrapping up some paperwork that might take a few more days.

Blum checked the time. Already past six. He showered and shaved, then dressed in khakis and a dark-blue linen shirt. Eschewing socks, he slid into a pair of Bally loafers, grabbed his sunglasses, and headed for the garage.

Precisely at seven, he parked in the tree-lined lot in front of Sunny Ridge Village, an attractive cluster of brick three-story buildings with saw-tooth balconies and steep shake roofs.

He found building 8 and pressed the button for unit C. Moments later, he heard a loud buzz and hefted open the door. Kay was waiting for him by an open doorway on the second level, up a flight of carpeted stairs. She wore a pleated, peach-colored, cotton skirt and a clingy, white blouse. She clutched a pair of white sandals in one hand and a hairbrush in the other.

"Sorry. I had to run some errands. Only need a few more minutes to finish getting ready."

"That's fine," Blum said. "I'm in no hurry."

She ducked back inside, leaving the apartment door open for him. By the time Blum entered the deliciously cool interior, she was dashing out of the living room down a hallway that led to the back.

"Help yourself to a drink," she called over her shoulder. "I'll just be a minute."

Blum grabbed a beer from the fridge and then wandered around the front room. In between a few bookcases, the sage-green walls were decorated with a few floral paintings, a lithograph of a horse galloping, and, incongruously, a poster of the cockpit of a commercial jet. Turning toward the bookcases, he spent a few minutes perusing the books on the shelves. Kay had a number of novels by authors he didn't recognize, some books on cooking and gardening, and some on horses. She also had a small collection on aviation, including a pilot-training manual and a technical guide for the Cessna 172.

That explained her reference to the "horizontal stabilizer."

"Sorry it's taking so long to get ready. I'm almost finished," he heard her call from the far room. He took another sip of beer and sat on a dining room chair. A moment later, Kay walked into the room.

As far as Blum could tell, all she had done was put on her shoes.

"That's much better," he said. "I was about to leave before."

She laughed. "No, you weren't."

Blum scratched his chin. "Shall we go?"

"Sure. Where to?"

"I thought I'd let you choose. Anywhere you like, as long as they have a decent wine list."

"Maybe Applewood? Ever been there?"

"No, I haven't. What kind of restaurant is it?"

"I guess you'd call it American," she said. "They have steaks and things, and people tell me they have some good wines."

"Well, great then. Applewood it is."

They made their way out to the parking lot.

"Wow," she said. "What a great car." After walking around the outside, she leaned in and examined the interior. "It must be a ball to drive. The dashboard reminds me of a cockpit."

Blum was impressed. The first thing most women said was that it must have cost a lot of money—or, worse, asked how much. Kay obviously appreciated cars as well as airplanes.

"Can you drive a stick?" he asked her.

"Sort of."

"Would you like to drive to the restaurant?"

"Oh, no," she said in shock. "It looks like it would be a handful. I'm used to my boring little Acura."

"Maybe after a few glasses of wine you'll change your mind," he teased, opening the passenger door for her.

Settling into the deep racing seat, she reached around for her seatbelt and found the lap straps. "No shoulder strap?"

"It's a four-point harness."

"Oh. Like in a plane." She found the other straps and clicked them in place.

"Exactly," he said, smiling.

The drive to Applewood took less than fifteen minutes. Even though he knew roughly where they were going, he let Kay give directions so he'd have an excuse to glance at her from time to time and admire how pretty she was. Her lips pursed with a faint smile as she held her chin high and let the breeze billow her hair in flapping waves. Blum was glad to see she was enjoying the ride.

Once inside the restaurant, they were taken to a table in the back of the dining room. A uniformed waiter appeared with menus.

"Would either of you care for a cocktail?"

Blum looked at Kay. She shook her head.

"I'll take a Tanqueray and tonic," Blum said, turning back to the waiter.

"Very good," the waiter said and disappeared.

They spent a few minutes going through the menu. The waiter returned with the gin and tonic and took their orders—a rib eye for him, a filet with Béarnaise sauce for her—then asked if there was anything else he could get for them.

"Would you like some wine?" Blum asked Kay.

She smiled. "Sure. I don't know much about it though. Why don't you pick something?"

The waiter handed the bound list to Blum. He turned to the listings for Bordeaux and chose the 2005 Chateau Talbot, which stood out from the rest of the grocery-store selections.

"So, what is it that you remembered?" Blum finally asked her as he returned the wine list to the waiter.

"It's about the CSR account. I remembered something about the money that went in and out." She paused.

"And . . ."

Kay stared at her hands, her brow furled. "Look. I know you could really use this information, but . . . I've never broken the rules like this before." She looked around to make sure no one could hear her. "I mean, I got a speeding ticket once, and I felt like such a criminal I didn't even tell my best friend about it for two months. So please understand this isn't easy for me."

"I understand," Blum reassured her. "This investigation isn't about bank accounts. It's about a missing person who could be injured or dead. Nothing will come back to you."

"I know. But you need to understand that I would lose my job if anyone found out. The only reason I'm even thinking about doing this is because no one took me seriously before when I tried to get someone—anyone—to do something about Feldmann. But now you're here, and you need my help. So I hope that justifies what I'm about to do . . . what I'm about to tell you."

The waiter's return interrupted their discussion. He placed the bottle of Talbot on the table in front of Blum, who nodded his approval. The waiter tore off the capsule, popped the cork, and then deftly poured a glass for Blum to taste.

"It's fine," he said. The waiter poured two glasses and disappeared.

Kay took a sip and nodded. "I don't drink that much wine, but that's really good." She looked around to make sure no one was close enough to hear them. "Alright. About a million dollars flows into the CSR account each year. Most of that comes from something called Agricultural Genomics Research International. Feldmann gets paid about a third of that in salary, and about half goes to buy equipment and materials from laboratory supply companies, computer suppliers, and so forth. The rest goes to some contract researchers."

"That's odd," Blum said. "So Agricultural Genetics—"

"Genomics," she corrected him.

"Genomics. Let's just call it AGRI." Having sounded out the acronym, Blum recalled Feldmann's license plate. "So, besides AGRI, no other money comes in?"

"A little here and there."

"What about the FDA? The CDC? NIH?"

"No. Not really. Occasionally, but of no consequence."

"Really? When I talked to him, he never mentioned AGRI. He told me mostly government agencies were funding his research."

"That's interesting," she commented. "I wonder why he would lie about that. You think AGRI wants to keep a low profile or something?"

"I guess so. Or maybe they just aggregate funds to feed to CSR. Did you learn anything about AGRI itself?"

"Nothing, really. It is an officially-registered 501c(3)."

"And you suddenly remembered all of this?"

She blushed. "I may have checked my notes."

"Ok, so do you happen to remember where AGRI's deposits came from? Which bank?"

"Some bank in Chicago. I think it's called Royalty Bank. No. Wait . . . Regency. Regency Bank. They're British, I think."

Blum's stomach tensed. His firm. He hoped the shock of hearing that didn't show on his face, but she seemed to sense something.

"Have you ever come across the bank before . . . in your investigation?"

"Not till now," Blum answered honestly. It made sense, though, that an organization that wanted to keep a low profile would choose Regency. Secrecy was a religion at the bank. Client numbers replaced names for all internal recordkeeping, and access to the list that matched those numbers to names was limited to the senior-most management on a need-to-know basis. That kept bank staff from being able to see the financial affairs of the important, and in many cases well-known, people. With a required minimum net worth of 50 million pounds (about 65 million dollars), Regency's somewhat paranoid clientele demanded precautions like that. The bank's set of security policies was known as "The Code," and employees were expected to obey The Code first, the Ten Commandments second, and any applicable laws after that.

Was it finally time to come clean about who he really was and why he was there? He was fast approaching the point of no return. Much more deception, and he could never tell her the truth and be forgiven. But that couldn't get in the way of finding his father's killer. He took a sip of wine and tried not to look into her eyes until the subject passed.

"So tell me more about your investigation," she said. "Who hired you?"

"Well," Blum said. "It sort of fell in my lap. Someone I knew died recently. I got a note from Meier telling me that he had something to tell me about the guy and he asked me to meet him."

Kay reached across the table and put her hand on Blum's. "It was someone close to you, wasn't it? I can tell from the way you're talking."

"Yes. It was." Blum cleared his throat, ran his fingers through his hair and swallowed hard. "Sorry," he apologized.

The plates of steaming food arrived. Blum poured some more wine into their glasses. His voice steady again, he continued with his story.

"I was supposed to meet him—Meier—but he never showed. I tracked down his apartment and went there to look for him. He wasn't there, and the place had been ransacked. I discovered he has an office at the university. And this is where it gets interesting," he said, pausing briefly to take a sip of wine. "When I went to check it out, it turned out to be in Feldmann's department. Feldmann recognized me, and that's when he invited me to his farm."

Kay sat upright. "Feldmann *knew* you? How?" She eyed him suspiciously.

Blum waved his hand dismissively. "My father knew him. They were both professors at the university. Dad didn't particularly like the guy. I met him once. He recognized me."

She stared at him without wavering.

He realized he'd been speaking about his father in the past tense, but Kay hadn't seemed to pick up on that.

"Look, what I'm trying to say is this—I think Feldmann is probably responsible in some way, and he might be preparing to kill more people. He's no friend of mine, if that's what you think. When I happened across the plane with the hole in it at his farm, it really shook me, especially after reading the article about you. That's why I came to see you. I had to find out if the story was true."

She relaxed some, but then concern flashed in her eyes. "You think he might kill more people—why? And how do you think he's going to do it?"

"Well, at this point I have a better guess at the how than the why. My thought is that he plans on releasing a pathogen of some sort from an airplane. That's what you saw them testing. The first bang you heard probably released something inside the cargo compartment. Then, the second explosion blew a hole through the fuselage, letting whatever was dispersed by the first blast leak out. If something like that happened at altitude, whatever's inside would be sucked out immediately."

"That makes sense," she said, thoughtfully. "And they must've needed to test that on a real plane. Wow. Expensive test."

"Very," Blum commented. "But, as I said, the *why* totally escapes me. Feldmann's a refugee from Hungary who left to escape oppression. He's a committed scientist, and I haven't come across anything that indicates he has any sort of agenda—other than feeding people."

"Maybe he's out to prove a point."

"What do you mean?"

"You know. Like, genetic research is getting out of control, or maybe he wants to create a crisis and then be the guy to fix it."

"Could be," Blum said. "I hadn't thought about anything like that."

"What do the police think?" she asked.

"I can't go to the police. At least not yet."

"You haven't told the police yet? Why not?"

"Apparently Meier thinks they might be involved somehow."

"But there're all kinds of police—city, county, state. They can't all be involved."

"I know, but I don't know which ones are, and besides, I don't even have enough hard evidence to prove that anything is actually going to happen. Look, when I worked for the FBI, one thing I learned is that most law enforcement people are much more interested in catching criminals than they are in preventing crimes. And what they really worry about is whether there's enough evidence to guarantee a conviction, so it's critical that all the evidence be admissible in court."

"So, what's that have to do with this?"

"Well, as I said, I don't know what crimes, if any, will be committed or when. I might know how, and I think I know who, but let's just say that some of the evidence was collected by, um, unconventional means, which would make it inadmissible in court."

"Ohhh," she said with a grin. "You checked your notes, too."

"So, if I go to them now with what I have, the most likely outcome is they tell me the only infractions they have any cause to investigate are the ones I've committed. And that's presuming I don't accidently go to the wrong cops. I really need a solid case before I can go anywhere."

"So what can I do to help?"

"Nothing else I can think of. You've been quite helpful already. You've confirmed what happened to that plane, and now I have AGRI to look into as well. Feldmann clearly didn't want to tell me about them. Perhaps that will lead somewhere. I have a couple of sources that might be able to help."

"No other leads?"

Blum shrugged, mentally going back through everything he knew. "Well, hmm. Did you ever come across anyone named Lawson?"

"You mean Victor Lawson? Yeah, he's one of the contract researchers that gets paid out of the CSR account."

"*Victor* Lawson? Are you sure?"

"Yeah...why? What is it?"

Suddenly a number of dots connected. "Someone named Lawson came up when I was at dinner at Feldmann's farm. Plus, I noticed a mailbox in Feldmann's office suite for a V. Lawson. And then, a friend of Meier's mentioned someone Meier knew named Victor. It has to be the same person."

Blum took out his phone and entered the name into a search engine. In addition to some links to websites, a row of pictures appeared. As he scanned the tiny images, the hairs stood up on the back of his neck.

"Holy shit," he muttered.

"What?"

"Victor Lawson's the guy I saw at Fortunato's when I was waiting for Meier to show up. I'm pretty sure he tried to follow me, too, when I left." Blum squinted at the tiny screen on his phone. "This would be a lot easier on a larger screen."

"Why don't we go back to my place and use my computer?" Kay offered excitedly.

"Right now?"

"You got other plans?"

*

Once inside her condo, Kay kicked off her shoes and removed her hair clip, letting her locks fall in disheveled clusters. "I can get us something to drink in a second. Let me switch my computer on."

She walked down the hall and turned into a room on the left. A minute later, she traipsed back out, her bare feet padding against the hardwood.

"What would you like to drink?" she asked. "I've got some white zinfandel in the fridge. I also have an unopened bottle of bourbon someone gave me as a gift."

Blum winced. "White zinfandel? Yuck. Um . . . I'll take a shot of that bourbon."

"Oh. A wine snob, huh? Well I like it." She grabbed the bottle from the refrigerator and poured some of the pale pink liquid into a wine glass; then, standing on her toes, she opened an overhead cabinet. Retrieving a bottle of what appeared to be Blanton's, she cracked the wax seal and peeled it open. Grabbing a tumbler, she poured in an inch of topaz liquor and carried the two glasses into the living room.

Kay handed Blum his drink. "Cheers."

Before Blum could reply, she turned and headed down the hall. "Come on," she said, leading him into a room lined with open shelves that supported a combination of books, knick-knacks and framed photos of Kay with various people. (Blum was selfishly glad to see there weren't any guys in the photographs.) A laptop sat on a small, sturdy table that jutted out from the right. Kay sank into a rolling office chair and pointed to another on Blum's left. "Grab that."

As Blum sat, she brought up a browser and went to a search page. "Victor Lawson, right?" Her fingers clicked away on the keyboard. In a second, a long list of links appeared on the screen. David scooted his chair closer to Kay so he could see the screen. She clicked on the first link, which brought up a research paper with someone Blum didn't recognize.

"Booooooring," Kay announced. She scrolled down the list of links until she found an announcement of Lawson's arrival at CSR. Peering at the article from the *Daily Illini*, they learned that Victor Lawson, who heralded from Boise, Idaho, joined CSR in 2011 after a four-year stint at Quantitative Disaster Analytics—a firm that developed computer simulation models of severe weather events and earthquakes for insurance companies. He had joined QDA after completing his PhD in mathematics from MIT in 2007.

Kay scrolled down to the bottom where she found a photograph of Lawson and Feldmann. "Is that him?"

Blum stood up behind Kay and leaned over her shoulder to get a better look. He studied the picture. "Yeah. That's him."

Standing so close, he could smell the vanilla and coconut of her shampoo, and he felt her bodily warmth against his face. She must have sensed his proximity because she leaned slightly forward, away from him, and held her blouse to her chest.

"Hey!" she said. "Eyes on the screen. I need you focused here."

"What?" Blum stood up straight. "No. I . . ."

Kay turned, laughing. "Relax. I just like teasing you." She scrolled on down the list of links, but they quickly faded into repetitions and references to other people.

Blum sat back in his chair and took a sip of bourbon. "Try adding Boise to your search."

Kay clicked away on the keyboard, scanning through the new listings. An item from the *Boise Times* dated June 12, 1997 read, "PROTESTORS HECKLED BY ANGRY CITIZENS."

"Click on that one," he suggested.

The top of the page displayed the newspaper's banner followed by large, block letters that repeated the title. Pasted below was a black-and-white photograph of a band of yelling marchers, heads shaved and carrying a banner scrawled with "GODLESS SAVAGES GO HOME!" Victor Lawson stood front and center.

The caption below the photograph read, "Members of ACID protest return of land to Native Americans. Members include Aaron Davenport, John 'Crater' McDunn, Victor Lawson, and Riley Pfister."

"Jeez," Kay exclaimed. "He's some piece of work, huh?"

"What does it say?" Blum asked. "I can't read it from way over here," he added with mock dejection.

Kay flashed him a grin over her shoulder then bent closer to the screen. "Let's see . . . ACID stands for Army of Christian Identity and Dominion. They claim that they're out to protect white Christians from Jews, Muslims, Mexicans, blacks, blah, blah, blah." She read further in silence for a moment, frowning more and more as she went. "Something about the state of Idaho returning land west of Boise to the Northern Paiute Tribe, which considers it sacred . . . ACID says that's a violation of white American sovereignty. Blah, blah, blah. God gave the land to *them*, not to a bunch of heathen savages. Blah, blah, blah. A hundred people showed up to heckle the

ACID protestors who . . . basically got pissed off and started throwing things. Then the police moved in and arrested the protestors."

"Then what?"

"That's it. That's the end of the article."

"Why would Feldmann hire someone like that?"

"Maybe he didn't know. For that matter, why would a guy like that go to work for Feldmann? I mean, he's Jewish, right?"

"What makes you think he's Jewish?"

"Feldmann's a Jewish name, isn't it?" she said, turning toward him.

"It can be, and Professor Feldmann is Jewish, but it's also a common German name."

She sensed his unease. "I didn't mean anything by it. I didn't offend you, did I?"

"Why would that offend me?"

"Because you're . . ."

Blum recoiled slightly, wondering what that might mean to her, and what it might imply for how she felt about him. "Jewish?" he paused trying to read her. "Yes, I *am* Jewish, by heritage anyways. But in terms of faith, I'm actually not much of anything."

"Oh," she said, blinking as she processed that. She turned back to the screen. "Let's see if there's anything else about the protest." She used her mouse to navigate back to the search page.

Blum hoped his reaction hadn't made her uncomfortable. He glanced around the room looking for any indications of how devout she was. No pictures of Jesus. No crosses. But she *had* said she was going to spend the afternoon with her church group.

"Here's one," she announced, bringing him back to the moment. She leaned forward and squinted at the screen, its light casting a bluish tint to the edges of her hair. "It says that . . . three members of the group were sentenced for inciting the riot." Her lips moved silently. "Victor wasn't one of them, though. He got off."

"Why?"

"It doesn't say. Maybe he knew somebody."

"Anything else?"

Kay shrugged. "Nope." She glanced at a clock on the shelf above the computer. "Oh crap. It's late, and I have to be in early tomorrow. I need to get to sleep."

Blum downed the last of the bourbon and got up. "I won't keep you, then. Thank you so much for your help." He held her chair for her as she stood.

"I had a lot of fun. I'm so glad I could be helpful."

Blum walked out into the main room. Kay followed.

"Hey," Kay said. "It's short notice, but I'm going to be singing tomorrow evening, and it would be great if you could come and hear me . . . if you want to."

"Singing? You're a singer?"

"Well. I just sing in the church choir. We do a concert each summer."

"Church choir? I'm not exactly the church type."

"No. It's not like that. It's really just a lot of pretty songs."

"Uh . . . I don't know . . ."

She smiled earnestly. "Tell you what. I'll cook dinner for you afterward. How's that?"

"Dinner? Well . . . sure. How can I turn that down?"

"Great." She was visibly pleased. "The performance starts at six, but I have to get there early. You can meet me there, if you want."

"That's fine. Where is it?"

"It's at the Wabash Congregation Hall on Graham Street. Near Hessel Park, if you remember where that is."

"I know where Graham Street is. If you tell me what you're cooking, I'll bring a bottle of wine."

"How 'bout chicken?"

"Sounds good to me," Blum said as he neared the door.

"Do you have everything?" she asked.

He patted down his shirt and pants to make sure he had his phone, keys and so forth. "I think so." He turned and faced her.

"I had a great time tonight," she said.

"Me too," Blum replied.

And now the uncomfortable should-I-or-shouldn't-I moment. He leaned in to kiss her, but she tensed up, and he stopped. He started to extend his hand instead, hoping his embarrassment didn't show. "Sorry," he mumbled. "I didn't mean to . . ."

She grabbed his hand and squeezed. Then she leaned in quickly and gave him a peck on the cheek.

"Don't worry. I like you. I just don't like to feel pushed."

"No problem. Well, good night, then." He smiled. "I'll see you tomorrow night at six. Wabash Congregation Hall, right?"

"Right. Good night." She waved good-bye to him as he turned and stepped into the hallway.

Blum made his way down the stairs as Kay stood in her doorway, the bright light from her apartment illuminating the dim stairwell. It wasn't until he was nearly out the front entrance that he saw the light fade as she shut her door.

13. IDENTITY

D avid Blum woke early but lingered in bed for over an hour, lost in contemplation. He knew he could access the deposit system at Regency, which meant he could dig up information on the AGRI account, but not without the account number, and he doubted Kay would give that to him. At least not yet.

As his thoughts drifted to Kay, he marveled at the swift transformation he'd seen from the coolly efficient compliance officer to the helpful, but reticent, witness recalling her experiences, and finally to the enthusiastic investigator, researching Victor Lawson.

Although he genuinely looked forward to seeing her again that evening, the church aspect nagged him. Did she really only want him to hear her sing? Or, deciding she liked him, had she now taken it upon herself to introduce him to Jesus? Questioning her intentions only made him cringe all the more at his own duplicity, and he wondered how long her interest in him would last when he finally admitted he'd led her on about being a detective.

Blum grabbed breakfast at the Bean There, then ordered a large cup of coffee to go and carried it back to the Greystone. Settling into the desk in his room, he fired up his laptop and began his research with AGRI, but no permutation of "A. G. R. I." or "Agricultural Genomics Research International" led anywhere. That struck him as odd, given that they were ostensibly a public-service institution. How could they function with no public face?

Next, he searched "Victor Lawson Boise" again and was presented with the same links that Kay had found the night before. Clicking on the *Boise Times* article, he read it in detail but found nothing new. He studied the photograph of the four screaming men, dressed in black shirts, the sun glaring off their shaved heads. Only Lawson looked at all familiar, despite his bald scalp, but the righteous anger in all their faces was scary. And that sign. "GODLESS SAVAGES GO HOME!" Its ignorance would have been laughable, if not for the implied threat of violence behind it.

Blum switched his search to "Victor Lawson ACID," but the only new item that contained all those words together was a journal article Lawson had written titled, "Mechanisms of Amino Acid Dissociation Reactions in Human Polymerases."

As Kay would say, "Blah, blah, blah." Or, maybe, "Boooring!"

Trying to avoid duplications with the initial list of links, he skipped all the way to page ten of the search. Nothing interesting. He moved back to page nine. Still nothing. On page eight, an article from the *Washington Post* titled "Modeling Superstar Accused of Data Theft" caught his eye. Blum clicked on it.

The article, parroting an AP news release, relayed how Victor Lawson, the lead weather-modeler with Quantitative Disaster Analytics, had been accused of stealing STORMPERIL 2010, a file of weather events all around the world. Insurance companies paid QDA over a billion dollars a year to model the impact of those events on their insured properties, making STORMPERIL QDA's crown jewel. The company had accused Lawson of stealing the data after the IT security people discovered that the master file had been breached and duplicated. Lawson was supposedly the only one who had accessed the directory at the time of the breach. The article ended saying that an investigation was underway.

Armed with that information, Blum searched on "Victor Lawson Data Theft" and was rewarded with a new set of links. Most were for other news services that had reported the same AP story, but, buried on page three, he found a news article from the *Miami Herald* that mentioned that Lawson had been exonerated after the file had been discovered on another employee's personal server.

Searching for just "ACID" would flood him with useless references, so he tried "Army of Christian Identity and Dominion" and found a few news stories from Idaho. The first article, from a TV station in Stanley, Idaho, reported that Riley Pfister had been convicted of plotting to kill two police officers. Blum recalled he was one of the protestors in the picture. The date on the item put it six months after the ACID protest in Boise.

The next article concerned a synagogue bombing in Boise. Previously, ACID had threatened to "rain fire down upon the false Israelites," making them the prime suspects, but nothing could be proven. That was two months before the march.

Wondering what a false Israelite was, Blum returned to the search page and scanned further. Near the bottom he noticed a link for the ACID website. He hesitated. The hotel's WIFI network might block offensive sites like that, or even record his attempt to go there. But, more than that, he wasn't sure he actually wanted to read it. It was like viewing a film-clip of a gruesome car accident— seeing it wouldn't change anything, but that didn't make watching it any less unpleasant.

When he clicked on the link, though, a notice popped up

indicating the website had expired. Backing up to the search page, he saw a number of links that included "Christian Identity" in them. He clicked on one and found himself staring at a screen edged with various cryptic emblems. Some looked familiar—a swastika, the SS death's head and double lightning-bolts—but most were not. Many of them contained a cross in one form or another, juxtaposed with fire, the sun, swords, or spears. Scattered about the screen were stick-like letters that appeared to be Celtic or Norse.

The center of the screen contained two rows of six boxes, each a link to a particular topic. One was labeled, *The Truth about the Jews*, another, *Lies the Government Tells*. Others read, *Protect Your White Christian Heritage*, *Teach Your Children Before Public Schools Poison Their Minds*, and *Government Thugs Are Coming for Your Guns!*

Out of morbid curiosity, he clicked on *The Truth about the Jews* and was presented with a black screen covered with tiny, white text. He read the first few paragraphs. The gist of it was that, according to them, Eve and Adam had a son, Seth, the progenitor of the white race, but Eve also had a son named Cain—the result of mating with the serpent (Satan), and Cain was the progenitor of Jews and Muslims. Blacks supposedly originated from apes that bred with the Jews. According to the website, Darwin had proven this scientifically, but he was barred from publishing the truth by the Jewish elite who controlled the government and educational systems. It went on to explain that the true Israelites—the descendants of Seth—migrated to Europe and became the Aryans. The false Israelites—today's Jews—were not God's chosen people but rather Satan's spawn.

Blum had seen enough. Repulsed by the garbage, he backed out of the website, returning to his home page. Then he carefully erased his browsing history, his cache, his search history, and all cookies. Closing the web browser, he leaned back and shook off the feeling of disgust. In a final act of catharsis, he completely shut off the computer.

He needed to learn more about the subject, but not from sources like that. He recalled a professor in his father's department who specialized in religious politics. He'd never met her, but his father had talked about her from time to time, and this sounded like something that might be up her alley.

Blum grabbed lunch and ran by a liquor store to pick up a couple bottles of wine for dinner. Afterward, he drove to Lincoln Hall, home to the political science department, and identified himself to the gray-haired receptionist on the second floor.

"Oh my gosh," she said, removing her turquois-framed glasses. "We're all so sad about what happened." Her eyes grew moist. "Solomon was such a dear."

"Well, thank you. Actually, I was hoping I could talk to Professor Wilmers. Is she in?"

The woman ran her finger down a calendar page inside a plastic sleeve taped to her desk. "It looks like she should be here. Down the hall to the left."

Blum followed the hallway to a cramped office where a handsome, middle-aged woman with salt-and-pepper hair stood and greeted him with a warm smile. She was dressed casually in a seersucker white blouse, faded blue jeans, and crude sandals.

"Professor Wilmers?"

"Yes," she replied.

"I'm David Blum—Solomon Blum's son."

"Oh, my. Come in and sit down." Her voice was soothing and genuine. "I can't imagine how you must feel . . . What brings you *here*?" she asked, settling her small frame into her creaking office chair and pointing to an armless metal side-chair. The rattling window air-conditioner just managed to take the edge off the sweltering heat outside.

"Well . . ." Blum hesitated. "I was looking through some of my father's things, and I discovered something tucked in the back of a book that I wanted to ask you about. Something a little disturbing."

"About your father?"

"Oh, no. It must have been something he came across. Since it involves religion, I thought perhaps he might have shown it to you at some point. Like an idiot, I forgot to bring it with me, though."

"So what was it?"

"A flyer from a group that calls themselves ACID—The Army of Christian Identity and Dominion. Have you ever heard of them?"

"No," she said, frowning. "But I'm familiar with Christian Identity."

"It's an actual thing?"

"Oh, absolutely. It's a racist fringe doctrine that's embedded itself in most right-wing hate groups, from Aryan Nations and Posse Comitatus, to various neo-Nazis, skinheads, and militia gangs. Eric Rudolph and Timothy McVeigh—the Oklahoma City bombers—were big adherents."

"So what exactly is it?"

"Well, it goes back to a seventeenth century idea called 'British Israelism,' which claimed that the ten lost tribes of Israel, whom they say were actually blue-eyed and fair-haired, migrated to Europe and ultimately settled in the British Isles. At first, it simply argued that Britons were also among God's chosen people. But, in the second half of the nineteenth century, the doctrine traveled to Canada and the United States, where it took on an anti-Semitic tone."

The words flowed easily, and Blum guessed it was a topic she'd taught recently.

"As it evolved, it became strongly anti-Semitic, and, by the nineteen thirties, had caught on with groups like the KKK, as well as a guy named Howard Rand, the leader of something called the Anglo-Saxon Federation of America."

Blum found himself fascinated by the lecture, but he didn't

know how much time the professor had, and he was afraid she'd suddenly look at her watch and tell him she had to be somewhere else. "And British Israelism evolved into Christian Identity?"

"Yes. Christian Identity came into being shortly after World War II when three men—Wesley Swift, Bertrand Comparet, and William Gale—launched it as a formal movement based on the most radical elements of British Israelism."

"It's been around *that* long? I'm surprised I've never heard of it before."

"It tends to stay under most people's radar. Later, Swift founded an Identity sect called the 'Church of Jesus Christ—Christian,' which in turn spawned the Aryan Nations. Over time, their reinterpretation of the Bible got more and more bizarre, ultimately concluding that Jews were the result of the Devil mating with Eve, and therefore the Bible, and all its rules, applies only to 'white' Christians. And, by white, they mean only Anglo-Saxons and Aryans."

"Making the Jews false Israelites." Blum remembered the phrase from the website.

"Exactly. With that as a premise, Identity adherents also believe that Jews, as the spawn of the Devil, are committed to destroying white, Christian society and establishing a New World Order. They think the U.S. government is already under their control. They call it ZOG, for Zionist Occupied Government." She chuckled. "Not the sort of stuff I learned in Sunday school, but, as I said, it's a fringe doctrine. It no more speaks for all Christians than ISIS does for all Muslims. Hate is hate."

"Anything in there about a millennium?"

Professor Wilmers raised an eyebrow. "Yes. As a matter of fact." She looked at David quizzically.

"It was mentioned in the flyer."

"Well, it all comes down to when Jesus returns. Unlike most

evangelicals, followers of Christian Identity are known as 'Post-Millennials.' They believe in the need for a global war between white Christians and everyone else, from which they will rise victorious and establish a Christian kingdom on Earth so that, after a thousand years, Jesus can return. A good number of them actually believe it's their duty to provoke that war in order to initiate the process."

That explained *Millennium* on Meier's list.

"The other part of that group's name—Dominion—probably comes from something called Dominion Theory."

"What's that?"

"Its followers believe that society is in moral decay because it's abandoned Christianity, giving rise to homosexuality, fornication, abortion, and teaching evolution in schools. They believe in the need to reassert the dominion of God in all aspects of life, including politics, law, and society in general. Sort of like the Christian Taliban."

"What about Pangaea? Does that mean anything in this context?"

Professor Wilmers squinted and frowned. "The geological term?" She shook her head thoughtfully. "I've never heard it associated with anything religious, but I guess it could be used metaphorically. Also on the flyer?"

"Yeah. There was a list of words scribbled on the back. Not my dad's writing, so I don't know who wrote them. What about *Ruhola*?"

"*Ruhollah*? It was the first name of the Ayatollah Khomeini who led the Iranian Revolution in 1979. No connection to Christian Identity, as far as I know."

Blum remembered Meier's question marks. "What if I'm not pronouncing it right? Is there anything in Christian Identity that sounds kind of like that?"

"Well . . . Perhaps Rahowa?"

"Maybe. Who's that?"

"Not who. What. It's short for Racial Holy War—the big battle between whites and everyone else that precipitates the end times. It became a greeting among some Identity adherents." She frowned in a look of distaste. "Nothing you want to hear your new neighbor say to you when you walk by. What else?"

"Does the number six million have any significance?"

"Of course that's the figure most often cited for the number of Jews killed by the Nazis," she said. "But, other than that, nothing I can think of."

"How about an 'infection of salvation'?"

She shook her head.

"So what draws people to something like this?"

Agnes Wilmers sat back and shrugged. "To some degree, it's not necessarily being drawn to this ideology, but rather radical ideology in general. People who feel disenfranchised are desperate to feel like they belong to something—something that makes them special. In addition, this sort of paranoia—the view that the world is a violent, threatening place from which they need protection—generally gets instilled when a child is quite young, and it's often the result of a violent home life or being exposed to some sort of existential threat, like war. As people like that grow up, their sense of vulnerability and the need to fight for survival can become generalized to their national, racial, or religious group. Combine that with a religion that tells you you're locked in an eternal battle between good and evil with everyone else, and . . . well, you get the picture. They feed on each other. You can see it happening all over the world today."

Wilmers shifted in her seat. "But it's hardly a direct cause and effect. For every zealot with a tinfoil fedora who goes to bed at night terrified of U.N. storm troopers or creeping Sharia law, there're another hundred who survive the same things and simply move on, or are instead motivated to help others. In some sense, religion is a language. And like any language, it can be used to say beautiful, inspiring things or horrible, destructive things. It all depends on the character and motivation of the speaker."

"So," Blum mused, "religion doesn't so much pick the channel as adjust the volume."

"Well put."

Blum shook his head. "Hey, thank you. This was quite informative. I appreciate you taking the time."

"My pleasure. And I didn't mean to scare you or anything. There are very few of the real crazies running around, but a number of these groups are bad enough to be designated as terrorist organizations. If you come across anything more specific, you may want to pass it on to the authorities."

"I will," Blum promised. He stood up. "I'll let you get back to work now."

"Hey, it was a welcome break. Champaign Urbana is pretty boring during the summer." She reached out and shook his hand. "Take care, David."

Blum nodded and walked out of her office, his mind racing.

14. SCRAMBLER

"Krieger," the voice on the phone said flatly.

Feldmann's stomach knotted, his resentment almost choking him. "Of course." He reached for the scrambler switch and set it to *continuous*. The green light flashed three times, and then glowed steadily. "And to what do I owe the pleasure?"

"Skip the bullshit. This isn't a social call."

"So, what do you want?"

"You can tell me what the hell's going on," the caller demanded.

"What do you mean?"

"Look. As you know, given the kind of people involved in this operation, we can't put armed guards outside everyone's office. We have to rely on anonymity for security. That means staying the hell off everyone's radar. Zurich is tired of your ego."

"My *ego*? I've spent decades doing unparalleled research that will never be published—research that could have won me a Nobel Prize. So don't talk to me about my ego."

"Damn it! Pangaea launch is only three days away. What in God's name were you thinking—inviting Blum to the farm?"

"David? He's harmless. Doesn't know anything."

"Who the hell knows *what* he knows, or what he might be up to? Besides, it's not your call. You need to clear those sorts of things with me first. Didn't you learn your lesson with his father?"

Feldmann chewed at his thumbnail. "You know damn well that wasn't my fault. I didn't tell him anything. That was Meier, and we took care of it."

"And the only reason you had to take care of it was because Lawson got talkative with his boyfriend."

"Exactly. It was Lawson—not me. You know, I'm really starting to worry about him. He's been acting erratically lately—"

"Lawson is *your* responsibility."

"*You* picked him, remember? You forced him on me, despite my reservations. I know he's been useful, but there's a downside to people like that as well. What do you think he'd do if he figured out he's not among the chosen?"

"Goddammit! We have a very narrow time window right now, and nothing can fuck that up. Another mistake and *we'll* have to step in to fix things. And I think you know what that means. No one is irreplaceable. Remember your esteemed colleague, Professor Detterly, at Princeton?"

Feldmann suddenly felt his bowels starting to liquefy. "No more problems. I promise. Alright?" He waited for a reply, but the line went dead.

Switching off the scrambler, Professor Feldmann tossed the handset back into the receiver. Then he marched, somewhat stiff-legged, to the bathroom down the hall.

15. THE WAY YOU SMILED

Arriving only minutes before the concert, David Blum pulled into the parking lot of the Wabash Congregation Hall and had to make a complete loop before he spotted an empty space near a garbage dumpster in the far corner of the lot. As he latched the top in place, the odor almost made him gag, and he silently hoped the smell wouldn't permeate the canvas cover. Appropriate, he thought. The sinner relegated to Gehenna.

Pushing his way through the double doors beneath the gabled roof, he could hear the small orchestra finishing their warm-up and settling down. An elderly lady in a lime-green dress rushed over from the open auditorium doors, flapping a program.

"Hurry. Hurry. They're about to start." She stuffed the program into his hands as he passed her. A dozen or so singers had already assembled on a small set of bleachers. The women wore frilly white dresses, and the men sported various combinations of suits or jackets and slacks. Blum spotted Kay on the top row.

The instant David sank into a cushioned chair near the back, the orchestra fired up, and the choir launched into "*Ave Maria.*" That was followed by a beautiful rendition of "*Nella Fantasia,*" and then a haunting "*Nessun Dorma*." From there the concert took a lively turn, with the rows of smiling singers belting out a string of show tunes and some pop songs. Kay sang one solo—an *a cappella* rendition of "You Light Up My Life." The concert ended with an audience participation performance of "He's Got the Whole World in his Hands," which Blum hypocritically mumbled his way through.

Afterward, he followed the audience out to the hallway where punch, iced tea, and cookies had been arranged on long folding tables decked with yellow crepe-paper streamers. Everyone seemed to know each other. Blum, the outsider, meandered through the crowd, searching for Kay. He found her talking to another woman around her age.

"David, come here," she said, as he approached. "I want to introduce you to my friend. She grew up on the farm right next to me." Kay turned to the redhead. "Betty. This is David."

He shook her hand and complimented them on the performance.

Kay set down her punch glass and hugged Betty. "Well, gotta run. See you Sunday." She grabbed Blum's arm and guided him through the milling people to the exit.

When they arrived at Kay's apartment, Blum retrieved the wine from the trunk. Once inside, Kay, still in her white dress, removed her shoes and walked through the living room to the balcony door. Sliding back the screen, she stepped outside onto the sun-drenched deck. She fired up the grill and stepped back inside.

"It'll take a few minutes to heat up," she told him. "I'm gonna get changed." She headed down the hall to her bedroom.

Blum carried the wine to the kitchen and fished through the drawers for a corkscrew. He popped the first bottle, a young Barolo, and retrieved two glasses from the cabinet he'd seen her open the night before. After pouring a good fill into both, he carried them back to the living room, taking a sip from his glass on the way. It tasted fine, albeit on the warm side from sitting in the trunk.

"The chicken's marinating in the fridge," he heard Kay yell from her bedroom. "Can you do me a favor and get it out so it can start to warm up?"

"Sure," David called back. He found the chicken soaking in an herbed liquid in a large zip-lock bag and set it on the counter. Then he got busy choosing some music. Spotting a copy of Mary Fahl's *The Other Side of Time*, he switched on the stereo, slid the CD into the tray, and hit play. The room suddenly filled with acoustic guitar and Mary's sultry voice.

Just as he was about to sit on the couch, Kay padded in, still barefoot, wearing faded jeans and an untucked pink shirt with a column of narrowly-spaced pearl buttons down the front. The slinky blouse clung to her every curve.

"For God's sake," she said, laughing. "At least take off your jacket. And go ahead and roll up your sleeves, too, if you feel really daring."

Blum laughed; he liked the way she smiled at him. He tossed his cream jacket on a chair and rolled up his shirt cuffs. He handed her the glass of wine. "Cheers." After clinking their glasses, they both took a sip.

Kay slipped into the kitchen and reemerged with the bag of chicken and a pair of tongs. She smiled as she passed him on her way back to the balcony, and he caught a whiff of her perfume. It smelled French and expensive. He watched as she set the two chicken breasts onto the hot grill. On contact, the searing meat hissed loudly and kicked up a brief cloud of smoke and steam, redolent of lemon, olive oil, and oregano.

She closed the lid and turned back to him, holding the goopy bag of marinade in front of her like a dirty diaper. He stepped aside as she hustled into the kitchen and disposed of it in the trash.

"There," she said. "Now don't let me forget to flip them in about ten or fifteen minutes." She buried herself in the refrigerator, pulling out a glass bowl of salad covered in plastic wrap and some peeled ears of corn.

"Would you like any help?" Blum asked.

"Just hand me my wine," she said. "I'll do the rest. You relax."

He retrieved her wine glass and set it on the kitchen counter next to her. Kay had assembled a tray with a loaf of French bread, a couple wedges of hard cheeses, and a pair of cloth napkins. Carrying the tray into the living room, he placed it on the coffee table and took a seat in an easy chair facing the kitchen. A few minutes later, she walked in and sat on the couch to his right, leaning toward him with her legs tucked to the side and her arm outstretched along the tufted back.

Blum swirled his wine. "So, how long have you lived here?" he asked, looking around the room.

"I moved in shortly after I started with the bank. At that time, it was sort of a stretch for me because they don't pay junior people that much. I was dating a guy, and we got pretty serious. I assumed we'd get married at some point, so I didn't see any point in moving up to anything fancier. Then he left me for his old girlfriend."

"I'm sorry. That's too bad."

"Yeah. It kind of threw me for a while. Anyway, the apartment was going condo, so I figured I'd buy in and then flip it in a couple of years. By the time I was earning real money and could afford an actual house, the financial crisis hit, and prices tanked. I was underwater on my mortgage, so instead of selling I did some renovation and bought some new furniture and carpets, and now I'm really enjoying not worrying about housing costs."

"It's nice," David commented.

"Were you ever married?" she ventured, looking at him coyly.

"I was engaged once. Years ago."

"So what happened?"

Blum stumbled over the words. "She died," he said, staring past Kay at nothing in particular. "Hit by an SUV."

"I'm so sorry."

"It's been five years now." He lifted his hands in a gesture of surrender.

"Anything serious at the moment?"

"If there were, I wouldn't be here."

She seemed to like that answer. "So when did you leave Champaign? Right after college?"

"Yeah. Back in two thousand. I joined the FBI and moved to Virginia for a while for training. Then I worked out of the New York office for a year, before switching to Chicago."

"Did you ever shoot anyone?"

He scoffed. "Why does everyone ask that when you tell them you're in law enforcement?"

"Did you?"

"No. I was in the white-collar crime area. No 'Freeze or die, FBI' moments for me. More of an accountant than anything. In fact, my biggest risks were paper cuts and carpal tunnel."

"Then why did you leave?"

"I had sort of a falling out with my boss. I got an offer to become an investment manager for twice my old salary, so I left."

"Do you ever miss it?"

"Sometimes." Blum took a sip of wine and lost himself in contemplation for a moment. "What I do now is fun, and it pays for a pretty comfortable lifestyle, but it doesn't really give me the same feeling of making a difference in people's lives. At least not people who really need any help."

Kay looked puzzled, and Blum wondered why that was so hard to understand.

"Your clients don't need help?" she asked, incredulous.

"They certainly won't starve without me."

"What about the case you're on now? Someone was *murdered*. Finding the murderer won't make a difference?" The smile had disappeared from her face.

Blum cringed. "I . . . I . . ." his face flushed as the words dribbled out of his mouth.

Kay sat upright and swung her legs onto the floor. "David, what's going on? You *are* a private detective, aren't you?"

"Alright, look," he said, hoping she was still listening.

Her mouth fell open. "You *lied* to me?"

Blum struggled for the right words. "Look, just listen to me. No, I'm not really a private detective. I was worried that you wouldn't talk to me unless you thought I was."

"Why?"

"What would you have done if I was just some guy asking you about that article?"

"I don't know. So why did you *really* want to talk to me then? You happened to read the article and thought it would be fun to talk to the crazy girl?"

"No!"

"And then what? Get me into bed like that sleazebag reporter?"

Now it was her turn to recoil in shame for a stupid slip. "Oh, God." She twisted her head away from him and covered her face with her hands. "You need to go. Now!"

"Let me explain."

"No. Just get the hell out of here." she yelled.

Blum stood up. "No! Wait. Please listen to me. Everything else is absolutely true. I *am* investigating a murder. Think about all the stuff we found together yesterday. I certainly didn't invent all that."

She leaned forward, her elbows resting on her knees as she

shook her head from side to side. "I don't care. You lied to me. I can't trust you."

Trying to comfort her, David touched her on her shoulder, but she shook his hand off violently.

"Get out. Just get out," she moaned. "Leave me alone."

"It was *my father* who died," he said, finally.

At that, she sat motionless, her face still buried in her hands.

Blum continued. "And, based on Meier's note and everything I've learned since, I have reason to believe he was murdered, so I'm investigating it. The police won't believe me unless I have proof. You know what that feels like. And then after I learned about what happened to you, and I saw the plane, I had to talk to you." Blum paused, looking at her, and sighed. "And that . . . that's why I'm here."

He looked down at her, trying to register her reaction. "When I came to your office, I never guessed we'd have more than one conversation, and I thought I had only one shot to get my questions out. I was sure you'd think I was crazy and kick me out if I told you the truth—before I could tell you the *whole* truth. I wanted to be totally honest with you, but each time I saw you, it got tougher and tougher. For that, I am so sorry. I knew I had to tell you at some point. I didn't mean for it to be so . . . accidental."

She remained still. No response.

"I shouldn't have lied to you."

Kay lowered her hands and turned slowly toward David. Her eyes brimmed with tears. "Your *father* was murdered?" She hunched her shoulders to dab her eyes on her shirt. "That's horrible." She stared at the floor. "So now you don't have anyone."

Blum bent over and grabbed one of the linen napkins. He stepped around the corner of the coffee table and handed it to her.

"Based on what you told me and what we learned together yesterday, I'm convinced that Feldmann, and probably Lawson, killed my dad, but I'm not sure why yet. Probably because he learned about whatever this horrible thing is they're about to do."

Kay dried her eyes. "God. I'm so embarrassed."

"Why? You didn't know. I'm the one who—"

"Not that." Her voice grew timid. "What I told you about that reporter. I was just a stupid teenager. The cops wouldn't believe me. My own father wouldn't believe me. And then that reporter pretended to take me seriously. It was such a relief." She sniffled and then wiped her nose on the napkin. "But then . . . afterward . . . all he did was make fun of me."

"It's already forgotten," Blum said. He leaned down and kissed the top of her head, cupping her still-damp chin in his palm. "And speaking of forgetting, I'm going to go and flip the chicken." Without looking up, she nodded her head.

Blum took his time tending to the grill in order to give Kay a chance to collect herself. When he finally stepped back into the apartment, she was busy setting the table, laying out silverware next to dinner plates.

"How's the chicken?" she asked.

"Fine. Another ten minutes or so. Are you sure there's nothing else I can do to help?"

She shook her head, and Blum noticed she still avoided eye contact. He retrieved the glasses and carried them to the table. She sat in the chair closer to the kitchen, and he slid her glass over to her.

"Listen, I'm really sorry. You know everything now. So, how about we start over?" he suggested.

She nodded and took a deep breath. "So . . . did you ever shoot anyone?" She smiled through damp lashes.

Blum was glad to see her sense of humor had returned. "No." He left it at that.

She ate her salad quietly, taking occasional sips of wine.

"Anything new in your investigation?"

"Well, I did learn more about that group, ACID, that Lawson was in. It's not clear it was ever very large, but its philosophy . . . my God. A lot of hate there. It looks like the group disbanded a while ago, though. The website's expired. One of their guys was sent to prison for plotting to kill a policeman. And Lawson's here, of course."

"So that's kind of a dead end?"

"For now."

When they finished their salads, Kay grabbed a platter and a fresh set of tongs and retrieved the meat. It smelled delicious.

"So what now?" Kay asked when they were reseated.

"I don't know. I'm pretty much at a loss." Blum plucked a steaming roll from a small bowl. "I wish I knew more about AGRI. It doesn't have a website, which is very strange for a public-service company."

Kay topped off her glass and David's with the rest of the wine in the bottle. She looked up at Blum furtively then turned away as she took a sip. Setting the glass back down, she stared at it before meeting David's gaze.

"I have some more information for you," she said, her voice strained. "But this could get me in a lot of trouble."

"More trouble than for what you've already told me?"

"I broke the rules before when I told you that stuff, but I got that information in the normal course of my work. What I'm about to tell you is something that I went looking for . . . with no legitimate excuse. That's why it's so important to know I can trust you . . . why I was so upset earlier when I thought I couldn't."

"So, what is it?" he asked as gently as he could.

"I went into the CSR account again today and printed off all their transactions for the past six months. I brought it home with me." She took a slow sip of wine. "God. I feel like I just admitted stealing money from the cash vault—it's only information, right?"

He reached out and covered her hand with his, giving it a firm squeeze. "Yes. It is only information . . . about some very bad people. No one will ever know. You did the right thing."

She nodded and, standing up slowly, walked back to her office, returning a moment later with a set of stapled papers. She handed the stack to Blum.

The top of the first page contained identifying information for the CSR account—the full account name, account number, and bank routing number. Below that, starting with last February, were line items for each transaction. Blum zeroed in on the large monthly deposits from AGRI as well as the payments out—mostly by check, identified by check number only, and some by wire—to Feldmann, Lawson, and a few technology vendors who were identified by account name.

Blum studied the AGRI deposits. Neither the originating bank nor the account name was identified—just the bank routing number and account number were listed—but Blum recognized Regency's ID. Now that he had the AGRI account number, he could access it on Regency's transaction system.

Turning the page around, he pointed at one of the AGRI deposits. "Last night, you said you had traced the originating bank on these inflows to Regency Bank in Chicago?"

"That's right."

"You remember I told you I work for an investment manager?"

She stiffened. "Why? You don't?"

"Relax. I do. But there's one more thing I need to add to that." He hesitated. Was she ready for another confession? "That investment manager I work for is . . . Regency Bank." He braced himself for her reaction.

She sat silent for a second, and then suddenly she reached across the table and grabbed both his forearms. "So you can see what's going on in the account, right?"

It wasn't the reaction he had expected, and he sighed in relief. "Yeah. I should be able to trace the money back to its source, now that I have the account number. I'll do that first thing tomorrow morning."

Kay squeezed his arms again. "This is so exciting." She smiled broadly. Then she dug into her chicken with gusto. Blum followed suit, complimenting her on the marinade.

"My mom's recipe," she said. "I used to love helping her make it . . . before she died."

"As I think I told you, I grew up without a mother, too," he said. "But I'm sure it was much more difficult for you, being a girl."

"Yeah. She died just when I probably needed her the most." Kay stared at her plate, her face almost expressionless. "Do you know what it's like going to your *dad* to ask about things like tampons? Especially *my* dad?"

"No," he said in all seriousness. "I can't imagine."

"Luckily, my friend Susan's mother kind of took me under her wing and more or less raised me after my mother passed. She was a really strong woman. Any self-confidence I have comes from her. She was the one who convinced me to take pilot lessons."

"I noticed your books. Do you have your license?"

"Almost. I aced all the written tests, and my instructor said I was a natural in the cockpit, but—"

"You ran out of money?"

"No, although it did get to be very expensive. The truth is I could never build up the courage to solo. I was fine when there was someone with me. They didn't even have to be as good a pilot as me. But the idea of being up there alone, with no one to rely on but myself, I couldn't do it. I started coming up with excuses at first. Then I just quit."

"How long ago was that?"

"It's been over ten years now."

"I'm sure you've gained a lot of confidence since then. Do you think you could go back and do it now?"

"Maybe. But, at this point, I'd basically need to start all over again." She shrugged. "Someday."

When they finished their dinner, Kay took the dishes to the kitchen. Blum noticed that the music had ended. Perusing her collection, he selected *Serenade* by Katherine Jenkins and played it. The second song on the album was "*Nella Fantasia.*"

"Sounds like you guys," Blum said to Kay as she emerged from behind the kitchen counter, drying her hands on a towel.

"Oh, my God, I wish. But thanks anyway. I'm glad you liked the show. I know you really didn't want to come. You thought it was going to be some sort of come-to-Jesus revival, huh?" She walked to the couch and sat down at the end, lifting her legs onto the seat cushion and clutching her bent knees.

"It crossed my mind, but I'm really glad I went. Otherwise, I wouldn't be here with you right now." He followed Kay's lead and, kicking off his loafers, took a seat on the opposite end of the couch, resting back against the side arm, his legs facing hers with their feet almost touching.

Kay studied her fingernails. She looked over at him. "About inviting you to my church. I hope you know I would never presume to tell you what to believe. Besides, I'm still trying to figure out exactly what I believe at this point."

"Oh?"

"Yeah. I grew up Methodist and was told God and the Bible had all the answers. It was very comforting to a scared little girl. Then I got out in the big world, and realized some of those things didn't quite make sense, at least not if you took them literally. For a long time, I didn't even think about religion much—except on Christmas and Easter. I mean, people seem to get so caught up in, 'I'm right, and you're wrong.' If there is a God, and I think there is, I have to believe what he really cares about is getting people to love and support each other, not whether we eat the wrong food or say the wrong words. That and stop killing each other because someone else's explanation of why it's important to be a good person is a little different from yours."

She stared directly into David's eyes. Her slightly pouty lower lip quivered with uncertainty, and he guessed she was worried she'd said too much.

It was hard for David to get his own words out without choking up a little. "I think that's the best description I've ever heard of what 'religion' should be all about."

The tension seemed to leave her body. Her shoulders relaxed, and her lips curled into a peaceful smile. Lowering her feet to the floor, she slid across the couch toward him. Shifting sideways, David leaned over, put his arms around her shoulders and kissed her lips tenderly. In time, he nibbled his way across her cheek and, after softly brushing aside her silky, vanilla-scented hair, he nuzzled her pulsing neck.

"Mmmmmm," she murmured.

Gently disentangling, he gazed into Kay's eyes. They were wide with pleasure and anticipation. He brushed across her chest with the back of his hand and felt her nipples harden as they pressed against her soft shirt.

"Before, you told me not to rush you. Am I rushing you?" he asked, gently.

"If I feel rushed, I'll tell you," she said and pulled him closer. Blum kissed her again, passionately, and her mouth opened wide. Their tongues met and explored each other. David slid his right hand upward and cupped her breast, massaging it gently and rolling her nipple between his finger and thumb. Then he moved his hand over and, one by one, undid the pearl buttons down the front of her blouse. The sides fell open loosely. He reached behind and unclasped her lacy bra, exposing two perfect, full breasts with bright pink nipples. All around the two points, the skin was tight and puckered. He lowered his head and ran his tongue over their warm skin, and she moaned.

Blum kissed her again on the lips. He let his right hand drift down to her leg and caressed it, first along the outside, then, as she spread her knees, along the inside, ending in the crevice between her thighs.

"It's been a little while," she said, almost apologetically.

"We can stop any time," he told her. "But then I guess you're not on the pill. I didn't bring anything . . ."

"Don't worry," she said softly. "I stopped at the drug store."

He kissed her softly on the nose. "You make up your mind fast."

"Women do that, you know. We decide about a guy pretty quickly. Then we wait to be convinced we're right."

"I guess guys make up their minds pretty quickly too," he said. "Only we don't take much time to be convinced."

"Or to convince," she added. "But not you," she whispered. "I knew the moment I saw you that you would be different. It was the way you smiled at me."

Blum kissed her again, then, standing, lifted her up and carried her to the bedroom, setting her down by her bed. He kissed her on her neck while he unbuttoned her jeans and unzipped her fly, gently lowering the waist over her hips and letting the pants slip down to her knees. With a slight wiggle, she shook them to her ankles and stepped out of the crumpled pile. She smiled up into his eyes, her thick locks of blond hair falling across her shoulders.

David stood back and admired her body, her curves accentuated in the cool glow of the moonlight from the back window, totally naked but for a pair of red lace panties.

16. HIDDEN PASTS

Blazing morning sun streaked across the bedroom ceiling. Shutting his eyes, Blum rolled over in the huge bed and reached for Kay, but she wasn't there. He pushed up onto his elbow and called her name. The apartment answered back with silence. Naked, he stumbled out of bed and searched for her in the bathroom and living room before finally spotting a note taped to the inside of the front door.

> DAVID,
> DIDN'T WANT TO WAKE YOU. HAD TO GO TO WORK.
> WHEN YOU LEAVE, PLEASE LOCK UP AND PUT THE
> DOOR KEY (ON THE COUNTER) THROUGH THE SLOT
> IN MY MAILBOX. I HAVE A KEY TO THE BOX SO I CAN
> GET IT. I HAD A GREAT EVENING. COME BY WORK
> AND SEE ME IF YOU GET A CHANCE.
> XXXX
> KAY

P.S. I LEFT YOU SOME COFFEE.

Blum looked at his watch. Ten thirty. After throwing on yesterday's clothes, he poured himself some coffee. He found a pen and a sheet of paper and began to compose a note to Kay, but his words of sentiment came slowly and sounded stupid. Better to drive over and see her later. He crumpled up the note and threw it in the trash.

On his way out, he paused at the mailboxes to slip the key into the slot labeled "K. Westfield." As he pushed his way through the outer door, he felt slightly sad, as if by returning the key he was somehow saying good-bye to her. Once outside, though, he quickly forgot the notion. The sun blazed fiercely, and billowy cumulus clouds sailed out of the western sky like an invading armada. Of course he would see her again, he told himself. Perhaps even that night, if he was lucky.

As he got in the car and clicked the seatbelt straps in place, he looked up at Kay's balcony and felt a wonderful peacefulness envelop him. They had made love twice—once right away, quickly, intensely, and with incredible fire. Then, basking in the comfort of their intimacy, the two had talked for what seemed like hours. After that, they had made love again, slowly, tenderly, melding softly. Finally, exhausted, they had fallen asleep with Blum nestled next to Kay's warm body. He could still see her eyes and lips and the curves of her back. He thought again about the feel of her breasts and thighs, and his body began to stir.

He longed to be with her again, but he wondered if she felt the same. And what would she be like when he really got to know her? She seemed to have her head screwed on straight, but he had been wrong before. Was he really ready to set himself up for another disappointment? Frustrated, he jammed the Cobra into gear and roared out of the parking lot of Sunny Ridge Village.

Back in his hotel room, he showered and dressed. Then he connected to the Greystone's Wi-Fi and logged into the Regency server using his coded key fob. He paused for a moment before accessing the Demand Deposit Account system. Given his role and the need to verify deposits, withdrawals, and wire transfers, he was granted full access, but he still felt uncomfortable. He was about to violate *The Code*.

Ignoring a stab of guilt, he clicked on the DDA icon. After entering his log-on ID and password, the main screen appeared. A user prompt requested an account number. Account names, other than for his own clients, were blocked, which was why having the account number for AGRI was so critical. He retrieved the CSR printout and carefully typed in the twelve-digit identifier.

Blum hit the return key. Immediately, account identification appeared on the screen, followed by transactions. The details were simple, but staggering in their implication. The account had a current balance just under seventy-five million dollars—not unusually large for an endowment, but, oddly, the entire amount sat in a checking account earning no interest. Even stranger, two different transactions, repeated over and over, accounted for almost all of the activity. One entailed half a million dollars a month wired in from another bank account, identified only by routing and account number. The other transaction entailed transfers out to an account at a third bank, also only identified by numbers. Blum checked the printout from Kay and confirmed that the recipient was CSR's account at First Urbana. The CSR account received about eighty-five thousand a month.

Blum minimized the DDA system window and checked the Federal Reserve's website for the routing number of the bank sending funds into the AGRI account. No listing appeared, indicating it was most likely a foreign bank.

Moving back to the Regency website, he located the internal directory and found the phone number for the "wire room"—the

159

people who effected electronic transfers of funds between institutions. He dialed it, and, after the receptionist answered, he provided his employee ID and personal code.

"I need to know the identity of a foreign bank. Here's the wire number." He read it to her.

There was a short pause, during which he heard a keyboard clicking in the background. "I thought so," the woman said. "It's us, sir. That's the SWIFT code for our London HQ."

"Great," he said, hoping his surprise didn't show. "I wanted to make sure." He hung up.

Good news. Being another Regency account, he could get the details on it as well. However, since it was a foreign account, he would also need the twenty-digit identifier on the back of his badge. He dug around in the computer bag, but it wasn't there.

Shit. Had he left it in Chicago? No. He recalled standing in the dining room at his father's house and holding it. Then he remembered. It had fallen out of his computer bag that first night, and he had put it in his back pocket before heading upstairs for bed. It must still be there at the bottom of the laundry pile in the closet.

Blum grabbed his computer bag and drove quickly across town to his dad's house. He parked on the next street and circled the block on foot to confirm no one was watching the place. Concluding he was safe, he entered through the side door.

The hot interior smelled musty but comfortingly familiar. He ran straight up to the bedroom and rifled through the pile of dirty laundry until he found the jeans he had worn the night he'd arrived. Feeling around in the pockets, he found the credit-card sized piece of thick plastic, thankful the intruders hadn't taken it.

Sitting at the dining room table, he retrieved the account printouts and his hand-scribbled notes and set them on the table next to his laptop. A few clicks took him to the DDA system, where he entered his ID and password. The screen defaulted to the Chicago transaction system, but, using a drop-down menu, he selected *Main Branch London*. A new screen appeared. He carefully copied the twelve-digit account number and the code off his ID badge and pressed the enter key.

As it had earlier that day, the screen suddenly filled with the account details, including the owner, "Agricultural Genomics Research International, UK." The balance stood at just over five hundred million dollars, with all deposits coming from an account in the Cayman Islands. In this case, though, the source account showed a name—Venus Holdings, PLC.

A quick search indicated that they were a Cayman Island holding company. Searching LexisNexis revealed a lawsuit from 2003 against something called Venus Mark of Van Ives, California. The suit mentioned Venus Holdings as their sole shareholder.

So, back full-circle to the United States. Absently, he typed the name into Google. The first listing to pop up was venusmark.com. Without reading the description, he clicked on the link. The screen filled with erotic images.

What the hell?

Venus Mark was an adult website.

According to the *Company Info* link, the outfit produced and distributed movies that catered to people with "special interests" that other studios didn't produce. Venus Mark even offered the option of creating one-off movies and virtual reality experiences to the customer's specifications for negotiated fees.

So, AGRI was a complete sham. Feldmann's Center for Scientific Research, ultimately, was being funded almost exclusively by pornography, with the money laundered through a fictional research institute.

Blum shut off his computer and sat back, running his hands through his coarse, black hair. Now what? With no way to look into

Venus's accounts, and with the discovery that AGRI was nothing but a mythical entity, he was out of leads. Lawson seemed to have stayed clean for the past ten years, so he was probably a dead end. At this point, Meier was a dead end as well. The only places left to look for evidence were CSR and Feldmann's farm, but breaking into either would be dangerous and, on his own, probably futile; searches of that nature needed to be handled by the authorities. And that meant it was finally time to call the FBI. They might simply ignore him, but it was time to quit playing cops and robbers and get back to work. He would have to avoid the Chicago FBI office, though; Petersen still worked there, and that would be a problem. He decided to call the Springfield office instead. No one there knew him.

Resigned to what he had to do, he repacked his computer and gathered his things. But then, with the tension of his search over, the depressing implications of his surroundings quickly closed in on him. Only four days had passed since he'd abandoned the house for the safety of the hotel. In that time, away from the familiar, his situation had morphed into something rather abstract and surreal. He had begun to feel like an actor in a movie, going through the motions, playing the part of someone else. But, now, standing in his childhood home, reality returned with an overwhelming sense of despair and regret.

He's gone, he told himself. Dad's gone.

Blum took a few ragged breaths. His entire body felt hollow. He could hear Kay's words ringing in his ears. "Now you don't have anyone."

Not ready to leave yet, he wandered upstairs to his father's bedroom. Stepping inside, he sat on the bed for a few minutes and looked around the drab room with its simple furniture—a bed and nightstand, a tall mahogany dresser, an armoire, and a low table with a few magazines strewn across it. He glanced down at the nightstand where an old electric clock hummed, its second hand still slowly tracing its way around the dial.

With a sigh, he stood up and walked over to the dresser. He absently ran his finger over the dusty wood of the chest-high top, where a comb, a pair of reading glasses, and an electric razor sat. He opened the top drawer. Inside, he found a collection of family photographs—posed studio shots of himself and his father, and a few of him as a toddler with his mother. Among the pictures were un-inscribed birthday cards from friends and relatives that David had heard of but had never met. All rather impersonal. Digging further down, he spotted a white cardboard carton about the size of a large cereal box. Unable to pry off the cover in the confines of the drawer, he carried it back to the bed.

Taking a seat on the corner of the mattress, he removed the lid and rummaged through more photographs, cards, and letters. These pictures were more personal—candid photos from vacations, school pictures of David over the years, from cute kid to dorky teenager with acne, to his carefully posed, oh-so-desperate-to-be-an-adult high school graduation photograph. He also found a rubber-banded stack of cards he'd made as a child and given to his father. A few were drawn in crayon, others with construction-paper figures cut out and glued on the front. Beneath them, he found cards from Aunt Shelly, even a few from his mother, and all of them contained handwritten messages of endearment.

He found it touching that his father had kept these mementos for so long. Then again, he thought, so like his father to keep his personal items locked away, hidden from everyone around him, as if afraid they might inadvertently reveal some emotion.

Gathering the contents together, he was about to return everything to the carton when he noticed a large envelope wedged into the bottom of the box. Using a fingernail, he managed to pry it loose. He dumped the contents onto his lap. Out spilled a few letters addressed to his father, along with a thick foolscap envelope. Blum examined the letters. One bore a cancellation mark from two years before he was even born. The other, from his Aunt Shelly, had been mailed only a month earlier.

He opened the flap on the older letter and removed the hand-written note.

> My dearest Sol,
>
> Please read this letter all the way through before you make up your mind about anything. I know I have no right to ask for any favors after what I am about to tell you, but please believe how sorry I am. I never meant to hurt you. I understand how important your work is to you. That commitment is part of what I so love about you. But at times, this intensity comes with a profound cost to me, and my needs. I've never doubted your love for me, but I don't think you have always given me the attention I deserve. That's left me feeling rejected and alone. A few months ago, when that sense of rejection was overwhelming, in a moment of weakness of which I am most ashamed, I'm sad to say I found comfort with someone else. I'm sure you could tell something was wrong. In fact, I'm half sure I wanted you to. That's no excuse, though. Clearly, there is no excuse.
>
> I want you to know how sorry I am and how I came to realize why I fell so far; it was only because your indifference could hurt me like nothing else in this world. I am pleading with you to give me another chance. If not, I will understand. You are a man of immense principles and loyalty, and I have violated that. I will never forgive myself, and I

would never expect you to either. I only ask that we try to start over—to rebuild that trust one fiber at a time.
Until I hear from you, I will be here at my mother's house. Please let me know one way or the other. I can't stand the thought of living with the agony of not knowing.
You will remain, always, my loving soul mate,
Myra

Blum shuddered, his chest burning. His muscles fell limp. He slid off the bed onto the soft carpet and leaned against the mattress.

His own mother! For the first time in his life, he was angry at her.

How could his father have ever forgiven such a betrayal? Was it out of love? Understanding? Or, maybe just total despair. The poor man. Whatever the reason, his dad had clearly taken her back. David had been born a few years later.

As the initial shock wore off, his pity for his father became tinged with resentment as well. If his father could have been that understanding with his wife, why had he remained so cold to his own son? Does a person only have so much capacity for affection, after which he simply lapses into indifference? Had his mother's affair consumed all that his father had to give, leaving David to fend for himself?

Almost afraid to read it, but curious to see what Shelly might have to say that would lead his father to hide her letter along with his mother's, David opened the other envelope. Shelly's neat script covered the entire unlined page.

Dear Sol,
You have to talk to David. There's so much you need to tell him, and he needs to hear those things from you. Ever since Myra's death, I've seen you shut down more and more. Everyone knew that Myra's mental condition took

its toll on you over the years. How you coped with every-
thing so nobly and patiently always amazed me. And, after
all that, for her to go and do what she did to you and David
is incomprehensible. You are a rock to have survived.

David's jaw tensed. What did she mean by "to you and David"?
The affair had ended two years before he was born. Had there been
another one?

I know you're afraid David doesn't appreciate what you've
done for him, but I'm sure he does. Even though he chose a
path different from yours (and probably different from the
one you might have liked him to take), I see so much of you
in him. I know he loves you, even if he never tells you so.
I think you need to sit him down and talk to him about
how you feel before it's too late. No one wants to leave
this world wondering if his father (or son) loves him. But
David's your son. It has to be your decision.
Perhaps he won't understand, but you need to try. As
you're so fond of saying, some battles are better fought
and lost than never fought at all.
With all my love,
Shelly

Of course he'd loved his father, David thought. How could his
dad have ever doubted that? Besides, they'd lived in the same
house for twenty years. If his father had been so worried about
how David felt, how hard would it have been for him to just walk
down the hall and ask?

And then the tragedy of it all hit him. When was the last time
he'd told his father that he loved *him*? Or conveyed how proud he

was of *him*? It had never dawned on him until that moment that his father couldn't simply know those things any more than he could— that he needed to hear them from David as much as David needed to hear them from his dad.

Almost as an afterthought, he opened the foolscap manila envelope and dumped the contents into his left hand. The untidy pile included his mother's driver's license, social security card, and a folded form.

He unfolded the velum document. The paper felt thin and slightly slick. Block letters across the top read, "CORONER'S REPORT, County of Champaign." Right below that were a series of boxes with labels for date, name, sex, height, weight, and so forth, each one filled with uneven, smudged letters and numbers from a typewriter.

He skimmed through the block of narrative in the large central box that mentioned physical examination and blood tests and focused on the bottom box: "Cause of Death: Ingestion of barbiturates leading to coronary failure. Suicide."

The last word wrenched him physically, like a rope tightening around his chest, threatening to suffocate him. His breath escaped in a primal moan, and tears rolled down his cheeks.

Oh God. So that's what Shelly had meant by, "to you and David." Not the affair—a betrayal his father had found a way to forgive—but the ultimate betrayal from which there was no escape, no chance to forgive. He thought about how his father must have anguished all those years, wondering what he could have done differently. And there David had been, too wrapped up in himself to notice anything other than his own stupid resentments.

Now David understood his father's silent contemplations—so many nights, sitting alone on the back patio, clutching his cigar and quietly sipping his scotch. And all that time, on top of everything else, his father had been wondering whether his son respected him, or even loved him. Any one of those nights, David could have just walked outside and put his hands on his father's shoulders and said, "I love you, Dad. I'm so proud of you." It wouldn't have changed the past, but it would have, at least to some small degree, helped ease the man's pain. Instead, David had sat selfishly in his own room, door shut, glaring out the window. Shelly was right; he was more like his father than he'd ever realized.

For a long while, David sat on the floor, staring through the far window at the trees outside, their leaves fluttering in the light breeze, sun-dappled green against the cerulean sky. Finally, when his tears subsided, he slowly repacked the box in reverse, burying the painful remnants in the envelope, stacking the personal cards and letters on top, and closing the lid. Carefully, he replaced the carton in the drawer and slid it shut. He picked up the comb from the top of the dresser and held it to his nose. It smelled like his dad, and, for a moment, he lost himself in a childhood memory of being held in his father's arms.

It took him a few minutes to even remember why he had come to the house. Oh, right. The badge. And then he'd learned the truth about CSR's funding. He needed to call the FBI.

Taking out his phone, he brought up his directory and scrolled through the entries for "FBI SPRINGFIELD OFFICE." Along the way, he passed the entry labeled "DAD" and paused.

He shut off his phone and stared at his reflection in the black screen. The tinted glass darkened his features, and for a moment he saw his father looking back at him.

Some battles are better fought and lost than never fought at all.

Whether he liked it or not, this was his battle to fight.

17. FAMILY TIES

Kay Westfield sat in her office, feeling very much like a guppy in a fishbowl. A week ago she had welcomed the chance to be seen at her desk, doing important work for the bank, in control of her world and her life. But today, everything seemed upside-down. Compared to what she and David were doing, the consequences of her job now seemed trivial.

Wanting to do something useful, she turned to her computer and clicked on "Retail Platform," then "Statements." A log-on page appeared, and she typed in her ID and password. It was rejected. She tried again, in case she had entered it incorrectly, but the same screen reappeared. As she'd feared, her sign-on must have expired.

What else could she do? She thought about any other sources of information she could use. Her first stop was the web site for the Office of Foreign Asset Control—"OFAC"—the Treasury's arm for tracing payments involving international terrorists, money-launderers and other nefarious entities. After clicking through a number of false paths, she found their searchable list of SDNs (Specially Designated Nationals) for that purpose.

Kay entered "Otto Feldmann" then "Victor Lawson," but no

matches were found. Next she tried "Center for Scientific Research" and "Agricultural Genomics Research International," but nothing came close to matching.

What else?

She brought up a search engine and searched "Victor Lawson," just as they'd done two nights ago. She found the same listings, including the article on the ACID protest. Out of morbid curiosity, she clicked on it and read the piece again. She shook her head in disgust. What drove people like that? Probably something they're born with, she decided. Or were they simply raised that way? She thought about her own father. He certainly held some of the same resentments. Where did they come from? Her grandparents—his parents—had always seemed pretty decent. She began to wonder what Victor's parents had been like.

She narrowed her search to only mentions of both "Victor Lawson" and "Boise." The first page showed mostly the same articles she'd already found, but the second page had an article from 1994 about how Victor had been accepted to Cal Tech after having completed only his junior year in high school. The university had made its decision based on Victor's grades, ACT scores, and a paper he'd published on "Stochastic Modeling of Molecular Kinetic Energy in a Mixture of Non-Ideal Gases."

"Boooring," she mumbled to herself.

Scanning through four more pages of references, she came across a short wedding announcement from 1983. It stated that Mary LeMar of Frost Valley, Montana had married Walter Lawson of Boise in a ceremony conducted at the First Christian Church, after which they had held a reception at the Niles Banquet Hall. It wasn't till she got to the last sentence that she understood why the article had even made the search list. It mentioned that Mary and Walter, along with *Victor*, Mary's five-year-old child from a prior marriage, planned to settle in Boise.

Kay glanced around through the lacy curtains covering the glass walls to make sure no one was watching what she was doing. Satisfied, she typed "Mary LeMar" and "Frost Valley" into a new search. After sifting through pages of irrelevant items, she found an article from the *Frost Valley Gazette*, dated February 12 of 1981, titled "Messy Divorce Finally Settled."

The article read like something out of the tabloids. According to the story, the divorce trial of Mary and Trevor LeMar had finally been settled by Judge Pascale after fierce accusations had flown on both sides. According to Mary, Trevor had beaten her nearly to death in front of her two-year-old son and then walked out on her, and, according to Trevor, that was okay because he was angry that the kid had been fathered by someone else. Mary hadn't disputed that point. In fact, she had apparently gone into minute detail about just how incapable Trevor was of fathering a child. Judge Pascale, in his learned wisdom, had magnanimously granted the divorce to Mary but had ruled for minimal alimony and absolved Trevor of any parental responsibility, stipulating no child support because, after all, "it's not his child."

So Victor had been born Victor LeMar, and at some point, he'd changed his name to Victor Lawson. Curious about his birth certificate, she found her way to the Idaho Vital Records website, ready to look up "Victor LeMar," but online access required a credit card payment to a third-party provider, and it wasn't clear if she could actually get information if she wasn't the person of interest.

Maybe there was another way.

She picked up her phone and dialed a familiar number in the bank's legal department.

"This is Devon Whistler. How can I help you?"

"Hey, Devon. What's up with my favorite attorney?"

"'Favorite attorney'—is that like 'model prisoner' or something?"

"And everyone says you're slow." She heard him laugh. "I need a favor."

"Sure."

"Can you track down a birth certificate for me?"

"Probably. Why?"

"I have a situation . . ." she said, stalling while she came up with a good excuse. "Um, it concerns an issue with the income benefi-ciary in a charitable remainder trust. I need to verify the identity, and I want to match our records. Is that something you can do?"

"Probably. What's the person's name?"

"Victor LeMar. Born in Idaho." She paused as if looking for pa-perwork. "Shit. I don't have the file here. I seem to recall he was born in 1977 or '78. Frost Valley, Idaho, I think is what the town was."

"Parents' names?"

"Mother is Mary LeMar—L-E-M-A-R. Father appears to be Trevor LeMar, but apparently he isn't the real daddy."

"Ooh. Sucks to be Trevor. Shouldn't be too hard. How soon do you need it?"

"How soon can you get it?"

"If I can't find it in an hour, I'll call you and let you know. A birth date would really help."

"I'll see if I can find the file. It may still be with the Trust department."

"Okay. Toodles." He rang off.

Kay looked at her desk clock and, seeing it was close to noon, decided to duck out for lunch. She started to walk to a diner up the street but decided to go to the Courier Café instead since it reminded her of David. When she returned to her office at one, the phone was ringing. Hoping it was David, she reached across her desk and snatched up the receiver.

"Yo, Kay." It was Devon. "No certs for Victor LeMar born in 1977, '78, or '79. You want me to go back farther?"

"Hmmm. Maybe." She took off her sunglasses and tossed her purse on the credenza, stepping around to her chair while still holding the receiver to her ear and dragging the phone cord across her desk.

"Wait," she said. "Try Victor Lawson."

"Victor Lawson? Not LeMar?"

"That's the issue," she said, trying to make it sound like an explanation. "We can't determine if it should be LeMar or Lawson."

"Lawson, huh? Okay. Let me give it a shot. Mother is Mary Lawson, then?"

"I don't think so, but maybe."

"I thought compliance people always dealt in certainties."

"We try to."

More clicking. "Wait. Hold up. I think I've got your guy."

"Really?"

"Yeah. Victor George Lawson. Parents Mary Lawson and Walter Lawson. Born July twenty-third, 1978. Is that your guy? I thought you said his mother was Mary LeMar."

"That has to be him. From what I know, her name *was* LeMar when Victor was born. And her husband's name was Trevor LeMar. She didn't marry Walter Lawson till 1983. Can you explain that?"

"Maybe they do things backwards in Idaho."

"Seriously!"

"Yes. *Seriously* backwards." He laughed. "Just kidding. Kid must have been adopted. When that happens, the parents can change the birth certificate. There has to be an original, but only the parents can get at that. Or law enforcement."

"Huh. Can you send me a copy of what you found?"

"Sure."

"Thank you, Devon." Kay hung up.

She opened a new search page and entered "Mary LeMar" and "Victor." Before pressing enter, she paused, then added "adoption." She hit return.

The very first link took her to a legal notice ("as required by *Idaho Adoption Laws and Statutes 16-1501, Part 6 (a)*") in the *Deer Creek Chronicle* making a public announcement that Mary Lawson and Walter Lawson desired to adopt a baby boy named Victor George LeMar. Kay brought up a map of Idaho and searched for Frost Valley. Then she looked up Deer Creek. The two towns were only miles apart in a small mountain valley northeast of Boise.

It took her five minutes, but she managed to track down the statute referenced in the legal notice and read it. The provisions covered reasonable attempts to notify someone who had parental rights that would be terminated by an adoption. Odd, she thought. Judge what's-his-face had lifted Trevor's parental responsibilities (and presumably rights, as well), so who needed to give permission? And, if it was Trevor, why would he object after all that time?

Returning to the search list, she scanned through a few pages of links, but none of them provided any insight. She changed the search to look for "Deer Creek" instead of "Frost Valley," and, on the second page of references, she found a link to an article in the *Deer Creek Chronicle* from all the way back in December 1979.

Unlike the previous articles, which had been available in text form, this link took her to a scanned image of an old, worn newspaper article. The paper had been damaged in a few spots, but she was able to read most of it. The story describing how Michael Wolf, who claimed to be the biological father of Victor LeMar, had sued Mary LeMar for parental rights under the recently enacted <something she couldn't read> *Child Welfare Act of 1978, 25 U.S.C. section 1902.* He had won the original court case, but the decision was overturned on appeal when the judge ruled that Victor had been born in July 1978, and the act hadn't become law until August. That seemed odd. If the act gave parents additional rights, it didn't seem to make sense that a judge would revert to an earlier standard. Puzzled, she did a search on the portion she could read. A moment later, her screen filled with multiple links to the same site. "Holy shit!" Kay said out loud, holding her forehead in disbelief.

18. GREATEST FEARS

Blum found Kay waiting for him in the bar at Applewood. "I discovered something really interesting today," she said as soon as she saw him.

"What's that," Blum asked, taking a seat next to her.

"Well—" She stopped suddenly. "David, what is it?"

Blum glanced away. *Was it that obvious?* "What do you mean?"

"You look . . . upset. What happened?"

Blum wasn't ready to talk about the letters just yet, and certainly not there. He inhaled sharply. "I guess it's all kind of catching up with me. The stuff with my dad. And being at the house today reminded me of everything."

"Of course. I didn't mean to . . ."

The awkwardness was broken when the bartender informed them that their table was ready.

After they'd been seated for dinner and given menus, Kay spoke up. "What did you find out about that AGRI account?"

"Well," Blum said, glad to shift away from his personal issues. "AGRI's just a clever front," he said. "It's really only a way to funnel money to CSR. AGRI London gets money in and sends it straight through to AGRI in Chicago. Almost all of that gets sent to CSR."

"Where does London's money come from?"

"Something called Venus Holdings in the Cayman Islands."

"What do they do?"

"It's a shell corporation that owns an American company called Venus Mark. They produce . . . um . . . adult entertainment."

"Really? Why would a company that makes pornography donate money to genetic research?"

He laughed. "I can think of a couple reasons. But, seriously, it's a great cover for laundering money. It generates a lot of revenue from anonymous sources, so it wouldn't be unusual to find untraceable purchases using prepaid cards and money orders, and the company can justifiably defend its privacy if anyone asks. Plus, with digital delivery of their, um, content, it would be easy to fake a lot of transactions."

Kay sat back, absorbing the implications. "So, CSR is being funded by someone who *really* doesn't want to be known. Can you trace the money in Venus's account?"

"No. I have no way to get information from the Cayman bank. So all this is very interesting, and it confirms that Feldmann's been lying about his funding, and probably his research as well, but it still doesn't tell us exactly what he's up to."

The waitress returned and took their orders.

"Okay," David said when they were alone again. "Now, what did *you* find out?"

"Well," she said, raising her eyebrow and smiling knowingly. "Our little anti-Indian rabble-rouser, Victor Lawson, is actually half Native American."

"What? How did you discover that?"

"I did some digging. His stepfather, Walter Lawson, adopted Victor when he was six—a year after Walter and Mary *LeMar* got married."

"So?"

"Victor's birth certificate says Victor George Lawson was born to Walter and Mary *Lawson* five years before their wedding."

"That doesn't make any sense."

"Apparently it does because, after an adoption, the state creates a new birth certificate with the new last names."

"So that shows he was adopted, but how does that prove he's half Native American?"

"It doesn't. But they had to post a legal notice in the paper for three weeks announcing their intended adoption so anyone with parental rights could offer up a protest. When I dug into that, I found out that some guy named Wolf—Michael Wolf—had tried to claim paternity of Victor under something called the *Indian Child Protection* Act, or something like that, of 1978. So, Wolf must be an American Indian."

"I take it he didn't win the case?"

"No. The judge decided it didn't apply since Victor was born a month before the act was passed."

"But then . . . Why would . . ."

"I know, right? It makes no sense. Victor, the fuming white-power activist, isn't so white bread after all."

David shook his head. "Bizarre."

Their steaks arrived, and they dug in, each in silent contemplation.

"Maybe Victor doesn't know about his real father," Kay said after a while. "He would have only been, what, a year old or so at the time of the court case with Wolf? Being branded illegitimate would have been bad enough, but back then, especially in a little town in Idaho, I have to imagine being a mixed-race child could be even worse." She took a sip of wine. "I wonder how different he would have turned out if he had known."

"Makes you wonder," David said. "Poor kid. Then again, maybe he *does* know, or at least suspects. As my father once told me, sometimes the things you hate the most in others are really just the things you fear about yourself."

Kay took a sip of wine. "So, now what do we do?"

"Well, I think it's pretty clear. I have to break into CSR and search Feldmann's office."

"Oh my God, David. No." Kay reached across the table and grabbed his hand. "What if you get caught? Or...worse? Why can't you go to the FBI now with what we know?"

"Because we don't really know that much. It's mostly just a bunch of suspicions."

"Don't you think it's at least enough to get them to do *something*? Especially since you used to be an agent there?"

"Look. There's something I have to tell you. I've never told anyone this before, but I didn't just quit the Bureau. I was forced out by my boss, an asshole named Petersen."

"What? Why?"

"We were investigating a regional bank, and I figured out someone had embezzled money from them. A lot of money. I couldn't figure out where the funds had gone, but I took the evidence to Petersen. He told me to focus on something else. Said he would look into it."

"But he didn't?"

"Worse. It turned out *he* was the one who had embezzled the money. I put the pieces together later and confronted him. To cover his tracks, he set me up. Made it look like I had stolen the money. He told me I had a choice: resign or face charges."

"Why didn't you fight it?"

"I wasn't sure I could win, and I couldn't stand the idea of my father thinking I was a criminal. So I quit. After I left, Petersen spread rumors about me so that if I came back with any accusations, it would look like I was only being vindictive."

"That was a while ago, though. Right? You don't think you could find someone who would believe you now?"

"Maybe. But I'm not willing to take the chance just yet. Whatever Feldmann's planning must be huge. AGRI London has almost half a billion dollars at its disposal. Maybe I could convince the FBI to start an investigation, but they'd probably just show up at Feldmann's office and start asking questions, which would only tip him off. I need to provide the FBI with enough proof to get them to storm in, guns blazing."

She winced. "But I don't want you to get killed in the process." She slumped back in her seat.

Blum emptied his wine glass. "Neither do I, but my mind's made up. Tomorrow morning, I'm going to scout out Feldmann's office suite. The last time I was there I really wasn't looking very carefully. Then I'm going to go back tomorrow night and search it."

"How could you even get in? Won't it be locked?"

"I have some keys I found in Meier's apartment, and I know one unlocks the front door of the building. I'm guessing the other one goes to either the office suite or Meier's office. Unfortunately, I may be short a key either way. I'll just have to see."

"What are you going to do if you don't get in?" Kay asked. "Or if you do get in and don't find anything?"

"Then I'll try to cut through the fence at Feldmann's farm and break into the greenhouse building. That has to be where the real work is going on, anyway."

"And if you can't get in *there*?"

"I don't know," he said. "But I'll make you this promise. Today's Thursday. Regardless of what I find out in the next few days, on Monday I'll take whatever we have to the FBI."

"You think a couple of days is going to be enough?"

Blum shrugged. "I hope so."

They left the restaurant and drove their separate cars back to Kay's apartment. Once inside, Kay set her briefcase on the dining room table.

Blum let out a long sigh. "There's something else I need to talk to you about."

"I knew something was wrong." She bit her lower lip. "What is it, David?"

He approached Kay and took her hands in his. "I went by dad's house today to get my work ID, and I spent a little time going through some of his things. I read some old letters and . . . well . . . I learned some things, including stuff I wish we'd been able to talk about before he died."

"Like what?"

"Well, for instance, a lot of the problems I thought I had with him were just stupid misunderstandings. On both our parts. In the end, either of us could have made the other a lot happier if we'd only bothered to talk to each other."

"Why didn't you?"

"Because we were both being pig-headed—waiting for the other one to go first."

She started to pull him toward her in a hug, but he pushed back.

"Wait. I'm not finished." He looked her in the eyes to make sure she was listening. "As painful as it was to find out how stupid I'd been, at least I got a chance to learn the truth. Unfortunately, my dad didn't, so he died thinking I didn't really love or respect him. And I'm not sure I'll ever be able forgive myself for that."

"That's so sad," she said, tears welling.

"Listen to me. I'm telling you this for a reason. I really think *you* need talk to *your* father."

"No," she protested, trying to pull away. "I know exactly how he feels."

"He probably cares for you more than you realize, and I'm sure you still care about him, no matter how angry he makes you."

"The last time I tried to talk to him, it didn't go well. At all."

"Please," David said. "If not for you, then do it for me. If you care for him at all, simply tell him that. And, if he makes you angry, tell him how it makes you feel and why it hurts you. Then let him talk, and just listen. If it all goes horribly wrong, you can blame it on me."

Kay sniffled and wiped her face with her shoulder to dry her eyes. Then, as he relaxed his grip, she pulled her hands free and hugged him. "I'll think about it."

"Seriously, please—"

"I said, I'll *think* about it."

Blum held her tighter. "I know," he said. "You don't like to be pushed."

She giggled into his chest. "No. I don't," he heard her say.

Blum disentangled himself, and, cupping her face in his hands, kissed her on the lips. "If it's alright, I could use a quick shower."

"Of course," she said, gently drawing his right hand to her face and kissing his palm. "The towels are in the cabinet next to the tub."

Blum closed the bathroom door and stripped down, setting his dirty clothes in a neat pile to the side of the sink. He adjusted the water and stepped into the shower, letting the soothing stream begin to ease his emotional pain.

Against the hiss of the warm water, he missed the sound of the bathroom door opening. The air felt suddenly cool. Squinting through wet lashes, he was startled to see Kay, now naked as well, step into the shower and slide up next to him. She looked up into his eyes and threw her arms around him. He hugged her tight, bent down, and buried his head in her neck.

19. TOUCHDOWN

With a black canvas backpack slung over his shoulder, David Blum stepped through the main door of Cotespath Hall under the watchful eye of the security camera and pressed the call button for the elevator.

The elevator dinged opened and Blum got in. As he pressed the button for nine, he mentally reviewed the list of items to watch for: security cameras, visibility from outside windows, types and manufacturers of door locks, locations of filing cabinets, etc.

A moment later, the elevator stopped, and the door opened on the ninth floor. Distracted by his mission, Blum nearly bumped into a pretty brunette dressed in a green dress who was about to enter the car.

"Sorry," he mumbled, stepping around her and out of the elevator.

"David Blum?" he heard her ask.

Turning, he recognized Feldmann's administrative assistant. "Yes. Oh, right, you're . . ."

"Tina. Tina Santini. I work for Professor Feldmann."

"I remember. How are you?" The elevator closed behind her.

"Are you here to see Otto?" she asked.

"Oh, yeah. And to return some books to Hans Meier."

"Neither one's here today. Feldmann's working out at his farm, and Meier hasn't been in for some time. But, if you give me the books, I can put them in his office for you."

"Oh, great," Blum said, sliding the backpack off his shoulder and unzipping it. He reached inside and removed two old, cloth-bound volumes he'd taken from his father's study. He hoped they would pass for something Meier would have owned and lent to his dad.

Tina turned back toward the hallway leading to the suite entrance. At the main door, she opened her purse and retrieved a keychain containing a few metal keys and a gray plastic keycard—just like the one on Meier's keychain.

She swiped the plastic slab across a sensor by the door, and the electromechanical latch responded with a loud click. Blum reached around Tina, pulling the door open and gesturing for her to go first. She smiled, as if surprised by the courtesy, and he followed her inside.

Lights were off in the front waiting area, but daylight streamed in from the large windows facing west, casting shadows of her desk and chair on the beige carpet but leaving the recesses of the room dark. Without pause, Tina walked halfway down the dim hall to the right, and, using a key, opened one of the office doors. Light streamed into the hallway.

"This is Meier's office," she told Blum. "We can leave the books here."

Blum handed Tina the two books, and she set them on the cluttered desk inside. He glanced down at the door lock and noted it said "Best." He also spotted a series of five small digits engraved above the opening. The first one looked like a one or a seven, followed by an eight or six, and then five-four-three.

"Hobby of yours?"

"Sorry. What?"

"Staring at doorknobs."

He shook his head, as if she made no sense at all. He shrugged. "My mind was elsewhere. Sorry. When did you say Professor Feldmann was coming back?"

"I didn't say . . . but he'll be out at his farm all day. I don't expect him back until Monday at the earliest. Is everything okay?"

"Yeah. I've just got a lot on my mind."

"I can imagine," she trailed off. Then she looked at him apologetically. "I'm so sorry, but I need to run right now, so I have to sort of shoo you out and lock up. But I'll tell Otto you stopped by. Can I give him a message?"

"Thanks, no. I'll call him Monday." He followed her back out of the suite into the outer hallway. He heard the door shut, followed by a loud click as the latch locked in place.

Tina pressed the elevator call button and then turned to face the elevator. A moment later, she pivoted back around.

"Hey," she said. "I know you have a lot going on, but, it occurred to me that maybe you could use some company—someone to talk to—given you're here in town for so long all by yourself. If you'd like, perhaps we could meet later for coffee or a drink or something."

Blum was about to decline, tell her he had plans, but then he reconsidered. She worked for Feldmann and spent her time in his office. Perhaps there was something she could tell him that might be useful, either about the lab or Feldmann himself.

"Sure," he said. "That would be nice." The elevator door opened, and they got in together. "What time?" he asked.

"I'll finish up here around five. Why don't you come by and pick me up out front?"

"Sounds good. You have any place in mind?"

"There's a cafe over on Lincoln. They serve everything from espresso to chardonnay, depending on what you're in the mood for."

"Great."

On the ground floor, the elevator opened into the lobby, and Blum followed Tina down the hall, past a stairwell to a side entrance. The exit led them to a concrete pad under a small overhang that provided little protection from the sweltering midday sun.

"I parked in the garage," he told her, hoping to break away and circle back to test his key on the door they'd just used.

"Me too," she said. "I'll walk with you." She stepped closer. "Hey. Can I borrow your phone for a second? I left mine in my desk."

"Sure." He reached into his hip pocket and slid out the phone. He powered it up and typed in his security code.

Tina tapped in a number, and then held the phone to her ear. A moment later, she said, "Hey, this is Tina. I need to cancel drinks today. I'll call you later." She hung up and handed the phone back to Blum.

"I hate to interrupt your plans. We could do this another day . . ."

"Oh. Don't worry. I see her all the time. Really."

"Well, alright then."

The two crossed an open grassy area, plodding slowly in the blazing heat of the late-morning sun to a sidewalk leading to the parking structure. They walked through the open archway at the near corner of the garage into the cave-like interior. Both of them were perspiring as they waited for the garage elevator.

"Man, it's hot today," he commented. "It's supposed to be even worse tomorrow."

"Yeah. Brutal. But I heard a cold front's coming through tomorrow night. Might even get some strong storms." The door opened. "What floor?"

"Four," he said.

Tina pressed the buttons for two and four. On two, the doors opened with a clunk.

"Well, then," she said. "I'll see you here at five." She waved back as the doors shut.

On four, Blum stepped out onto a nearly full parking deck. To his right, a ramp led slowly down. Straight ahead the pavement was level. The layout didn't look right, but he checked the floor number painted on the wall next to the elevator door and confirmed he was on the fourth floor. Tina had apparently led him to a different elevator than the one he'd used earlier. He shrugged and walked straight ahead, figuring he'd wander until he got to his car. At the far corner, though, the ramp to his right led upward. Sure enough, he found an elevator at the end, but the sign next to it displayed the number five, and he hadn't passed his car. He was certain he'd parked on the fourth level.

Confused, he turned around and walked back to where he'd started. Still not spotting his car, he continued down the ramp that was now on his left. To confirm his location, he walked up to the stomach-high wall and peered over the edge. The single-lane drive below looked like where he'd pulled in, but he noticed a silver car exiting, not entering. Now frustrated, he turned to the left again and walked to the next corner. The elevator door there was labeled three.

"What the hell?" he said aloud.

"Another victim of the double helix," he heard a man's voice behind him say. "It happens to everyone."

Blum turned around and saw a gray-bearded African-American man with thick black-framed glasses standing in front of an open car door about twenty feet away.

"Huh?"

"The parking garage," the man explained. "There're two interwoven spirals—one headed up and one down. It's easy to end up on the wrong one. When that happens, you can walk all the way from the top floor to the bottom and not find your car. You have to switch to the other spiral using the drive that runs through the middle."

"Oh," was all Blum could think of to say. "Thanks."

The man laughed. "Simply cut through, and you'll be fine."

Blum waved to the man, then followed his directions and quickly found his car. He started the engine and let it idle as he unzipped his backpack and retrieved Meier's keychain. He examined the two keys carefully. Both had *Best* logos on them. The one with the duller finish had opened the front door to Cotespath Hall. He flipped over the other key and looked at the numbers engraved on it—76543—the same as Meier's office. And the keycard opened the CSR suite. He had everything he needed.

Blum pulled out of the garage. Today might be a good day to check out the farm, he decided. With Feldmann there, it would be interesting to see if the Infiniti showed up. At a minimum, he needed to get a sense of the layout of the ground cover in order to select the best spot to cut through the fence. So, after a quick lunch, he headed west on Springfield Avenue through Champaign, past Sunny Ridge Village, and on into the countryside. Fifteen minutes later, he pulled over and parked on the gravel shoulder a quarter mile from the farm. He retrieved his backpack and set out on foot for the spot on the north fence opposite the far end of the runway.

The sun bore down on him as he walked to the farm, passing tall stalks of corn on his left and fields of soybeans across the road to his right. As he surveyed his surroundings, the paint-by-numbers simplicity of the landscape's palette struck him—light green grass next to dark green fields of soybeans or corn—the latter fringed with golden tassels—all set below a deep-blue sky. Here and there, the monotony was interrupted by the black, tarry road surface flecked with gray gravel, distant grain silos in silver or white, and the occasional red barn. But, all told, nowhere near the riot of colors found in town.

Finding a good vantage point, hidden from the road by a shallow culvert, he dropped his backpack to the ground and peered through the woven chain links, studying the cluster of buildings in the distance. He searched for any signs of movement around Feldmann's house, but the heat waves radiating up from the fields distorted his view of the horizon and made it hard to discern any details. He opened his backpack and retrieved his digital SLR. Zooming the lens to about 50mm, he clicked off a few shots to capture the general layout.

After ten minutes or so of studying the buildings on the horizon and seeing nothing, he sat against the fence and grabbed a bottle of water. As he tilted his head back to take a gulp, his eyes followed the zigzag of chain links up to the glittering coil of barbed wire. Only then did he notice the small white rings at the base of each V-shaped support that appeared to separate the angled struts from the fence posts. Curious, he set his camera on his backpack and carefully scaled the fence. Up close, it became clear that the white rings were actually ceramic insulators, which meant the barbed wire was almost certainly electrified.

Back in Boy Scouts, he'd learned a trick for detecting whether an electric fence was live or not by using a sheath knife with an insulated handle—a process that turned something that could be extremely painful into something merely uncomfortable. Not having a sheath knife, he improvised, taking his silver fountain pen from his pocket and holding it between the folds of his wallet. He climbed back up and touched his makeshift detector to the wire and held it there. Seconds later, a momentary jolt of electricity ran down his arm and legs. The impulse was just strong enough to cause him to drop the wallet and pen, but not enough to knock him off the fence. Satisfied, he jumped down, hoping his action hadn't triggered any detectors.

Returning his attention to the compound, but not sure exactly what he was waiting for, Blum sat on his haunches and stared down the asphalt strip to the buildings in the distance. The soft background static of crickets, punctuated by the staccato *wizzu-wizzu-wizzu* of cicadas, serenaded him as a gentle breeze wafted in aromas of corn, wildflowers, and vegetation. In the midst of such peaceful, bucolic splendor, Blum found it hard to believe that a deranged professor was up to something so evil he was willing to kill to keep it secret.

After half an hour, the heat grew oppressive despite the southerly breeze caressing his face, and he became restless. He stood up and stretched for a bit, contemplating whether to move on to another spot. But then a new sound emerged in the background—a whining, mechanical hum, faint, but growing steadily louder. At first, he thought it might be an approaching car or tractor, but, as the sound got clearer, he realized the pitch was too high.

He stared up and down the road, trying to spot the source of the sound. As the seconds ticked by, the engine noise continued to intensify, but still nothing appeared. Then, all at once, a deafening mechanical scream exploded onto his senses, and he ducked instinctively behind the culvert. From over the top of the wall of corn on the opposite side of the road, a twin-engine aircraft burst out of the blue sky and roared low over the narrow road, its wheels hanging down like the talons on a giant eagle. After clearing the fence, it cut its engines and dropped quickly. Blum grabbed his camera and followed the plane until it touched down on Feldmann's runway. It didn't look like Feldmann's King Air, which meant the professor had visitors.

The twin pivoted and taxied back toward him. As it passed the hangar, it spun around and stopped. A minute later, the door opened and a short ladder dropped down. Blum quickly replaced the zoom lens with a long telephoto and held the camera to his eye. Using it as a monocular, he watched two men climb out of the plane. The heat waves distorted the images, but every now and then a short gust of wind would lessen the effect, and he would snap pictures.

Feldmann and Lawson, along with a tall, silver-haired man, appeared from the hangar and greeted the two visitors. Blum got pictures of them, too. As he watched, a small Jeep rolled up to the plane and parked near the tail section. The driver got out, and, working together, the men unloaded a large, white crate into the back of the Jeep. Blum kept snapping pictures. In a few minutes, the Jeep drove toward the greenhouse and disappeared behind a row of trees. The men followed on foot, disappearing as well.

Blum quickly retrieved his binoculars and focused them on the greenhouse. Struggling to find a spot where neither lens was blocked by fence wires, he watched the side door open and the crate get dragged inside on a dolly. One by one, the men entered the huge building, and then the door shut behind them.

For another half hour, as the hard sun beat down on him, drying his eyes and parching his throat, he kept the binoculars trained on the access door, but nothing happened. He gulped down another bottle of water. Finally, concluding no one was going to come back outside, he repacked the bag and, glancing around to make sure he hadn't left anything behind, pulled up a tall strand of Jimson weed and used it to brush the dirt, hiding his footprints.

As he drove back toward town, he tried to imagine what might be in the white crate. He also thought about what he might be able to learn from his coffee date with Tina. What a stroke of luck, he told himself, her inviting him like that.

20. CAT CURVES

Blum had hoped that by arriving early for his meeting with Tina, he'd have an excuse to go back up to the office suite and look around. However, when he pulled into the circular drive in front of Cotespath Hall, Tina was already sitting out front, sipping a Diet Coke, waiting for him.

As he pulled to the curb and stopped, she looked up, smiled, and tossed the can in a trash bin. Grabbing her purse, she walked over to the roadster.

"Nice car," she exclaimed. "It must have cost a fortune."

"Well," Blum said, opening the door for her. "They give you a discount when you buy more than one."

She smiled her thanks and stepped as daintily as she could across the wide sill, finally sinking back into the low seat.

"My. They didn't design this thing for ladies in dresses, did they?"

"No. More like racers in helmets and Nomex suits. You comfortable?"

"Snug, but comfy," she said, searching for the seatbelt.

"Here," David offered. He lifted the lap belt and handed it to her, then pulled the shoulder strap around the back of the seat. "There's another one of these on the other side."

"You've got to be kidding. Oh well, tie me up. I can take it." With some help, she managed to click together the four straps.

"Okay," Blum said, firing up the engine. "Where is this place you were talking about?"

"It's only a few blocks away. Hardly seems worth the ride in a car like this. If you're not in a hurry, there's another place I know. It's a couple of miles away, though."

"Fine with me. Which way?"

"Head east on Florida."

Blum pulled away from the curb. "So," he asked her over the staccato of the engine. "Where are you from?"

"I was born in Italy, but I grew up outside of Chicago, in Wilmette. I went to college in Connecticut. Now I'm here."

"Oh? Where did you go to school?"

"College? At Yale. You're from here, right?"

"Yeah. Grew up in Champaign and stuck around for college."

"Now where do you live?"

"Chicago, just north of the Loop. I work for an investment company—helping rich people spend their money."

"Sounds like fun."

"It has its moments. How about you? What did you study?"

"Biology and Finance."

"Interesting combination." He caught the light at Florida Avenue. "So, what's the good professor like to work for?"

"Feldmann? He's okay. For the most part, he keeps to himself. He's not that talkative."

"Really? When I had dinner with him he gave me the full tour, and he barely *stopped* talking."

"Did he give you a tour inside his big greenhouse too?"

"No. Why?"

"He's always there doing his research, but he never talks to anyone about it, and he hasn't published anything in years."

"He did show me his experimental crops."

"What sort of crops?" she asked.

"Oh, some of his giant corn. He actually served that for dinner. And there's something he's doing with plants that attract insects to help control pests."

"That stuff's ten years old. Everyone's seen that. He didn't show you anything he's done *recently*, did he?"

"Like what?" Blum asked.

"I wish I knew. It sort of pisses me off, actually. I turned down a job with Monsanto for this because I thought I might learn about all the cutting-edge research they're doing at CSR. Plus, it seemed like a nice break before I applied to graduate school. Instead, I spend my time effectively begging for money and organizing travel for visiting agricultural delegations. Feldmann shows them his big ears of corn and his fancy plants, and they go away amazed. The rest of the time, he spends plowing away on research with his sidekick, Lawson."

"And Meier?"

"Meier? Meier hasn't done any research for him, at least not directly."

"But his office . . ."

"Lawson pulled strings to get him that office. Meier's advisor is Prandler."

"Prandler?"

"Another professor. Junior guy to Feldmann. No, it's only Feldmann and Lawson." Tina suddenly pointed to the right. "Turn here on Philo."

Blum turned south. "Now where am I going?"

"It's about a mile down on the left."

"Who's Lawson?" Blum asked. "I haven't met him."

"He's a post-doc. From *Boise, Idaho*," she added, as if that clarified everything. "He's been working with Otto for four or five years now. Big, ugly guy with a head like a watermelon. Nasty temper . . . and paranoid, too."

"How so?"

"Oh, I don't know. Like one day, he accused me of stealing his calculator. He stood in front of my desk for half an hour telling me how he *knows* I hate him, and that's why I'm always taking his things. In the end, the damn thing was sitting on his filing cabinet the whole time." Suddenly she pointed to her left. "It's right there. The Chimney Spark Tavern. You see the sign?"

"Got it," Blum said. He pulled the roadster into the restaurant lot, parking it between two SUVs.

Crossing a small lobby area, she led him into the crowded main bar—a long, cavernous room with brick walls and vaulted ceiling, crisscrossed with polished beams. Blum spied an empty booth and pointed Tina toward it.

A sandy-haired cocktail waitress in a plum dress stopped by, holding a tray under her arm. "What can I get you two?"

Blum looked at Tina.

"Absolut and soda," she said.

Blum ordered a Rangpur and tonic with lime, and the waitress disappeared.

"Do you usually drive this far for a drink?" he asked.

"If you go anywhere near campus, it's only wall-to-wall students. Sometimes it's nice to hang out with adults. I like it here," she added, looking around the room. "They have good food, too, if you're hungry."

"Maybe later." As Blum sat back, he felt his cell phone dig into his hip. He removed it from his pocket. "That guy Lawson—what's his area of specialty?"

"Cat curves," she said.

Blum glanced over at her to see if she was joking, but she looked perfectly serious. "Cat curves?"

"Weather modeling with computers. Predicting catastrophes. Cats." She sounded bored, staring down at the table. "So, you went to the U of I, huh? What was your major?"

"First tell me what a cat curve is," he said, not wanting to let the conversation drift away.

She looked like she would rather discuss snow tires. "It's a probability distribution of potential damage from things like hurricanes and earthquakes."

Blum stared at Tina, waiting for more information.

"You really want to know about this?"

"Yeah. It sounds interesting."

She shrugged. "To measure the odds of a couple of bad events wiping them out, insurance companies hire specialty firms—and there's only a few—to build huge models of potentially destructive weather and earthquakes all over the world, based on historical data and how wind and water and everything interact. They use these models to simulate hundreds of thousands of potential years of events. Then the insurance company sends them a database of where all their insured properties are, what they're made of, how much they cost and so on, and the modeling firm figures out what each potential year of outcomes would mean in terms of claims. A lot of the years will have very few claims, but some years will have devastating losses."

The waitress returned with their drinks.

"Cheers," Blum said.

Tina raised her glass and then took a sip. "Cheers."

"So where's the curve?"

"You're like the first person I've ever met who finds this interesting." She cocked an eyebrow at him as she took a sip. "Anyway . . . since

199

all of the potential years have the same statistical likelihood of occurring, if you sort all those years from best to worst, you get a probability distribution of potential losses. And that's what a cat curve is."

"And Lawson works on those? For *Feldmann*?"

"He worked on them for one of those modeling firms before he joined the department. He's some sort of genius math programmer that helped his company come up with a better data set than any of the other firms."

Quantitative Disaster Analytics, Blum thought. And the database must be STORMPERIL 2010, the one he'd been accused of stealing.

"So how do you know so much about this?" he asked her.

"As part of my finance work, I took a course on Monte Carlo simulation."

"And that is . . ."

"Writing programs that simulate complex systems using the probabilities of different things occurring and their correlation— the likelihood they'll happen together."

"Give me an example."

"Well, for instance, my project in school was modeling the value of a stock portfolio. You're in investments, so you know that depends on things like each company's earnings, interest rates, and people's willingness to take risks. The earnings are affected by the overall economy, which affects interest rates and people's expectations for the future, which drives their willingness to take risks. But," she paused to take a sip of her cocktail, "each one of those things isn't *determined* by the others . . . they're probabilities that only tend to *affect* each other. And then there's all the random stuff that can happen to each individual company that's not related to what's going on with the others. So you can't simply solve a bunch of equations and come up with *the* answer. Instead, I wrote a program, kind of like those weather programs, that came up with a bunch of possible outcomes. By examining the set of potential outcomes, I could show what might happen with varying levels of certainty."

"Sounds like a blast."

"Yeah," she said in a moment of self-reflection. "It actually was kind of fun."

"But wasn't it models like that that caused the financial collapse back in 2008?"

"Well, more like overconfidence in models. As my finance TA warned us, 'Simulation is a lot like masturbation—you do it too much, and you start to believe it's the real thing.'"

Blum laughed. "And what's Meier studying?"

"Something boring like fertilizer."

"I can see you have a passion for agriculture."

Tina snorted. "I love it." She kicked off her shoes and rested her feet on the seat next to Blum. She took a sip from her drink and lifted her chin provocatively.

"Feldmann isn't around the office much these days?" Blum asked casually.

"Oh, he's been back and forth. I guess the big project, whatever that is, is all out at the farm, and, since he didn't have any classes this summer, he's been spending most of his time there. Now that students are returning, he'll probably be around Cotespath more."

Tina stirred her drink. "I was wondering . . . how well did your father know Otto?"

"I remember my father mentioning his name from time to time, and we had him over to the house once for dinner, but they weren't really close or anything."

"In that case, why did Otto go to your dad's funeral?"

"How did you know he was there?"

"He had me look up the date and time for him. I'd never heard him mention your dad's name before, and, given how focused he's been, it seemed odd for him to do that for someone he didn't know very well. It's not like him to just be considerate. There's always *something* in it for him."

Blum thought about his dinner invitation, and he wondered what Feldmann might have been after.

The waitress returned. "Can I get you another round of drinks? Maybe some food?"

Blum's thoughts flashed to Kay. He hadn't told her what he was doing, and she was probably wondering why he hadn't called her yet. He already felt guilty for just being there. Having dinner with Tina felt almost like cheating on Kay, but he still had more questions to ask.

He looked at Tina, who nodded. "Sure," he told the waitress. "We'll take another round. And some food might be good."

Tina chimed in, "I'll take a mushroom and Swiss burger. Oh, and you have to try their fries. Greasiest things you've ever seen, but boy are they good."

"Okay," he said. "I'll have a cheeseburger with cheddar, and some of those fries."

The waitress scribbled on her pad, smiled, and headed away.

Tina turned back to David. "How much longer are you going to have to hang around town? Is there a lot of paperwork for you to take care of?"

"Not really. My dad's lawyer is handling most of that."

"So then why're you running around returning books and talking to crazy professors? If I were you, I'd be somewhere else, trying to forget all about this place. It must be hard spending your time around so many reminders." Tina reached across the table and put her hand over his. "I'm really sorry, David."

She looked at Blum with a surprising warmth, and the sudden intimacy embarrassed him. "Thank you," he said, sitting back. "I do have some personal stuff to take care of. I should be done soon."

Tina downed the rest of her drink. "Excuse me a second. I need to use the little girl's room." She scooted out of her seat and disappeared toward the back of the bar.

Blum used the opportunity to text Kay, telling her that he was busy tracking down some information and that he'd call her later. As an afterthought, he told her to go ahead and eat without him.

Tina returned and slid into her seat.

"Something up?" she asked.

Blum coughed. "Checking messages." He tossed the phone back on the table as the waitress returned with their food.

As they ate, Blum let the conversation drift to unrelated topics—college experiences, Blum's job in Chicago, and Tina's desire to return to graduate school for an advanced degree. After a while, he decided to steer the discussion back to the lab and its security.

"You know, I've been wondering who pays for all the research," he said, trying to make it sound like an idle comment.

Her eyes narrowed, but then she shrugged. "Oh, the government mostly, but also private companies and some nonprofits."

So, he told himself, either she's lying, or she doesn't know the truth about Feldmann's funding. "And who owns the results?"

"What do you mean?"

"Well, if a company pays for research, don't they want exclusive ownership of it? How do they feel about it getting published?"

"I guess they work that out in advance. I really don't get involved in that."

"Has anyone ever hacked into your computers or tried to break in? You know—like one company trying to steal another's research?"

"Not that I know of. It is sort of strange how the local McDonald's is locked up better than our labs, but the office really is a pretty quiet place, except when Otto gets angry and starts cursing in Hungarian. He can be really frightening at times."

"I'll bet," Blum said. "He seems pretty intense. Does he make you work ridiculous hours? Late nights? Weekends?"

"Oh, here and there, when there's a rush or something. Usually, though, with him mostly working at his farm, I'm the last one out of the office at five."

Blum liked what he heard. Lax security and offices deserted in the evening.

He glanced out the window. Sunset was close.

"I hate to say this, but I need to get going soon," he said.

She looked at her watch, and then shrugged. "Seven thirty? It's not *that* late."

"Yeah, but I've got some packing to do," he said. "If you see the waitress, ask for the check. I'll be right back. Just need to use the restroom."

Blum slid out of the booth and wove his way to the back of the bar between crowded tables and milling patrons. A few minutes later, he returned, and, not bothering to sit, glanced at the tab, and set down enough cash to cover it and a tip.

"Oh, let me get some of that," Tina protested.

"Next time," Blum said, grabbing his phone off the table. He flagged down the waitress and gave her the money. Turning back to Tina, he held her hand as she stood. She thanked him, and he led her back through the lobby and out to his car.

"I walked back after lunch today," she told him. "Can you drop me at my apartment? It's just east of campus."

"Yeah. No problem."

After a spirited drive, they arrived at Tina's white, two-story colonial, and Blum helped her out of the car.

"This was fun," she said. "I'm glad we got the chance to talk."

"Same here," Blum said, mentally congratulating himself for the intelligence he'd collected.

She waved and scampered up the front steps.

Blum pulled away from the curb. Within half an hour, the sun would set, providing him the cover of darkness he needed to break in and search the CSR suite.

21. FINAL ASSEMBLY

Otto Feldmann stared around the sterile room—white ceiling tiles above white walls, white-laminate cabinets and Corian countertops, blue-white fluorescent lights glaring down on white floor tiles. Only Lawson's blue nitrile-rubber gloves and pinkish face, partly covered with a white surgical mask, violated the otherwise achromatic environment. That was until Feldmann opened the white crate, exposing hundreds of colorful cans of shaving cream.

The pair worked in sequence. Lawson unscrewed the lid of a shaving cream can, exposing the hidden compartment inside. Next, he filled the can halfway with milky liquid using a ballcock at the base of a glass tank. Handing the can to Feldmann, the professor screwed the small explosive charge and GPS control-mechanism into the fake lid. He pressed the test button and, seeing the green LED flash, screwed the lid into the can and set it in another white crate next to him.

Feldmann marveled at the design. The sodium azide charge's mild detonation characteristic was perfect for the purpose. Better still, it lacked the typical signature of nitro-based explosives that alerted airport residue chromatographs. The final result appeared to be a typical can of shaving cream—absolutely at home in anyone's checked luggage. The can's weight would match as well, if anyone bothered to check, and the cans even felt right when shaken. Even if a few screeners got suspicious and pulled the odd can, it wouldn't matter—Lawson's calculations included sufficient redundancy to ensure enough would make it onto the right planes. By the time the world figured out the cans' true function, it would be too late for anyone to do anything about it.

The liquid itself was his own creation—micro particles containing his virus suspended in a medium of artificial cytoplasm, then encased in a UV-blocking, biodegradable outer shell—all small enough to atomize for dispersal.

"This is it," he commented to Lawson. "Only two more days."

Despite Lawson's mask, Feldmann could see that his assistant was smiling.

22. OLD FACES

Blum parked two blocks north of Cotespath Hall and reached for his phone to call Kay. When the screen lit up, he was shocked to see icons arranged on a black background—not the backdrop of a Rothko painting that he had expected, and he realized he must have gotten their phones mixed up back at the tavern, grabbing hers and leaving his on the table. Both phones were locked, so neither person could use the one they had to call the other. For a moment he considered driving straight back to her apartment; she could go out again any time, and he needed his phone. But the later he went to Cotespath, the more suspicious it would be if he were spotted in the building.

Stick to the plan, he decided. He turned off the ringer and stuffed the phone back in his pocket.

Cutting through the parking garage, he crossed the grass quadrangle, walking slowly, soaking up the background noises and becoming accustomed to the flow of cars and the occasional pedestrian. As he approached Cotespath, he studied the side exit. The single overhead flood lamp cast a distinct cone of light onto the concrete apron below, illuminating a vortex of swirling insects in its path. He hoped Meier's key would work on that door as well. If so, he could take the stairs and avoid the camera by the elevators. If not, he'd simply have to keep his head down in the main lobby and hope no one was paying attention to the video monitors.

Blum crept out of the shadows, into the glare of the lit alcove, and inserted the key. To his relief, the lock turned, and the door swung open, emitting a faint squeak.

Stepping into the back lobby, Blum let the door shut behind him and felt the cool, dry air chill the patches of sweat on his shirt. He could hear a faint buzz of line current and the soft whir of air conditioning in the background, but nothing else. Half way down the hallway, he found the stairwell door and slipped inside. After easing the metal door shut, he turned and began to climb the concrete steps.

By the ninth floor, his legs felt heavy and weak. He paused to rest. Then, taking in a deep breath and exhaling slowly through pursed lips, he cracked open the door. To his relief, the dark hallway on the ninth floor was as deserted as the first. He headed in the general direction of the elevators, and, after a minute of wandering, found the section where he'd been earlier. His heart thumping, he tiptoed across the lobby and pressed his ear to the suite door. No sounds from inside.

Extracting the keycard from his pocket, he waved it over the sensor as he'd seen Tina do earlier. Once again, he heard the loud "click" of the electromagnetic latch releasing. Feigning nonchalance, he pulled back the solid door and stepped inside, ready to face whomever might still be there. To his relief, the suite was dark, save for the faint outside light filtering through the blinds behind Tina's desk. The door shut behind him, muffling the background hum from the hallway, and he heard the latch reengage. The soft carpet and ceiling tiles in the enclosed area further muted sounds, creating a comforting, cocoon-like atmosphere.

Blum crossed the foyer, past Tina's desk and a small alcove with a photocopier, and walked down the unlit hall to the staff offices. Using the key to unlock the door, he stepped into Meier's office and peered out the window for a minute, scanning the walkways below. Not seeing anyone, he let down the mini-blinds and clicked on his penlight.

Papers and journals sat in stacks on every surface, in some cases piled so high that they had tipped over under their own weight. Blum read through the titles, but they meant nothing to him. He poked around on the shelves and in the drawers on Meier's desk, but everything appeared totally innocuous—including the two books he'd dropped off earlier. After ten minutes, he gave up and left the room, careful to pull the door completely shut behind him.

Knowing it was a long shot, he tried Meier's key on Lawson's lock. As he had expected, it failed to turn. Frustrated, he grabbed hold of Lawson's office door and gave it a forceful tug. To his amazement, the latch sprang free, and the door flung open, almost hitting him in the face.

"I'll be damned," he said.

Seeing that the blinds were closed, he shone his penlight around the room. Lawson's desk sat barren except for a computer with four screens and a ruler. Journals, all carefully aligned with the front edge of each shelf, filled the low rows of bookcases on the back wall under the window.

Just as Blum was about to step inside, he thought he heard faint footsteps. He immediately shut off the penlight and closed the door, stopping right before it latched. He turned back toward the lobby and stared into the darkness. Had he imagined it?

He walked out into the waiting area and listened again. Still nothing. Then he noticed two shadows moving across the crack of light under the main doors. He gasped when he heard the latch click open.

Certainly it would be better to try to bluff his way out than get caught hiding somewhere. He dove around Tina's desk, sat in her chair, and grabbed the desk phone. Right as the door swung open, he flicked on the desk lamp and twisted the chair to face down the hallway.

Out of the corner of his eye, he saw a blue-uniformed man enter the suite. Blum turned back slowly and tried to act bored. He acknowledged the guard with a slightly raised right hand, as if to say, "Give me a moment," then turned back to the dark hallway of offices, nodding slightly to his imagined counterpart on the other end of the line. Mentally cringing, he waited for some sort of reaction.

The uniformed man approached the desk and stood still. Blum pivoted his chair and glanced up, staring into hawk-like brown eyes below a graying crew cut. Still bluffing, Blum put his hand over the mouthpiece and asked the officer, "Can I help you?"

"I was going to ask you the same thing." The man glared down at him, waiting.

Into the receiver, Blum said, "I'll call you back," and hung up. Then, to his confronter, he said, "I work here."

"So do I. And I've never seen you before. Who are you?"

Only one possible name came to Blum's mind. "Hans Meier," he said. "I work for Professor Prandler. You can check the nameplate on my office door." He pointed into the dark hallway, hoping the security guard had never met Meier.

"Is your name on your driver's license as well?" the guy asked, calling Blum's bluff.

"My wallet is in my car." Blum tried to sound irritated. "Are you *really* going to make me go and get it?" He didn't like the way the guard stared over his shoulder down the hall. Had he noticed that Lawson's door was ajar?

"I'll tell you what," the cop said. "Let me use that phone."

Blum turned the phone toward the guard and watched him punch a number on the pad. He still tried to look bored and a bit irritated, but he lost his breath when he heard the guard speak.

"Professor Feldmann? This is Officer Barry Ford over at Cotespath. Sorry to bother you at home. I was just now checking your suite, and I found someone who claims he works for Professor Prandler." There was a pause. "Yeah. He was sitting at your secretary's desk talking on the phone. He says he's Hans Meier, but I've never met Meier." There was another pause, during which the cop stared intently at Blum, sizing him up. "He's about six foot—maybe a little taller. Dark hair. Clean-shaven. Brown eyes."

Nothing at all like Meier.

Blum's heart pounded like a jackhammer. Could he possibly launch himself from the desk chair and sprint past the guard? The cop was armed, but would he shoot someone right here in the lab? Blum pushed the desk chair back slightly and pulled his feet under his body, ready to spring.

"I see," the cop said. "That's what I thought." He nodded at Blum.

Blum reached out for the edge of the desk and gripped it for leverage.

The cop smiled at Blum. "He says you're okay, but he wants me to clear out the office so I can lock up for the night. He says you'll understand."

Blum was baffled, but played along. "Sure. I'll come back tomorrow and finish up." He looked around, as if he might accidentally leave something of his there. Then he stood up and slid the chair under the desk, hoping his weak knees didn't show. He bid the guard good night and stumbled out of the suite to the elevators. He could hear footsteps following him, but didn't dare turn around. When the elevator door finally opened, he stepped in and glanced back as he turned to press the *Ground* button. The guard was nowhere to be seen.

As the door shut, Blum tried to comprehend what the hell had just happened. Feldmann certainly knew the guard hadn't been talking to Hans Meier. He probably suspected it had been Blum and simply asked for the description as a confirmation. So why let him go?

His gut told him something was wrong. Perhaps they were waiting for him outside; the guard's job had been to chase him into their trap. Blum frantically slapped the button for the second floor. The elevator lurched to a stop, and the door parted to another dark hallway.

Running to the back stairwell, he took the steps two at a time. He opened the door and peered into the deserted first-floor hallway. Nobody. Keeping his back to the wall, he slunk to the side exit. He tried to see if anyone was waiting for him outside, but the floodlight on the overhang totally obscured everything beyond the lit pad.

Blum dove for the door and sent it flying open. He sprinted into the dark, anonymous night in the general direction of his car. He didn't slow down until, two blocks from the lab, he collapsed onto a cement bench, his chest heaving.

The escape had been too easy. Why would Feldmann let him leave when he knew damn well he was being lied to? It also bothered Blum that he'd given up any remaining pretense that he was only an innocent orphan settling his father's affairs, and he certainly couldn't be seen at Cotespath again. Even so, it was revealing that Feldmann didn't seem to be particularly concerned that he might find anything incriminating at CSR. And that left only the farm.

When his lungs no longer burned, he stood up and made his way to his car. He needed to call Kay, but first he had to get his phone back from Tina. He cursed the waste of time.

Taking a circuitous route to avoid going anywhere near Cotespath, Blum drove east of campus. He pulled into a parking space up the block from Tina's house and walked back along the tree-lined street. As he turned onto the walkway to approach the front door, he happened to look up and saw Tina standing inside a large window, apparently talking with someone in the room. Thank heavens she hadn't gone back out.

Given the steep angle upward, all he could see was her head and a patch of white ceiling above it. Curious as to who might be with her, he walked out into the deserted street to get a better view. From the shallower vantage, he could see Tina down to her waist, along with the top of a bookcase on the far wall. A second later, a man stepped in front of the window with his back to the outside. Blum waited a bit for the man to turn around, but he stayed facing away. Finally, deciding he'd wasted enough time, Blum headed for the porch steps. At that moment, the man turned and briefly faced the window.

Blum gasped.

The silver-haired burglar who had broken into his house!

A speeding car rounded the corner and honked for Blum to get out of the way. Blum jumped to the curb and looked back up at the window just as the man turned and pointed right at him.

Blum's knees went weak. He had to get away.

He turned and ran down the street to his car, his mind racing. He cursed his hubris—so proud of himself for smooth-talking Tina into telling him about CSR, when all the while she had been playing him, setting *him* up.

He reached the Cobra and tore open the door. The engine sprang to life, and he screeched away from the curb. At Green Street, he started to turn left to head to Kay's, but then he slammed on the brakes. Along with his computer, all the evidence he had—Meier's note, the account printouts, everything—was in his hotel room. His mind raced as he tried to remember if he'd told Tina where he was staying. It didn't matter, he decided. He had to risk going back there. Go in. Grab everything. Leave before they could get there too. He spun the car to the right and floored the accelerator.

Not wasting time with the underground garage, Blum parked in the surface lot and ran into the lobby. The bored, tattooed woman who'd checked him in was standing behind the front desk, paging through a magazine.

He stormed the counter. "Has anyone called about me?"

She didn't bother to look up. "If they did, there'd be a flashing light on the phone in your room," she said.

"No. What I mean is, has anyone called *just now*, asking if I'm staying here?"

She glanced up from her magazine, resting her finger on the page so she wouldn't lose her place. "No. Not since I got here. But I've only been on duty since eight."

"Good. I'm going to be checking out. Make up my bill. I'll be back down in a couple of minutes, as soon as I get my things together."

"You bet," she said.

Not wanting to wait for the elevator, Blum dashed up the stairs and ran to his room, his mind reeling. He bolted into the dark hotel room. The door slammed behind him. Something hard whacked his shins. He tumbled forward. As his face slammed into the soft carpet, the lights flashed on. His head swimming, he looked up to see a man standing over him, holding a gun.

23. A BIG MISTAKE

A s Blum's head cleared from the shock of the fall, he recognized the man holding the silenced Beretta as the other burglar from his dad's house—the short one with thick, black hair. The man pointed the barrel at Blum's head and motioned with it for Blum to stand up.

Blum stumbled to his feet. The man walked over to him cautiously, keeping the gun pointed at Blum's midsection. Blum knew immediately he was dealing with a professional. An amateur would have held the weapon at arm's length, but this guy kept it back at his hip, away from a parrying blow. With expert precision, his captor frisked Blum under his arms, around his belt and crotch, up his back and down his legs. Satisfied, he ordered Blum to sit in the armchair in the corner. Out of options, Blum obeyed.

"What do you want?" Blum asked, feeling the warmth of the chair sinking in through his clothes and realizing the guy must have been sitting there for a while.

"Now we wait," the man said, taking a seat on the couch across the narrow room.

As the tense minutes passed, Blum studied the man who faced

him. He looked well-groomed, southern European, and Blum guessed he was about thirty years old. He seemed totally at ease and, in fact, almost bored.

Blum tried to guess his captor's next move. The fact that the gun was silenced, and that he hadn't been executed outright, probably meant the guy didn't intend to kill him here in the hotel room— at least not right away. Perhaps he was to be taken somewhere? But then what? Die of a "heart attack" like his father? Maybe that was it. They were waiting for the "doctor" to arrive. The gun only ensured cooperation. Feldmann must have let Blum leave the lab because he expected to find him here.

A sharp knock on the door interrupted his thoughts. It was followed by two knocks that seemed to come from the top of the door, followed by two that obviously emanated from the bottom. The man with the gun stood up and walked to the entrance, turning his body so that it always faced Blum. Then, reaching up backwards, he opened the latch and walked back into the center of the room. An elderly man, carrying a black leather bag in his right hand, followed behind the man with the gun. Blum didn't recognize him. The young guy sat on the chair by the desk. The gray-haired man pulled out his cell phone and punched in a number, waited a bit, and simply said, "He's here," then listened for a few seconds and hung up.

"Ezra's on his way," he told the younger guy who, from the deference in his voice, seemed to be in charge. "Perhaps we should get started, Carlo. This could take a while."

"Who's Ezra?" Blum asked, trying to keep his voice from cracking.

"Shut up!" the older guy ordered. He unzipped his black bag and pulled out an H&K USP .45 pistol with a suppressor, setting it on the desk next to him.

Blum sat in the padded chair gripping the armrests, his knuckles white with tension, until he realized how scared he must look. He forced his hands to relax, but sweat built up across his forehead. A large drop dribbled to his right eyebrow. Instinctively, he lifted his hand to wipe it away. In an instant, the old guy snatched up the pistol and thumbed off the safety.

"Just wanted to rub my eye," Blum said.

"Ask next time."

"Alright. I'm asking." Blum raised his shoulders in question, and the old guy nodded okay. Blum lifted his arm and wiped away the sweat, using the opportunity to shift slightly in his seat, testing his balance, but the chair felt too soft and too low for him to jump up easily. If he tried, he would likely just fall backwards. Carlo had picked the seat well. Blum slumped back, discouraged.

For a moment, the three men just eyed each other without saying a word. Then, like an alarm, the angry tone of the desk phone burst onto the silent room. The old guy snatched his gun from the desk and Carlo sat upright. The phone rang again.

Carlo looked at Blum, and then at his partner, who picked up the receiver.

"Yes?" A pause. "Yes . . . My what?" Another pause. "Oh, yes. No, actually I've decided to stay at least one more night . . . Yes. That would be fine. Thank you." He hung up. Blum suddenly remembered that he'd told the clerk he was checking out. Carlo looked interested, but didn't ask any questions. The older guy shook his head as if to say, "It was nothing."

Blum's leg began to cramp. "I'm thirsty," he ventured. "May I have a drink of water?"

Carlo looked at him. "No." Carlo's phone buzzed, and he answered it. He listened for a second, then, without saying a word, hung up. "Ezra says to go ahead and start, Zeke."

The older man, Zeke, nodded, leaned forward, and eyed Blum with newfound intensity. "What is your name?"

The question caught Blum off guard. "David Blum," he said—wondering if that was really what Zeke meant.

Zeke frowned. "You don't sound very sure. Who are you *really*?"

"Why don't you ask your little whore, Tina? She knows who I am."

Carlo started to do something—stand up or speak perhaps—then seemed to think better of it.

"I'm going to ask you again," Zeke said. "And I want a straight answer. Who are you?"

"I'm David Blum. You know that."

"David Blum is in London. His secretary confirmed it."

"Denise? That's what I *told* her to tell people."

"If you really are David Blum, why didn't you go to Solomon Blum's house after his funeral?"

"I did," he protested. The line of questioning was bizarre. Then he remembered. He'd arrived late and entered through the kitchen door. They must have either not seen him or given up waiting for him. "I got there late."

"And then Feldmann invited you to his farm. Right?" Carlo cut in.

"Yeah. That's right. Just like I told your 'assistant,' Ms. Santini." Blum glared at Carlo.

For an instant, Carlo stared back at him, and then he stood up and turned. Blum used the opportunity to make a move. He heaved himself up from the chair—throwing it back against the wall to provide forward momentum—and dove for Carlo's gun. But Carlo was too fast. With a swift kick to Blum's shins, he knocked Blum to the ground. Blum heard scuffling around him and felt the crunch of metal against the back of his skull. Lights flared in front of his eyes, and he collapsed forward, face first, into the carpet.

His senses numbed, he was only vaguely aware of being dragged by his hair. He felt himself being scooped up and thrown back into the now-upright chair. He started to slump forward, but the clenched hook of an arm under his jaw yanked him upright, and he felt the barrel of a gun press into his temple.

A sharp knock on the door froze his captors. The initial knock was immediately followed by two knocks at the top and two at the bottom as before. Carlo stood up and walked to the door. He looked through the peephole and then opened the latch.

"Ezra," he said in greeting.

Carlo returned with the new arrival, and, as Blum had guessed, Ezra was the older burglar he'd seen in the window at Tina's apartment. So where was Tina?

Ezra crossed the room and sat on the couch that faced Blum as Carlo leaned against the desk to Blum's right. Carlo seemed slightly agitated, but Ezra looked cold as sleet.

"Why are you here?" Ezra demanded.

Blum focused on the lamp on the desk and forced his mind to clear.

Ezra leaned closer. "I'll ask you for the last time, why are you here?"

"I'm here for my father's funeral. Even *your boss* knows that."

"Our boss?" Carlo asked.

Ezra glared at Carlo, and then turned back to Blum.

"What are your orders?"

"Orders? I don't have any orders. My father's dead because you killed him. And now the FBI knows about that," he lied.

"Knows what?"

"That you killed him and made it look like a heart attack. I talked to my former director. Agents will be here soon." Blum tried to judge the reaction of the group. He felt the grip on his throat loosen a tiny bit.

"What information did you give them?" Zeke hissed into his ear.

"For one thing, the license number of the Infiniti that you guys got into after you broke into my house. I saw you from the bushes, you know." Ezra and Carlo glanced at each other. "So you and your boss are blown."

"Our boss?" Carlo muttered again, standing up.

"Why would you think that we—" Ezra motioned around the room "—killed your father?" Zeke tugged at Blum's windpipe for emphasis.

Blum embellished the truth. "Because Hans Meier wrote a note, saying Otto Feldmann killed my father and that you guys made it look like a heart attack. And it's in Meier's handwriting, so, even though you killed Meier too, it'll still stand up in court."

"Feldmann?"

"Yes, it named him specifically," Blum lied.

"Why do you think Meier's dead?" Zeke asked, tightening his grip on Blum's neck.

"I went to his apartment. You guys tore it up pretty badly, but you didn't find the note because I already had it. And Meier had it delivered to me right under your noses—after the funeral. So what does Feldmann want done with me? Another heart attack? Or do I simply disappear like Meier?"

"Feldmann?" Ezra furled his brow.

"Oh, shit," Carlo said quietly. Then he said it again louder. "Oh, shit!"

"Be quiet, Carlo," Ezra ordered. He looked at Blum closely and carefully. "What *exactly* did you tell the FBI?"

Blum pressed further, encouraged by the discord he seemed to be creating. "I told them that Feldmann either killed my father or had him killed. The same for Meier. I gave them the note and the license number. I also told them that Feldmann's research isn't what it seems—that it's funded by a sham charity that's being used to launder money."

Ezra exploded. "Who the hell do you work for?"

"I just work for a bank," Blum said. "But you killed my father, and even if you kill me, you can't stop what I've done."

Ezra wasn't listening. Carlo was still pacing and muttering, "Oh, shit."

Ezra turned to Blum. "I'm afraid you've made a very big mistake," he said grimly.

24. THE DEVIL YOU KNOW

"What do you mean, a mistake?" Blum asked. From the look on Ezra's face, Blum sensed that somehow the immediate danger was passing.

"We're not your enemy," Ezra said. He removed his jacket, revealing a shoulder holster, and tossed the garment on the bed. "We're both on the same side here."

Blum tried to process this information. "So who are you then? Not FBI, obviously. CIA?"

"No."

"Homeland Security?"

Carlo paced even faster. "He's fucked it up. He's fucked it all up," he muttered. Even Ezra's granite face showed concern.

"No. We work for a private organization—"

"In that case, who hired you?"

"We took this one on ourselves, as it appears you did. Through some accident, which I need you to tell me about, you've managed to stumble into a very big and grave situation. And without knowing it, you've thrown a wrench into the works." Ezra stood up and cracked his knuckles.

"Why should I believe you?" Blum asked.

"Let me tell you a little about what we know. Perhaps that will convince you. Then it will be your turn."

"What makes you think *you* can trust *me*?"

Ezra stared directly into Blum's eyes. "I'm a pretty good judge of whether someone is lying. I've had a lot of training and quite a bit of experience. But mostly I believe you because I've listened to everything that happened to you since you arrived at dinner this evening, including your little escapade at CSR."

"How the hell . . ." Blum's jaw clenched.

Ezra laughed. "I'm sure you noticed that Tina switched phones with you at dinner. The phone she gave you has a monitoring application on it."

Blum shuddered at how easy it had been to trick him. "But how did she know what kind of phone I had?"

"If you recall, she asked to use yours when you ran into each other this morning. It was a simple task to find one exactly like it and load the app. Tina and I heard the whole conversation, and, well, it struck me that if you worked for Feldmann, you wouldn't have needed to break into his office. Moreover, when you were caught, you would have simply told the guard to call Feldmann. On the other hand, if you worked for his organization, there's no way you would have given up any part of his plans to us just now. That said, I needed to meet you in person to verify this. Besides, sometimes you learn the most from someone's reaction to a question you already know the answer to."

Blum's mind raced, trying to make sense of everything.

Ezra sighed. "So I'm going to tell you some things, and then I need you to reciprocate. There's a lot I'm not at liberty to reveal, but here's what I can say. See if it lines up with what you know. We first became interested in Feldmann because of Victor Lawson. He was flagged back in 1997 for his involvement with a white supremacist organization called ACID. We've kept tabs on him over the years."

Blum was intrigued. "So someone *paid* you to keep track of Lawson, all those years? Who?"

"We do these sorts of things on our own," Ezra said. "Just in case. In 2012, he traveled to France to visit a company that sells equipment for the dispersal of biological agents. That company was also on our surveillance list because it was known to have sold such equipment to the Iraqi military in the nineties. And that led us to Feldmann." Ezra paused and looked at Blum.

All of this confirmed what Blum knew. "And?"

"And now you go."

"What do you mean?" Blum asked.

Ezra leaned forward. "Now you tell me something, like, for instance, how did you get into the office suite tonight?"

"I used Meier's keys," Blum said.

"Meier gave you his keys?" Carlo asked. "Where is he?"

"I don't know," Blum said. "I found the keys in his apartment. As I said, I went there and found it destroyed by someone searching for something."

"And why did you go to the office tonight?" Ezra asked. "What were you doing there?"

"I wanted to search Meier's office. And hopefully Lawson's and Feldmann's, as well. To see what I could learn." Blum paused. "So, why were you watching my house after the funeral? I hadn't even been to Feldmann's office yet."

"We followed Feldmann there."

"And why did you break in while I was having dinner at Feldmann's farm?"

"We wanted to see if you were who you claimed to be," Ezra said. "We were worried you might be working for Feldmann, or, worse, for his organization."

Blum was puzzled. "What do you mean by 'or his organization'? And why would that be worse?"

"Because he seems to have fallen out of favor with them." Ezra dragged a chair away from a low dressing table by a side window. He turned it around and sat on it, facing Blum. "Every bit of evidence pointed to David Blum being in London. We really got suspicious when we tracked you down to this hotel under the name of Jack Wentworth."

"When I saw you inside my house, I got scared and checked in here under an alias. But why confront me tonight? What changed all of a sudden?"

"A little background. We intercepted cell calls to Feldmann from Europe. At first, they weren't scrambled, and it seemed as though Feldmann reported to someone there. Someone who is part of a larger organization."

"Who?"

"That's something I can't tell you," Ezra said. "Anyway, after his controller started encrypting his calls to Feldmann, we could only monitor their frequency and duration. But we recorded the calls, and we finally broke the scrambler code earlier this year." Ezra frowned. "Unfortunately, they've switched the coding again, so we've lost that ability. But one of the things we learned from what we were able to decode was that Feldmann's direct controller was actually someone right here in the local area. The calls were being routed through Switzerland to protect his location. This guy has been in place for years, but recently they sent someone new from headquarters in Zurich to keep closer tabs on Feldmann—possibly to, um, take care of him. We thought that person might be you."

"You thought I was here to . . . what? Kill Feldmann?"

"It was a possibility. You showed up in Feldmann's office the day after Meier disappeared. He seemed to know you, even though Tina had never seen you there before. It made sense that you might be someone who was sent to keep an eye on him—someone he had met previously whom he would trust. Someone who'd be in a position to kill him if the order came through. We called your office yesterday and again today, and your secretary said you were in London. Then you showed up at Cotespath this morning, and we began to worry. The last straw was spotting you watching Feldmann's farm this afternoon. We were afraid the order to kill Feldmann had come down, and it would be a real nightmare if someone killed him right now."

"Why?" Blum asked.

"Feldmann is a known entity. We can watch him, monitor his communications, and track his activity. Tina managed to get hired as his secretary. She hates the role, but it's given us some valuable information. If Feldmann is removed, and Lawson would almost certainly be killed along with him, then we'd have no link to this local controller or whoever would take Feldmann's place. Look. We don't have much time left. I need you to tell me exactly what you told the FBI."

"Before I do that, I want to know who you *really* are. You say 'a private company,' but what the hell does that mean?"

Ezra looked at Carlo, who shrugged. "Let's just say we're a public service organization, based overseas and privately funded. Our goal is to prevent humanitarian disasters."

"Like Human Rights Watch or something?"

"We don't just watch," he said without any hint of humor.

Blum stared from Ezra to Carlo to Zeke. They stared back, waiting.

Ezra cleared his throat. "Look. We have surveillance in place, and we're ready to strike when the need arises. We know whatever Feldmann and his team are planning is imminent. Outside investigators coming in now and trying to do everything by the book with warrants and lawyers will destroy any chance of stopping him before he kills a *lot* of people; they will slow us down, and we don't have the luxury of time. We need to stop whoever is coming from the FBI, at least for the time being." Ezra paused, his expression dire. "*If* Feldmann gets suspicious, or *if* his controller has him killed, the whole operation will be driven deeper underground. So, I need you to tell me *right now* what you told the FBI and what they're going to do when they get here."

Blum's mind raced. He needed time to think. "I'd be a fool to trust you," he said, stalling.

"You see?" Carlo exclaimed and began to pace again. "It's too late."

Blum knew he had to make up his mind quickly. So far, everything they'd told him they could easily guess he might know. Except Lawson's radical affiliation. And then he remembered how they had asked him why he didn't go to his father's house after the funeral. Feldmann had talked to him there, so anyone working directly with Feldmann would have known that.

"Alright," Blum said. "I guess I need to tell you the truth."

Carlo sat down. Ezra and Zeke looked at Blum expectantly.

Blum said, "I lied."

"What?" Carlo bolted upright.

Zeke grabbed his gun. Ezra ducked out of the firing line of the two men.

"It's okay," Blum said, holding up his hands. "What I mean is I haven't told the authorities anything. It all seemed so bizarre. I didn't think anyone would believe me. At least not without definitive proof. No one else knows anything."

"No one?" Ezra demanded.

"No one." Blum thought about Kay. She knew almost everything he did. If he needed to, he would tell them about her later, but for now he didn't see any point in getting her involved.

For a moment, his mind drifted to Kay and the realization that he still hadn't called her. She must be so upset by now, he thought.

"Thank God," Carlo said. Zeke relaxed and put his gun down.

"You have to tell us what you know," Ezra said.

Blum spent the next hour relaying the evidence that he had, starting with Meier's note. He told them what he had learned about ACID and the list of terms he'd found in Meier's apartment. He also described the plane he'd found in Feldmann's hangar, but left out any mention of Kay, other than to say that he had found an old newspaper article that described an explosion on Feldmann's farm back in 2000.

"We checked into that," Carlo said. "It was only a propane tank that ignited."

"But I saw the plane," Blum said. "They must have covered up the incident somehow—famous professor and all that."

Zeke shook his head. "Do you really think he could kill *six million* people with one bomb? We figured maybe a few tens of thousands—a hundred thousand at the most."

"I don't know. It was just something on the list. *Six million chosen*, along with *everyone dies*."

"Okay," Ezra said to Blum, wringing his hands with seeming finality. "Here's what you need to do—" Blum's heart raced; they were making him part of the team. "You need to pack your things and leave. Tonight. Go back to Chicago. We'll let you know when you can return to town. Probably within a few weeks."

"What?"

"It's too precarious for you to stay here. We have to have you out of the way."

"No," Blum protested.

"This is not a game. As long as you're here, Feldmann will be wary—especially after you got caught in his office tonight."

"But I can be helpful." Blum didn't like the defensiveness in his voice. "Damn it. Don't you get it? Feldmann killed my father. I *have* to stay!"

"Absolutely not," Ezra said. "We can't have some *banker* getting in the way."

"Look," Blum snapped. "I'm not leaving, so we might as well find a way to help each other out. I've been trained in law enforcement. I used to work for the FBI. I've been to the farm. I know my way around there. Besides," he said, thinking of what he could use for leverage. "I have something else you might find helpful."

"What's that?"

"Pictures. From the farm this afternoon. A plane landed and—"

"You got pictures? Let me see them," Ezra demanded.

"First, a deal. I'll stay out of your way, but I want you to agree to keep me informed. I'll do the same."

"Absolutely not," Carlo said, but Ezra seemed less resolute. He looked at Carlo and frowned. He looked back at Blum. "What do the pictures show?"

"A plane landed and two men got out. I got pictures of them and the people on the ground who met them."

"Alright," Ezra said, after weighing unknown factors. "I'll talk to our supervisor and see what he says. No promises."

"I understand," Blum said.

For the next half hour, the group pored over the images. Unfortunately, no one recognized anyone but Feldmann and Lawson. The faces of the pilots were new to them; and the images of the taller man and the driver were too obscured to recognize.

When they were finished, Zeke stood up and stretched his arms. "It's late," he said. "I'll leave the rest of the evening to you young-sters." He slipped his pistol back into the leather bag and slung it over his shoulder. "Ezra, I'll call you in the morning. Carlo, you have a good evening. Mr. Blum, I hope we didn't scare you too much."

And, with that, Zeke left.

"Do you have anything to drink?" Carlo asked.

Now that the tension had dissipated, Blum felt exhausted. "I've got a bottle of scotch in the dresser. Top drawer. Help yourself."

"Perfect," Carlo said, standing up.

Blum walked into the bathroom without bothering to close the door.

"David," Carlo called to him. "Do you want a glass, too?"

"Sure," he yelled, zipping his fly. He walked back into the room as Carlo poured two glasses of the liquor.

"And you?" Carlo asked his partner.

"None for me," Ezra said, gathering his things. He put on his jacket and checked in the mirror that the bulge of his gun didn't show. "I'm going to head out. Carlo, you'll stay with Mr. Blum tonight. See that he doesn't get into any trouble."

After Ezra left, Carlo carefully locked the door. "Sorry about being an uninvited roommate, but, until we clear everything with our boss, we need to keep an eye on you."

Blum shrugged. "I'd do the same in your position. Besides, it's late. What else do I have to do?" He desperately wanted to call Kay, but that was clearly out of the question now.

"Don't be so hard on Tina, either," Carlo said. "She was only doing her job. Besides, what were *you* doing at dinner?"

Blum shrugged, sheepishly.

"You know, she's quite taken with you." Carlo added.

"Is she?" Blum responded, flatly.

"Yes. She thinks you're quite the charmer. I'm sure she'll be glad we didn't have to shoot you tonight. She really wants to see you again."

"Why would she tell *you* that?"

"I'm her brother," he announced, proudly. "She tells me everything."

"You're awfully generous with your sister."

"Well, as with Feldmann, better the devil you know, eh? Besides, you two might be good for each other, you know. You certainly seem a cut or two above the losers she usually goes after." Carlo smiled. "Just don't tell her I said that."

Blum grinned. "I think you just did." He reached down and removed Tina's cell phone from his pocket and waved it at Carlo. "If I know your sister, I'm willing to bet she's still listening."

The smile disappeared from Carlo's face.

Blum held up his glass. "To the devils we know."

25. THE BEGINNING OF THE END

"Professor Feldmann can't be that bad," Peter Creighton shouted over the din of the crowded campus bar.

"You have no idea," Victor Lawson replied, taking a long slug from his third bottle of Budweiser. He looked around the beer-soaked room at the throngs of blithering college kids, back in town for the fall semester.

Creighton swirled his half-full beer glass and squinted into it, as if analyzing a flask of solution. "I remember when you used to worship him."

Victor was barely listening. At last, his moment had finally arrived. All the planning, calculations and testing, all the preparation, and all the waiting—praying—for the heavens to align, were about to pay off. And throughout, God had been there with him—inspiring him, and guiding him. A deluded atheist like Feldmann would never be able to see the truth—never understand what science really was—translating God's master design into the language of the material world.

For Lawson, there was no greater proof of God than the perfection of Euler's Identity—that simple mathematical equation that needed only three elementary operations to link the five most basic mathematical constants in one single equation: $e^{i\pi} + 1 = 0$. How could anything but an almighty being create a universe where such an elegant equation held true? Feldmann might dismiss the idea, but Victor was sure of God's hand in the world. And their mission.

And that meant God had chosen Victor as His agent on earth. How many men in history could say something like that? And suddenly the whole painful saga of his life made sense to him. He had been born to a mother but not conceived by the "father" who raised him. (And certainly not the vile man his mother had tried to convince him was his real father!) He had lived as an outsider, shunned by those who didn't understand him, a threat to those in power. He had suffered for his beliefs, and, like Jesus, had risen from that pain and been chosen by God to lead mankind to salvation. Like Euler's Identity, it all fit together too well to be anything other than the work of the divine.

"Hey," Creighton said. "Where the fuck are you, man?"

"Huh?"

"I was saying, if he's that bad, go work for someone else."

"It's way too late for that," Lawson replied, staring aimlessly at the oblivious kids.

"Come on. Cheer up. It's not the end of the world."

"Yes, it is," Lawson said absently, downing the last of his beer. "Tomorrow is the beginning of the end."

26. THE RIDE BEGINS

The blare of the hotel room phone rattled Blum awake. He looked at his watch and saw it was almost ten. Grabbing the handset, he barely managed to utter, "Hello?"

"It's Carlo," a voice said.

Blum looked around the empty room. "Where are you?"

"I'm in the restaurant downstairs having breakfast. My sister's here with me. Why don't you join us?"

"She's still talking to you?"

"Reluctantly. On a serious note, I have something important to go over with you."

"Give me a minute," Blum said. He hung up, climbed out of bed, and dressed from the crumpled pile of clothes on the floor.

Dragging himself downstairs and entering the sunken breakfast area off the main lobby, he spotted Tina and Carlo sitting at a table along the back wall of the room. Blum waved, grabbed a plate of scrambled eggs and a few sweet rolls from the buffet line, and then poured himself a cup of coffee.

"Good morning," he greeted the two as he took a seat. Carlo, like Blum, wore the same clothes he'd had on the day before. Tina was dressed in jeans and an orange, sleeveless knit top with a shawl collar, and her hair was pinned up in a neat bun.

"Good morning," she said. She didn't look too upset.

Carlo scanned the room to make sure no one could hear him. "This afternoon you need to go and meet with someone. He goes by Jason, but of course, that's not his real name. He's the coordinator on this project. He's agreed to let you be involved on a limited basis, provided he meets you in person first. And, for now, that's all I can tell you."

"Okay," Blum said. He turned to Tina. "Good to see you again."

"And you, I guess, despite calling me a whore."

Blum blushed. "Sorry about that. I thought you'd just set me up to be killed."

"All in a day's work." Tina shrugged. "Oh yeah. Before I forget . . ." She reached into her purse, pulled out his cell phone, and pushed it across the table.

"And here's yours." Blum retrieved Tina's phone and gave it to her. He took a slug of coffee. "By the way, if it's okay to ask, how *did* you get a job as Feldmann's admin?"

Tina looked at Carlo, who nodded his ascent, but he cocked his head slightly as if to say "within bounds."

"Well, the initial plan was for me to apply to graduate school at Illinois in genetics in Feldmann's department. Given my academic background and grades, my prospects seemed great, but I came to Urbana and met with Feldmann and he told me it was too late to apply for the coming year, and, besides, I didn't have the background they were looking for. I told him I'd work as an intern while taking some undergraduate prerequisite courses and apply for the following year, but he said they didn't really do that sort of thing.

I was insistent, and finally he told me that the only thing he had to offer was office admin, given that the prior one had just quit. It wasn't exactly what I had in mind, but it seemed like an ideal way to keep tabs on what was going on at CSR, so I accepted it."

"That was lucky."

Carlo wiped his mouth with his napkin. "We need to get going in a minute. Jason's address is 2412 East Osage." He repeated it again slowly. "Do not write it down. You understand, I'm sure. Our safety, and that means your safety too, depends on precautions like that. Jason is expecting you. One thirty. He values punctuality."

Blum repeated the address. "I'll be there." He turned to Tina. "You too?"

"No. I'll be at CSR. Feldmann's insisting I come into the office today, even though it's Saturday. He does that from time to time. I think he simply likes to know where I am when something important is going on out at the farm."

Carlo stood up. "Which is why Zeke and I'll be out there today on surveillance duty."

Tina stood as well. "*Ciao*," she said, and then followed Carlo from the room.

Blum downed the last of his cup of coffee, reflecting on how exciting Carlo and Tina's lives must be. He paid for breakfast and returned to his room to call Kay. As he began to dial, though, an uneasy feeling crept over him. If they could plant a surveillance device on Tina's phone, why not on his? Was this a test? Give him his phone back and listen to make sure he was telling the truth? Blum turned off the phone. He considered removing the battery as well, just to be sure it was totally inactive, but if they *were* monitoring it, that might make them suspicious. Frustrated, he shoved it back in his pocket. If he got the chance, he'd buy a burner phone later.

At one-thirty, after driving around for half an hour to make sure he wasn't being followed, Blum parked two blocks from the address on Osage and walked the rest of the way to the brown, wood-shingled bungalow. He pressed the doorbell and waited. Glancing around on the front porch, he saw typical family sorts of things—some chopped wood for a fireplace, a porch swing in need of repair, and a broom and rake. Not at all what he would have expected for the house of a spy boss.

He heard the door open and turned. A tall, burly man with black hair and hawkish brown eyes peered out through the narrow gap.

"Yes?" he prompted.

"I'm here to see Jason," Blum replied.

"And you are?"

"My name is Blum. Carlo sent me."

The man nodded and opened the door wider, revealing a large semi-automatic strapped to his belt. "Come this way."

The exterior of the house might have seemed the picture of suburban banality, but the interior was an unobtrusive fortress. From what Blum could see, all the windows had metal bars with key locks, and he noticed a number of security cameras.

"*Bonjour.* I've been expecting you," a gentle voice said.

Blum turned to greet a short, bald man of about fifty with skin the color of molasses. He had bushy eyebrows over black-framed glasses and a slightly far-off gaze, as if he were staring at a distant battle. He held his hand out and gave Blum a hearty pumping. "Call me Jason. *Mon Dieu*, you gave us quite a scare last night. But then, I imagine we did the same to you. Please come with me," Jason invited in a faint French accent, his "with" sounding more like "wiss."

Blum followed Jason through a short, undecorated hallway to a back room lined with metal bookcases. Drapes were pulled over all the windows, and Blum presumed they were seldom, if ever, parted. Despite a continuous breeze of circulating air conditioning, the room held a pleasant aroma of pipe tobacco.

"Please sit," Jason said. "Can I get you something to drink?"

"Coffee would be great, if you have any."

Jason pressed a button on an intercom. "Tom?" he called, presumably to the man who had answered the door. "Coffee, *s'il te plaît*, for our guest."

Blum glanced down at the items on Jason's desk and noticed a photocopied report. The layout of the front page caught his eye. He recognized the format as that of an FBI personnel file. As Blum sat down in an oak chair opposite Jason, he bent closer and saw that the dossier was his own, and the transmission date at the bottom indicated it had been sent that morning.

"We have been studying the pictures you took," Jason began straight away. "They're very interesting, but, unfortunately, two of the faces are simply too fuzzy to identify."

Jason opened a drawer of his antique desk and removed an envelope of prints. He threw the top one on the desk. "We've identified Feldmann, of course, and Lawson. Carlo told me that you said that three people on the ground met the plane."

"Yes. That's right," Blum said, leaning over the desk and looking at the pictures. "Feldmann, Lawson and . . . that guy there." He pointed to one of the men. "Unfortunately, I never got a good shot of him."

"Yes. Most unfortunate. Here's a profile, but it doesn't tell much. So disappointing because the man is almost certainly Feldmann's control."

"Who is he?"

"They call him Krieger. Albert Krieger. We've eliminated everyone around here with anything close to that name, and we haven't been able to figure out who he really is." Jason pulled another photograph out of the stack. "And these two were on the plane?"

"Yes. Do you recognize them?"

"No. But I've forwarded the images to some people who might." Jason looked at Blum intently. "I know you're curious about who we are. Carlo told you some, but let me provide a few more details." He retrieved a sand-blasted Dunhill lovat from a wooden stand on his desk. "Mind if I smoke?"

Blum shook his head, and Jason filled the bowl with tobacco from a small ceramic urn with a pewter lid. He lit it with a large wooden match, puffing madly. The room instantly filled with the mellow smell of English Cavendish, laced with a touch of Latakia.

"Our story goes back to 1947. As fate would have it, a group of four men and two women were staying at the same hotel—an old eighteenth-century manor just outside of Spa, Belgium—and, one evening after dinner, they found themselves sitting together on the back terrace. As they talked and learned more about each other, it became clear that all of them had barely survived the atrocities of the past fifteen years, and all had lost the majority of their families—in battles, in ghettos and concentration camps, or simply freezing or starving to death in their homes."

"Survivors of the Holocaust," Blum commented absently.

"Yes, some," Jason said. "Three were Jewish, but two were Protestants who found themselves in the wrong place at the wrong time, and one was a Catholic widow who was punished for trying to do the right thing. War might start out discriminating, but it always ends up slaughtering the innocent—regardless of sides. Shaped by those experiences, they all agreed that governments could not be trusted to prevent future atrocities because, as they saw it, governments tend to be run by selfish, corrupt people. And, even when leaders start with the best of intentions, they have to operate in the spotlight, judged by the world, where failure on a noble endeavor is worse than success at doing nothing at all."

Blum shifted in his seat. "Isn't that why countries have spy agencies and secret armies? CIA, MI6, and such?"

"Organizations like that can operate under cover, true. But, regardless, they often get corrupted by the whims of their leaders." Jason puffed at his pipe a bit. "So, these six people agreed that something else needed to be done. They decided that there were plenty of aid organizations, but such charities treat the effects, not the disease. What was needed was an international organization with no loyalty to any single country that would do *whatever it takes* to prevent future humanitarian disasters.

"They were all quite wealthy, and they agreed to pool their fortunes and fund an endowment of sorts to finance a new, stateless organization—one that would operate globally. Those six became its original board of directors and recruited like-minded people from the ranks of discharged soldiers, law enforcement personnel and scientists."

"So, who hires you? And how can you be so sure that their motives are honorable?"

"We aren't hired. We monitor potential threats all over the world on our own, and our board of directors decides what our assignments are. Our endowment, which has grown considerably over the years, covers all expenses, so we are not beholden to anyone but ourselves. But we do have limited human resources, so we have to choose our endeavors carefully. Some situations are simply beyond our capabilities, and others are clearly only police matters where playing by the rules works, and we leave that to law enforcement. What we specialize in are those situations where we can intervene and make a difference because we do things others won't."

"Like dealing with Feldmann . . ."

"Precisely. This situation is beyond the capabilities of conventional law enforcement. If this were being handled by official organizations, they'd be tripping over protocols, international jurisdictions, and egos. They'd spend all their time fighting about who's in charge while jealously protecting their own interests and, invariably, leaking information to the press. Instead, we engage with them in a symbiotic relationship, of sorts. Over time we've built credibility in the right circles."

"They know who you are?"

"They have no idea who or what we are. All they know is that when we send them intelligence, it's irrefutable and instantly actionable. When we're finished with our work, we often let them come in and clean up, and they get to pat themselves on the back for their accomplishments. Our only pride is in what we *prevent* from happening."

Jason relit his pipe.

"So, what *do* you know about Feldmann?" Blum asked.

"What do *you* know?"

"Well, let's see . . . Jewish refugee from Hungary teamed up with a white-supremacist, planning on blowing up an airplane to distribute some sort of biological agent that will kill a lot of people, perhaps trying to precipitate some kind of racial holy war. All of which makes no sense to me."

"None of it?"

"Maybe, if you took Feldmann out of the equation. I mean he really seems like the odd man out, doesn't he?"

"Go on," Jason encouraged.

"Well, let me think. Perhaps they plan on making this look like an Islamist plot. Feldmann gets support for Israel, his religious homeland, or annihilation of some portion of the Middle East, and Lawson and his friends get the final battle in the Holy Land they've been dreaming of. Oh, and Jesus gets to come back and congratulate them all for their good work. Except . . . Feldmann doesn't strike me as a religious zealot. Any indication he is?"

"No. As best we can tell, he's a complete atheist."

"So what's *your* explanation?"

Jason puffed at the pipe. "Your diagnosis is mostly right. Only, it gets more interesting. The people in Zurich that seem to be pulling all the strings are part of something called the Global Future Alliance. Until a few years ago, we didn't think they were particularly dangerous, at least not in terms of actually doing anything. In addition to a somewhat inflammatory news site, their big focus seemed to be hosting an annual, invitation-only conference attended by hundreds of academics, business leaders, and government officials, all of whom share what some might consider, shall we say, less-than-enlightened points of view. Then, they discuss the future of the world. A few speeches have raised eyebrows, but nothing to keep you up at night."

"How is Feldmann connected?"

"He's a regular attendee."

"Lawson also?"

"No. Not that we're aware of. Probably too much of a, how do you say, 'hot head.' But we managed to get one of our own invited three years ago. The conference itself was uneventful, but she did uncover a 'special session' attended by a small subset of members—fifteen or so, including Feldmann—held at an offsite location away from the main conference."

"What did they discuss?"

"We don't know. 'Closed door,' 'invitees-only,' and all that. The interesting thing she did piece together was that the members of that session were all in very different fields." Jason opened a yellow file folder on his desk and paged through it. He put his finger down in the middle of a page. "Public health, psychology, politics, law, economics, sociology, human ecology, agriculture, nuclear engineering, civil engineering, urban planning, genetics—that was Feldmann—and military science."

"Quite a diverse group. But what's so strange about that? If you're discussing the future of the world, you'd want a diverse set of views."

"Yes, you would. But a few fields seemed strangely absent."

"Like what?"

"What about computer science? Or communications? Why nuclear and civil engineering, but not electrical or mechanical engineering? Why nobody for robotics, nanotechnology, alternative energy, or any other more futuristic field?"

Blum shrugged.

"Unfortunately, they meet in different locations each time. Only *they* seem to know where that's going to be in advance, so we haven't been able to wire the meeting room before they get there. Also, it appears the members are screened for listening devices before they go in. No chance to plant a bug on one of them."

Blum straightened in his chair. "Dead end, then?"

"Not completely. As usual, the weak link proved to be the human one. Last year, our agent managed to seduce the psychologist, a Princeton professor named Alex Detterly. Lubricated by alcohol and oral sex, he bragged to her about being a member of a select group of people who were willing to do more than just talk about the future. He told her they were doing 'extraordinary things' to shape it, but he wouldn't elaborate. We planned to try to blackmail him with his infidelity into revealing more, but that's no longer an option."

"Why?"

Jason cocked an eyebrow. "The week after the conference, he 'fell' in front of an Acela train pulling into Princeton Junction. We think his hotel room might have been bugged. The Alliance must have pegged him as a security risk."

"Huh. So Feldmann's only a part of the puzzle. But why the whole Global . . . whatever-you-call-it conference? Why not simply meet as a small group without all the fanfare? It seems like a lot of unnecessary attention."

"Cover," Jason said. "These are very visible people, famous in their own circles and beyond. Some have security clearances with their governments and would have to inform those governments of any international travel. If they all ostensibly ended up somewhere on vacation together by coincidence, that would raise eyebrows. But showing up at the same conference each year is quite understandable, even expected. From there, it's easy enough to slip away for a private meeting without being missed."

"Where does this Alliance get its money?" Blum asked. "All this must be very expensive."

"We've tracked it through a circuitous set of accounts back to something called Venus Holdings. They appear to get their money from—"

"Pornography."

"Precisely, but how did—"

"I tracked CSR's funding back to the same entity."

"So CSR and the Alliance *are* linked!" Jason nodded, smiling. "We assumed so, but hadn't been able to prove it." He puffed on his pipe. "Your bank seems to keep its secrets better than anybody."

"We do our best," Blum said.

Jason looked at his watch and frowned.

"Now what?" Blum asked.

"Now we wait." Jason said. "I suggest you make yourself comfortable for the time being."

Blum stretched his arms and settled back in his chair. He didn't have to wait long. Tom returned a few minutes later. "Carlo called. He saw them load the crate back on the plane. Then the two visitors boarded, and the plane took off."

Jason wheeled around to face Tom. "You're tracking them, *n'es pas?*"

"Of course. Flight plan's for Wichita, but we're monitoring their flight path as well."

Jason nodded. "Find out if we have a team anywhere near Wichita. We need to have someone there when the plane lands."

"Why not intercept them?" Blum asked. "Alert Homeland Security and have them scramble fighters or something?"

"Too risky. If they get scared and dump the bomb, the consequences could be deadly. Besides, we don't know that it's not just an empty box that they loaded. I don't want to tip them off before we know what's going on and where the bomb is."

Blum scowled. "What the hell is in Wichita?"

"It's the geographic center of the U.S. for one thing. Depending on how far this stuff can dissipate, that might be a good place to release it. It could also be a good central transfer point to another flight somewhere else."

"Any other instructions?" Tom cut in.

"Just track that plane and make sure it doesn't deviate from its flight plan. Let's hope to hell it doesn't land in the middle of nowhere and ditch that cargo."

Tom disappeared.

While Jason immersed himself in his thoughts, Blum sat quietly, afraid to interrupt. Despite the desperation of the situation and the potential maelstrom to come, he felt surprisingly elated. For the first time since he'd left the Bureau, he was back on the inside—at the center of decision-making and information sharing. And, very soon, he was likely to close in on his father's killer. Whatever was going to happen would likely occur in the next twenty-four hours. The anticipation built up inside him until he could barely sit still.

Blum glanced up at Jason, who appeared to be studying him with a look, not of suspicion, but amused satisfaction, perhaps even wry enjoyment, as if to say, "Exciting, isn't it?"

Suddenly, the intercom buzzed. "Jason? We just intercepted a message from Zurich to Krieger. Open line."

"And?" Jason asked, leaning toward the plastic box.

"Message was, 'Clean up tonight. Shut down tomorrow.' I guess that's it, huh? They're going to kill Feldmann tonight."

Jason stared at the ceiling for a moment and then turned back to the intercom. "Alright. Contact everyone; tell them to remain on high alert. Then report back to me on everyone's position. I want to be able to mobilize immediately if we have to."

"Roger that," Tom replied.

Jason turned to Blum. "Strap yourself in, Mr. Blum. The ride is about to begin."

27. A BLOW TO THE HEAD

Victor Lawson sped east toward Champaign and away from the onslaught of tumbling clouds that chased after him. From time to time, he glanced in the rearview mirror and saw flashes of lightning against the angry black wall of the approaching squall line. The spectacle was almost enough to forget the demeaning assignment Feldmann had sent him on—driving twenty miles just because that bitch, Christina Santini, wasn't answering her phone. Who the hell cared if she was at work or not? CSR was clean. There was absolutely nothing she could discover there. The little twat could be thumbing her nub in the ladies' room for all he cared.

Or was he just being naïve? Did Otto really care where the fuck she was, or was this just an excuse to get him away from the compound? Maybe there was something going on there they didn't want him to know about. Was that it? His work was done; they didn't think they needed him anymore. So now they were shutting him out.

His fear turned to anger. And after all he'd done for them!

And there was that new guy, too. The little blond shit he'd seen hanging around outside the compound. He'd even spotted him at the CSR office once. Otto had never mentioned him and, in fact, had denied even knowing about him. So, what was *he* doing there?

Lawson fumed at his gullibility. For a moment, he considered aborting the trip and confronting Feldmann. But he'd only get the same answers he always got when he asked about his future. "Don't worry. We'll take care of you." What the fuck did that mean? No. He needed to watch his back and bide his time. Run this fucking errand and get the hell back to the farm.

Lawson floored the accelerator and hurled the black Mercedes toward the lights on the horizon. As he approached the edge of town, a childhood fantasy came back to him. The open garage door and his stepfather kneeling over the lawnmower, his back to the outside. The workbench covered with tools. The weight of the hammer in his young hand. The crunch of the skull as the claw pierced his father's skull and embedded itself in the soft, warm brain. Only this time, he saw himself approaching the open hangar door. Feldmann stood just inside, facing away from him. The hammer sat on a toolbox . . .

28. TUMBLERS ALIGN

Tina Santini sat typing her fourth grant application of the afternoon. It was bullshit work, and she knew it. Just like her entire assignment, as far as she was concerned.

In the three years since she'd managed to get hired as Feldmann's secretary, her initial excitement had faded into routine, then tedium, then frustration. Now, it bordered on anger. She used to conduct weekly searches of Feldmann's office, gaining entrance with a copy of his key she'd made surreptitiously shortly after joining. The searches had never turned up anything meaningful, but doing so had at least made her feel useful. Then, six months ago, Ezra and Jason had decided that the situation had grown too sensitive and called off the searches. When she protested, Ezra took away her key.

Too agitated to sit still, she stood up and stretched her neck and shoulders. Turning to the window and lifting the mini-blinds, she marveled at the drama playing out to the west. Nearby, warm sunlight still bathed the expanse of campus buildings and courtyards, and it looked very peaceful from her rather private vantage point. But, out on the horizon, the approaching cold front had pushed dense clouds toward town, darkening the far edge with a creeping twilight. She'd heard it was supposed to rain hard that night, with high winds and a possibility of severe storms. Thank God, she thought. It might finally cool down.

Feeling a slight headache coming on, she opened the top desk drawer and dug around for her bottle of aspirin. In the process, she spotted a large bobby-pin wedged below one of the dividers. She'd noticed it before but never paid any attention to it. A worthless bit of trash left behind by the previous secretary. Today, however, it struck her as particularly valuable. The flat spring-steel looked a lot like the metal of the lock picks she'd used during her training. Studying the four-inch pin, she decided the metal was a little thick, but certainly the right width and flexibility.

It couldn't hurt to have another quick look in Feldmann's office, she decided. He was safely out of the way at the farm, and no one was going to come in on a Saturday afternoon. If she didn't find anything, she'd simply keep quiet, and if she *did* find something to report, no one would care that she'd ignored orders. Again.

Tina folded the pin back and forth at the joint until it broke into two pieces. The ribbed half she bent at a right angle to form an inch-long L at the end. A perfect tension tool. The other piece she could use as a crude rake. Slipping her purse into a desk drawer, she crept down the hall to Feldmann's office.

Well, here goes, she told herself. *Let's see what you remember.*

She knelt down on the carpet and slid the short end of the L into the bottom of the keyhole, putting tension on the lock core by pushing downward on the long end. While she did that, she slowly raked the other piece of bobby-pin back and forth under the pins. Yes. The old feeling was coming back. After a few minutes, she could tell she was close because the core turned slightly. But then the pins bound up, and she had to release the tension, letting the pins reset, and start over again. The next time, she started with the rear pins and worked forward. That felt better. After five minutes she could tell she was down to only one pin, but it was binding badly. Again, she released tension and let the pins reset.

She flexed her fingers and started one more time with the difficult pins. Then she moved to the rearmost pins and finished with the front ones. Twenty minutes of careful work later, she felt the magical sensation of the tension tool going limp in her fingers as the core broke free.

Now it was fifty-fifty whether she'd chosen the right direction to turn the lock. If she'd picked the lock in the wrong direction, she would have to reset it and start all over again.

The tension tool wasn't strong enough to force back the bolt, so she put it and the rake in her pocket and used one of her keys to turn the core more forcefully. She felt the bolt retract and the door swung open in front of her. With her throat in a knot, she glanced up and down the hall to make sure no one had shown up. Then she stepped into Feldmann's office and swung the door closed until it almost latched.

She was immediately struck by how quiet and benign the little room seemed without Feldmann's intense presence. Even so, the excitement of the situation had her stomach fluttering.

At first, she poked around aimlessly at the stacks of items on his desk—an old, metal monster positively littered with papers and used coffee cups. After five minutes or so of fruitless searching, though, her elation faded into frustration. She searched inside his desk drawers, then carefully pulled each one out and looked underneath. She rifled through the notes on top of his bookcases. Nothing incriminating, as far as she could tell.

In time, she moved on to the two-drawer filing cabinet next to Feldmann's desk. Pulling open the top drawer, she fished through the contents—an agricultural journal in what she presumed was

Hungarian, as well as a couple of English scientific magazines. She closed the drawer and opened the one below, eagerly scanning the tabs on the file labels, but her disappointment grew as she read each one. They were all just the grant applications she had prepared for him.

She'd broken in only to read her own typing! Disgusted, she slammed the drawer. Deciding there was nothing to find, she left the office, shutting the door firmly behind her.

"Damn," she cursed. What a waste of time.

What about Lawson's office? Since he knew she had a key, she had always assumed he wouldn't leave anything incriminating there, but, with nothing better to do, she retrieved the keychain from her pocket and opened his office door. Fifteen minutes of rifling through desk drawers yielded nothing, so she turned to his filing cabinet.

Seeing that it was locked, she retrieved her picks. The push-lock on the cabinet had fewer pins than the one on Feldmann's office door, but the keyhole was smaller, making it harder to work her tools. Four or five times she had to remove the rake and start over again. It was terribly frustrating. Once, she bent her pick and hit the cabinet in anger. The noise brought her back from her senseless tantrum. She stood up and took a few deep breaths, then bent down and started on the lock again.

Thinking back to her hours of training, she recalled how some locks would spring open within a few seconds, but others would only yield after hours of work. Even the same lock could be easy one time and impossible the next. Locks were like people—they had personalities and tempers. And, like little children, they seemed to know right when you were frustrated the most, and that's when they behaved the worst.

At last, though, after restarting ten times or more, she felt the tension tool turn. She twisted it a little harder while pressing on the lock to relieve tension from the core. It turned smoothly. As she pulled her fingers back, the button popped out.

She slid open the top drawer and fished through the contents, which, as best she could tell, were simply papers Lawson had submitted to various journals for publication. Nothing that looked useful. She closed it and opened the bottom drawer. It felt particularly light. Peering inside, all she found was a worn leather glasses case. She shut the drawer in disgust and reached for the lock but then paused. Something was odd.

Lawson didn't wear glasses.

She reopened the drawer and took out the case. It felt empty, albeit with a slight rattle. She opened the flip-lid and peered inside. Nothing. She clicked the lid shut and heard the same rattle. Puzzled, she flipped open the case again. The shell-like lining looked loose, and she pulled it back with her fingertips, exposing a flat, rectangular piece of plastic the size of a postage stamp. Inverting the case, the plastic square fell into her open palm, revealing a row of copper contacts along one edge.

An SD memory chip. And one that Lawson had taken some effort to hide.

Tina replaced the leather case in the cabinet and shut the drawer. She walked back to her desk and looked for an SD slot on her computer, but it didn't have one. Of course not, she realized. As an admin, she got one of the ancient computers. Only researchers and professors got new models.

"Shit," she muttered. The researchers' computers were all password-protected. Then she remembered the empty office. She had the password to *that* computer.

Entering the stuffy little room, she shut the door, switched on the machine, and waited for it to boot up. Then, entering the generic username and password for the department, she pushed the memory chip into the slot on the front of the CPU.

A box came up asking her if she wanted to view the contents, and she clicked Yes, praying the chip itself hadn't been password-protected. She felt a tingle of excitement as the screen filled with a list of files. She opened the first one, labeled "CALC_NUM_ DISB.M" and saw that it contained a computer program. It looked like MATLAB, the language she'd learned to write her Monte Carlo simulation back in college. While she'd long since forgotten how to write a program, she still remembered enough to puzzle through someone else's.

After browsing through that first file, she felt weak. As she scanned the contents of subsequent files, she found it almost hard to breathe. Turning slowly, she stared out the window at the sunlit trees against the dark clouds simply to convince herself she was still a part of the world and not lost in some nightmare. Reluctantly, she turned back to the monitor and read further, the gravity of the situation sinking in with each line of code.

How could they have so underestimated what they were dealing with?

29. THE APPROACHING STORM

The room had grown prematurely dark. Jason turned on a floor lamp next to his desk and then glanced at his watch. "It's almost six," he told Blum. Then he switched on the intercom. "Tom? Anything from Tina?"

The box blared back, "Nothing yet. I've been trying her cell and office. Apartment, too. By the way, the closest team we had was in Oklahoma City. They're on their way. Let's hope this storm system coming through the Midwest delays that plane. Even so, our guys may not make it in time."

"Keep trying to reach her." Jason squinted at the squawk box. "You still there?"

"Yeah. Hold on. Something's coming in. I—" The line went dead for several moments. "Hey. Carlo called in. Feldmann's Mercedes just pulled out of the farm. Looks to be heading toward town. Do you want him to follow it?"

"No. We need to keep eyes on the farm. Tom, I want you to go find Tina. I'll take over on coms. Check Cotespath Hall and her apartment if necessary. I don't like the fact she's out of contact."

"I can go," Blum offered.

Jason considered the proposal. "Alright. I can use Tom here. But if you can't find her, come straight back. And, if you do find her, bring her right here. No side trips."

"Absolutely," Blum said. He stood up and grabbed his jacket. "Be back shortly."

Blum jogged to the Cobra. The humid air felt heavy on his shoulders, and the sweet smell of rain seemed much closer. Blum tossed his jacket on the passenger seat, climbed in and fired up the engine. Before he could slip it into gear, his phone buzzed and he grabbed it from the jacket pocket. The low-battery signal was flashing.

Kay. Damn it. It tore him up not to be able to answer. Dare he send a text? Could Jason's team monitor that as well? He decided to risk typing something innocuous. "BUSY. WILL CALL LATER." Jason couldn't be upset about that.

A moment later, he got her texted response. "WHERE R U? R U OK?"

Right as he began to type an answer, the phone went dead. Shit. He hadn't charged it since he'd left Kay's condominium the day before. Too late now. He tossed the useless device in the door pocket.

As he headed west toward campus and the approaching squall line, the wind around him grew stronger, and the giant sycamores that lined the street bowed and swayed. High overhead, against the blackening sky, he noticed four crows, dipping and cawing as they flew into the rush of oncoming air.

Tina's apartment was almost on the way to Cotespath, so he stopped there first. He rang the doorbell and banged on the outside entrance. When no one answered, he drove on to Cotespath Hall. Pulling into the parking garage, he spotted a silver Infiniti that he guessed was Santini's. A quick check confirmed it was empty. He snatched his gun from the glovebox and shoved it in his waistband, throwing on his jacket to conceal the weapon.

Traversing the courtyard, he entered through the back door. He jogged to the elevators and smacked the call button. When the doors opened on nine, Blum crossed the desolate hallway to the entrance for CSR. Finding it unlocked, he opened the door and stepped inside. No Tina. The whirring fan on her computer caught his attention, and he noticed the reflection of the monitor in the window behind her desk. So where was she?

Blum checked the tiny room with the copier first, but she wasn't there. Perhaps the bathroom? Just as he was about to leave the CSR suite, a noise from the carpeted back passage to Feldmann's office stopped him in his tracks. Walking back through the reception area, he peered down the dark corridor. One of the doors sat slightly ajar. As he approached, he heard a faint whimper from inside. Quietly, he slid the Kahr from his belt. He took a step back. As he ducked and kicked open the door, he heard Tina scream.

30. CALCULUS OF DEATH

B lum's kick smashed the office door back against the interior wall. Tina let out a shriek as her hands flew to her face at the sight of the gun.

Blum scanned the room. It took only a second to confirm she was alone. "Sorry," he said, "I thought you were in danger." He stuck the Kahr in his belt.

She lowered her hands and stared back at him but remained strangely quiet. Trembling slightly, she turned back to face the computer screen.

"Oh my God, David," she said softly, "It's horrible. Feldmann is the devil, alright."

"What are you talking about?"

"It's not just *a* bomb," she said, her voice trembling. "It's hundreds of bombs."

"*Hundreds*?" He stumbled over the words. "Why . . . ?"

"It's always the same, isn't it? To gain recognition for his cause or whatever. What does it matter why?"

"What did you find?"

"A memory card. I picked the lock on Lawson's filing cabinet and found it hidden in a glasses case. It has a bunch of files on it. Computer programs. Data sets. Output." She still seemed dazed, almost trancelike.

Blum stepped behind her and looked over her shoulder at the screen, filled with lines of cryptic words and numbers. "What am I looking at?"

"It's a computer simulation program," she said absently. "It calculates how many planes they need to blow up. Four hundred eighty-seven."

"They *calculated* how many planes . . ."

"Yeah. Calculus of death. How sick is that?"

"Based on *what*?"

She shook her head. "Variables with names like persistence rate, infection rate, and dispersion coefficient. It uses data files of geocoded population—basically, how many people live where—all over the world. The program also accesses a data file called STORMPERIL."

"That's the weather file that Lawson created."

"Yeah. And there's a file of global airline flights with three-dimensional GPS coordinates of their routes. It looks like the program somehow optimizes which flights to target and where, taking into account likely weather patterns. It's all programmed to tell them how many planes it will take to ensure a minimum infection rate with a ninety-nine percent probability."

"And that gets them to six million people dead very quickly," Blum said. "Not to mention the fifty or hundred thousand people who die on the targeted planes. But with this list, we might be able to stop those flights."

"Perhaps," Tina said, still staring at the screen. "What are you doing here, anyway?"

"Jason sent me. Someone in Zurich gave Krieger the order to kill

Feldmann and Lawson tonight. We couldn't reach you."

She shook her head. "My phone's in my purse back at my desk."

"Jason wants you back at his house. We'll take the memory chip with us."

"No. I have to put it back. Lawson could come looking for it. He'd know someone took it, and they might change plans. Let me copy it. It'll only take a minute."

"Okay, but we have to hurry," Blum said. "Feldmann's car left the farm a little while ago. It might be headed here."

"I have a thumb drive in my desk," she said. "I'll copy it onto that." She pushed past Blum and ran down the hall, returning a moment later. Inserting the drive into the USB port, she began copying files, tapping her fingers nervously on the desk.

Blum paced around the room. "How much longer?" He looked at his watch. Six-forty. Jason must be sweating bullets.

"Hold on . . . It'll be finished in a minute." She squinted at the screen. "Where did you park?"

"In the garage. Right next to you."

"If Feldmann shows up, he can't find you here. Go get your car and meet me in front."

"I'm not leaving you here alone."

"Don't be stupid. I work here. Feldmann insisted I come in today. He'll expect me to be here. But, if *you* get caught here with me, there's no talking our way out of that. I'll be right behind you."

Blum weighed the risks. She was right about getting caught in the office again. "Alright," he said. "I'll see you downstairs."

Blum dashed back to his car. Firing up the engine, he screeched his way down the spiral ramp to the ground level. Unfortunately, the exit dumped him onto a street with no direct route to Cotespath, forcing him to navigate around the block to the circular drive in front. Negotiating the last curve before entering the drive, he spied an empty, black car parked across the street from the front door. Feldmann's Mercedes! And it hadn't been there before.

Blum yanked the Cobra into a side driveway and shut off the engine. He jumped out and crossed the street. Sprinting to the building, he flung back the front door and dove into an empty elevator. Time was critical, but he knew an opening elevator could be a warning signal to anyone on the ninth floor, so he pressed ten instead.

At ten, he leapt from the elevator and dashed to the stair entrance. He raced down to nine, taking the steps two at a time, his left hand on the railing to steady himself and his right hand clutching the Kahr at the ready.

Opening the stairwell door, he jogged down the empty hall toward the elevator lobby. Just as he was clearing the corner, he heard a series of "clump-clump" noises, then the sound of the suite doors slamming shut and the solenoid latch reengaging. He sprang into the lobby, his gun ready to fire.

A shiver shot down his spine when he saw Tina lying unconscious on a lab cart being pulled into the elevator. Blum dove for the closing door, but he was too late. The last thing he saw was a sheet being thrown over her face as the steel barrier slammed shut.

The stairs would be too slow. Blum smacked the call button for another elevator and cursed aloud. He had to assume that whoever had taken her had at least heard him, if not seen him as well, and that meant he had to get to Tina quickly.

When the elevator arrived, Blum dove in. A moment later the door opened onto a deserted lobby. Blum dashed for the front door, hitting it full force and slamming it back against its hinges as he ran to the curb. The cart sat ominously deserted by the side of the walkway, and the car was gone. Looking frantically up and down the street, Blum spotted the Mercedes in the distance driving away.

As he turned to get his car, he noticed something on the ground next to the cart. A cell phone. Not Tina's, so most likely her captor's. It must have fallen out of the guy's pocket as he maneuvered Tina into the car.

Running down to his car, he climbed in and slid the gun under the passenger seat, where it would still be within reach. The engine fired up immediately, and he bounded out into the street, almost hitting a bicyclist. Oblivious to the rider's cursing, Blum floored the accelerator, squealing his tires, and shot down the campus back road. Up ahead, the Mercedes had just turned left, heading north.

At the intersection, Blum hit his brakes late, causing him to skid sideways into traffic. A blue sedan screeched to a stop, barely missing his front fender. Blum zoomed around the car and, seeing the Mercedes seven or eight cars ahead, passed on the right and moved up three cars. As he did, he got a momentary view through the sedan's back window and recognized Lawson at the wheel. Without his cell phone, Lawson couldn't tell Feldmann what had happened, which meant Blum had to get to him before he reached the farm.

As Blum expected, Lawson turned left on Green, heading west toward the farm. The traffic light turned yellow. Spotting a left turn lane up ahead at the intersection, Blum checked for oncoming traffic. Seeing none, he shot out across the center line, cutting ahead of the lead car and zoomed into the left-turn lane right as the light turned red. The car he'd skirted pulled in behind him as he skidded to a stop.

Or was he headed in entirely the wrong direction? Shouldn't he drive directly to Jason and let him know what Tina had discovered? Jason's team could have lost track of the plane at this point, and Jason needed to know what they were up against. His team could rescue Tina. They were equipped to handle this sort of thing; he wasn't.

The left turn arrow turned green. The car behind him honked.

How could he jeopardize everything for Tina? She might already

THE PANGAEA SOLUTION

be dead. Blum banged his fists against the steering wheel, agonizing over what to do. What if he failed? And besides, she knew the
risks. The turn light went red. The angry driver behind him leaned
on the horn. Blum whipped the steering wheel to the right and
dumped the clutch, leaving a trail of burnt rubber as the roadster
dove across two lanes and sped east toward Jason.

But, if Lawson had found her with the memory chip, Blum *had*
to stop the car before it reached the farm—before Lawson got a
chance to warn Feldmann. Blum screamed in frustration. He had
to make a decision: follow Lawson or return to Jason? Either way,
there was no turning back.

Fuck it! Jason could wait. Save Tina.

Blum snapped the steering wheel to the left, briefly sending the
car into the oncoming traffic. Simultaneously, he yanked the hand
brake. As the back end of the car screeched in a wide arc, he unwound
the steering wheel, let down the brake and floored the accelerator,
launching him back the way he'd come and toward the Mercedes.

Within seconds, he'd closed the distance he'd lost, but Saturday
evening traffic thickened as they approached the heart of campus,
and Blum could see Lawson half a block ahead, mired in a throng
of vehicles. They passed through two lights, and traffic got worse.
Sunset was still a half hour or more away, but the muddy, black
cloud cover created a nighttime darkness. Streetlights flickered to
life, and drivers switched on their headlights.

Blum tried to move up, but a car from a side street turned right
on red and slipped between him and the car in front. He risked
another pass on the right. Now there was only a dented gray van
between him and Lawson. As the line of cars approached the next
intersection, the traffic light turned yellow.

The Mercedes pulled through without hesitation. The van
slowed, and then sped on through as well. Blum gunned the engine,

268

and the car jerked forward. Suddenly a large, tan sedan jumped the light and pulled out into the intersection, cutting off his lane. Counting on the car to keep moving, Blum swerved to drive behind it, but the sedan stopped dead. He stomped on the brakes and laid on his horn. The car didn't budge.

"Move!" Blum yelled at the driver. But now the light had turned green the other way, and the traffic on the cross street streamed around the pair of cars. Blum glared at the driver—some stupid woman with red glasses—who sat grinning at him. He unclipped his belt and stood up.

"Move out of the damn way!" he yelled.

Up ahead, the Mercedes disappeared into a thick column of traffic.

31. NIGHT RUN

David Blum slammed the door to the Cobra and stormed the big sedan that blocked the intersection. Behind him, cars honked angrily, and people yelled. As Blum approached the car, the window slid down.

"Move your God damn car!" he shouted, but the lady's grin only grew wider.

"Oh, God. I'm terribly sorry," she said with mock concern. "I must have flooded it. What should I do?"

Blum couldn't tell if she was crazy or just being a brat. "I don't have time to screw around. Move your damn car!"

He heard the locks click and the passenger door open. He tensed, sensing a trap. To his shock, Kay Westfield emerged on the far side.

Before he could say anything, he heard her call to the driver, "I'll be right back," and slam the door.

"What the hell are you doing here?" he yelled.

"We were headed to a bar on campus, and I saw your car."

"Well, tell her to move! I don't have time for this."

"Why haven't you called me?" she demanded, stepping in front of his car. "I'm not going anywhere until you talk to me." She stood there, arms akimbo, in defiance.

Motorists, viewing the scene as some sort of love spat, seemed to realize the futility of honking and found their way around the standoff in the center of the intersection. As one car passed, Blum heard a guy yell, "Slap her good!" Another person shouted, "Kiss and make up!"

Blum grabbed Kay and pulled her toward him. "I'm not screwing around. That was Feldmann's Mercedes that just drove by here—I was chasing it. I have to stop that car from reaching the farm."

"Why?"

"I don't have time to explain. Now tell your friend to move. I have to go *now!*"

Kay looked at Blum and seemed to realize how serious he was. "Take me with you."

"No. It's too dangerous."

"If you want her to move . . ."

Blum stared up the road at the thick train of cars. Every second he wasted, the Mercedes made its way farther from him and closer to the farm. In desperation, he agreed.

"Susan," she called. "Move your car. I'll call you later."

"What?" her friend yelled out the window. "If you think that—"

"Move the car!" Kay ordered in a tone that shocked even David.

Susan, shaking her head, pulled away and drove through the intersection. David and Kay dashed back to the Cobra and jumped in. The red light took forever. Overhead, the low canopy of clouds twisted and turned, and, just below the dense ceiling, small wisps of light-gray scud streaked by like blowing tufts of wool.

The instant the light turned green, Blum shot across Sixth Street in a scream of tires as he dodged between cars in the heavy traffic.

Mentally, he began calculating how far behind he must be. Kay's stupid friend had wasted probably three minutes. Lawson wouldn't seriously speed until he was out of town. With traffic and lights, he was traveling, say, thirty miles an hour—half a mile per minute. That put him as much as a mile and a half ahead. Blum was about three and a half miles from the edge of town, which meant Lawson was about two miles—four minutes—from the open countryside where he could then speed up. Blum zoomed up to fifty. At that rate, he would be about a half mile or so behind Lawson when he could really accelerate.

Kay hadn't said a word since they'd left Susan. Blum glanced over and saw her gripping the dash with one hand, dead-faced, lips slightly parted, staring straight ahead, and he wondered what he'd gotten her into.

Deep in thought, he almost didn't see the light turn red. He slammed on the brakes and swerved slightly as a car crossed in front of him. He drummed the steering wheel nervously as the engine growled like a tethered beast. The signal was taking too long. He checked the intersection. No traffic. He leapt through and flew ahead.

When he turned to check on Kay, he was shocked to see her holding his gun and looking at him questioningly. He realized it must have slid out from under the seat when he'd stopped suddenly.

"Be careful," he yelled over the engine howl, but then he saw that she seemed to know something about guns, holding it firmly and pointing it down at the floor.

Blum returned his gaze to the road ahead where the traffic was beginning to thin. When they crossed Prospect Avenue and headed further west through residential Champaign, he spotted Lawson's car a quarter of a mile ahead. As the black Mercedes topped a small rise, the greenish-brown clouds overhead seemed to almost rub the roof.

A second later, like an explosion in heaven, a brilliant flash of lightning lit up the entire scene in daylight, and the boom of thunder rocked the Cobra on its suspension. Kay gasped, and Blum turned to see her drop the pistol on her lap. She looked at him, embarrassed, and then set the gun back on the floor by her feet.

The storm had obscured any remnants of the setting sun, leaving the streets dark as night. At the next light, he turned north on Mattis and was finally able to pick up speed. Lawson, a few hundred yards ahead, turned west on Springfield on his final leg out of town. Blum caught the yellow traffic signal and spun through the intersection. Finally, afraid he might get hit if he didn't, he switched on his headlights.

As they raced west, they zipped past the entrance for Sunny Ridge Village. An instant later, they sped past a trucking company, then a plant nursery, then an auto-repair shop and a gas station. With no one left between him and Lawson, Blum stomped on the accelerator. The engine's eerie growl grew into a wicked scream. Suddenly, they plunged into darkness as the streetlights ended and they hit open farmland. Kay gripped the dash harder, but then her arms, heavy from the acceleration, fell back and rested in her lap.

On the three-four gearshift, the exhaust barked briefly before the clutch caught, and the roadster squatted down for another blast of acceleration. Seconds later, they zipped under the overpass for Interstate 57, the howl of the engine echoing back like a rabbit punch to the ears.

Blum quickly narrowed the gap between him and Lawson to a quarter mile, but Lawson began to speed up, too—doing at least a hundred. Then Blum saw brake lights ahead, and he lifted his foot from the accelerator. The brake lights ceased and headlights swung to the left.

Lawson was turning south off Route 10 and onto one of the county roads, perhaps trying to see if Blum was going to follow him.

Seconds later, Blum stabbed at the brake and downshifted into second. He took the left at forty, slid a bit on a patch of gravel, then shot forward, bounding up a small hill and leaping over a set of railroad tracks to where the road dipped back down. He floored the gas, wound out the engine, and shifted to third. Lawson's taillights now appeared as two red pinpricks up ahead. Blum shifted to fourth at close to one hundred and accelerated from there.

Driving down the narrow country road at two miles per minute, Blum felt like he was sprinting on a high wire. The asphalt surface, buckled with ridges and gullies from years of traffic, tossed the car up and down on its firm suspension. Twice, the back end scooted out—only a few degrees—but it felt like halfway around to Blum, who wrestled the machine back into line with strong but delicate movements of the steering wheel.

At one point, while passing over a narrow bridge where the road rose abruptly, the car left the ground for a brief instant. The Cobra reared up, its headlights pointing at the low ceiling of clouds as Blum stared ahead at the empty blackness where the road had been. He braced the steering wheel, now limp in his hands, for the landing while the engine, freed from the burden of powering the car, raced wildly to the redline. Then, before Blum could even absorb what had happened, the car touched down with a screech of tires that whipped the Cobra sideways. The body glanced off the low guardrail, flaying aluminum and paint from the left front fender.

Kay screamed as David spun the wheel frantically to straighten out the car, and, like an angry beast, the Cobra heaved upward, lifting its right wheels off the ground. Blum tugged the steering straight, and the car bounced down. Without pausing, Blum brought the Cobra back under control and sped onward.

"It's okay," he yelled to Kay. But when he stared ahead, squinting into the darkness, he could no longer see Lawson's taillights.

At the next crossroad, he slowed and shot a glance to his right. Far off down the side road, he spotted a pair of glowing red dots.

He slammed the brakes and spun the car into a sharp right turn. Blum briefly took the Cobra to nearly one-forty, but backed off when the rough surface threatened to hurl them from the tar ribbon into the adjacent field. After a minute, he saw brake lights flash ahead and headlights swing around to the left.

Rather than chase Lawson directly, Blum decided to cut him off on his final approach to the gate, so, at the next crossroad, he double-clutched down through two gears to second, throwing the car into a left turn. The new road, which now paralleled Lawson's southerly route, was wider, and Blum took the car up to one-fifty. Flashes of lightning burst around them, exploding like artillery, but neither passenger could hear the thunder over the savage wail of the V-8 motor.

Four miles south, Blum turned right and gunned the engine, racing to the next intersection, a mile ahead. Ignoring the stop sign, he screeched to a halt in the middle of the intersection and stared northward, searching for Lawson's headlights. A few seconds later, he saw a car blip past, a mile to the north. So, Lawson was taking the long route.

"Do you see him?" Kay asked. It was the first thing she'd said since she'd gotten in the car.

"Yes. But he's going around the far side of the farm. I don't know why. We'll catch him when he heads south."

Blum slapped the lever into first gear and took off. As he approached the next intersection, he pulled over and shut off the engine. He turned to Kay. "Give me the gun," he said.

She felt under the seat for the pistol, found it, and handed it to Blum.

"Okay. I need you to get out of the car and go hide in the corn. There's going to be shooting, and I don't want you to get hurt."

"Wouldn't I be safer in the car? I could crouch down."

"If Lawson has a gun, he'll shoot at me first and the car second. You'll be safer the farther away you are. Run in a hundred yards and lie down, as low as you can get. When things quiet down, I'll call for you. If you don't hear me, then keep going. You should be able to find a farmhouse in a mile or so." He stepped out of the car.

Kay hesitated. "But I want to help."

"There's nothing you can do. Now go! I don't have time to argue." Blum turned his back on her and jogged to the edge of the corn by the intersection. He stared up the road. It should only be a short while, he thought, before the black Mercedes slows to turn the corner. Lawson, not seeing any headlights in his mirrors and finding a clear road in front of him, would turn south and head for the gate two miles ahead of him and a half mile to the east.

Blum only had six bullets. He decided he would start by trying to hit Lawson. He gave himself four shots for that—three head on and one through the side window as the car passed. After that, he would go for the tires. He had no idea if a nine-millimeter slug could actually puncture a tire, but there was little else to try. And so he waited, squinting into the distance.

As the pounding of his pulse intensified, a scary realization hit him. Kay had no idea what he knew. If he got killed, Jason would never get the information he desperately needed to have. He should have told her. Too late now. Concentrate.

And then Blum saw the blue-white glow of headlights coming over the rise up ahead in the road. He ran through his mental checklist—front-sights on target, align rear sights, thumb clear of the slide, lock wrist.

When the car was only a hundred yards away and Blum could hear the whine of its tires on the smooth tarmac, he tensed his arm. It occurred to him that for the first time in his life he was about to shoot to kill. Before it had only been abstract silhouette

targets or bull's-eyes. He closed his mind to the thought and focused his aim just above the headlights and slightly to the right of
center. But then he heard a female voice call to him.

Kay. God damn it, he thought. Why didn't she do what I told
her? Ignore her.

Fifty yards. Blum took two deep breaths and held the second
one. Steady now . . .

"Don't shoot! Don't shoot!" he heard her scream. "It's not him!
Don't shoot!"

Kay burst out of the wall of corn almost directly in his line of
fire, her flying hair rimmed in a halo of yellow, backlit from the
headlights behind her.

"It's a pickup!" she yelled.

Blum dropped his arm quickly and held the gun against his side.
Sure enough, a big red pickup roared past him, spraying him with
a cloud of dust in its wake.

"You could have been killed," he said solemnly when she reached
him, panting.

"I know, but it's a good thing I stuck around."

"We have to get to the front gate," Blum said, grabbing Kay. "We
might still be able to catch him there."

Even though he drove like a madman to the entrance, it was too
late. He spotted the Mercedes pulling in the main drive and heading up the path to the house when they were still a quarter-mile
away. A few seconds later, it disappeared into the foliage.

32. CROSSING THE STYX

Blum screeched to a halt and cursed.

Suddenly Kay flooded him with questions. "What is Lawson doing driving Feldmann's car? What's going on?" She glared at him. "And why won't you talk to me?"

Blum realized he hadn't even been listening. "I'm sorry. You have no idea how serious this is."

"So tell me."

Blum found it hard to concentrate. He wanted to tell Kay the whole story, but he didn't have time. He gave her only the main facts. "There was a lady in that car who discovered a memory card with some files that detail Feldmann's plans. If we can get the chip, we can stop Feldmann from blowing up hundreds of planes and killing millions of people."

"Why didn't you tell me all this before?"

"Because I just found out last night. I was with the people she works for, and I didn't want to get you involved. That's why I couldn't call. Lawson caught her in his office right after she found it. I saw him drag her away, and I was chasing him when you stopped me. Unfortunately, that woman and I are the only people who know about that memory chip besides Lawson. And now you." He thought for a second. "I need your help."

"Anything."

"I need you to drive back to Urbana and deliver a message for me to a guy named Jason. He's in charge." Blum unclipped his seat belts and stepped out onto the asphalt road.

"Can't you just call him?" She pulled out her cell phone.

"I don't have his number. Only an address."

She stared at Blum, eyes wide. "I won't know where to go. Why can't you come with me?"

"I need to get in there, get that chip and save that woman. I owe it to her." Blum walked around and opened Kay's door. "I'll give you the address. Go there and tell Jason that I sent you. Tell him that Feldmann's people plan to blow up almost five hundred airplanes and that the original computer chip with all the information may still be hidden in Lawson's filing cabinet in a glasses case. Then, tell him they need to come here and storm this place with everything they have before it's too late."

"Can't I just wait for you?" Kay pleaded, looking up at David. "*Please.*"

"I have no idea how long it'll take me. I don't even know if I can make it in, but I have to try. So *you* have to get the message to Jason."

"Alright," she consented. "But I haven't driven a stick in years, and I was never very good at it. And your car scares me." She undid her belts and climbed out.

"You'll be okay. It works like any other car." Kay still looked frightened. "You have to do this," he told her. "I wish it could be different."

She threw her arms around him and hugged him tight. "Me too."

Blum pushed back and stared at the fence. "The problem is the fence is electrified, and I don't have any bolt cutters . . ." He fell to his knees, his breath quickening, and began to dig furiously at the loose dirt at the base of the fence.

"What are you doing?"

"Maybe I can tunnel under."

A few inches down, the bottom of the fence met a cement slab. "Shit. There's no way . . . I don't know what else to do."

"Take a breath, okay?" She grabbed his shoulder. "I think I know another way you can get in."

"You're right. You got in." Blum stood up. "All I have to do is run the car through the fence—"

"Not like that. There's a place where a creek goes under the fence. A sort of tunnel. Maybe you can get through there."

"Show me."

"We have to drive there. It's on the other side of the farm."

"Okay," Blum said. "But you should drive so you can practice."

"Alright." She helped Blum to his feet, and they ran back to the car.

Kay slid into the driver's seat. "You have to move it up. I can't reach the pedals."

Blum got in the passenger side and showed her how to adjust the seat. He told her to start the engine. She turned the key, but forgot to press the clutch pedal, and the car lurched forward and stalled.

"Oh, my God," she said. "I'm so sorry." She looked at him sheepishly. But on her next attempt, she started it correctly, and the car idled roughly.

"It's a simple 'H' pattern," Blum explained. "First is forward and slightly to the left. Second straight back from there, and so forth. You won't need fifth."

"It feels like the shift lever is bent," she said.

"Don't pay any attention to that. Just move the knob."

Roughly at first, but then more smoothly, she drove around the farm to a bend in the road where a creek passed under the barbed-wire fence. Blum got out and surveyed the flat, cement-slab bridge. It was about ten feet wide and extended for ten or twelve feet beyond the fence. He climbed down the gully on the far side of the road and, rolling up his sleeve as far as it would go, lay down and shoved his arm into the inky stream. He felt around for the opening and, from the curvature on the arched upper rim, guessed he would be able to fit inside. Of course, he had no idea if the tunnel got narrower further in or was blocked by a grating of some sort. He climbed back up the bank to his car.

"Do you think you can get through?" Kay asked.

"I don't know for sure, but I think so." He began to strip.

"What are you doing?"

"I want dry clothes on the other side." He bundled up his pants, shirt and shoes. "Get me my gun, please."

Kay retrieved the Kahr and brought it to David. He put it inside the bundle of clothes and tied the wad together with the sleeves of the shirt.

"If I make it all the way through, throw the clothes to me on the other side. I'm going to tell you the address now, so start practicing it."

To the sound of Kay repeating Jason's address, Blum, dressed only in his underwear, climbed down into the dark gully, slipping a few times on the slimy rocks along the steep bank. He stared into the black stream for a few seconds before stepping in. The creek felt cold and oily as it washed around his midsection. He stared down at his mostly naked body and the reflection of his face, both of which looked obscenely pale against the dark water.

Slowly at first, and then more rapidly, he took deep breaths, concentrating on forceful exhalations and deep inhalations until he felt slightly dizzy and his fingers began to tingle. Then, closing his eyes, he crouched down into the crevice between the embank-ment and the cement bridge.

The water tickled its way into his nostrils and ears and chilled his scalp. Closing his mind to the sticky, cold discomfort, he felt his way slowly into the tunnel. A parade of sparkling lights flickered in front of his tightly closed eyes. Inch by inch, he used his fingertips to crawl forward. At any moment, he expected to run his hands over a broken bottle or some other sharp object that might cut the exposed skin of his belly.

A few feet in, he hit something sharp protruding down from the roof of the tunnel. Carefully, he studied it with his fingers. It felt like a portion of steel reinforcement for the concrete. He ducked down and proceeded.

Another few feet in, his hands closed around something soft and spongy. A wad of newspaper or rags, perhaps. He squeezed it gen-tly and heard a rush of fine bubbles. His fingers squished through the jelly and closed in on a spiny, cat-sized rib cage. He jerked his hand back. But then, realizing that he had nowhere to go but for-ward, he pushed the rotten carcass away and crawled onward.

Blum's biggest fear was getting trapped—tangled in roots or wedged into a crevice and unable to escape before he blacked out. He had to move slowly to be safe, but already, his lungs felt stale and his diaphragm contracted spasmodically from time to time. He picked up his pace.

Just as the need for air was becoming unbearable, Blum reached up and felt the edge of the tunnel. Elated, he kicked forward and swam for the surface. An instant later, his head smashed into an overhead barrier. He nearly gulped water as he shot his hand up and felt a rough, concrete ceiling above him. He'd been under water for almost two and a half minutes, and his air was gone.

Like a trapped animal, he clawed forward. Something scraped

down his back, and he felt a burning between his shoulder blades. He kicked harder, still running his hand along the ceiling. A few seconds later, he felt the roof lift away. He found the lip of the exit and scrambled through. Rising carefully with his arm extended upward, he felt air on his hand, then his arm, and finally his face. He was through! Blum's lungs heaved in and out, sucking in the muggy night air. Standing up, he trudged out of the filthy creek. His mind felt numb. He could hear noises, but not distinct sounds. He fell to the grass face first and didn't move.

After a bit, he got up to his knees and coughed.

"I thought you were dead," Kay called to him through the fence. "Are you okay?"

Hearing her, Blum coughed again, and slowly stood up. He wrung the water from his hair and combed it back over his head with his fingers. "I'm fine now," he told her, resting his hands on his knees and still panting. "Can you throw me my clothes?"

Kay tossed the bundle in a steep arc but didn't throw it out far enough, and on its descent it caught on the barbed wire. Blum glanced at Kay, who looked apologetic, but then the bundle rolled off and fell at Blum's feet.

"What's the address?" he asked her, as he got dressed. She told him. "Alright, now go! Be quick, but don't take any chances. You have to get the message to Jason. You're the only one right now that can save all those people. I may not come out again, so it's only you."

"Don't say that," she said. In the dim light, Blum could see her pale fingers clutching the wire.

David put his shoes on his bare feet.

"I know you can do it," he told her. "It's your chance to fly solo— just like you told me about."

"Yes, I know, but I'm still scared."

And with those words, Kay climbed into the driver's seat. Blum watched her as she strapped herself in and studied the various controls. He held his breath as she started the engine, put the car into first, and then drove away down the road. He saw the car jerk once and heard gears grind, but, after that, she accelerated smoothly to speed.

Checking his gun one more time, he put it in his pocket and continued to stare down the dark road as the Cobra's taillights grew smaller and smaller. Then suddenly, seemingly from nowhere, a large blue sedan roared past him, heading toward Kay.

His mind raced through a series of questions. Is it? Could it be? He saw a passenger silhouetted against the car's dash lighting, lifting a submachine gun. He watched in horror, feeling totally helpless, as the two cars passed over a distant hill and disappeared. As the sounds of the engines faded away, Blum heard the long, plaintive wail of a locomotive horn from somewhere in the distance.

33. FLYING SOLO

Kay Westfield sat in the Cobra, steeling herself for what lay
ahead. She grabbed the fat shift-knob and felt the ball buck
in synchrony with the pulsing of the noisy exhaust. After
pressing the clutch pedal—she wasn't going to make that mistake
again—she forced the lever into first. Like the clutch, the shifter
felt big and stiff and hard to move. She let out the clutch slowly and
gave the gas pedal a nudge. The car leapt forward effortlessly. She
sped up and shifted awkwardly into second, cringing as she heard
the gears grind. The car stumbled, but then she accelerated, and
things smoothed out. A moment later, she shifted to third, leveling
out her speed at sixty.

When she glanced in the rearview mirror, she noticed headlights far behind her. At first, she dismissed them, but as they grew
larger, a feeling of dread crept over her. She sped up with little
effect. The vehicle still closed in quickly. Suddenly the headlights
seemed to race forward.

Oh, my God. They're coming after me!

Kay braced herself and stomped on the gas pedal. The exhaust
wailed, and the air left her lungs in a low moan as her stomach

pressed against her spine. She kept her foot planted on the floor until the engine sounded like it might explode, then she shifted to fourth and accelerated again. Stealing a look in the mirror, she was relieved to see that she'd gained a couple hundred yards of distance.

Kay tested the feel of the steering wheel and then pressed harder on the gas. The engine responded. The speedometer needle crossed 130—faster than she'd ever driven before. Despite the desperation of her situation, the sense of control—of playing out her destiny—made her feel strangely peaceful. She sat up taller and gripped the wheel more securely.

Kay Westfield was flying solo.

Ahead, the glowing gray ribbon of road spun toward her, lit up in the twin-cones of the powerful headlights. A sign indicating a railroad crossing flashed past. A moment later, she heard a long, piercing whistle. Glancing into the darkness off to her right, she saw the cycloptic headlight of a freight train speeding across an expanse of open soybean fields toward her. Close, too. No more than a few hundred yards.

Kay scanned the road ahead, desperately searching for the crossing point. With no warning, the asphalt seemed to disappear in front of her, and the car pitched downward, pointing into a wide ravine at the gleaming tracks twenty yards ahead. The red signal-lights flashed their dull right-left warning as the train flew toward the crossing, now barely a hundred feet away.

Stop or go?

The dark sedan leapt over the edge of the ravine behind her. In a split second, Kay made up her mind and floored the accelerator. The car swayed from side to side as it screamed forward. The train blew its deep horn again—a loud, unmerciful warning. Twenty feet. Now she could hear the locomotive's engine over her own. Kay felt the front wheels hit the first rail as the deafening tornado of the train bore down on her. The steering wheel whipped from her hands. After that, the only sound Kay Westfield heard was her own scream mixed with the roar of the oncoming train.

34. STORMING THE GATES

Blum continued to stare at the horizon even after the cars had disappeared over the distant hill. As he turned away, an overwhelming sense of loss gripped him—what had he done? But the Cobra was fast, and Kay was strong, he told himself; perhaps she would escape after all. Clinging to that thought and closing his mind to her potential fate, he focused on his objective.

With his gun secure in his rear pocket, he set off across the large field toward Feldmann's house. The dull glow from the low clouds lit his way, and from time to time erratic flashes of lightning streaked between the clouds.

As Blum trekked across the loose, broken soil, he stumbled on football-sized clods of plowed earth. He found it tiring and frustrating, and the more he attempted to hurry, the more he struggled. All the while, the low clouds boiled overhead.

Ten minutes later, and only halfway to the farmhouse, Blum felt the rain begin—just a sprinkle at first, but quickly the drops became huge, cold, splattering missiles that smacked him in the face and pelted his shirt. The dirt clods grew slick and treacherous, further slowing his pace.

Soon, the rain changed to hail. Marble-sized pellets of ice stung as they glanced off his head, shoulders, and back. He cursed the heavens but trudged onward through the torrent. Finally, he heard the clattering timpani of hail pummeling the metal roof of the hangar, and he knew he was getting close. Over the cacophony, he could also hear a loud roar, like a jet plane somewhere in the distance, but he had no idea what that was.

Reaching the end of the plowed field, he ran across the grass to the hangar and took refuge under the overhang from the deluge.

Once the rain died down to no more than a drizzle, he crept to the side door of the hangar and opened it. The vapor lights were out, and it took his eyes a few minutes to adjust to the darkness. As soon as he could see, Blum walked to the tool rack in back and found a utility knife. Pocketing the tool, he felt his way back to the door and peered out. The area between the hangar and the house looked deserted—no alarms sounding, no people moving around.

Blum crouched and ran across the grass to the farmhouse, using scrub bushes for cover until he reached a low brick wall. Shifting his gun to his waist, he peered around the corner. Confirming he was alone, he made his way to the front of the house where a porch light illuminated the Mercedes parked at the base of the stairs. Despite the rain, the trunk sat open; no doubt that was where Tina had been transported.

Blum approached the car from the dark side. Using the utility knife, he cut the valve stem on the front tire of the Mercedes. The car slumped down as the air-stream sputtered and quit. Blum peeked around the corner of the car, studying the front of the house. No lights appeared. No noises of alarm. He made his way back to the low wall and crouched behind it.

A moment later, he heard a door slam behind him—away from the house and on his exposed side. He whipped his head around.

At the base of the large greenhouse across the grassy field, light streamed from an open doorway. Blum stared into the long, glowing shaft and saw the silhouette of a man standing there. The man, probably Feldmann, yelled something and then disappeared inside, leaving the door open. Paralyzed with fear, Blum waited for guards to come rushing out to get him.

Could he possibly shoot his way out with only six bullets? Any decent shot could pick him off well before he could reach the fence. And, even if he did make it, then what? Try to scale over and risk being electrocuted? He'd certainly be too breathless at that point to swim back through the tunnel.

To his surprise, though, another man stepped into the doorway—from the outside. A big man—Lawson—seemed to be carrying a sack over his shoulder. He turned, and the sack moved. No, not a sack. Tina.

Blum had no idea how long Lawson would stand there before stepping inside and shutting the door. He didn't hesitate. He sprang from his hiding place and sprinted across the open grass to the cavernous building. He lifted his gun, but it was futile at that point. Before he had covered even half the distance to the open door, he saw it swing shut and then slam with a deep, resounding boom. The sound bounced off the farmhouse and steel hangar and rolled away across the rain-soaked fields. Like a rejoinder from heaven, a dull thunderclap echoed the boom and left the night even more silent than before.

In desperation, Blum continued his race to the face of the brick monolith and tugged at the locked door, but the huge slab of cold steel didn't even rattle on its solid, safe-like hinges.

No longer concerned about being seen, Blum ran along the cliff-like face of the building, desperately searching for a way in. He jogged a full hundred yards to the far corner but found no reachable window or doorway. Turning the corner, he stared along the far face, fifty yards wide, and, halfway down, he spotted a break in the brick.

At the midpoint of the wall, he found a metal panel, twenty feet wide and almost thirty feet tall that appeared to roll upward like a garage door into a motorized lift mechanism. The housing for the mechanism formed a ledge that looked to be about a foot deep and the width of the door. Another ten feet separated the ledge from the roof, but a heavy standpipe curved from the door, up and over the top of the building. If he could make it to the lift housing, he could reach the pipe and climb to the roof where he hoped he could break through the glass greenhouse.

The door consisted of interlaced aluminum slats with an inch-deep recess separating each pair—just enough room to get a foothold. He began to climb, keeping his cheek pressed against the cold metal and not daring to look up or down. He simply counted the bolts as they passed. One . . . two . . . three . . .

After a while, when he raised his hand to grip the next row of slats, his knuckles hit the bottom of the metal ledge. He slid his hand out from the wall as far as he could, searching for the outer edge, but it just kept going. From the ground, the mechanism had looked so small, but now he realized it must protrude almost two feet.

He started to panic. What if he couldn't get a grip on it? Climbing down would be more dangerous than climbing up, and he wasn't sure he even had enough strength to make it all the way back down. Already, his knees were beginning to buckle and his fingers were getting numb. If he fell from where he was, he'd be crippled, if not killed.

With great care, he tilted his head back and looked up at the ledge, finally managing to make out the point where the mechanism ended and the images of the distant clouds began. Now that he could see what he was doing, he realized that his hand had very nearly reached the edge before. Yes. If he leaned out a little farther, his fingers could clear the corner . . . up an inch . . . two inches. Something different. A lip of some sort. Could he grab it? Yes. But, would it hold his weight?

Blum tugged hard with his right arm but felt no play in the smooth metal. He knew it was his only shot. He pulled harder. As he did, his feet slid off their slippery metal perches, and he found himself dangling thirty feet off the ground by one hand. He shot his left hand up, got hold, and then hung like that for a moment.

The top of the mechanism housing was another foot higher. Blum could see an open gutter running along its upper edge. He let go with his right hand and tried with a slapping motion to reach the gutter, but his fingers fell short. He vainly tried to lift himself higher with his left arm but wasn't strong enough to pull up far enough.

Now he could feel his fingers getting weak. In less than a minute or so, his grip would fail, and as numb as his hands were, he wouldn't even know what had happened until he felt himself falling. In desperation, he began to swing his body from side to side, slowly at first, but then faster and higher until his shoulders rose six inches at either peak. Finally, when his right shoulder swung as high as he dared take it, he flung his arm up and grabbed the gutter. He caught it, and it held.

He let go with his left hand and swung it to the gutter as well. From there it was a simple kip and vault to a push-up over the ledge. Blum swung one leg onto the cold, rough surface and then, rolling over slightly, dragged his other leg up and lay on his back. He rested like that for a minute, staring up at the sky. Finally, using the standpipe for support, he stood up and leaned there against the wall, waiting for the feeling to return to his fingers.

When he felt strong enough, he climbed the pipe to the roof and made his way across the wide expanse of tar toward the metal-and-glass greenhouse that he'd seen from the ground.

The poster-sized glass slabs reflected images of the twisting sky overhead and caught flashes from a new wave of arriving thunderheads. Crouching over one of the angled panes, Blum stared down into treetops below and realized that what had appeared to be a separate greenhouse structure on top of the main building was actually the faceted dome of a massive skylight over the entire structure. Purplish lights lit the interior, but the fogged windows obscured details.

It took ten minutes in the dark, but Blum finally found something he could use as a hammer—a two-foot length of steel framing he was able to rip from the air-conditioning unit. Choosing the largest pane, he turned away and closed his eyes. The first two strikes against the slab only bounced off, but the third one did the trick. He heard a shattering crash and opened his eyes just in time to see the pane crumble completely, showering down in a hailstorm of splintered glass.

Leaning forward, he stared though the hole into the eerie abyss. Violet lights silhouetted the branches and leaves of the trees below. Most of the limbs looked too weak to hold him, but off to the left he could see a strong bough that paralleled the ceiling. He studied the system of tubular struts that crisscrossed below the glass roof and figured he could use them to climb to the tree branch.

Careful not to cut himself on the shards around the frame, Blum stepped through the jagged-edged hole and onto one of the cross pipes. He found a guy-wire and used it to steady himself. Inside, it felt hot and steamy, and sweat began collecting along his brow and neck. From deep below his perch, he could hear strange noises filtering up through the heavy canopy of dense foliage as he steadied himself, preparing to maneuver towards the chosen limb. The sounds varied from random clicks and buzzes to a melodic roaring noise. Something about them seemed almost alive, but unlike any animal he had ever heard.

"You're in," he told himself as he climbed over to the exposed tree limb. But just as he stood up on the branch, a numbing burst of blue-white light shattered the night. The shock wave hit Blum, flinging him off his feet, into the open air. He knew he was falling, but his body, knocked senseless by the lightning bolt, was powerless to respond. Leaves whipped past. A branch struck his leg and sent him spinning. Another slammed his head. A flash of sparks.

35. EYES IN THE DARKNESS

David Blum lay unconscious on the packed earthen floor of the giant terrarium. Lit up in a pool of pale purple light, his chest rose and fell as he breathed the hot, humid air. The lightning strike to the metal greenhouse skeleton had shocked the inhabitants into silence, but, as the minutes passed, activity slowly resumed. The first to stir were the least intelligent creatures—the insects. Flies, moths and cockroaches tested the air with dangling feelers, and, finding no new threat, buzzed and flapped and crept on in their lifelong quest for food. Next to resume activity were the reptiles and amphibians. Frogs and turtles surfaced in the little pond and, sniffing and testing, decided it was safe to crawl back out into the open. And so it progressed through the birds and on to the mammals.

In time, creatures began to approach the center clearing. In particular, the cockroaches that picked and searched for food among the dirt and rotting leaves began to scurry closer. Although they had run in fear from the lightning burst, disturbances in their world often meant things falling, and things falling meant fresh food.

One roach stood at the edge of the little clearing where Blum lay

sprawled. Carefully and repeatedly, it tested the air with its dancing and rubbing antennae. When at last it was satisfied that everything had fallen, it scampered out into the open. Halfway to Blum,
it stopped and repeated its smelling and testing routine. It rolled
its two lead-shot eyes and preened each antenna with the other
and then proceeded, creeping within a few inches of Blum's carcass before it stopped again. A second later, the cockroach scampered headlong onto Blum's chest. As the first roach searched for
an open wound, others began to follow his scent trail, and, in less
than a minute, there were a dozen or more bugs crawling across
Blum's comatose body.

Something about the prancing feet and tingling antennae sent
a message deep down into Blum's brain. A yell or a slap would have
left him senseless, but the crawling insects touched a primordi-
al nerve, flashing danger signals that banged on the door of his
imprisoned consciousness. Like a bubble released under water, it
took a few seconds for the reaction to reach the surface. As the
gas cloud wiggled its way up the pool of his psyche, it grew larger
and gained speed. When at last it erupted, Blum instinctively tried
to sit up, but his bruised body wouldn't let him. Instead he simply
rolled his head and opened his eyes.

The last thing Blum remembered was standing on a limb far
above ground. It took him a few seconds to recall the blistering flash
of light and the instantaneous explosion that had sent him spinning to the ground. It was then that he noticed the cockroaches.

At first, he thought they were ugly birds, for they were as big as
crows, and their awkwardly folded wings looked like tail feathers.
But then he saw the antennae, and that made him notice the feet
and jaws. And the peering eyes.

Blum swept his right arm across his chest and sent the pack
scurrying. The bug that had first crawled onto him held tight to an

open wound on his belly. As sensation returned to his wakening body, Blum felt the prickly probing and sucking of the insect's mandibles. In a panic, he grabbed the rat-sized creature and squeezed hard. It felt like a scrabbling crab in his hand—the legs and feelers clawing for freedom. He wrestled it loose and, with a last wrenching twist, crushed his thumbs into the brittle underbody. The insides dripped out between his fingers and dribbled like syrup onto his chest. He threw the slippery mess away and wretched violently. When he opened his eyes again, he saw the other roaches scurrying over to the squashed carcass to enjoy the feast.

Blum found the strength to heft up on his elbow and look around. He saw that he had landed in a small clearing lit only by purple grow lamps. All around him grew a wall of dense undergrowth, but in the shadows, he could make out constellations of curious eyes peering in. Most were small pinpricks, but others seemed as big as quarters. He forced himself up to his hands and knees. As he rose, some of the eyes retreated momentarily but quickly returned.

Blum couldn't see all the way to the ceiling, but from the outside dimensions of the building, he figured he must have fallen twenty-five feet or more. He realized that only the dense growth on the way down had kept him from being killed by the fall. After another minute or so, he stood up. Though he felt a bit wobbly, his legs seemed to have survived uninjured.

He knew he had to get out of the terrarium and find his way to Tina. But how? He was literally lost in a forest with no idea which way was which. Fortunately, he only had to head so far in any direction to reach a wall.

As he stood there deciding which way to go, he noticed some of the eyes coming closer. Blum waved his arm and chased them back, but they soon returned. Under one bush, right at the fringes of light, he thought he could make out waving whiskers and probing noses. One of the noses moved out into the light—a large, pointed, pink nose, like an anteater's, that twitched and darted as it sucked in air. Attached to it were foot-long whiskers that looked like strands of stiff nylon. It sniffed frantically at the ground, then lifted and sniffed the air. Behind it, still in the shadows, were two dime-sized eyes.

Blum searched for a place to run, but everywhere he looked more eyes stared back at him. Without warning, one of the sniffing creatures scampered into the pool of pale-lavender light, and Blum faced a gigantic rat, as big as a dachshund, with bristly gray hair and a scaly, silver tail. It saw Blum and squealed like a pig. Its lips pulled back, and it hissed wetly through dripping, nail-like teeth. And then it charged.

Blum kicked madly at the bolting creature and caught it across the side of its open jaws, but the rat moved lightning fast and bit down on the soft leather of his shoe. Blum felt the gnawing teeth sink into the flesh of his big toe as he tore his foot back. The rat held on, swinging under Blum. Afraid the rat would bite again, Blum spun on his left foot, trying to fling the snarling beast away, but it refused to let go.

The weight of the animal tugged awkwardly at Blum's balance, and he stumbled, stepping on the rat. The rodent bit again, and this time his toe split open as his shoe filled with blood. In desperation, Blum jumped and landed with full force on the attacker. His heel crunched down on the skull, and the animal's brains squished up around the leather shoe like gray feces.

Not waiting for a second attack, Blum turned and fled into the forest. Through the darkness, he stumbled forward, his hands extended and his fists clenched together to protect his face. Twice he felt flesh flay from his knuckles as they glanced off a tree trunk or pole. Despite the pain, he kept going.

A low branch caught Blum at the waist, and he somersaulted forward over it. His hands hit soft ground, and then his face hit his hands. He bit a mouthful of dirt and coughed hard as he sprang back to his feet, afraid of being attacked again.

But everything was quiet.

He continued forward, more cautiously now. Shortly, his hand touched a cold, flat surface. A wall. A wonderful tiled wall. Something normal. Something he knew. Encouraged, he felt his way along the barrier. Fortunately, little vegetation grew right up against the wall, so he was able to walk unimpeded as he ran his fingers along its surface. At times, he heard noises around him—slippery, stealthy noises.

In two minutes, he had covered fifty yards but had discovered no door. Blum did find a corner—a blessed, real-world corner, just like in real-world buildings where rats were rat-sized, and bugs were smaller than his fingers.

From time to time, he also heard heavy footsteps in the depths of the forest, and swore he even heard low, raspy breathing. Or was he only imagining it? Twice, Blum stopped and listened. He even turned around. But in the darkness he couldn't see a thing. He needed a light.

A lighter.

Blum felt in his trouser pocket. Yes. He still had his father's gold lighter with him. He pulled it out and felt its cold weight in his palm. He also remembered the utility knife in his back pocket. He would have preferred to have his gun, but that had been flung to hell when he'd fallen. He retrieved the knife and extended the half-inch blade. Pathetic, but better than nothing.

Not wanting to consume fuel until he was sure he would see something, Blum waited and listened. Nothing. No footsteps. He moved onward. By this point, his injured foot had grown numb, and he could hear the squish of oozing blood with each step. Still no doorway.

Repeatedly he fought the temptation to use the lighter to scan ahead, reminding himself that the light wouldn't project more than a few feet, and would waste fuel—fuel he may need to scare away an attack.

Blum stopped again to catch his breath. This time, he heard the footsteps come closer. Finally, unable to hold back any longer, Blum dialed up the flame control, snapped open the lid and spun the striker. The butane ignited a three-inch torch of yellow and blue.

It took an instant for his vision to adjust. Nothing—at least not at first. But then he saw two quarter-sized eyes glaring back at him, and he heard a deep, rasping growl. Blum clicked the lighter shut and ran along the wall, oblivious to the dangers he might stumble across.

Fifty yards ahead, he felt a break in the surface. He almost missed it at first, but something registered with his numb senses. He dug out the lighter and flicked it on. There in front of him stood a four-foot-wide, metal door. The edges fit tight against their frame. He spotted a lever-type release and gave it a yank, but the mechanism was locked on his side.

Blum heard twigs breaking behind him and knew that his attacker was dangerously close. Frantic, he crouched down and examined the latch itself. The door opened out, and he could see the bolt exposed between the door and the jamb. If he was lucky, he could use the utility knife to push it back into the door.

He panicked though when he realized that he would need two hands to slip the bolt and work the latch—nudging the bolt with the blade, then pulling on the door to prevent the sprung bolt from slipping while he moved the blade to press further. And he needed to repeat the process over and over until the latch was completely withdrawn.

Deciding to try to hold both the door and the lighter with his left hand, he shifted the burning lighter to it. The flame was visibly shrinking, and he knew the butane was running out. Grabbing the lever with his left hand, Blum tugged on it, being very careful not to drop the lighter. He heard footsteps behind him and turned quickly to look. The lighter fell to the ground and went out.

Blum dropped to his knees, patting the ground around him. He could hear precious butane escaping—valuable seconds of light gone. He heard a loud groan from the bushes. His hand closed on the lighter. He spun the striker, reigniting the flame, and immediately he heard heavy footsteps retreat back into the underbrush. But now he was almost out of fuel.

Blum put the end of the lighter in his mouth with the flame pointing out. Then he quickly tore off his shirt, held it out at arm's length, and lit it on fire, tossing it toward the bushes where he'd heard the noises. He immediately returned to working the latch.

After two or three movements—each one nudging the latch only a few millimeters—he noticed the fire was dying out for good this time. He had only seconds left, but now the door began to rock in its frame. Then the flame disappeared completely, and he heard the footsteps charge towards him.

36. NO PLACE TO HIDE

B lum dug at the latch. The bolt retracted. The door opened.
Light flooded in. Blum threw himself into the bare, ce-
ment-walled hallway beyond and slammed the door behind
him. He leaned back, utterly spent and barely able to remain upright.

As he stood there—half naked, bleeding, defenseless, and bathed
in the rays of fluorescent strip lighting—he shut his mind to the mon-
sters he'd left behind. Instead, he forced himself to focus on why he
was there. To find Tina. To stop the killings. To stop the nightmare.

He winced when he looked down at his shoe and saw the shred-
ded leather. The rat had torn out a section the size of a golf ball, and
he had no idea how much of his toe he'd lost with it. All he could
feel was a throbbing ache centered somewhere below his instep.

For now though, the solid, smooth cement felt good against his
bare back, and, all told, he had to consider himself lucky. The fall
could have killed him, or the rats, or whatever had been chasing
him through the darkness.

He surveyed the hallway where he stood. The fifteen-foot-wide
concrete floor extended at least a hundred feet in either direction
under a series of pastel-painted pipes and ventilation ducts that

hung from the tall ceiling. At the far end of the hall to his left he spotted two doors, so he limped down to the first one and felt the latch. It turned easily. Blum took a deep breath and eased the door out a crack, knowing it could be another entrance back into the bizarre greenhouse.

Peeking inside, he quickly realized it was only a closet, barren except for an unused trash can. Shutting that door, he checked the next one. It, too, was unlocked. It felt heavier than the previous one, and he heard a faint rush of air enter the room as the weather-stripping at its edges cleared the frame. He reached along the wall and found a light switch. Overhead fluorescent lights flickered on and lit up a narrow workroom with white counters, cabinets, walls, and floor tiles. To his left, he spotted a Corian counter with a few pieces of lab ware—a large Erlenmeyer flask, a row of gallon-sized plastic jugs with blank labels, and a pile of used blue nitrile gloves. And, for some strange reason, four cans of shaving cream.

Stepping up to the counter, he prodded one of the cans with his pinkie to test whether it was full or not. It rocked easily, and the lid rattled in place. Puzzled, he pushed it harder. The can tipped over, rolling toward the back wall. Along the way, the nozzle assembly spiraled out leaving an empty can.

Blum studied the nozzle. It was clearly more than a spray mechanism for shaving cream. A small, black-plastic box, half the size of a pack of gum, protruded toward what would have been the inside of the can, and from it extended a cigarette-sized glass tube filled with a white powder. Blum noticed a small push-button switch on the side of the box, and a set of two LEDs.

Seeing this, he guessed at how it would work. The glass tube contained some sort of explosive, and the black box looked like the control mechanism. At the right time and place, as determined by Lawson's computer programs, the control mechanism would trigger the charge and distribute the contents of the can. Blum didn't know a lot about explosives, but the small amount of material in the tube hardly seemed like enough to blow open the fuselage of a plane. Perhaps that was only a primer, though, and the contents of the can were the main charge. If the can were placed next to a container with the virus, the explosion would blast the deadly contents everywhere. That had to be it.

Not wanting to touch the device for fear of setting it off, Blum left it on the counter. He shut off the lights and stepped out of the room. He walked down the hallway in the other direction. When he got to the end, he found that the hall turned right at the end. Peering around the corner, he tried his best to make out details in the far shadows.

At one point, he thought he saw something move in the distance. Startled, he pulled back around the corner and listened. But then, as he stared at the tile wall opposite him, he began to see muddy patterns spinning and turning in front of his eyes. He was exhausted, he realized, and he knew he'd lost a good bit of blood. The pain in his foot was getting worse, and he was beginning to find it hard to balance without holding onto something. His vision was fuzzy too. He closed his eyes. It would be so easy to simply let go and collapse into sleep. He fought to focus his thoughts as he shook his head. When he opened his eyes again, the patterns disappeared.

He glanced around the corner one more time, and, seeing nothing, crept into the barely lit passage. The hallway stretched out for at least fifty yards with no doors on the right side, and Blum guessed he was traveling parallel to the greenhouse.

In time, he happened onto a door on his left and tried the knob. It turned. He opened it cautiously, and faint light spilled into the hallway. The air from the room smelled ghastly, as if a sewer had backed up, and Blum recoiled from the stench. He almost shut the door, but then, in the orange glow of an overhead light, he noticed a half-naked man propped against a pipe along the far wall of the dingy, cement cell. He could see a gag tied around the guy's slumping head—a scruffy mop of blond hair hiding his features.

Blum stepped into the room, and as he did, the man slowly looked up. At first the guy looked frightened, but then his unshaven face sagged into an expression of pain and bewilderment. Despite the growth of facial hair, and the covering of filth, Blum thought he recognized the face from the photograph in Beau Delaney's apartment.

"Hans Meier?"

The man nodded a painful "yes."

Blum walked over to Meier and ungagged him. Meier coughed and spat out a dark clot of blood and mucus. He tried to speak, but his throat wouldn't respond. He tried again, and when he couldn't for the second time, he began to cry. Blum looked on, helpless.

A moment later, Meier looked up at Blum. Then he motioned with a slight nod of his chin to his wire bindings. Blum untwisted the strands and released the arm. No longer supported by the pipe to which he'd been attached, Meier fell forward. Blum grabbed Meier's hand to help him up. It felt strangely cold and gelatinous. Then, without warning, the leathery gray skin Blum held slid off the end of Meier's arm, and the fetid liquid remains inside splattered to the floor. In shock, Blum dropped the glove-like cover of dead skin. As the rotted-meat smell engulfed him, he gagged.

Meier cried louder. He tried to sit up but succeeded only in rolling over on his back, the limp, lifeless arm staying trapped underneath. Blum pictured the black, rancid blood pumping back into Meier's weak body now that the bindings were released, spreading to Meier's organs—his heart and lungs—and sowing its poison. Blum knew Meier would not live much longer. Meier probably knew it too.

"Feldmann," Meier said softly. "Stop Feldmann. Told your father."

"That's why I'm here," Blum said. "I know about the airplanes."

"What . . . what do you know?" Meier asked, barely able to breathe.

"About the plan to blow up the planes."

"More."

"I know. He's trying to distribute some sort of virus that's going to kill millions of people. Six million. Isn't that right?"

"No. More . . ."

"How many more?"

"No . . . Don't understand . . . Six . . . million . . . live." Meier babbled something else, his eyes staring at nothing.

"I don't understand. Then who *dies*?"

Meier wasn't closing his eyelids at all anymore. Blum waved his hands in front of Meier's face but got no response. He heard Meier mutter something else. At first, Blum thought it was only a loud breath, but then he heard it again more distinctly. He bent down lower, wincing at the rotting fumes of breath that blew against his cheek.

"What is it? I can't hear you."

"All . . . the . . . others."

"Which others?"

"Everyone."

"Who is everyone?"

"Everyone but his kind," Meier said with a finality that shook Blum to the pit of his stomach.

Then, all at once, the words struck deep into Blum's subconscious, and a wave of overpowering fear and guilt engulfed him—a memory from the distant past, long since forgotten in a drunken haze, now came back to haunt him. He knew exactly what the plan was all about, and the implications beat him with their incriminations.

Suddenly, Meier turned his head toward Blum, and the dead, milky eyes pointed right at him. The face was a mask—human, but nearly lifeless. Meier seemed to take a long time inhaling his next breath. "Everyone," he moaned in a deep, windy baritone. And then he died.

Blum had never before witnessed a death in process. One moment, a life—a brain full of memories and plans, thoughts and ideas—and the next, only a cooling mass of water and cells. Blum nudged the heap in front of him but got no response. He stepped back and stared into the corner of the dim room.

He should have realized what was happening when Tina told him what she'd learned. The whole picture fit; the planes, Feldmann's research, Lawson's weather modeling, the Global Future Alliance. How could he stop it now? Kill Feldmann? Would that make any difference at this point? Someone else had the bombs already. He'd wasted so much time. He had to get back to Jason. Had to get away from the farm.

Blum backed out into the hall, shutting the door behind him. A shadow passed over his head. He turned. A fist smashed him squarely across his jaw, slamming his head against the concrete wall with a splintering crack that sent him to the floor in a crumpled heap.

37. PANGAEA REVEALED

SUNDAY, AUGUST 18

Glimmers of consciousness returned to Blum in shallow waves that ebbed and flowed; then, as his senses returned, the pain in his neck and head and swollen foot took hold and wrenched him fully awake. He lacked the strength to open his eyes, but he could feel rough hemp rope biting into the flesh across his shins and forearms and around his chest, binding him to some sort of chair.

He could feel his head resting heavily on his sweating chest, and he felt small drops of liquid—he couldn't tell if they were sweat or blood— drip from his nose to his belly and then dribble down to his waist. The air felt warm, but not hot, and it smelled clean in an artificial sort of way. The only sound he heard was his own breathing.

In time, Blum opened his eyes. The harsh light glared, forcing him to squint. He glanced down and was mildly relieved to see that the puddle in his lap was only sweat and drool. He realized that his tongue was protruding, and he withdrew it. He tried to swallow, but his parched throat refused. Too weak to raise his head, he rested.

After a few minutes, as he managed to focus his thoughts, he began to piece together exactly where he was. He remembered Meier's hand in his, the cold glove sliding from the black flesh and the spilled-oatmeal sound and nauseating stench as the rotting tissue hit the cement floor. He saw again the look of utter hopelessness on Meier's face. He also recalled leaving the room and shutting the door, then turning—and the crushing blow that had knocked him over.

Right then, perhaps in response to a movement of his, Blum heard someone behind him make an unintelligible comment and then clear his throat. The shock of not being alone gave Blum the energy to look up. He stared ahead at a bare wooden desk and, behind it, a wooden chair, and beyond that a blank cement wall. Someone stepped up to his side, but he didn't have the strength to turn and see who it was. A second later, the man walked in front of him, and he recognized Feldmann, dressed in a white lab coat. Feldmann stared at him for a moment, studying his face, then walked behind the desk and sat down.

"So," he said. "You are awake. I'm afraid my assistant hit you harder than he should have. Ah, well. No matter now." The professor folded his hands and seemed to make up his mind about something. "As I am sure you have already surmised, I am the man responsible for your father's death."

"I know," Blum said in a weak, scratchy voice.

"Of course. That's why you're here, no? But did you know that I'm also the man who killed your grandfather?"

Blum stiffened and sat up straighter. "My grandfather? The Russians—"

"That was the story, but, no, it was me."

Blum coughed. "How? You were only six."

"I shot him with my father's pistol."

"Why?"

"Because he recognized my father—knew who he really was." Feldmann looked at Blum for emphasis. "It's quite an interesting story. I'm sure you will be amazed." He studied Blum's face for a reaction. Blum just stared back dully.

"During the war," Feldmann began, "my father was a member of the Arrow Cross—the Hungarian Fascists. He was proud of that, even after fascism got to be a dirty word."

"But . . . you're Jewish."

The professor snorted. "I didn't, um, convert until later. But I'll get there. In 1945, he found himself temporarily assigned as a Hungarian translator for a German SS unit at a detainment camp right over the Austrian border. Your grandfather was the leader of a resistance group. He was boastful of that, as a matter of fact, but he refused to tell my father's team where they could find the rest of his band. They tortured your grandfather for over four hours. *Four hours!* I'm sure you've never been tortured, but, believe me, that's longer than you could possibly imagine." He let the sentence trail off and swept it away with the back of hand.

"But, in the end, he finally cracked—or so they thought. He told them about a location—a hidden attic in an old house in a village just across the river in Hungary. So they went and found the hiding place, but everyone was gone. Your grandfather must have known when they were leaving, and that's why he held out for so long—to give them time to escape." The professor shook his head in disbelief.

"By the time the team got back to the camp, your grandfather was gone. An order had come down to send a work detail to town to help with firefighting. Later, they got word that the building he was in had collapsed, and everyone was killed."

"But he didn't die there."

"No."

"So, then what?"

"Then what? Then everything. The Allies were close. Hitler was dead. The whole world was collapsing. My father knew the area would soon be overrun."

Blum looked down at the knots in his arms. On the left, the rope bit into his forearm, and his hand was turning grayish-blue from lack of blood, but, on the right side, the knot seemed a bit sloppy. He flexed his forearm and felt the tiniest bit of play. He looked back up at Feldmann to see if he had noticed, but the professor was too engrossed in his story. Besides, Blum judged, the edge of the desk appeared to hide his wrists from view.

"So, my father escaped to Budapest and lay low as the Red Army moved westward. When things settled down, he got married and had me and led a rather boring life—until 1956, when the Soviets returned in force. Afraid someone from the old days might turn him in to save himself, he decided we needed to leave Hungary. My mother was weak and scared, though, and she refused to go. So he grabbed me, his six-year-old son, and we traveled back to Szentgotthard, where he grew up, and made arrangements to cross into Austria."

"So," Blum said. "At least that part of your story was true."

"Yes," Feldmann said, frowning as if it would be absurd to question his facts. "Of course, that's the same town where your grandfather had lived, and, as events would reveal, still did. Apparently, he'd escaped from the burning building. But he spotted my father that night on the way to the dock and recognized him. I watched the two men fight. My father's gun fell from his belt." Feldmann tilted his head, reliving the memory. "So, I picked it up and shot your grandfather." He shrugged. "And then we went to the dock."

"Where my father was waiting."

"Yes. Exactly. And, after we crossed, my father spread a rumor that the Russians had killed your grandfather. It was what everyone wanted to believe, and so they did. And, claiming our name was Feldmann, he told everyone my mother had been Jewish and had been killed by the Russians as well. The Austrians went overboard for me after that—guilt, I guess. Two years later, we moved to Berlin, where I lived until things started to get crazy again. The Russians built the wall. Eichmann was on trial. My father thought I would be safer in America, so he arranged for me to be adopted by a Jewish family in Cleveland. Since it was my dead mother who was supposed to have been Jewish, I could feign ignorance, and my foster family was only too eager to teach me. Of course I didn't believe any of it, but it was fun to see how convincing I could be."

Blum wondered about Tina as he continued to work on his wrist binding. Was she still alive? "Spare me," Blum said. "Tell me what happened to my father."

"Of course," he said. "You deserve to know. Lawson met Meier while teaching a class. Meier was quite a prodigy, and they discovered that they both shared a common interest . . . if you know what I mean. Hoping he could count on Meier to be a dutiful little Aryan, Lawson told him a bit more than he should have. But instead of joining the winning side, Meier went running to your father. Apparently, he'd taken a course from him and knew you used to be a federal agent. Your father could have been a real threat, but he was stupid. Decided to be the hero. Hah! We'd followed Meier to your dad's house and guessed what was happening. We knew he was coming, so it was easy to have Lawson 'head him off at the pass,' as you Americans are fond of saying."

"The cops said it was a heart attack."

"The cops . . . Yes, well . . . Anyway, it was pretty simple for Lawson to get your father to pull over to the side of the road and give him an injection of an agent I developed. In large doses, it causes almost immediate cardiac shock, and, because it's biological and not pharmacological, it doesn't show up on a standard tox screen. It's really an amazing creation. With smaller doses, it's a lot messier, though. It can take up to three days for the infection to kill you. No symptoms, and then POW! Horrible headaches, vomiting, dizziness. Looks a lot like food poisoning. But we weren't going to do that to your father. We're not cruel. It's simply that the world is on the brink of an irreversible crisis, and something needs to be done. Timing right now is critical. We've waited years for the weather patterns to align. They may not repeat again before it's too late. We couldn't afford even a week's delay. It was his fault really—for interfering. You must realize that."

Blum spat in contempt.

Instead of being upset, Feldmann just shrugged. "We did what we had to. Nothing can stop us."

"But why?"

Feldmann turned and stared directly into Blum's eyes. "Survival."

"Whose survival? Yours?"

"Mankind!" Feldmann said, as if it were self-explanatory. "Before it's too late."

"Is this where I get the speech about Aryan superiority?"

"Not at all. Let me tell you something. It's not about one group of people being better than another, but it is about differences and conflicts. Yes, I was raised on a diet of anti-Semitism, and then I had to learn to hide it when I moved to America. But, over time, I realized I had been fed a lie. Among themselves, the people in the Jewish community lived fine—they supported each other and existed in relative harmony, just as the people I had known in Hungary and Austria and Germany. In time, I came to realize that it's at the boundaries—where cultures and religions and races meet—where conflict arises."

Blum used every opportunity when Feldmann looked away to flex and relax his right forearm, turning it slightly each time—trying to gain some play in the ropes. He could feel the utility knife in his back pocket. If he could only get his right hand free, he could use the knife to cut the remaining ropes.

"Malthus had it wrong. We will always be able to produce enough food. That isn't the problem. What will ultimately destroy the human race, if we don't reverse course, is disease, lack of water, and, ultimately, violent conflict. As the population of the world grows and people are forced closer and closer, the problem gets worse. Yes, they find some diversity interesting, even fascinating for a while. But, deep down, people are quite naturally suspicious, even afraid, of other people that are too different. In today's society, those who don't understand the big picture label this very natural reaction as prejudice and racism."

Feldmann rubbed his chin. "The only way to eliminate conflict is to eliminate the collision of those differences—let people who are homogenous remain that way, separate and free of conflict—the way people lived for millions of years, until, due to overpopulation, they were forced to live together—to fight for survival."

Feldmann stared at Blum earnestly, and Blum could tell that Feldmann desperately wanted him to agree. When Blum only stared back stone-faced, Feldmann seemed to search for another way to explain the point.

"You don't understand, do you? Even though the goal that is so entrenched in our very nature—ensuring the survival of our species—has not changed, the world has. Survival of the individual has become too easy, and, as a consequence, the world population has exploded to the point where the biggest threat to human existence is that very success. This new situation requires new rules. Survival of the species today means that we must be willing to sacrifice individuals."

Blum strained one more time and was finally able to withdraw his right wrist from one of the loops holding him to the arm of the chair.

With the extra slack that provided, the rest of the loops slid off easily.

"I know that idea offends your sense of morality," Feldmann said. "But let me tell you something. Despite what you think, there's no such thing as 'right' and 'wrong.' Morals are nothing more than social DNA that has evolved over millions of years to protect mankind. Survival of the species used to mean protecting every individual, so people learned to settle their disputes without violence. Those sorts of 'Thou shalt not kill' principles got written down and taken for, um, gospel. And ever since then, people have been raised on a diet of those rules, and they take them as absolute truths. They've never questioned their basis. Never considered the need to revise them."

Blum nodded. He needed to keep Feldmann talking to give himself a chance to retrieve the utility knife. "And you have, I suppose?"

"Many have. It's not just my opinion. It's simply a conclusion anyone reaches if they look at it logically—without the baggage of a bunch of acquired emotions."

"And you think that justifies killing how many millions—*billions*?"

"We're not going to kill anyone," Feldmann said with a conspiratorial wink. "Yes, well, perhaps a few, but that can't be avoided."

"But . . . all those planes . . ."

"What about them?"

"The bombs. You're going to—"

"Ah," Feldmann said. "So your father *did* talk to you before he died. Ah well, it's of no consequence now. The wheels are turning. The devices are on their way. In only a few days, it will be done."

Blum had grown up in an academic family. He knew that "publish or perish" was more than just an employment reality—it was a religion. He sensed Feldmann was burning to finally "publish" his great accomplishment, even to an audience of one, and the longer Feldmann kept talking, the more likely Blum was to get a chance to cut himself free. "I don't understand," Blum said. "How could that be?"

"Actually, we began by discussing the option of simply culling most of the world's population, but it was rejected because it quickly became clear the system couldn't possibly absorb the immediate consequences of all that death. The world would break down into physical and political anarchy. So, I embarked on a different course of study. And then, fifteen years ago, I achieved the breakthrough that made it possible to accomplish our goals without the need to actually kill anyone."

"Death without dying?"

Feldmann raised his eyebrows with pride. "Yes, actually. I found a way to use a specially constructed SCAA virus to render men and women sterile by creating a variation of something called a repro-five mutation. It took me years to determine what that DNA sequence needed to be and how it could be delivered intact." Feldmann nodded in a moment of self-congratulation. "My greatest accomplishment. And by using infertility, I eliminated the issue of mass death. My plan achieves the same ultimate goal, but it's much more elegant."

Feldmann looked back at Blum. "Dispersal was an issue. We initially tested detonating bombs in luggage, but the heat and shock of the blast tended to kill the viruses, and after 9/11, security became much too tight. Then we discovered a simpler method that's actually much more effective. You see, in an airliner, fresh air enters the cabin, passes through it, and then is sucked down into the luggage compartment. After it passes through there, half of that is expelled to the atmosphere. Using a low-yield propellant, one that isn't easily detected, we simply burst the canisters in the luggage compartment and let the cabin exhaust system do the rest—spreading our virus to the four winds for global distribution. A few people catch a mild case of the flu, but that's all anyone notices."

Feldmann suddenly turned to Blum, raising his hand for

emphasis. "Picture it. At first, nothing happens. Life goes on. People grow up. People get married. People go to work. People live out their lives, get old, die and are buried according to their customs. Everything as before, except, no babies. And that's the wonder of it all. No sudden deaths. No pile of bodies to dispose of."

Of course, Blum thought. *Everyone buries their own.*

"We grew the virus in maturing rats. They make a good host, and the rats are not affected. We kept them growing beyond a normal size to increase the efficiency of the process—hence our little menagerie upstairs."

"And the roaches?"

"An early test of the concept—and a good food supply for the rats." Feldmann spent a moment to gloat silently at his accomplishments. "Of course, the other essential requirement was that we have a way to provide immunity to the right people—the 'chosen ones'—who need to survive. We were able to do that with a slightly altered form of the primary virus—an inoculation of sorts—that prevents corruption of the fertility genomes in those infected."

An infection of salvation.

"Those people were selected carefully to ensure a high degree of homogeneity—of race, religion and culture. The big question was how many people would be needed. We brought together some of the greatest minds in the world to figure it out—experts in their fields— to explore the implications for human survival, preserving vital infrastructure in key areas, maintaining political and social order."

The Global Future Alliance, and their special sessions.

"The answer turned out to be a surprisingly small number of people—only about six million or so, at least at first. By the time the transformation is complete, there will be more of them of course."

Six million chosen.

"After a few years, the effects will begin to be noticed. At first there will be reports of severe drop-offs in birth rates around the world. 'Experts' will be called in. They'll do tests. They'll look for environmental factors—pollution, pesticides, or defective medicine. A few well-placed journal articles from us will keep the world busy following dead-ends. They won't find anything to explain the phenomenon. More tests. By the time the cause is discovered, it will be too late. And then, forty or fifty years from now, like passing a hard stool, there will be a brief period of pain, and then it will all be over."

Blum was still waiting for Feldmann to turn away so he could get the chance to grab the knife and free his other wrist.

"And then, like a bank with its doors open and no one around, the whole world will be ours. *The whole world!* The Amazon will regrow. Animals will repopulate Africa. Air pollution will disperse. Everyone will live healthy, well-fed lives. With the population reduced, the spread of disease will diminish. The world will be like a child again—young and innocent, with hope and anticipation. Like Pangaea once more, it will be a new beginning for the world. A chance to start over. A chance to do it right. Won't that be amazing?"

Feldmann was now raving uncontrollably—not actually expecting a real reaction. His glare was directed at the heavens, and his fist pounded on the desk. Blum used the opportunity to reach inside his back pocket and retrieve the utility knife. Concealing it in his palm, he slid his hand under a loose loop of rope as if it were still tied.

"We will achieve what others have attempted, but failed," the professor bellowed. "Humans can't live packed together like rats. They need room to live."

"*Lebensraum*," Blum said grimly.

Feldmann frowned. "Don't say it with such contempt . . . such *superiority*. *Lebensraum* might be a word the Nazis invented, but the concept was pioneered right here in North America long before anyone had heard of National Socialism."

"What the hell are you talking about?"

"Don't forget that when the European settlers came here four hundred years ago, this continent was already populated with millions of indigenous people. At first, you were content just to trade with them for bits of land, but soon you realized that you needed more room to expand. Your economy and your survival depended on it. And so you took the land from them, at first in bits and pieces, but later in great swathes. You systematically killed off their food supply and waged wars against them, and you forced them into exile farther and farther to the west until, when there was no more room, you rounded them up and herded them into *de facto* concentration camps—'reservations.' You anointed the program 'Manifest Destiny'—told people it was God's will that they take the land. And its great proponent, Andrew Jackson, is commemorated on your twenty-dollar bill."

Feldmann's voice turned to scorn. "And then you self-righteous Americans dared to look down your noses at the Nazis. You cried, 'No fair,' when someone else was doing it, when the only difference was that *you* got away with it. And your country was better for it." Feldmann glared at Blum. "What? No quick retort?"

Before Blum could even respond, he heard a door behind him fly open, and a winded voice spat out, "Jerry's dead."

38. THE MAN FROM HEADQUARTERS

"What do you mean, he's *dead?*" Feldmann glanced over Blum's shoulder at the intruder, looking puzzled, but not concerned.

"Just what I fucking said." Lawson stepped into view. "I just found his body in the filing room. Shot."

"He's not even supposed to be down here," Feldmann said.

Both men looked at Blum, and it occurred to him they thought he had done it. "I don't have a gun," Blum responded quickly.

"You could have hidden it," Lawson said.

"Why would I do that?" Blum asked. Lawson eyed Feldmann, waiting to hear his response.

"There must be some other explanation," Feldmann said. "We're the only people here."

Blum remembered what Tina had told him about Lawson's paranoia. "That's right, Victor. You two *are* the only people here . . . now that Jerry's dead. So, if you didn't do it . . ." Blum let his words trail off as he shook his head.

"Don't be stupid," Feldmann said. "There must be some

reasonable explanation. Are you sure he was shot? He didn't fall and hurt himself?"

"I saw the fucking bullet holes," Lawson exclaimed.

"Your work's done," Blum said to Lawson, who stood with his back to Feldmann, biting at his thumbnail. "Besides, I'm not sure where you fit in any more. You know—not being 'one of them,' that is. One of the chosen ones."

Lawson sniffed loudly as Blum continued, turning his gaze to Feldmann. "You must have told him, right? About his real father—his biological father? The Indian—Michael Wolf."

"That's crazy. You're lying," Lawson growled.

It struck Blum that Lawson didn't seem as surprised by the allegation as he should be. He recalled what Kay had told him. "I've *seen* your birth certificate and read the articles about your adoption," Blum said.

Lawson turned his head and looked at Feldmann. "He's lying. I'm . . . My mother would never . . ."

"Alright!" Feldmann barked. "Enough of this! He's talking nonsense. For God's sake, Victor, back off! Sometimes, I swear, you're like a little—"

Blum saw Lawson's jaw clench and his fists ball. "A little *what?*" he yelled over his shoulder to Feldmann while continuing to glare at Blum. "A little kid? That's how you used to describe Jerry, right? So, why did you kill him?"

Blum didn't wait for Feldmann to respond. He stared into Lawson's glaring eyes. "You're next, you know."

Obviously trying to quell Lawson's rage, Feldmann reached out and put his hand on Lawson's shoulder. "He's simply—"

That was it. Lawson's nostrils flared, and he erupted, pivoting quickly and swinging his right arm, smashing Feldmann's nose with the ball of his monstrous hand. "Don't ever fucking touch me!" he bellowed.

Feldmann stumbled, falling backward into the desk chair. Lawson turned and rounded the desk, diving for Feldmann's neck. Feldmann, moving faster than Blum thought he could, yanked open a desk drawer. Blum was shocked to see Lawson freeze, then back up. As Lawson retreated, Feldmann lifted his arm, and Blum saw a gun in his hand—a Colt M1911 .45 caliber.

"Now, back off!" Feldmann ordered. "This is nonsense. Enough!"

"Tell me what the fuck is going on," Lawson demanded. It sounded more like a plea than an order.

Blum watched Feldmann's grip on the pistol. It was not uncommon for a scared person to accidentally fire a gun, especially a single-action pistol like the Colt. But the hammer was down.

My God, Blum realized, Feldmann didn't seem to notice he still had to cock the hammer, and perhaps even cycle the slide, before he could fire the gun.

Feldmann glared at Lawson, who stared back at the pistol.

"Nothing's changed," Feldmann said. "Don't be so easily manipulated."

"Of course he'd say that, but you know very well he's going to kill you next," Blum said, knowing his only chance at escape was to keep Lawson enraged. "And probably your mother as well. He doesn't want people like you around. Just like your birth father . . ."

"Shut up!" Feldmann ordered Blum.

"You bastard!" Lawson yelled. "After all I've done for you." He raised his fist.

Feldmann lifted the gun. His knuckles turned white for a second, then again. He looked puzzled and glanced at the pistol. Lawson seized the opportunity. He lunged at Feldmann and grabbed the old man's throat. Feldmann took a swipe with the heavy pistol at Lawson's wrists, but his arm was too short to reach Lawson's face. Feldmann dropped the Colt and gripped Lawson's forearm.

The gun clattered to the floor by Blum's feet. Blum yanked his right arm free and leaned forward, stretching as far as he could to get to the weapon, but it lay a few inches out of reach. He slid out the blade on the utility knife and hacked away at the ropes on his left wrist, finally managing to cut it loose. He heaved forward again, but, even with both arms free, he just couldn't reach the pistol.

Lawson, now clutching Feldmann by the neck, pushed his thumbs into the old man's larynx, causing Feldmann's face to turn a brilliant shade of crimson. The old man's tongue hung halfway out of his open mouth, but his eyes, still alert, glared fiercely at Lawson. As Lawson pulled Feldmann toward him, Feldmann's hands managed to reach the other man's face. Protecting his eyes, Lawson tucked his chin down as Feldmann clawed at Lawson's scalp. After three frantic swipes, Feldmann succeeded in grabbing a handful of black curls and pulled, tearing off a patch of hair still attached to a flap of flesh.

In desperation, Blum gripped the edge of the desk with both hands and threw the chair he was tied to over to the right. His shoulder hit the floor, trapping himself under his own weight. With all the strength he had left, he pushed up and tipped himself on his back. His feet, still tied to the legs of the chair, now pointed at the fighting men. Feldmann was waving a wad of Lawson's scalp in his hand, and blood ran from Lawson's head where it had been attached.

Frantically, Blum felt around for the Colt but couldn't find it. Finally, realizing that his head was resting on it, he reached back and grabbed the gun. Betting that the magazine was full, Blum worked the slide. A fresh shell ejected onto the floor. Feldmann had been only a hammer-pull away from saving his own life.

Blum pointed the gun at the tangle of snarling men—unable to maintain aim on either one—and pulled the trigger. The explosion deadened all sound. Both men stopped moving. Blum waited, unable to breath. A moment later, Lawson appeared to step back from Feldmann, but then the giant man slumped to his knees and crumbled to the floor. Blood streamed from his chest right below his shirt pocket. Feldmann turned to Blum in shock.

"Get back against the wall!" Blum yelled, barely able to hear his own words over the ringing in his ears.

Feldmann backed up with his hands massaging his neck. He was trying to say something, but his throat wouldn't respond. Blum, keeping the pistol on Feldmann, cut his chest and ankles free, pushed himself back off the chair, and sat up on the floor. As he managed to climb to a kneeling position and then stand up, he fought to close his mind to the fact that he had just killed someone.

"Where is Tina?" he demanded.

Feldmann squinted. The question obviously surprised him, and Blum realized that Feldmann had never made the connection.

"She's with me," Blum explained. "Is she still alive?"

"We can deal," Feldmann said weakly. "She's okay."

"Where?"

"Right upstairs. I can show you."

Feldmann started to walk toward Blum. Blum kicked the chair forward, hitting Feldmann in the shins. He raised the gun and aimed it at Feldmann's nose. The old man closed his eyes. All the anger Blum had felt over the past two weeks flooded over him. He thought about his father lying in his car, dying of a heart attack because of Feldmann. He thought about Kay, no doubt chased down and killed for Feldmann. He leveled the gun and gripped his right wrist with his left hand to steady his aim. He hoped the flash wouldn't obscure the image of Feldmann's head exploding backward against the wall. He knew that a .45 was a slow bullet. He'd heard you could even see it coming toward you like some awful, deadly insect. That would be good. He hoped Feldmann *would* see it. He decided to wait for Feldmann to open his eyes.

But then he reconsidered. Acting out of anger was wrong. He'd killed Lawson, but only in self-defense. Feldmann was no longer a threat. No need to kill him. You're not an assassin, Blum told himself. If you shoot him now, you're no better than he is.

Feldmann seemed to sense Blum's change of mind and opened his eyes. He looked more confident.

"Take me to Tina!" Blum ordered. He kept the gun pointed at Feldmann.

Feldmann stepped toward the door, and Blum backed off to the side to keep a safe distance. Feldmann paused with his hand on the knob. "We can make a deal. I mean, think about it—you had the same idea. You clearly understand why this is the right thing to do. What we're doing isn't even cruel like what you suggested. You must see that this is the only answer."

Blum sneered. "You don't give up, do you?" He lifted the gun a little higher. "We've tracked your packages on their way to Wichita. They're not going to make it onto those airliners. It's over."

Feldmann turned to face the door. His shoulders slumped. "God in Heaven! Do you realize what you've done? Mankind is self-destructing. Operation Pangaea is its last hope for survival."

"Shut up and show me where Tina is."

Before Feldmann could utter a sound, the door flew open, knocking him back toward Blum. A piercing yellow flash from the hallway lit the room, and Blum heard a loud *Foomp!* Feldmann's head jerked sideways as if suddenly looking away from the flash, but then Blum noticed a small, black hole in Feldmann's forehead, like a third eye. A stream of blood flowed down to his chin. Feldmann's body sagged, and then crumpled to the floor.

The door opened wider, and Blum faced a young man with blond hair, dressed in a blue windbreaker and holding a silenced pistol. Caught by surprise, Blum dropped the Colt and started to put his hands up. Then he realized—of course—Jason had sent his men into the farm after all. And that meant Kay had escaped. She was alive. He breathed a sigh of relief.

"Who are you?" the man demanded.

"It's alright," Blum said. "I'm with you. Lawson caught Tina in Feldmann's office and brought her here. I followed them. Lawson's dead. I shot him. They caught me and were about to kill me."

The man nodded and grunted. "Boss should have told me to expect you. Typical fuck up." He motioned to the gun on the floor, indicating it was okay for Blum to pick it up. "I guess we're done here for now," he said, sounding rather indifferent to what had just happened. "I shot the housekeeper earlier."

"Oh?" The silenced pistol explained why he hadn't heard the shot.

"Sure. He could've been trouble."

Blum was taken aback by the man's callousness, but assumed that cynicism must become a natural defense in his business.

"Well, let's get going then," the stranger added. "Nothing else is going to happen here tonight."

"What about Tina."

"What about her?"

"We have to find her. We can't just leave her here."

The guy shrugged. "Sure. You know where she is?"

"Feldmann said something about right upstairs. Follow me." Blum didn't wait for the man to respond and walked past him into the hall. He glanced down the corridor to his left and spotted a concrete stairway. He hobbled toward it, hearing the other guy following a close distance behind.

The door at the top of the short flight led to a hall with a tile floor. Blum could see a door at the far end, as well as two more doors along the left wall. He tried the first knob on the left. The door opened to a brightly lit, white-tiled bathroom. Tina crouched, huddled in the corner and strapped to the sink pipes with leather belts at her ankles and wrists. Blood dripped from her dark hair, and Blum noticed slash marks down her naked back. Her jeans were dirty and sticky with blood as well. She turned toward him when she heard him enter—her eyes scared but alert.

She looked at him in disbelief, but then her face relaxed into an expression of utter relief as she recognized him. Blum stepped toward her, letting the door spring closed behind him, leaving Jason's man in the hall.

"It's okay," he told her. "Jason has sent someone in. Feldmann and Lawson are dead. Let's get you out of here." He knelt down and untied her bindings. "Will you be able to walk?"

She turned to him, tears in her eyes, and hugged him. "I'm sorry," she sobbed. "I should have been more careful."

Blum wanted to give her something to cover her nakedness, but he didn't even have his own shirt. Deciding to ask the cold bastard in the hall for his jacket, he stood up and turned around, but, as he reached for the handle, the door opened. The blond guy stuck his head in, looking impatient.

Blum turned and smiled at Tina to reassure her, but she looked shocked. She shook her head. Blum turned back to the doorway.

The man frowned. "Look. Just shoot her and let's get out of here. I want to get some shut-eye before we clear out tomorrow."

Blum's stomach wrenched. The gunman wasn't sent by Jason—he was the assassin sent by Zurich to kill Feldmann and Lawson. Any second, he'd see Tina untied and realize Blum wasn't who he thought. And he was still holding his gun!

"Of course," Blum said, thinking fast and trying to keep his voice from wavering.

He lifted his gun and pointed it at Tina. He had no idea how many shells had been in the magazine, but he took his chances. He spun to his left and pulled the trigger twice. Tina screamed. The man fell forwards, slamming the door shut. Blum kicked it open, but it hit the man's body and bounced shut again. Blum put his weight into it, pushing the body out of the way. When there was enough room, he squirmed through the gap and pointed his gun at the man again. No need. The guy was lying still, face-up in a widening pool of blood.

"He's dead," Blum called to Tina. His ears numb, he could barely hear the words himself.

He took her hand and led her from the room. She stumbled, and he put his arm under hers. They limped down the hallway to the large door at the end. Blum opened it, and a rush of fresh air swept in. Stepping outside, he could hear crickets singing in the bushes, and, overhead where the clouds were breaking up, he could see stars. The air had turned cooler, but refreshing, and it felt glorious to be outside again after what seemed like an eternity in captivity.

"Do you know where the Mercedes is?" she asked him.

"It's no use to us. I let the air out of one of the tires. It can't go anywhere."

"No. The thumb drive. I hid it in the trunk where Lawson locked me. I didn't want them to find it on me."

"So, you *did* get a copy."

"Yeah. Lawson caught me right after I put the original back."

"It's this way," Blum told her, leading her to the far side of the old farmhouse.

Tina followed him across the wet grass, arms crossed over her naked breasts. When they reached the black sedan, she stepped past him and leaned into the still-open trunk. As she bent over, the skin across her back stretched, reopening one of the gashes, and it began to ooze blood.

"I've got it," Tina said through the pain. "Let's call Jason."

Blum smashed the front-door window of Feldmann's house and opened the latch from the inside. While Tina searched for a phone to call Jason, Blum limped around, making a quick search of the house to ensure they were alone. In the process, he managed to find a shirt for himself and a sweater for Tina. When he returned, Tina was sitting at the kitchen counter holding the receiver. He handed her the sweater.

"The phone line is dead," she told him, hanging up. She slipped on the sweater, wincing as the heavy knit grazed her lacerated back; but then she pulled it over her head and down across her bare torso. "What now?"

"I don't know," Blum said. "I guess we'll have to walk to the next farm." As he said it, he began to wonder if either of them could actually make it that far. At this point, he found it hard to stand up, and he knew it was possible that Tina could be in worse shape than he was. But it was their only hope. Certainly, after all they'd been through, they couldn't give up with only a mile's walk to go.

Blum spotted a six-volt lantern by the back door. He clicked the switch, and was glad to see it light. "Alright then," he said, trying to sound reassuring. "Let's go. It's already getting light. It won't seem that bad once we get moving."

Tina nodded and stood up. The two walked outside and started around the house to the front drive, but, as they cleared the corner by the car, Blum spotted headlights approaching the distant gate. The vehicle stopped outside, and Blum heard a rattling followed by a few loud cracks. He pulled Tina to the ground behind a low hedge.

"Let's see who it is," he told her. "Maybe we can steal the car if they come in."

A minute later, Blum watched the vehicle pull into the drive and head toward them, but now that he was crouched on the ground, he felt his head swimming. His vision blurred again, and he could barely hold his chin up. He tried to shake it off, but the specter of sleep tugged at his consciousness.

What seemed like a second later, he realized that he'd nodded off because Tina was now standing over him. Two men with submachine guns stood next to her. He remembered his gun and tried to lift his hand, but he didn't have the strength. Then he heard Tina telling him it was okay. Blum looked up. It was Carlo. And Ezra. He slumped to the ground.

Blum awoke once more, finding himself propped up against the rear window in the back of a panel-van, feeling it bounce down the front drive of the farm toward the gate. There were a number of people in the van, but he couldn't see well enough in the unlit interior to recognize any of them. Looking out the window, he saw a brilliant flash of light. His eyes cleared. The concussion hit the van and rocked it. The giant greenhouse lit up in flames. Then the walls collapsed, and the glass roof fell into the center of the inferno. A second later, Feldmann's house exploded as well.

Soft hands squeezed his arm. "It's okay," Tina whispered into his ear. "We're safe. Close your eyes and go to sleep."

39. AFTER THE STORM

D avid Blum dreamed he was swimming in a large tank of warm water. Above him, blurred images of people stared down at him, waiting for him to surface. He was aware that he'd been holding his breath for an awfully long time, but it neither surprised nor concerned him because he knew it was only a dream. Eventually, he would have to come up for air, but for now, he felt comfortable and safe, surrounded and protected by the giant womb of the pool.

Blum stayed in this state for some time—knowing he was unconscious but not wanting to wake up. In fact, it wasn't until much later when one of the people seemed to reach into the water, and he swatted to send the hand back, that he finally emerged from his coma.

A nurse—a big, brawny woman—was wrestling his arms back down to the bed. Blum let out a string of obscenities and, in his stupor, was vaguely aware of them being answered in kind.

As his senses cleared, he realized he was lying in a hospital bed. He could smell alcohol and clean linen, and from a loudspeaker in the ceiling piped the typical background paging noises of a hospital. "RN1, please call Two North. RN1, please call two-seven-eight-one."

Realizing that he was now fully awake, the nurse let go of his arms.

"Where am I?" he asked. His last memory was bouncing around in the back of a van.

"You're in Barnhardt Hospital. You've been under for some time."

"How long?"

"Well, you were admitted early yesterday morning. Sunday. It's Monday afternoon now."

"How did I get here?"

"Your uncle brought you in. He's been waiting outside, off and on, that is, for you to wake up. Very busy man, apparently." She smiled at him. "You're lucky he found you under that tractor when he did."

Tractor? Then it hit him. Jason must have given the hospital that story to explain his injuries. "How am I?" he asked.

"Well, you've lost a lot of blood, and it looks like you lost part of your big toe, but the ER doc thinks it should heal well enough not to be a permanent issue. You'll need crutches for a while, and it might be a month or two before you're tap-dancing again." She scanned his chart. "I think they'll take you off the IV later today. Then, if the doctor says it's okay, you should be released tomorrow."

"Can I see my uncle now?" Blum asked. He caught himself before he said "Uncle Jason" in case Jason had told them a different name.

"Sure. I think he's still out there. But take it easy. If you start to feel weak, just tell him you need to rest. He can come back again after dinner."

"Okay."

The nurse smiled and left the room as hundreds of unanswered questions flooded Blum's thoughts. Overall though, he felt profoundly relieved. He remembered the drive away from the farm, and he knew that Kay must have somehow survived the chase and made it to Jason. Blum wondered how the two of them had gotten along.

The door to his room opened, and in walked an exhausted but confident-looking Jason. He nodded, then closed the door and walked over to David's bed, sitting in the upholstered chair next to it.

"So, David, how do you feel?"

"I've been better," Blum replied.

"So have I," Jason said seriously. "You must have a whole host of questions, but first let me tell you what I can about what's happened, starting with Tina. She is okay. She was beaten rather badly, but otherwise not seriously injured. After some stitches, she went home to recover. She waited in town till this morning to see you, but, since it could have been days before you woke up, she flew on to Brussels this afternoon."

Blum thought again about the wounds he'd seen on her back, and he realized that Tina must have been tortured for hours. Like his grandfather, somehow she hadn't broken.

Jason shifted to a more comfortable position in his chair. "The storms Saturday diverted the plane to the south, so our operatives made it to Wichita in time and ambushed the two men when they pulled into a private hangar. After we confirmed the bombs were still on board, we handcuffed the pilots to the plane and notified the FBI. We warned them about the contents, and they took care of the rest. In case there was a backup plan in place, baggage on international flights is being specially searched, and the routes have been changed for a while to avoid flying near the GPS locations that would trigger release. A giant mess for international travel, but best to be safe, n'es pas?"

"What about the farm? The greenhouse?"

"Completely destroyed. The official word is that the buildings were leveled by a tornado, and that propane lines were severed, setting off the explosions. The press is accepting it. Feldmann didn't seem to have any close friends, and anyone in the area that would know any different is either dead or not talking. There *were* some reports of people seeing strange animals, but those rumors have been around for years, so no one is paying any attention to them. Oh, and Albert Krieger, Feldmann's controller, has unfortunately fled. We intercepted a message that he's in the Netherlands, but DHS has no record of anyone named Krieger leaving the country legitimately. He may be traveling under a false identity. Or, perhaps, Krieger was only an alias." Jason shrugged.

"How is Kay?" Blum cut in. He was dying to know. Blum was surprised Jason hadn't mentioned her yet.

"Who?"

Blum turned cold. "Kay. Kay Westfield."

"Who's she?"

"She must have talked to you Saturday night. I sent her to you to get help."

"I've never heard of her. No one came to me Saturday."

Blum told Jason a brief account of what had happened, including the part about the car chase. He wondered if Jason would be angry with him for having given Kay his address.

"That's all very interesting," he said without concern. "And it does explain a few things."

"Like what?"

"Shortly after Lawson returned to the farm, Carlo and Zeke were on patrol and spotted a sports car driving away. Thinking it might be trouble, they tried to follow it. The driver got scared and tried to outrun a freight train at a crossing. At first, they thought the train had hit the car, destroying it, but then they saw that it had merely clipped the back end and knocked the car off the road on the far side of the crossing. They saw a young woman—it must have been your friend—and concluded it was only a teenager out hot-rodding."

"What happened to her? Did they just leave her there?"

"Oh, no. While they waited for the train to pass, a marked police car approached on the far side of the tracks. They backed off, not wanting to get involved and figuring that the situation was under control. They called in a report, but we didn't think it had any connection to Feldmann. You were supposed to be in Urbana. I never guessed it was *your* car."

"Did Carlo say whether she was okay?"

"They told me they didn't see her move while they were there. I guess that's not what you wanted to hear."

Blum's heart sank. "So what *did* make you move in if it wasn't her message?"

"When Tina never reported in and you didn't return, we decided to launch an early morning raid. We set up thermal and audio surveillance—parabolic and linear-phase microphones—from the fence to try to figure out how many people were there and where. Shortly before sunrise, we heard gunshots. Figuring Feldmann had been killed by the assassin Zurich had sent, we moved in immediately. That's when we found you and Tina."

"So you have no idea what happened to Kay?"

"None at all."

"You're not worried that she has your address?"

"Everyone else has left town already. I'm on my way to the airport, and my house is cleaned out, as is Tina's apartment." Jason shrugged. "What do you think she would tell the police?"

"I made it clear to her that she should only talk to you."

"Let's hope so. I guess you'll simply have to hold your breath on this one. After all, you two are the ones who would be at risk at this point."

"If I can't reach her, I'll have to call the police," Blum said. "I'll be circumspect."

"Be careful. As far as the authorities are concerned, all the dead bodies have been explained, so you're in the clear. It wouldn't be good to go poking." Jason looked at his watch, then back at Blum. "David, I don't have much more time if I'm to make it to my flight, and I need to talk to you about your future."

"My future?"

"Yes. You proved yourself admirably the other night. Tina told me what you went through. *Mon Dieu!* Quite an ordeal. Anyway, you're clearly capable, and now I'm sure you must have some of the fire in you that keeps us motivated." He paused, looking at David seriously. "I want you to come work for us."

"I don't know."

"Why not? You don't think Feldmann was the last of his kind, do you? What about his controller, Krieger? Wouldn't you like to track him down? Bring him in?"

"Before you give me the full recruiting speech, there's something I should probably tell you. It may change your mind."

"What's that?" Jason asked, leaning closer and taking on a slightly cool demeanor.

"The big plan—Feldmann's big idea—reducing the population to clear out the world. Starting over again with just a few people . . ."

"I don't understand."

"Years ago, when I was only eighteen or nineteen, my father had Feldmann over for dinner. We all had a bit too much wine to drink. We got to talking. Crazy shit. You know, how to solve all the world's problems. Feldmann went on a tear about how overpopulation was ultimately going to kill off the human race by a combination of resource depletion, pollution, disease and, ultimately, internecine warfare. I was only a teenager, and you know how they can be— they think they've got the whole world figured out. Well, I threw out there, as a joke really, that if we could eliminate people—most of them, that is—then the ones that were left could sort of start over, like thousands of years ago, but with what we know now about technology and medicine and so forth. I only meant it to sound absurd. Anyway, after he left, my dad gave me a stern lecture on all the horrors that human beings have unleashed on each other when they put aside their sense of humanity in the name of 'common sense.' I hadn't put the pieces together until Meier told me what was going on."

"So? From all you've told me, those guys were headed down a path like that long before that dinner. You don't hold yourself responsible, do you?"

"No. That's not what's bothering me. It's this—when Feldmann took me through his justification, especially the 'We're going to save humanity without killing anyone' part, I have to admit it made sense to me. I *still* see the logic in all that. I mean, I know in my gut that it's wrong, but *why* exactly, I can't say. And it sounds kind of lame to just say, 'It's wrong.' It *makes* rational sense. So where's the flaw in his argument? And, if I can't see it myself, what does that say about me?"

"There's no flaw in his reasoning," Jason said bluntly. "But you said it yourself—you *know* it's wrong. You can't prove that with all the logic in the world. You simply know it. Feldmann was the consummate soulless scientist—all brain and no heart. And Lawson, for that matter, was just like him—all scripture but no soul—no empathy. Neither one could tell right from wrong despite convincing themselves that they had all the answers. Both were blinded by their own certainty—Feldmann in his facts and logic, and Lawson in his sermons and dogma. None of those things alone could make them good people. Only the people who raised them could have done that. Consider yourself lucky, David. You clearly had very good parents. Despite their flaws, and I'm sure there were many, they gave you the greatest gifts of all—a conscience and a sense of compassion. I'm sure they were very proud of you."

Blum inhaled slowly trying to keep his eyes from watering. "Yeah," he said, mostly to himself. "I guess they weren't so bad, after all."

"David, seriously, will you consider joining us? We need people like you."

"I don't know," he said. "I'd planned to spend some time in Champaign. Kay . . . I've grown rather fond of her. I want to stay here, at least for a while. No matter what, I need to make sure she's okay. She went through a lot for me. I owe it to her."

"That's very noble, but don't get too sentimental. This isn't your home anymore. Give it some time. Who knows? You might change your mind."

David felt a strong urge to say yes to Jason's offer, no matter how much he wanted to deny it.

Jason frowned. "Look, you don't need to decide now. I'm going to give you the number for a travel agent in Los Angeles. It's a cover. If you want to reach me, ask for Felix, and tell him that you want to book a . . . what shall we call it? How about a 'homecoming tour'? That's it—a homecoming tour. Have you got that?"

"Sure," Blum said.

Jason scribbled a number on a scrap of paper.

"I'll think about it," Blum said.

"Good. Oh, and there's one more thing you might be interested in. The local CSR account was closed out on Friday. The money was wired to an account in your bank. We don't know the name or number on the account, but you might want to check out AGRI if you still can. You never know. We would certainly welcome whatever information you can provide. Call the same number I gave you. Be cagey, of course. I'm sure you know the drill."

"I will. And thank you for talking to me. I'm just glad it's all over with." Jason stood up, patted his sides and then cocked his head. "It's never over, David. Remember that. The battlefields change, but the war goes on. Get better soon. Talk to your girlfriend. When you decide where your future lies, give me a call." Jason put a small beret on his bald head. "I would enjoy working with you again, as would the others." He smiled at Blum and then walked out of the room.

Blum sank back into his pillows and stared out through the half-closed blinds at the trees outside his window. Beyond them, wispy fair-weather clouds streaked across an azure sky, revealing a transparency that hadn't been there for a long time. Summer was fading quickly.

Unable to remember Kay's cell number, and with no computer or cell phone, Blum used the bedside phone to call information. The operator gave him the number for her apartment and then connected him, but he got her voicemail. Touched by a twinge of paranoia, he hung up before leaving a message. Afterward, he felt silly. He almost called back, but he told himself he'd try again later. Feeling suddenly tired, he lay back on his pillow, and, in only a moment, slipped off to sleep.

Blum was woken later by an orderly serving a dismal dinner of chicken and rice with a bowl of vegetables that tasted straight from an autoclave. After dinner, he grabbed the phone and dialed Kay again.

The phone line connected. He waited for the mechanical hiss that led into the voicemail introduction he had heard before. Instead, he was overjoyed to hear a dull, sleepy Kay squeak out, "Hello?"

"Kay? It's David. I've been trying to reach you."

"Where *are* you?"

"In the hospital, but I'm okay. How are you?"

"I'm fine, but I've been so worried about you. What happened?"

"It's a long story, but it worked out alright. I'll tell you all about it when I see you. But you have to tell me what happened to *you*."

"Well, after I left you, some car started to chase me. I even drove in front of a train to try to get away. David, I was so scared. And I wrecked your car. I'm sorry. I think it can be fixed. I know how much you loved it, and it must be awfully expensive, but I'll try—"

"Never mind about the car. What happened to you? Were you hurt?"

"I only got banged up a bit, and I have a lump on my head. Lucky for me, the county sheriff happened to be driving by. And, you know what? It was Kresge, the same cop who came out to talk to my dad and me that night after the prom. I don't think he recognized me, though. Anyway, he took me to the sheriff's station in Sadorus, which was just down the road. The EMTs gave me first aid. I was kind of shaken up but basically okay. I wanted to get to that guy's house like you told me to. I really did. I tried to get away, but . . . I hope I didn't screw things up. Did I?"

"No, you didn't screw it up. As I said, it all worked out. Did you tell the sheriff anything?"

"Well, I told him that I really had to get somewhere—that it was really important. He asked me about it, but I told him it was personal. And, like I said, I was really shaken up, so he gave me some medicine to calm my nerves, and then I fell asleep on a cot in the station."

Blum shifted the receiver to his other ear. "He didn't ask you anything else?"

"No. When I woke up Sunday morning, the sheriff wasn't there, so after the EMT examined me, I had someone look up your father's address and had your car towed there. Then a deputy drove me to my apartment."

"And that was it?"

"Yeah," she said. "I drove to the address you gave me, but no one answered. I was so scared. I thought you were dead. I heard about the explosion and the fire, and I was sure you were buried down inside somewhere."

"No. I got away."

"So, what happened to Feldmann?"

"You know, I probably shouldn't talk about that on the phone."

"Do you want me to come over?" Kay asked.

"That would be great, if you're up for it. But you sound really tired."

"I've barely slept for the past two nights, but it's so wonderful to finally hear your voice again. I'll be right over. Tell me where you are."

"I'm at Barnhardt Hospital. I don't know what room number, but they can tell you at the desk. And Kay?"

"Yes?"

"I'm so glad you're alright. I was worried sick about you, too."

They said their good-byes, and Blum hung up.

Half an hour later, he heard a soft knock at the door, and suddenly there was Kay Westfield, wearing a flowered sundress, looking tanned and beautiful despite a large bruise on her forehead. She approached the bed slowly, clutching a small bouquet of flowers in front of her like a shield. She stopped just short of his reach. Suddenly, her smile disappeared, and she started to cry.

"I'm so sorry, David. Look at you. You look horrible," she whimpered.

He chuckled. "Go ahead. Make me feel better."

She dropped the flowers on the bed and hugged him tightly as she sobbed. "And it's all my fault."

He winced as her hand clutched a sore spot, and she backed off. "Oh God, did I hurt you?"

"I'm okay. Now come over and give me a real kiss."

She bent over the bed, carefully this time, and kissed him firmly, sweetly, on the lips, her tears falling on his face. Then she stood up and looked at him, wiping her eyes.

"How long do you have to stay here?"

"I can get out tomorrow. That is, if you can look after me."

"Of course, I will. You can stay at my place."

"I don't want to put you out. We can stay at my father's. There's a couch on the first floor that folds out into a bed. I can sleep there."

"Okay," she said, her tears clearing. "I'd love to take care of you. What will you need? Do you have food in the house? You'll need bandages and stuff. I can go get some. Will they give you crutches? If not, I can get you a pair . . ."

She went on like that for some time—not waiting for Blum to answer one question before moving on to the next. Blum smiled at her concern. What a wonderful person, he told himself.

When they had settled all the details of his convalescence, they talked about Saturday night. Blum told her about the greenhouse and the strange animals he'd encountered. Kay was fascinated, but also deeply relieved that her mystery had finally been solved.

"So what really happened to Feldmann?" she asked. "The news said he died in the fire. Did he really?"

Blum motioned for Kay to shut the door, which she did.

"I'm not allowed to tell you everything," he explained. "And you can't ever breathe a word of any of this to anyone. Right now, as far as everyone is concerned—the police, the FBI, the people who Feldmann worked for—what just happened here is past history. If stories come out, then someone may come back and give this place another look. And it wouldn't be safe for you to have been mixed up in this. Do you understand?"

"Yes, of course. So what *did* happen?"

"He was shot."

"Did you shoot him?"

"No," Blum said, relieved that he could be open, at least about that.

"Did you shoot anyone?"

"That's one of the questions I can't answer."

She nodded, considering the implications of his response. "Why was Feldmann doing all that?"

"Well, we were on the right track," Blum said. He gave her a high-level description of what had been contemplated.

"That's horrible," she said, staring down at the floor, pausing in thought. Then she looked up. "What about that lady—the one in the car. Did she get out?"

"Yes. She's fine. She's in Europe now."

"Oh, good," Kay said, sounding relieved. (About being fine or being in Europe, Blum couldn't tell.)

They stared at each other for a minute, both deep in their own thoughts but smiling. Kay broke the silence.

"Guess what? I called *my* father today."

"How did that go?"

"Okay, I guess. At least we're talking. And that's a big improvement. It was really hard, but I told him I forgave him, even if I don't agree with him. I realized I missed him more than I thought, despite everything, and even though he never said it to me, I know he missed me too. So, thank you."

"For what?"

"Talking me into it."

"You mean pushing you into it?"

Kay laughed. "You know, I'm going to look forward to taking care of you. And I'm going to get the doctor to order you to do whatever I tell you." She giggled and then added rather seriously, "I was afraid I'd never see you gain. I thought you were dead, but then I prayed—I know you don't believe in that—and here you are, and you're okay, and now we're together again. I don't know what I would have done if you'd left me. I guess I've felt alone for so long, that, well, I know I never want to feel like that again."

"Well, I'm kind of glad you're alive, too," David replied, not sure what else he could say.

"Oh, goodness. That's really a heavy load to dump on you. And now it sounds sort of like I . . . well, don't worry. I'll take care of you, and then . . . we'll see. Right now, you just get better." She stood up and looked straight into his eyes. She hesitated, her lip quivering. "I love you," she added quickly, as though scared that if she said it more slowly she wouldn't be able to finish. She gave Blum another quick kiss and ran out before he could say anything.

Blum sat back and reflected on the whole conversation, replaying every word she'd said, and, as he did, a peaceful warmth spread through his entire body.

40. HOMECOMING

Tuesday evening, less than two weeks after reading the note from Hans Meier that had drawn him into the whole nightmare, David Blum sat in the overstuffed couch in his father's living room, his right leg resting comfortably on a leather-covered ottoman. He held Kay tightly to his chest and slowly sipped a glass of Bowmore. It was a cool night, and Kay had lit a fire in the fireplace. A nearly full moon shone through the tall windows, and its light mixed with the flames, casting dancing shadows on the walls.

Blum had noticed that Kay seemed a little quieter than he'd expected she would be. He wanted very much for her to share in the excitement he felt about what he wanted to tell her, and her seeming distraction frustrated him more than a little. Twice, he'd asked her if something was wrong, but she had told him that she was only tired. Finally, he decided he couldn't wait any longer.

"Kay," he said, gently nudging her back from where she rested on his chest. "I've been doing a lot of thinking."

"Mmm?"

"Yes. And I've come to some conclusions about what I've been doing and about what I want to do."

"Like what?" she asked, her eyes half closed.

"Now listen. This is important to me."

"Okay," she said, opening her eyes and looking into his.

"Kay. We haven't known each other for all that long, but we've been through a lot together in the past week—probably more than most people go through in a lifetime. I have to get back to work at some point, but I've been thinking . . . Maybe I can arrange things so I can base myself here. I travel a lot, and, besides, Chicago isn't *that* far away. And if I can't work it out to be here, I'd like you to think about joining me there. I only want to be with you. Nothing could make me happier. I know this is rather sudden."

She smiled, and tears welled up in her eyes. "That's exactly what I want, too. It's what I was sort of trying to say yesterday, but then I realized how serious it sounded, and I didn't want to lay all that on you. But, yes, I want to be with you, too. Maybe I can take a leave from work—for a little while—and then we can see what happens."

Kay slipped her arms around David and hugged him tightly. He fought back the urge to squirm as she once again grabbed at a bruised portion of his back. In a moment, she sat back and smiled again. Then she shut her eyes, and David noticed that she seemed to slump down a little lower in the couch. Perhaps it was only the after effects of the past few days.

"I feel really weird," she said softly.

"I feel odd too. I haven't been in any sort of serious relationship in a long time."

"No. I mean like . . . a little sick."

"Really? Do you feel feverish?"

"No. I . . . my stomach hurts—and my head too."

"Let me get you some water." David started to get up.

"No. It'll pass. It happened to me earlier."

"What happened?"

"I got sick. I threw up earlier this afternoon—and then I felt better."

"Do you want to lie down?"

"No. I'll be—"

Suddenly, Kay rocked forward and gagged. A spurt of vomit hit the coffee table and dripped over the edge. She looked up apologetically, cupping her chin with her palm. "I'm sorry."

"Are you okay?" Blum pushed himself up to a standing position, using the edge of the couch for support.

Kay looked very pale, and her lips were slightly bluish. "I can't . . . breathe," she said, almost as a moan. She leaned over, face first, against the back of the couch and began to gag again.

"Was it hard to breathe before?" Blum asked.

"No . . . just a . . . headache." She began to wheeze.

Feeling helpless, and now a bit frightened, Blum limped to the hall phone and dialed 911. "I'm not taking any chances," he called to her. "You may have suffered a concussion."

When he returned to the living room, he found Kay on the floor by the couch, propped up partly on the coffee table. Blood dripped out of her mouth and down her chin, and she looked deathly scared.

"What's . . . happening . . . to me?" she pleaded.

A sudden terror gripped Blum—a cold steel hand clutched at his shoulder and, in his mind, he heard Feldmann's bellowing laughter. A ghostly voice whispered to him, "In smaller doses, it can take up to three days to work. Very messy that way."

Blum shoved back the table and rolled Kay onto her side. She was still breathing, but her forehead felt cold. He kissed her cheek. It too felt cold, and strangely stiff. For a brief moment, she opened her eyes.

"I love you," he told her. "Be strong. The ambulance is on the way." He wanted to tell her that she was going to be okay, but he didn't want his last words to her to turn out to be a lie.

When he saw the flashing red and white lights shine through the windows, he hobbled to the front door on his crutches. Two EMTs in white were already halfway up the walk with a gurney. They loaded Kay quickly and slid the cart into the ambulance. Blum insisted on riding in back with her.

"Did she use any drugs that you know of?" one of the medics asked.

"No," Blum said, not even looking up. He didn't know what to tell them. He knew it was a bacteria—a deadly bacteria that had also killed his father. He had no way to explain how he knew that or what could be done about it. "She said something about possible food poisoning," he told them, feeling utterly helpless. He squeezed Kay's hand tightly and hoped that, somehow, the doctors could keep her alive.

At the hospital, Kay was wheeled into an emergency room, and Blum was told to wait in the lobby. He stumbled to a seat and buried his face in his hands.

How the hell could this have happened? All he knew was that someone associated with Feldmann must have tracked her down and infected her. But how? Where? Was he infected too? He didn't think so—he felt fine.

What was taking the doctors so long?

After a while, he decided he couldn't stand to wait in the lobby any longer. The insipid, watered-down environment galled him, from the vague, soupy paintings to the bleaching fluorescent lights and tinkling tones of the easy-listening music. He needed fresh air and the sounds of the real world to clear his mind.

He told the receptionist that he would be right outside. Limping down a short flight of stairs, he pushed his way through the glass side door to a walkway along the back of the building. The air outside felt almost cold. The leaves that only last week had been so lush and full now sounded dry and brittle. Summer had vanished, he realized, pushed aside by Saturday's storms, and autumn had snuck in quickly in its place. A sudden gust of wind tugged at his hair and flipped his collar up against his chin, making him shiver slightly.

Blum was furious with himself. How could he have gotten Kay involved in all this? At that moment, he wished he'd never met her, never talked to her or gotten to know her. Never put her life at risk. And now the only man who'd known the secret of the disease that was destroying her was dead himself. Blum checked his watch. She'd been in there for twenty minutes. Maybe there was a way to stop the effects. Maybe she could be kept alive until her body found a way to fight the invasion.

He felt his phone buzz in his pocket and absently grabbed it, noticing an alert that he'd received an email. Irritated by the distraction, he reached for the "clear" button, but his heart skipped a beat when he spotted a message he'd missed from earlier in the day—from Kay. He opened the message, which prophetically she had labeled, "Maybe it's too late." The single line of text read, "Just got this today. Oh well." Below it was an attached file.

Blum opened the attachment, which appeared to be some sort of form. Zooming in on the heading, he realized immediately that it was the wire instruction for the closed CSR account that Jason had mentioned. Blum carefully scanned the page. All the information was there: the receiving bank, account number, and the amount—seventy-five million and change. He made his way to the bottom of the form and checked the date. Sure enough, it had been sent last Friday. So, Feldmann must have initiated the transaction shortly after the plane with the bombs had landed.

Blum scanned across to the signature. What horrible handwriting, he thought. How do you get Feldmann out of that? He shook his head when he realized that it wasn't Feldmann's signature. It was Albert Krieger's!

Krieger must have been nervous when he signed because he seemed to have corrected the spelling on his last name. Blum zoomed in. The base of the "i" had a wide loop, and the first "e" had a funny leading slope to it that wasn't there on the second one. In addition, the "r" at the end looked as though it had been added after the writer had lifted his pen. In a moment of confusion, he must have signed the wrong name and then corrected it.

Blum squinted at the screen, trying to picture what it must have looked like when first written. And then it hit him. It said "Kresge." Kresge was Krieger!

Why hadn't he thought of that? Kresge—always the man on the spot. He banged his temples with his fists. Good old Detective Kresge, who never failed to show up when there was trouble with Feldmann. He had talked to Kay and her father when she'd seen the explosion at the farm, and then he'd convinced them to drop the issue.

On a hunch, Blum found the email with the accident report on his father. Skipping past the location and details, he scrolled to the signature at the bottom. Kresge. Meier must have known, or at least suspected, as much, and that's why he'd warned Blum about going to the police.

And, just by "coincidence," Kresge had been driving toward the farm on Saturday night after Feldmann had caught Tina. And then he'd found Kay in Blum's car . . . had taken her to the station . . . and given her *medicine*!

What the hell was taking so long?

Blum looked up and saw a shadow in the lighted doorway. The receptionist. She motioned for him to come inside. She wasn't smiling.

The doctor met him at the top of the stairs. Even though he was considerably shorter than Blum, he put his hand on David's shoulder in a condescending gesture.

"I'm sorry," he said. "Whatever it was attacked her internal organs. Ultimately, it was her heart. It simply failed."

Blum wanted to cry, but he fought back all emotion and stayed stoic.

"Do you have any idea what happened?" the doctor asked.

"Food poisoning, I think," Blum said, clenching his teeth. "She said she felt sick after lunch." He wanted to get away as fast as possible, to escape and drive through the night until he was a thousand miles away.

"Do you know where she ate lunch?"

"No. I don't."

"Are you a relative?"

"No. Just a friend. Her father lives in Ivesdale."

The doctor left, presumably to contact Mr. Westfield, and Blum stumbled to the main lobby to ask the receptionist to call him a taxi.

An hour later, David Blum sat on the back patio rocker in the dark, cigar in hand, slowly sipping a glass of scotch and trying to come to grips with all that had taken place.

Like two converging weather fronts, Feldmann and Jason had collided over the prairie and kicked up a brief, violent storm. The ensuing barrage had taken its toll. Feldmann, Lawson, and Jerry were dead. So, too, were Blum's father and Meier. And now Kay was dead as well. A year from now, only a handful of people in town would still care about, or possibly even remember, what had occurred these past two weeks. And no one who was left behind— Kay's father or her friend Susan, the receptionist at the hotel, Beau Delaney, or the doctor who had just pronounced one Kay Westfield dead of food poisoning—would ever know the full significance of what had just played out.

Ten days ago, if he'd heard on the news that some woman from Ivesdale, Illinois had died of food poisoning of an unknown source, he would have simply ignored it and moved on. But he *had* met her, and he'd grown to love her. And now she was dead because of him.

So where did that leave him? He'd shot two people—in self-defense and to prevent a horrific disaster—but now what? Go back to work at the bank, wining and dining his clients, as if nothing had ever happened? Helping the rich get richer and smiling dutifully when one of them complained about a ding in his Bentley?

And then David knew what he had to do—what his father would have wanted him to do. Slipping his cell phone from his pocket, he retrieved the scrap of paper that Jason had given him and dialed the number carefully. He heard a heavy buzz on the line, and a voice announced, "World Travel."

"Is Felix there?"

"No. Can I take a message?"

"Yes. Tell Felix his friend David wants to book a homecoming tour. Oh, and tell him I found out the name of the other traveler we want to meet—the one whose name he didn't know."

"Felix was hoping you would call," the woman said. "He'll be pleased."

David hung up and turned off his phone. He took a sip of scotch and contemplated his future—what he was leaving behind and what lay in store for him. And, as he did, from all around him rose the throbbing pulse of crickets and cicadas. The lonely chorus grew and grew, until its drumbeat filled his senses and consumed his entire consciousness.

A REQUEST...

The tagline of the *Washington Post* is, "Democracy dies in darkness." Well, so do book sales. As an independent author, my greatest marketing resource is readers like yourself. So if you enjoyed this book, please recommend it to your friends, mention it in your blog, or add a like on Facebook. And, if you would, submit a quick rating/review on Goodreads, as well as Amazon, B&N, iBooks, Kobo, or wherever you buy your books. Anything would be appreciated.

If you want to see more of my writing and the things that inspire me, check out my website, www.charlesjacobs.com, where you'll also find my blog, Homeschool Spy Lessons.

Thank you,
Chuck

CPSIA information can be obtained
at www.ICGtesting.com
Printed in the USA
FSHW021848100220
67004FS